# THE BRILLIANT LIFE OF
# *Eudora Honeysett*

# THE BRILLIANT LIFE OF *Eudora Honeysett*

A Novel

ANNIE LYONS

wm
WILLIAM MORROW
*An Imprint of* HarperCollins*Publishers*

This is a work of fiction. Names, characters, places, and incidents are products of the author's imagination or are used fictitiously and are not to be construed as real. Any resemblance to actual events, locales, organizations, or persons, living or dead, is entirely coincidental.



HarperCollins books may be purchased for educational, business, or sales promotional use. For information, please email the Special Markets Department at SPsales@harpercollins.com.

FIRST EDITION

*Designed by Bonni Leon-Berman*

Library of Congress Cataloging-in-Publication Data has been applied for.

ISBN 978-0-06-302606-3 (hardcover)
ISBN 978-0-06-305715-9 (international edition)

20 21 22 23 24 LSC 10 9 8 7 6 5 4 3 2 1

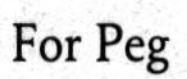
For Peg

I want death to find me planting my cabbages.

—MICHEL DE MONTAIGNE

# THE BRILLIANT LIFE OF
# *Eudora Honeysett*

# Chapter 1

WHEN EUDORA HONEYSETT hears the *flip-clunk* of the letterbox on this particular Tuesday morning, her heart skips before she pulls it back down to earth like a rapidly descending hot-air balloon. It will be junk mail as usual. Unsolicited junk. As she struggles to a standing position, retrieves her stick, and anchors herself to gravity, Eudora marvels, not for the first time, at humanity's ability to fill the world with unwanted junk. The oceans are stuffed with plastic, the landfills with broken three-year-old fridges, and her doormat with an endless littering of pizza leaflets, advertisements for retirement homes, and flyers from individuals offering to repave a driveway she doesn't have. Occasionally, she casts a critical eye over the expensively produced retirement-home brochures filled with photographs of smiling elderly couples toasting their successful move to the old person's equivalent of a Premier Inn. Eudora can't imagine anything worse. She was born in this house and intends to die in this house, hopefully sooner rather than later.

Death is an inevitable preoccupation for a woman of Eudora's years, but she can't recall a time when it wasn't lurking in the background. It's partly due to growing up during a world war, she supposes. She doesn't fear it though. She is wryly amused by the world's innate ability to deny death but wholly unsurprised too. People are too busy staring at their telephones, endlessly searching for some truth that will never come, idly sniggering at infantile video clips of goodness knows what, never stopping to notice the universe around them or the people in it. They certainly never notice her. Eudora Honeysett is invisible, and she doesn't care one jot. She has lived her life as best she can. She is ready for the next step, the final destination, or whatever half-baked euphemism people insist on using these days.

Death. The end. She's rather looking forward to it. It may be a black hole or, if she's lucky, she'll be reunited with all the people she's ever loved. This is a short list but then why do people insist on having hundreds of friends? She heard a discussion on the radio the other day about "toxic friendships" and how you need to rid yourself of these kinds of people. Eudora's advice would be to avoid them in the first place. Keep yourself to yourself. *Mind your own beeswax*, as her mother was fond of saying.

She retrieves the post from the mat with a certain amount of difficulty and is pleasantly surprised to find an A4-sized envelope with a Swiss postmark addressed to her among the rubbish. Eudora experiences that skip of anticipation again, this time well-founded. She's been expecting this, looking forward to it even. She carries the envelope with the other items balanced on top to the kitchen, holding it out like a holy artifact, worthy of respect and awe. She sifts through the other post. There's another letter addressed to her—one more wholly unnecessary hospital appointment. Eudora understands that it's the NHS's duty to preserve life, but sometimes she wishes they'd leave her alone. Sometimes she wishes there was an opt-out clause, a way of making it all stop. Eudora throws the letter to one side and grasps the A4 envelope in her faltering grip. Glancing at the clock, she reluctantly places the precious item to the side. She will save it for later so that she can give it her full attention.

Eudora gathers her belongings in preparation for leaving the house. She welcomes this daily routine. She may be world-weary, but she refuses to stay indoors all day, slumped in a chair like many of her peers. Her body is winding down like an old clock, but she is damned if she's going to accelerate the process. Eudora gets up every morning at eight and leaves the house by ten. There are far too many slovens in the world. Eudora does not intend to join their ranks.

She picks up the bag containing her swimming things and leaves the house. The bright sunlight is rather dazzling, and it takes a few moments for her glasses to adjust, bringing shade and comfort. Eudora notices that the estate agent's "for sale" sign in front of the house next door has been changed to "sold." She shivers with dread at the prospect of new neighbors. Hopefully they will keep themselves to themselves like the last lot. She notices the postman to-ing and fro-ing from house to house and avoids his gaze. They've been on bad terms since she scolded him for taking a shortcut in front of her house, tramping a path through her daylilies so that they failed to bloom last year. He used to stop and chat occasionally but now he looks the other way. She doesn't care. He was being inconsiderate and needed to be told.

Eudora makes slow progress but remains doggedly determined. She soon falls into a steady *tap, step, step, tap, step, step* rhythm using her walking stick, or "third leg" as the smiling social worker called it. Her name was Ruth and she was enthusiastically positive. Eudora didn't share her cheer but didn't mind it either. Ruth was kind, and in Eudora's world, this commodity was in short supply. It was wise to embrace it whenever possible.

Ruth had appeared as if by magic one day last year after Eudora's fall. One minute, Eudora was walking along the pavement, and the next, she was kissing it. Unfortunately, a man with two irritatingly yappy dogs witnessed the incident and insisted on calling an ambulance. Eudora had tried to assert that she would be fine if he could simply direct her back to her house. She was then overwhelmed with sudden panic as she tried and failed to recall her address. In a flash it came to her.

"Quay Cottage, Cliff Road, Waldringfield, Suffolk."

The man frowned. "Suffolk?"

"Yes," insisted Eudora.

His expression was kindly. "I don't think so, my love. This is south-east London. Not Suffolk. I'll call that ambulance. You might have a concussion."

And so the process began with a hair-raising ambulance trip leading to a lengthy wait in the Accident and Emergency department. It was during this time that Eudora experienced something of an epiphany. She'd never considered the terrifyingly closed atmosphere of a packed A&E waiting room to be a conduit for enlightenment, but Eudora had lived long enough to know that life never ceases to surprise.

It was the woman with barely any teeth and the hairy mole on her cheek who set the fires of Eudora's mind ablaze. She looked like a witch from a children's fairy tale, except there was kindness that shone from her rheumy eyes as she talked, which she did incessantly as soon as Eudora made the questionable decision to sit beside her.

"Not long now for you and me," she wheezed, glancing up at Eudora.

"One can only hope," replied Eudora with a polite smile. "Although it's very crowded. I fear we may be here some time."

The woman shook her head. "Not in here, you silly goose. I mean we've not got long to live."

Normally, Eudora would have been offended, but she could see that this strange little woman was something of a kindred spirit. "Well, that too," she admitted. "But unfortunately, we don't have much control over these things."

"I thought about killing myself," said the woman as if she were discussing what she might have for lunch.

"Good heavens above!"

The woman eyed her with amusement. "Don't pretend you haven't. Everyone our age thinks about it."

A horror from the past elbowed its way into Eudora's memory. "Certainly not," she said, sitting up straighter in her chair.

"Mind your backs!" shouted a paramedic as she and a colleague burst through the door with an elderly man on a trolley. A host of medical professionals appeared from nowhere, checking the man's vital signs as they hurried him through. "He's going into arrest!"

The waiting room seemed to hold its breath as they disappeared down a corridor. "Don't want to end up like that poor old bugger, do you?" said the woman, tapping Eudora's arm. "Being poked and prodded when you're on your way out. May as well take control of your destiny if you can."

"But how?" asked Eudora, curiosity getting the better of her fear.

The woman tapped the side of her nose and winked before reaching into the bag that she wore slung across her front like a life belt. She held out a dog-eared leaflet, which Eudora accepted as if it were a dirty sock. "Give them a call."

"Elsie Howlett?" called a nurse.

The woman rose steadily to her feet. "Take care, Eudora," she said without a backward glance.

It wasn't until much later, after Eudora had undergone rounds of tests and consultations with overworked, red-eyed doctors and breezily efficient nurses, that she realized she'd never told Elsie her name. Eudora supposed she must have overheard her conversation with the paramedic. Against her better judgment and for want of something else to do, Eudora had read Elsie's leaflet from cover to cover. It had set her brain into overdrive as a frenzy of thoughts rushed through it like a series of fireworks igniting one after another. As the doctor addressed her with hand-wringing sympathy, presumably in response to the fact that she was extremely old and he couldn't offer a cure, a switch flicked in her mind and a decision was made. When she was finally given permission to leave, she clutched Elsie's leaflet to her chest and approached one of the nurses.

"Excuse me, I was wondering if I might be able to see Elsie Howlett, please?"

The nurse's face fell. "Are you a relative?"

"No. I'm a"—Eudora searched for the appropriate word—"friend."

The nurse glanced behind her as she spoke. "I'm not really supposed to give information to nonrelatives."

"Oh right. Well, I'm her sister then."

The weary nurse managed a half-smile. "I'm sorry, my love. Elsie passed away about half an hour ago."

"Oh," said Eudora, squeezing the leaflet into a ball. "She died."

The nurse touched her lightly on the sleeve. "Yes. I'm sorry."

Eudora looked into her eyes. "Don't be. She was ready to go."

The nurse nodded uncertainly. "You take care."

As Eudora traveled back from the hospital, blinking into the autumn sunshine from the questionable comfort of the patient transport vehicle, she felt as if she'd been reborn. The NHS now had her in their well-meaning grasp, but Eudora had Elsie's wisdom and bloody-minded determination on her side. She couldn't imagine a more potent force.

⁂

Ruth had been another one in the long list of people determined to preserve Eudora's existence at all costs. She arrived on a drizzly day in October. Eudora had been housebound for nearly a week and was frustrated to the point of fury with her uncooperative joints. When Ruth presented her with the walking stick, Eudora experienced an unexpected wave of fondness for this woman. It was a gift in the truest sense of the word. Her freedom was restored, the outside world hers for the taking. She could start to put her plan into action.

This fondness rapidly dissolved as Ruth produced a folder and a pen from her bag and pulled out the inevitable form.

"Eu-dora Honey-sett," she said as she wrote.

"With two t's," said Eudora. The misspelling of her name was a lifelong bugbear.

"And you live alone, Eudora?"

Eudora would have preferred "Miss Honeysett" but managed to stifle her disappointment. "Yes."

"Any relatives at all?"

"No."

Ruth's expression folded into one of sympathy. "Friends?"

"I have a cat."

Ruth glanced over at Eudora's fat, lazy excuse of a feline, who was asleep on the back of the sofa. She smiled. "I'm guessing he's not much help when it comes to shopping or cleaning the house."

It was meant as a joke but only served to provoke defensiveness in Eudora. "I manage," she said firmly.

"I'm sure you do, but I want you to know that we offer all kinds of support. I can put you in touch with agencies who offer cleaning and laundry services, or even organize a carer to come in every day."

Eudora stared at the woman as if she'd suggested a Bacchic orgy. "I don't need any help. Thank you."

Ruth nodded. It was a knowing nod—a nod that had heard this response many times before from all manner of elderly people like Eudora. "Please be assured that the help is there if you need it. I'll leave one of my cards in case you change your mind."

Eudora had thrown it straight in the bin as soon as Ruth left. Montgomery the cat curled around her feet, almost tripping her up, as he demanded food by issuing forth a series of loud meows.

"We don't need anyone, do we, Montgomery?" said Eudora, filling his bowl with biscuits. She placed it on the floor and attempted to scratch the cat behind his ears before receiving a sharp nip in response.

Eudora reaches the leisure center and is grateful for the anonymity that her swim membership brings. She has a card that enables her to sweep past reception. The only issue is with the card-activated barrier. Eudora loathes and detests all technology and very nearly rescinded her membership when they installed these monstrosities. However, she has become well-practiced at the skill of swiping and manages to sail through to the changing rooms with little effort now. She goes to the same changing cubicle, puts her belongings in the same locker, and makes her way to the pool, nodding to the swimmers she sees every week while blessedly avoiding verbal communication. Once in the pool, she ignores the initial chill, disregards the cheerful young woman who remarks on the temperature of the water, and launches herself into aquatic bliss. This is the only place where Eudora feels something akin to joy. For a moment in time, she is weightless and pain-free. She has always been a strong swimmer and glides through the water now with a similar ease to when she swam as a teenager. The aches are still there but they melt into the background as she stretches and reaches her way along the pool.

Eudora doesn't swim for long—half an hour or so—but it's enough to bring her what she needs: a sense of purpose and sufficient impetus to face another day. She climbs out of the pool feeling the inevitable weight of reality again as she retrieves her stick and traipses back to the changing room.

As she leaves the leisure center a while later, she notices two women arguing over a parking space. The air is filled with vibrant expletives. Eudora stares openmouthed, unable to mask her horror. When did the world get so loud and angry? One of the women notices her.

"What the fuck are you staring at, grandma?" she snarls.

In her younger days, Eudora might have replied, scolded her to stop being rude and respect her elders. But those days are long gone. Eudora can see that this woman is unpredictable and beyond reasoning. You were vulnerable when you were old. Everything is fragile and in danger of breaking.

"Excuse me," mutters Eudora, ducking her head and shrinking away. She hurries as best she can. One of the most frustrating aspects of growing old is the slowing of life's pace. Up until the age of seventy, Eudora had been able to nip here or pop there, but her nipping and popping days are over. In this age of rush, rush, rush, she is redundant.

She casts a furtive glance over her shoulder. The women are still arguing. One of the leisure-center employees has come out to try and reason with them as a queue of horn-blaring cars forms. Eudora realizes her hands are shaking and decides to stop off at the shop, which marks her halfway point to home. Although she dislikes most aspects of modern life, Eudora has nothing but praise for these scaled-down supermarkets, which have appeared on almost every main street in recent times. Not only are they convenient, well-placed, and large enough for her to remain anonymous while she shops, they also carry the reassuring presence of a security guard.

She nods to this particular gigantic bear of a man standing with arms folded by the front door and breathes in the sacred cool of refrigerated goods. She walks steadily around the store, retrieving a pint of milk before finding herself in front of the bakery display.

Her mother never entertained the idea of shop-bought cakes when Eudora was a child. There was always a homemade sponge or fruitcake in the tin and often half a dozen lemon curd tarts made with leftover pastry. Eudora's eyes alight on a plastic carton containing what promises to be apple turnovers. A memory flickers in her thoughts, bringing with it an unexpected wave of comfort.

She finds herself reaching for the pastries and carrying them to the register before she has time to change her mind.

Eudora continues her journey home with a renewed sense of calm and a secret thrill at her unexpected purchase. On rounding the corner of her street, she is startled by a cacophony of barking as two small dogs encircle Eudora with their leads in a flagrant attempt to upend her.

"Chas! Dave! Come here right now!"

The dogs dance back the other way, releasing Eudora, who scowls into the face of their owner.

"I am so sorry, Miss Honeysett," says the man. "Pardon my French, but these two are little buggers. Are you all right?"

Eudora experiences a conflict of emotions. Her annoyance is abated by his use of her proper name but heightened by his cursing and south-east London accent. Added to which, Eudora has no idea who this man is. She guesses him to be a few years younger than her but probably no more than five. His white hair is thin, his appearance relatively smart—a blue-checked shirt with pressed navy trousers. He has laughter lines at the corners of his eyes. She's never trusted people with laughter lines. "I'm quite fine, thank you. Do I know you?"

The man holds out his hand with a smile. "Stanley Marcham. I scraped you up off the pavement when you'd had a few too many last year."

Eudora stares at him in horror.

He laughs. "I'm joking. But I *was* there when you had that fall. How are you feeling now?"

Eudora hears the sympathetic concern and wants to

be away. "Never better. Thank you. Now if you'll excuse me . . ."

Stanley nods. "Of course. Places to go, people to see."

Eudora sniffs. "Quite. Good day."

"Mind how you go."

Exhaustion overwhelms Eudora like a wave as she closes the front door on the world. She manages to make some tea and a sandwich and carry them into the lounge before sinking into her chair with relief.

She wakes hours later, tea cold, sandwich untouched, limbs heavy with weariness. Sleep never seems to refresh her these days. It merely keeps her going until the next rest. As her mind returns to full consciousness, she remembers the envelope and the pastries. This is sufficient motivation for her to leave her chair and fetch the items along with a fresh cup of tea. As Eudora moves around the kitchen, she is struck by a thought. Rummaging in the back of a drawer, she finds what she's looking for. Returning to the living room, she pushes the candle into the turnover and sparks a match. Its flame illuminates the framed photograph behind, of her mother and father with five-year-old Eudora sandwiched between them.

"Happy birthday, Eudora," she whispers before blowing out the light and making a silent wish for the future. She removes the candle and picks up a turnover for a bite. It's syrupy sweet but she's hungry and devours half of it before drinking a mouthful of tea to dilute the taste. Eudora wipes her hands and mouth on a handkerchief and picks up the envelope. This is what she's been waiting for. This is her real birthday treat.

She retrieves the letter opener, which had been her father's. It's shaped like a small silver sword. Eudora can remember being fascinated by it as a child but never allowed to touch it. She slices through the envelope and pulls out a stapled sheaf of pages. Her heart quickens as she reads the heading:

**KLINIK LEBENSWAHL–OFFERING CHOICE AND DIGNITY IN DEATH AS IN LIFE**

She takes a bite from the half-eaten pastry, turns the page, and begins to read.

## 1940
## LYONS TEA SHOP, PICCADILLY

"Choose anything you like. Anything at all." Albert Honeysett's eyes glittered with possibility.

"Are you sure, Daddy? Don't we need to eat in moderation?" Eudora had read this on a poster. She wasn't sure what it meant but it sounded important.

Her father laughed. The laugh was huge and warm and always felt to Eudora like an embrace. "Dearest Dora," he said. "Always so good and kind. Don't worry. I put in a call to Mr. Churchill only this morning and he said that as it's your birthday, you're allowed a special treat."

Eudora giggled. "In that case, please may I have one of the fancy pastries and a glass of lemon cordial?"

"An excellent choice," declared Albert, nodding to the waitress that they were ready.

Eudora sat up straighter in her chair with her hands in her lap and peered around at their fellow diners. Apart from a scattering of men in uniform, you would hardly have known there was a war on. She admired the women with their smart hair and neat appearance. She smoothed down her own wrinkled dress—a baggy gingham affair with misshapen collars, which her mother had made from an old tablecloth.

Eudora would never say it out loud of course but she found the war thrilling; the idea of their heroic soldiers fighting for freedom, and Mr. Churchill leading them to victory, was quite the most exciting thing that had ever happened. She had gone to stay with her mother's uncle in Suffolk for a while soon after war broke out, but her parents decided that it was safe for her to come back to London. She was sure that it would all be over soon. Life could carry on as it had before the war with their happy family of three.

The waitress appeared moments later with their order, and as Eudora noticed the candle on the top of her cake, she decided that life was perfect.

"Happy birthday," said the waitress, placing it in front of her.

"Thank you," replied Eudora.

"Happy birthday, Dora," said her father. "Make a wish."

Eudora blew out the candle and closed her eyes. *I wish. I wish. I wish this moment could last forever.*

The air-raid siren screamed its response. *Maybe Hitler's in charge of wishes today*, thought Eudora as her father took her hand and led her to the shelter. It was a squash and a squeeze, but Eudora didn't mind because she was safe with him. Nothing bad ever happened when Albert Honeysett was around. In the half-light of the shelter, he pulled her closer, kissing the top of her head.

"I've got a surprise for you," he said, pulling a napkin-wrapped parcel from his huge overcoat pocket.

"My pastry," said Eudora. "Thank you, Daddy."

"Happy birthday, Dora."

"Would you like a bite?" she asked.

She could hear the smile in his voice. "No. You enjoy it. It's your treat for being such a good girl. You make Mummy and me very happy."

Eudora nestled closer, making sure she savored every bite, the sharp-sweet taste of apples reminding her of days spent picking fruit from Uncle John's orchard.

"It's a shame Mummy couldn't come today," she said, wiping her mouth on the napkin when she'd finished.

"Actually, I wanted to talk to you about that."

Eudora stared up at her father. There was a note of caution in his voice. Her skin prickled in the close heat of the shelter.

"You see, Mummy is very tired at the moment because she's going to have a baby."

Eudora froze, unsure of how to react.

Her father seemed to sense this. "Now, you don't need to worry because it's going to be wonderful. You'll have a new playmate and someone to be your friend for always."

Eudora felt reassured. That did sound nice. Most of her friends at school had siblings. She sometimes wondered if she was missing out.

"And of course the baby is going to be the luckiest child in the world to have you as a big sister."

Eudora nestled her head against her father's chest, breathing in the peppery scent of tobacco.

"And there's something else." There was that note of caution again. Eudora held her breath. "I'm going away for a while."

"Where? How long for? When will you come back?" The words tumbled from her.

He squeezed her to him. Eudora started to feel claustrophobic. "I can't really say, and I don't know for how long. So I need you to be very brave and look after Mummy and the new baby while I'm away."

Questions flooded her mind. *But why now? And why can't you say how long? And why can't you tell me that it's going to be all right?* Eudora pressed her lips together tightly to stop them spilling out because she knew he would never lie to her and, more than anything, she feared the truth.

The all clear sounded but the two of them stayed where they were until everyone else had gone. Her father held her tightly. Years later, Eudora realized that, rather than comforting her, Albert Honeysett had been clinging to his child, painfully aware of the uncertain future ahead.

"So, will you look after Mummy and the baby for me? Please?"

She gazed up at him. She thought she saw the reflection of a tear but decided it was a trick of the light. "Of course, Daddy. I'll look after them until you get home and then we can do it together."

Her father nodded before hurrying them to their feet. "Good girl, Dora. I knew I could rely on you."

As they emerged, blinking, into the light, Eudora stared up and down the street. Everything looked exactly as it had an hour previously. She could see two women through the window of the tea shop, sitting at the table where she and her father had sat earlier, drinking tea and eating sandwiches as if nothing had happened. She watched the buses and taxis hum along the street, the people milling back and forth, continuing with their lives. Business as usual.

In contrast, as she walked along Piccadilly hand in hand with her father, it was as if every cell of Eudora's being had changed. It wasn't until adulthood that she recognized this as the moment her childhood ended. If she'd known the dark times that lay ahead, Eudora probably would have begged her father to let them run back to the shelter and stay there forever.

## Chapter 2

THE NEXT MORNING, Eudora is woken not by her alarm clock but by the sound of a lorry reversing. She retrieves her glasses and looks at the clock: 7:27 A.M. She frowns at the intrusion, but as her brain slides into consciousness, Eudora realizes that for the first time in many years she has slept through the night without waking. And then she grasps the unfortunate fact that her bed will need to be changed as a result. She takes a deep breath and hauls herself into a sitting position, contemplating the effort of the task ahead. The words of Ruth, the endlessly encouraging social worker, spring into her mind.

*Please be assured that the help is there if you need it.*

Then Eudora remembers the booklet she read from cover to cover last night. It galvanizes her into action.

"Come along, Eudora. No sense in idling. Let's get this done and make that telephone call."

Stripping the bed is easier than remaking it. Eudora has to take several breaks during the process, cursing the inventor of duvets and fitted sheets as she works. She remembers changing the beds with her mother—the holy trinity of sheet, blanket, and eiderdown all smoothed with hospital-cornered precision. Eudora had succumbed to the infernal duvet trend when her mother became ill, deciding that it might make life easier. And it had. For a while. But then she got old and discovered that elasticated sheets and plastic poppers are the enemy of arthritic fingers.

By the time she's finished, Montgomery has sloped upstairs in search of food. He jumps up onto the freshly made bed with a petulant meow. Eudora shoos him off, receiving a sharp hiss in reply.

"You really are the most bad-tempered cat," she tells him. He fixes her with a cold green stare before yawning to reveal dagger-sharp teeth.

Like the duvet, she'd bought the cat in a moment of weakness, thinking he would be good company during her twilight years. Sadly, Montgomery has morphed into the equivalent of a long-endured husband—cantankerous, offhand, and only interested in being fed.

Eudora uses her last remaining energy to dress. She won't go swimming today. There is a far more important task at hand.

She pulls back the curtains to be confronted with the sight of a removals van, vast as an ocean liner, parked across next door's curb and hers as well. A gang of men of different sizes and with varying quantities of body tattoos are loading items of furniture into it with practiced efficiency. One of them glances up at her with a cheery smile. Eudora drops the curtain. She doesn't need distractions from the outside world today.

As she carries her soiled bedsheets to the landing, the cat plants himself with defiance across the top step.

"If you trip me up, there'll be no one to feed you," she tells him. He stares up at her with momentary distaste but seems to take the point, slinking down the stairs with practiced arrogance.

Eudora stuffs her washing into the machine's gaping mouth and feeds the ungrateful cat, who devours it and exits the house in record time. She settles with tea and toast in the living room, taking tentative bites before realizing that she's ravenous. Once finished, Eudora switches on the radio and decides to close her eyes for a moment before making the phone call. They're talking about a woman who ended her life at a Swiss clinic. She'd worked as a geriatric nurse and couldn't bear the idea of old age, having seen the indignities and hardship people had to suffer firsthand.

"Wise woman," murmurs Eudora as she drifts into sleep.

A sharp knock at the door jolts Eudora back to startled consciousness. She closes her eyes again, but whoever it is seems determined, as they rap the knocker with renewed vigor. Eudora struggles to her feet and makes her way to the door. She is relieved to see that the chain is on, enabling her to peer through the narrow gap. A young, shaven-headed man carrying a large holdall leans forward with a leering smirk.

"All right, missus. 'Ow are you today?" he says in that voice people reserve for the old and infirm. Eudora is used to this but detests it all the same.

"What do you want?" she demands with as much fierceness as she can muster. She feels emboldened by the safety chain.

The young man frowns but plows on with his pitch. "My name's Josh and I'm part of a scheme to help young offenders reintegrate into the community." He speaks as if reading a script and holds up a card, which Eudora can't read. For all she knows it could be a library card. Although she doubts it.

"What do you want?" she repeats. She longs to shut the door on him but is too afraid.

Josh unzips his bag and holds up a dishcloth. "I'm selling these. Best cloths out there. Five quid a pack."

"I do not require any dishcloths."

Josh is undeterred. "'Ow about tea towels then? 'Free for a fiver?"

"No. I don't want to buy anything. Please leave."

He stares at her for a second, all traces of friendly patter replaced with glinting menace. "Silly old bitch," he growls before hauling the bag onto his back and stomping down the path. He pauses at the gate, staring back at her with contempt. "'Ope you die soon," he adds before clearing his throat and spitting on the ground.

"That makes two of us," says Eudora, shutting the door with trembling relief and turning the deadlock.

Fear often spurs people into action, forcing them to make a clear choice between fight or flight. Eudora doesn't have the strength or ability to fight anymore but she senses that her own unique version of flight is the right one to follow. A one-way flight and an end to all this.

The world is too much for Eudora, and it isn't even hooligans like Josh who are the worst. Everyone is selfish and caught up with themselves these days. They have no time to notice her or others like her. They consume news or food as if they're trying to eat the whole world; they watch and judge and spit out their opinions as if they're the only ones worth listening to. Eudora is invisible to these people, but she has stopped noticing them too. They're welcome to their "post-Brexit, Donald Trump, condemn everyone, be kind to no one" world. There is no helping them now. Soon enough, she won't be around to witness their continuous decline into moral torpor. Good riddance and good night.

Back in the living room, her hands are shaking as she reaches for the phone. Eudora puts on her reading glasses, finds the number on the back of the booklet, and carefully stabs the buttons.

"*Klinik Lebenswahl. Kann ich Ihnen helfen?*" Eudora is surprised to hear German. A reflex part of her brain considers ending the call, such is her long-held loathing of Germans. Other people may have forgiven what happened in the war, but she never will. In the nick of time she remembers that this clinic is Swiss-German. There is nothing to fear.

"Do you speak English?"

The woman's voice is soft and soothing. Eudora is immediately reassured. "Yes, of course. How can I help you?"

Eudora opens the booklet. She wants to get the terminology right. "I would like to book myself in for a voluntary assisted death," she says firmly. The rush of adrenaline at finally uttering these words out loud is dizzying.

"I see. And is this the first time you have called us?"

"No. I telephoned to request a booklet after I read about your organization." She decides not to mention Elsie. This is her decision. The ending to her story. "Thank you for posting it to me," she continues. "I have now read the booklet from cover to cover and made my decision. I would therefore like to book myself in. Please."

*Manners, Eudora, even when discussing your death.*

"I see," repeats the woman. "Well, as you may know, we have a protocol to follow."

"What protocol?" demands Eudora.

"We must be sure that you have thought about everything properly and fully, that you understand all the implications, that you have discussed it with those close to you, and that you are absolutely sure this is the only option available to you."

Eudora clears her throat. She has had enough of this woman's honeyed tones. "I am eighty-five years old. I am old and tired and alone. I have nothing I want to do and no one I want to see. I am not depressed, merely done with life. I don't want to end up dribbling in an old people's home, wearing adult nappies in front of a shouting television. I want to leave this world with dignity and respect. Now, can you help me or not?"

There is a moment's pause. "Yes. We can help you but there are procedures to be followed. If you are sure, I can send you the forms, which will start the process and we will take it from there. Is that what you would like?"

"Yes. Please," replies Eudora, her voice wavering as she realizes that finally someone somewhere is listening. "Thank you."

"You are welcome." She hesitates before continuing. "This is an unusual situation for me. Forgive me, but I do understand what you are asking. My grandmother felt the same as you. She wanted to be as good at dying as she'd been at living."

"Did she manage it?" asks Eudora, her curiosity aroused.

"She did. It's how I ended up working here."

Her honesty gives Eudora courage. "What's your name?"

"Petra."

"Thank you, Petra. So, will you send me the forms?"

"Of course. I am thinking that you are not able to travel to us so we will be conducting this process by telephone?"

"Will that be a problem?"

"It shouldn't be, but you will need to provide various forms and have detailed conversations with Doctor Liebermann. Do you know about the costs?"

"I can pay."

"That's fine. Forgive me for asking. So, if you would be kind enough to give me a few details, please."

Eudora does as she asks. "And can you tell me how long it takes?" She doesn't feel that she needs to add the obvious words, *to die.*

"It depends. But I would say between three and four months from when you sign. You can change your mind at any time of course."

*I won't,* thinks Eudora, feeling relieved that she'll be gone by Christmas—the loneliest, unhappiest time of the year.

"I will be your contact for the whole process," Petra tells her. "Please call me at any time with questions or concerns. I am here to help."

"Thank you, Petra." Eudora hopes the woman can hear

how grateful and relieved she is, how much this means to her. She hangs up a short while later with a mixture of euphoria and exhaustion. The die is cast. Eudora hobbles to the kitchen. Standing before the almost blank calendar, she counts forward four months and writes one word in a shaky, spidery script.

*Freedom.*

Eudora smiles. She is in control for the first time in years. She won't be defeated by old age; she will defy it, cast it aside like an unwanted skin. The end will be on her terms and her terms alone.

She is roused from her reverie by a knock at the door. At first she fears it's that hateful young man returning to terrorize her, but the knock is gentler and more considered. She takes a while to reach the door, leaving the chain on as she answers. She peers with a frown into the face of a little girl who wears a blank expression but who, on seeing Eudora, changes it to a frown, mirroring the old woman's.

"Yes?" demands Eudora.

Another face appears above the child's—a nervously smiling woman with unkempt hair whom Eudora eyes with disdain.

"Sorry to bother you," says the woman a little too loudly.

The child's frown deepens. "Mum. Why are you shouting?"

Eudora raises an eyebrow.

"Sorry," says the woman to the child. "Sorry," she repeats to Eudora. "We just wanted to introduce ourselves. We're your new neighbors."

"Oh," says Eudora.

"Why have you got this chain on your door? Is it broken?" asks the little girl.

"It's to keep out unwanted intruders," replies Eudora with meaning.

"We're not intruders, so you can open it properly, if you like."

Eudora does not like, but she is never rude. She unhooks the chain.

"That's better," says the little girl. "I'm Rose Trewidney, by the way."

Eudora regards Rose Trewidney for a moment. She is dressed in a cherry-red T-shirt calamitously teamed with a purple ra-ra skirt.

"And I'm Maggie," adds her mother. "We've moved up from Cornwall today. It's been quite a journey, but we've made it. It seems like a lovely neighborhood, rather fewer beaches than Cornwall of course."

Maggie laughs, although Eudora has no idea why. She remains silent as this woman fills the air with words. She is aware of the little girl gazing up at her.

Eventually, Maggie runs out of words. "So anyway, we just wanted to say hi."

"Will that removals lorry be there long?" demands Eudora, nodding in its direction.

Maggie glances over her shoulder. "Oh, erm, hopefully not. Is it in your way?"

"It is parked over the space in front of my house."

"Right, well, I'm very sorry about that."

"What's your cat called?" asks Rose, ignoring the tension building above her head.

"Montgomery," says Eudora irritably.

"Aww, Montgomery. Here, Montgomery," says Rose, kneeling down, making kissing noises to entice him.

"He's not very friendly," warns Eudora.

The cat makes a beeline for Rose and, to Eudora's amazement, not only allows her to stroke him but starts to purr when she makes the potentially life-threatening move to pick him up.

"Aww, you're a lovely boy, aren't you? We used to have a cat but he got run over."

Eudora stares as Rose hugs the cat tightly while firing a series of questions at her. She finds herself with no choice but to answer.

"What's your name?"

"Eudora."

"And how old are you?"

"Eighty-five."

"I'm ten. Do you live here alone?"

"Yes."

"And do you have any children?"

"No."

"That must be lonely."

Eudora frowns. "It isn't."

"Do you like the Queen?"

"Of course."

"Me too."

Her mother interjects. "Rose, I think we've taken up quite enough of Eudora's time," she says. She mouths an apology to the old woman. "Come on. Let's go and sort out your room."

"Oh. Okay," says Rose. She kisses the cat on his head and plonks him on the floor before following her mother back down the path.

"Bye, Eudora. Bye, Montgomery. See you soon."

Eudora closes her front door and stands there for a moment, wondering what on earth has just happened. A sound emits from her mouth—a strange, foreign sound—quiet and wholly unexpected. The cat stares up at her in surprise as he hears his owner chuckle for the first time in his living memory before he skulks away in search of food.

## 1940
## SIDNEY AVENUE, SOUTH-EAST LONDON

Stella Honeysett announced her arrival to the world with a scream as piercing as the siren's wail that forced her laboring mother into the Anderson shelter, which Albert had built before he left.

"To keep my angels safe," he told Eudora as she helped him cover its corrugated-iron structure with tarpaulin. Then she watched while he shoveled great spadefuls of earth on top.

"Snug as a bug," he said, standing back to admire their handiwork. He glanced down at Eudora with a smile. "Now, will you help me replant my poor old marrow on top? I had to dig him up to make way for your new nighttime home."

"Of course, Daddy."

"Good girl. And then we can make it nice and cozy inside for you and Mummy."

"And the new baby," said Eudora, adopting what she hoped was a responsible expression.

Albert leaned down to kiss the top of her head. "I can see that I'm leaving Mummy and your new brother or sister in good hands."

Eudora beamed up at him like a flower turning its head toward the sun. Although she didn't want her father to leave, Eudora knew that he was doing his duty and that she, in turn, must do hers. She was sure that if she did exactly as her father asked, God and Mr. Churchill would send him back to them unharmed.

"Someone's gone up in the world," came an accusing voice from over the fence.

"Good afternoon, Mr. Crabb," said Albert, propping his shovel against the new shelter and approaching their neighbor. "You and Mrs. Crabb are more than welcome to use our shelter if London's bombed—there's enough room for six people."

Mr. Crabb looked appalled. "Adolf Hitler is not going to chase me from my bed."

Eudora's eyes grew wide as an image of their terrifying enemy chasing Mr. Crabb around his bedroom flooded her imagination.

"We didn't let Fritz beat us last time, and we're damn well not going to let them beat us this time!"

Eudora gasped. Albert placed a reassuring hand on her shoulder. "Well, you're both welcome if you change your minds. Now, if you'll excuse us," he said, leading his daughter away.

Mr. Crabb was still muttering about "the bastard Boche." Eudora clung tighter to her father's hand. She sometimes woke to hear their neighbor crying out in the dead of night. It was a chilling sound, not of anger but more like an animal, trapped and desperate. The first time she heard it, she ran from her room and bumped straight into her father on the landing.

He had knelt down, pulling her trembling body close. "It's all right, my darling Dora. It's all right. Mr. Crabb can't help it. He lost his son during the war, you see, and he's having a nightmare. That's all. It's a terrible nightmare. Do you understand?"

Eudora didn't but nodded her head rapidly to pretend that she did. Any shared confidence with her father was treasure to Eudora, a precious gem to be cushioned in her heart forever. She always tried to be kind whenever she saw Mr. Crabb, but there was something about his wild gaze and unpredictable nature that terrified her.

Eudora helped her father drag an old rectangle of carpet into the shelter and held pieces of wire mesh across wooden frames while he nailed them together to craft makeshift beds. Albert placed roll-up mattresses on top of the bed frames and stood back satisfied.

"Shall we try them for size, Dora?" he asked, his eyes sparkling as he lit a candle and placed it inside a flowerpot.

"Okay, Daddy," said Eudora, wriggling into the tiny space. "It's very cozy." She giggled.

Albert took his place on the other side and smiled at her. "See? I told you. Snug as bugs," he said, reaching out across the divide. She placed her small hand in his and wished, as she always did with her father, that they could stay like this forever.

Life hadn't changed that much since the start of the war. She had to carry her gas mask with her at all times and listen out for the air-raid sirens but apart from that, they carried on as before. Her father would listen to the news on the wireless every evening. Eudora would sit by his feet and try to do the same. She didn't understand much of what was being said, but she heard her father reassuring her mother that they were safe in London. This was enough for Eudora. Her father would never lie to them. As long as he declared them to be safe, all would be well.

"What on earth are you two still doing out here?" Beatrice Honeysett's sharp words brought a swift end to Eudora's reverie as her mother frowned down into the shelter.

Albert let go of his daughter's hand and jumped up. "Come and see what Dora and I have made," he said with a gallant bow.

"How on earth am I going to get down there?" demanded Beatrice, running a hand over her burgeoning belly.

"I'll help you, Mummy," said Eudora, her heart leaping as Albert shot her a wink.

Beatrice huffed and puffed her way into the shelter and sat heavily on one of the homemade beds. "It's a bit dark and cramped," she said.

Albert took a seat beside her and put an arm around her shoulders. "I think madam will find it rather cozy in time," he said, planting a kiss on her cheek.

"Oh, get away with you, Albert Honeysett," scolded Beatrice, but she was smiling. She took another look around. "You've worked very hard."

"I helped Daddy make the beds," said Eudora. "And we planted his marrow on top of the shelter."

Beatrice looked from her husband to her daughter and back again. "You two. What a pair you are."

Albert held out his arms to Eudora, pulling them both into a tight embrace. "My precious girls," he said.

"Well, let's just hope this baby doesn't decide to make an appearance during an air raid," said Beatrice.

Albert had been gone a month and London was barely a week into the Blitz when Beatrice went into labor. Eudora was relieved that Mrs. Crabb had decided to take up the offer to share their shelter during the now nightly air raids. She found her mother's keening to be altogether more terrifying than Hitler's bombs and was grateful for their neighbor's presence.

Eudora held her breath and squeezed her mother's hand as their next-door neighbor took charge of the situation. Mrs. Crabb was rake-thin and smelled of peppermints. She was a trained librarian but still seemed to know exactly what to do as Beatrice brought new life into the world in the same moment that many other lives were being snuffed out by the enemy.

Eudora fixed her eyes on the wavering candle flame and prayed. The clamor of the bombs seemed to intensify, and then there was silence. Eudora exhaled before being knocked sideways by a huge explosion, which shook the shelter with a violence that was truly terrifying. Her heart drummed ten-to-the-dozen as lumps of metal clattered against the sides and she glimpsed what looked like a sky on fire through the tiny gap in the shelter. Eudora longed to cry but knew she mustn't. Her father would want her to be brave. Her mother's eyes were wide with pain and fear, seemingly oblivious to the horror outside. Eudora screwed her eyes tightly shut and prayed for a miracle, for her father to save them. And then, through the damp darkness, she heard a small voice.

"Pack up your troubles in your old kit bag and smile, smile, smile."

Eudora blinked in astonishment at the sound of Mrs. Crabb singing before realizing that her mother had gone quiet, her face set and determined, eyes tightly shut as she pushed with all her might. The siren screamed out the all clear, and Stella joined in, emerging bloody and furious into a chaotic, fractured world. Mrs. Crabb wrapped her in a blanket before handing her to Beatrice.

"Promise me you'll get these girls out of London," she said, her voice heavy with a mother's loss. "Promise me."

Pale and exhausted, Beatrice stared up at her and nodded. "I promise."

They emerged hours later to find that Mrs. Crabb's house had suffered a direct hit; the front wall was all that remained, like the opening to a doll's house. They found Mr. Crabb at the end of the garden, still in his bed, blown clean from the house. Mrs. Crabb went to live with her sister in Devon, and although Eudora was sad about Mr. Crabb, she got the feeling he would be satisfied that Hitler hadn't succeeded in expelling him from his bed.

# Chapter 3

A SENSE OF restless anticipation descends over Eudora during the following week. Her heart soars whenever she hears the post drop onto the mat and dives as she discovers nothing but junk mail. Her one consolation is hope; hope for a smooth process bringing an ending to life on her terms.

*My death. My way.*

The mere thought of this makes day-to-day life more endurable.

One morning, she is following her customary routine of dressing, eating breakfast while tuned in to the *Today* program, and leaving the house by ten o'clock. The day is breezy but warm. Eudora pauses on the doorstep, permitting herself a moment to feel the sun on her face before setting off along the road. She spots Stanley Marcham farther along the street, walking his infernally yapping dogs and is glad for once that the ravages of old age prevent her from catching up with him.

Eudora is lost in thought as she reaches the leisure center and perturbed to find that her usual locker and changing cubicle are both occupied. Irritated, she casts around for another before hearing someone call her name. She is so unused to hearing it spoken out loud these days that if it weren't for the unusual nature of her moniker, she would have assumed the person to be addressing someone else.

"Eudora!" call two voices in unison.

Eudora turns to see Maggie, grinning like a lunatic, with Rose standing beside her.

"Hello," says Eudora, her heart sinking at the inevitable exchange.

"I thought it was you," says Maggie brightly.

Eudora wonders at the obviousness of this statement. "And so it is." She notices that Rose is wearing large green goggles, giving her the appearance of a boggle-eyed frog.

"Do you swim here regularly?" asks Maggie.

"Every day if possible," replies Eudora.

"Wow. That's amazing. I wish I could get my mum to go swimming."

"Granny likes to sit and watch the world go by," says Rose.

"Mmm. I've told her she needs to move more. You've got to use it or lose it, right?" says Maggie to Eudora.

Eudora has no idea what she's talking about so opts for a peremptory nod. "If you'll excuse me . . ."

"Can I come 'round to see your cat again, please?" asks Rose.

"Rose, you can't just invite yourself 'round to people's houses," says Maggie, embarrassed.

"Why not? How else do you get to see them?"

Maggie looks to Eudora for help, but the old woman remains silent.

Rose seizes the opportunity. "So can I come? A bit later? I've got a present for you."

Eudora regards the little girl for a moment. There's something about her tenacious character that she admires. Eudora also senses that Rose won't take no for an answer and, although she habitually avoids human company, can't see the harm of letting the child visit her recalcitrant feline.

"Very well. Two o'clock. Don't be late."

"Yes, ma'am!" cries Rose with a salute.

Eudora's lips twitch before she disappears into the changing room with a shake of her head. Rose and Maggie are splashing about in the shallow end when she emerges into the bleached light of the main pool. Eudora ignores them and walks toward the swimming lanes. Sinking into the shallow end, she relishes the soft weightlessness of the water on her skin. After a few lengths, Eudora rests for a moment. She notices Rose and her mother laughing together. The little girl is standing on the side while Maggie waits in the pool, arms outstretched, encouraging her to jump. She sees joy mirrored in their faces as Rose leaps and Maggie catches her. Eudora takes a deep breath and dives under the water to drown it out.

Her post-swim weariness seems to slide away as she arrives home later to find a large, thick envelope with a Swiss postmark sitting on the mat. Eudora can't wait a moment longer. She drops her swimming bag in the hall before carrying the envelope into the living room. Once again, she uses her father's letter opener, pulling the sheaf of documents onto her lap. There is a note attached, written in a looping European hand:

*Dear Ms. Honeysett,*

It was a pleasure to talk to you today. I enclose the forms as requested. Please call me if you want to discuss any of this or just to talk. I know what a big decision it is and am here if you need me.

*Kind regards,*

Petra

There is something about these words that touches Eudora. She is not used to thoughtful people. She presses a hand over Petra's writing before turning to the forms. There is a lot of information required. She isn't surprised but tires quickly as she begins to work her way through them.

*Come along, Eudora. He who hesitates is lost. You've made the decision. Keep going.*

It takes her a couple of hours to complete everything. She puts the forms into an envelope and seals it.

Eudora sits back in her chair, a sense of satisfaction spreading through her body like an embrace. She considers making herself a sandwich, but as her eyelids grow heavy, she decides to take a moment to rest. It's been a busy morning. All this living and dying takes it out of you.

She wakes with a start.

"Yoo-hoo!" calls Rose through the letterbox.

"Yoo-hoo indeed," mutters Eudora, hauling herself to her feet. As she opens the door, Eudora fights the urge to shield her eyes from the alarming clash of Rose's outfit—purple, yellow, orange, and green all mingled to startling effect.

"I'm experimenting with fashion," explains Rose, registering her surprised expression. "And we made you these." She holds out a plate of honey-colored biscuits.

"You'd better come in," says Eudora.

"Okay." Rose follows Eudora to the living room. "These are a delicacy where I come from," she says, placing the plate on the little side table. "They're Cornish fairings—ginger biscuits, really."

"Thank you," says Eudora.

"Shall we have a drink? That's what I usually do with my granny."

"If you like." Eudora hopes Rose isn't trying to recruit her as a surrogate grandmother. She'll be sorely disappointed if she is.

"Shall I get the drinks?"

"Can you make tea?"

"No."

"What can you make then?"

"Squash. I'm excellent at squash."

"I may have some fruit cordial in the cupboard."

"I'll find it," says Rose, skipping off toward the kitchen. "Do you want one?"

"People usually say '*would* you like one' to be polite."

"Oh. Okay. So do you?"

"What?"

"Want one?"

Eudora fears this is going to be one of the longer afternoons of her life. "Very well."

Rose nods and disappears from the room. Eudora can hear cupboards being opened and closed and wishes she were sprightlier so she could at least keep an eye on her. Rose starts to sing to herself. It's strange to hear this sound in the usual quiet of her house, but not unpleasant. She appears moments later carrying two bone-china mugs filled to the brim with cloudy lemon liquid. Rose smiles as she hands one to Eudora, who frowns at the drink but takes it all the same.

"Cheers!" says Rose, clinking her mug against Eudora's. "Biscuit?" She offers the plate.

"Thank you," says Eudora, taking one. The drink is tooth-numbingly sweet. Eudora winces as she takes a sip and places it on the table. She nibbles the biscuit. It's also sweet but in a warm, comforting way that reminds Eudora of the ginger cake her mother used to make. "These are delicious," she admits.

"I know," says Rose. She drains her drink, wiping her mouth with the back of her hand. "Who's that for?" she asks, gesturing at Eudora's precious envelope.

"Meddlers for nosy parkers," says Eudora.

"What does that mean?"

"It's something my mother used to say. It means 'none of your business.'"

"Fair enough," says Rose. "Mum says I'm very nosy, but I just like to know what's going on."

"I suppose that's fair enough too," says Eudora.

"Can I ask another question? You can say no if it's too nosy."

"Very well."

"Is that you in the photograph?" Rose points at the framed picture on the side table.

"Yes. That's me in the middle."

"And is that your dad?"

"It is. And my mother."

Rose peers at the photograph for a long time. "I love old pictures. They make me want to go back and see what it was like."

"Why?" asks Eudora, intrigued. She didn't think people cared about the past anymore.

"Because I love history. I love all the stories about the war and what it was like. It's much more interesting than life now. Do you ever wish you could go back?"

Eudora gazes at the photograph. "All the time." She is aware of something brushing against her ankles and looks down in surprise to see the cat, nuzzling his way around their legs.

"Aww, Montgomery, there you are," says Rose, scooping him into her arms and rubbing her chin against the top of his head.

Eudora watches in amazement as the cat nudges her in reply.

"What shall we do now?" asks Rose.

"I actually need to go out to the post office," says Eudora, eyeing the envelope.

"Great. Let's do that."

"Are you sure your mother will allow it?" asks Eudora, hoping this will deter her.

"Good point. I'll go and check. You get ready. I'll meet you outside."

Eudora is ruffled but for some reason does as she is told. There is no sign of Rose as she leaves the house, so Eudora decides to seize the opportunity. Her mother has probably forbidden it, and besides, Eudora would prefer to make this trip alone.

She is only a few yards along the street when she hears Rose calling, "Eudora! Wait up—I'm coming!"

Eudora knows pretending not to hear is futile. She pauses to wait for the little girl to catch up. They walk along in silence, Rose hopscotching from paving stone to paving stone.

"When I was a little girl, my father used to tell me to avoid the cracks in the pavement otherwise the bears would get me," says Eudora.

"That's funny," says Rose.

They reach the post office to find a small queue with Stanley Marcham holding court at the front. He is laughing at something the man behind the counter has said. Eudora isn't surprised. She had him down as a joker as soon as she saw him. As he turns to leave, Eudora pretends to be interested in a display of jiffy bags. Stanley spots them nonetheless.

"Hello there," he says.

"Mmm," replies Eudora.

"Hello there," echoes Rose.

"Is this your granddaughter then?" he asks, eyes sparkling at Rose.

"Good heavens, no," says Eudora.

"We're friends," declares Rose.

Eudora is astonished. "Are we?"

"Aren't we?" asks Rose.

"Of course you are. And how lucky you are too," says Stanley.

"I'm Rose, by the way," she says, holding out her hand.

Stanley takes it with a smile. "And I'm Stanley. Very pleased to make your acquaintance, Rose."

Rose giggles.

Eudora has reached the front of the queue. "Excuse me," she says, moving forward to the counter, irritated by their easy chatter.

"Bye, Stanley," calls Rose over her shoulder before turning back to Eudora. "He was nice."

"Mmm. Airmail to Switzerland, please," Eudora tells the man. She notices he doesn't joke with her. In fact, she can't ever remember having had a conversation with him.

"Have you ever tried these?" asks Rose, plucking a bag of sweets from the display in front of the counter.

Eudora squints at the packet. "Haribo Cherries. No, I haven't."

"You should. They're *really* nice."

The man sticks a stamp and an airmail label to the envelope, placing it in the large gray sack behind him. "Anything else?"

*No. Just this date with destiny, thank you*, thinks Eudora.

She glances down at Rose. Her gaze is so open, as if she's seeing the whole world for the first time. "May I have these too, please?" she says, picking up the sweets and showing them to the man. He flashes a grin at Rose and smiles at Eudora.

"That's £7.79 in total, please."

Eudora hands over a ten-pound note and carefully counts the change back into her purse. As they leave the post office, she hands Rose the sweets.

Rose stares up at her. "Thank you, Eudora." The little girl opens the packet and offers it to her. "Try one."

Eudora can't get her fingers inside, so Rose carefully cups her hand and tips a sweet into her palm. Eudora is struck by the novel sensation of this child's soft, warm touch. She puts the sweet into her mouth and is amazed. The flavor of cherry is strong and rather wonderful. "Thank you, Rose."

"No, Eudora. Thank *you*."

"Mind your backs, ladies," says a voice. Eudora turns to see a postman hauling the large gray sack of letters and parcels he's collected from the post office toward his waiting van. She watches as he flings it inside, pulls the door shut, and races off to his next stop. It's a reassuring sight. The deed is done. All she can do now is wait.

### 1944
### QUAY COTTAGE, CLIFF ROAD, WALDRINGFIELD, SUFFOLK

---

"Again, Dora," demanded the small girl.

Eudora smiled and lifted the rickety wooden swing seat carefully to avoid the risk of splinters. "Ready?"

"Ready!"

Eudora let go, feeling heady with love as the air was filled with her sister's ticklish laughter. The oak tree's branches creaked as the swing flew back and forth and she felt the dappled sunlight kiss her face through whispering leaves. Eudora remembered being pushed on this swing by her father. She sent up a silent prayer for his safe return. His last letter had sounded positive.

*I miss you, my darlings. I hope to be home soon.*

Hope. That perfect word. Eudora embraced it like a talisman.

"Higher! Higher! Higher!"

Stella was a demanding child, but Eudora didn't mind. She doted on her younger sibling, relishing the fact that her mother entrusted Stella to her care. Eudora also remembered the promise she'd made to her father before he left. It was as constant as the beating of her own heart.

Stella's cries were increasing in pitch and intensity now. Her laughter had a piercing, hysterical edge. Eudora wondered if it might be wise to stop.

"Shall we take a break, Stella? Go inside and have a drink? It's very hot out here."

"Noooo, Dora! Noooo! Again! Again! Again!" shrieked Stella.

"What on earth is all this racket?"

Eudora winced at the sight of her mother, neck flushed scarlet, storming toward them, tea towel in hand. Some girls' mothers completed their outfits with neck scarves or pearls. Eudora's mother's accessory of choice was a tea towel.

"Sorry, Mummy. We were just playing," said Eudora. In this time of war, she took her role as peacekeeper very seriously. She was sure Mr. Churchill would approve.

Beatrice Honeysett eyed her daughters. Eudora noticed a softness around her mother's eyes when her gaze was fixed on her, but it hardened as she turned her attention to Stella. She pointed a finger toward her youngest child.

"I don't want to hear any fuss or shrieking from you, young lady. Don't you know there's a war on?"

Stella jutted out her chin and stared at her mother. Beatrice's eyes narrowed at this gesture of open defiance, her breathing intensifying as she studied the child's face. Eudora's eyes flicked from one to the other and noticed her mother shrink slightly at Stella's knife-sharp gaze—clear blue and as open as the wide Suffolk skies, a carbon copy of their father's. Beatrice's sadness quickly gave way to anger. Her fist tightened its grip on the tea towel as she began to whip it toward Stella.

"Wicked, wicked girl!" she cried.

Instead of inciting fear and shame as it might have done in Eudora, Stella squealed with mocking laughter, dodging both the tea towel and her mother's fury, darting away toward the far end of the garden. Beatrice lurched forward, ready to follow, but Eudora caught hold of her.

"It's all right, Mummy. It's all right. I'll look after her. You go and rest for a while. It's so hot. We're all just too hot."

Beatrice's eyes swam with tears as they fixed on her eldest daughter's face. Eudora saw a never-ending pit of sorrow in that gaze. It frightened her.

*I need you to be very brave and look after Mummy . . .*

Eudora breathed in fresh courage from the memory as she searched for the right words. "It's all right, Mummy. Daddy will be home soon. We can go back to London and everything will be all right."

Beatrice squeezed her daughter's hand. "You're a good girl, Dora," she said before retreating inside.

Eudora could feel sweat trickling down her back, the heat of the day as burdensome as if she were carrying stones in her pockets. She looked toward the end of the garden and spotted Stella staring back at her from behind an apple tree. She wore an expression of malevolent glee on her tiny, perfect face as if it was all a huge game and she was sure she had just won.

Eudora sighed and held out a hand. "Come on, Stella. Come and help me make the pie for supper." It was ridiculously hot to be making a pie, but she knew her great-uncle expected something hearty after a day working in the fields, even in summer.

The kitchen was welcomingly cool, and Eudora set about making pastry, rubbing fat and flour through her fingertips, while humming a tune.

"What's that song, Dora?" asked Stella, who was sitting at the kitchen table, drinking milk.

"We-ell meet again," sang Eudora. "Don't know where, don't know whe-en!" Despite her mother's outburst, she was in a happy mood. As her father had taught her, Eudora had been following the news on the wireless and felt sure victory was close at hand. Her mother refused to listen to the radio. She found it too depressing, but Eudora couldn't help herself. She owed it to her father, as if she was protecting him somehow by tuning in. She knew it was silly but she also harbored a secret idea that he would know she was listening. His letters sounded optimistic too. Eudora knew he couldn't share what was really happening, but she gleaned that he was okay and that was enough for now.

Every day was a step closer to him returning home, and every night Eudora would kneel beside her bed and pray with all her might. She persuaded Stella to do this too, even though the child had never met their father. Stella fidgeted as they prayed but always rewarded Eudora with an obedient "Amen" at the end.

Despite her deep love for the child, Eudora knew her sister had a troublesome streak.

"There's something of the devil in that one," warned her great-uncle after they'd caught Stella pulling the wing from a butterfly one day. Even Eudora agreed with the punishment of her being locked in their room with no food for the rest of the day. She'd expected Stella to kick and scream as she led her upstairs at her mother's behest, but the child was strangely calm and remained silent and expressionless as she sank onto the bed. Eudora sat down beside her for a moment, folding her hands in her lap.

"Why did you do it, Stella? How could you be so cruel?"

Stella glanced up at her sister with a lack of contrition that sent a chill through Eudora. "I just wanted to see if it could still fly. But it couldn't." She turned away from her sister and lay down, her large blue eyes staring into the middle distance.

Eudora told herself that Stella was just a child. Children could be cruel sometimes. She was sure Stella would grow out of it. It was hard for her growing up during the war, having never met her father, with a mother who seemed to resent her and a great-uncle who spent the day in the fields and the night drinking. Eudora felt like the only one who could steer a path through the vagaries of life, and she was determined to take care of Stella at any cost.

"Could you fetch me some carrots for the pie, please, Stella?" asked Eudora.

"Okay, Dora," said Stella, skipping out through the back door. Eudora smiled and went back to her humming.

*We'll meet again, Daddy,* she thought. *I know we'll meet again.*

Pastry finished, she turned her attention to the rabbits, which her great-uncle had caught the day before. Eudora had become an expert at skinning and butchering rabbits. She'd cut herself on the sharp knives the first few times she'd performed this task but now she was a dab hand. She'd become extremely adept at all manner of domestic tasks since they'd moved here, almost taking over her mother's role. She didn't mind. The doctor said Beatrice's nerves were bad, and Eudora saw it as another strand to keeping her promise to her father.

Stella skipped back into the kitchen holding the carrots aloft like a trophy. "Got them!"

"Good girl. Can you rinse them for me, please?"

"Okay, Dora."

"Look at you. Like two little housemaids doing all the

chores." Eudora turned to see Beatrice standing in the doorway. She'd thought her mother would be pleased to see them getting on so well, but she detected a hint of jealousy in her tone.

"I'm washing the carrots!" cried Stella, spinning around and splashing dirt and water everywhere.

"You're making a terrible mess!" scolded Beatrice, color rising to her cheeks.

"It's all right, Mummy. I'll clean it up. Shall I make you some tea?" said Eudora.

There was a sharp knock at the front door. Beatrice put a hand to her heart. "Oh my shattered nerves. Whoever can that be?"

Eudora froze. *Daddy. Let it be Daddy.* "Shall I go?"

Beatrice dismissed her with a wave of her hand. "No, no. You make the tea. I'll go."

Eudora craned her neck to see who was there as her mother opened the door. "Who is it, Dora?" asked Stella, nudging in front of her sister.

As soon as Eudora saw the boy, she knew. "Angels of death" they called them. She couldn't hear his words, but she heard the mumbled "Sorry. Sorry." Eudora closed her eyes and pushed the kitchen door shut. She wrapped her arms around Stella and covered her ears as the scream went up. It was a scream that filled the whole house, the whole village, the whole world, and, to Eudora, it felt as if it was a scream that would never end.

# Chapter 4

THE FOLLOWING DAY hangs hot and heavy. Eudora longs for a swim but can't face the walk. She throws open the windows and back door to allow what precious breeze there is to waft through to the living room. She lingers a moment at the back door, blinking out at her parched lawn. There is more soil than grass. It's baked and cracked like an overdone pie crust. Her next-door neighbor used to cut the lawn while he was doing his own. He was a little slapdash with his efforts, but she was grateful for his kindness. He also barely spoke, and she was grateful for that too. She has no idea who will cut it for her now that he and his family have moved. Eudora can just about manage to tend her flowerbeds, but even this is starting to prove a struggle. Hopefully these concerns will soon be a thing of the past.

After breakfast, Eudora resolves to make the best of being trapped at home and settles down to put her affairs in order. First, she considers whether to make a will. She's not sure there's any point. There's no one to inherit her estate. In the absence of beneficiaries, the Crown will get everything. Eudora would like to hope they will spend it wisely, but she doubts it. She hasn't trusted a single prime minister since Churchill, and as for her local politician, she wrote him off the day she attended one of his monthly meetings and he addressed her as "Eudora." He hasn't done anything about the uneven pavements on her street yet either. Montgomery sidles into the room and casually rubs his head against her ankles.

"That tickles!" exclaims Eudora. He does it again. Eudora reaches down to scratch his head. He nudges her hand in reply. "Someone's in a good mood today," she remarks, watching him take up position in an inviting patch of sunshine on the back of the sofa before falling asleep, his nose rested on folded velvet paws. On impulse, Eudora seizes her writing pad and pen.

She writes,

*These are the final wishes of Eudora Honeysett.*
*I am of sound mind and wish for the following to be adhered to after my death.*

She taps her pen against her top lip before continuing.

*I wish for my house and all its contents to be sold, and the proceeds, along with any money remaining in my bank accounts, to be used to help fund the NHS. I wish for my cat, Montgomery, to be given to Rose Trewidney, who lives next door to me.*

Eudora glances at the concertina file containing all her financial documents on the shelf beside her chair. She ought to write something specific about these. Her thoughts are interrupted by the rumble of the garbage lorry pulling onto her street.

"Oh blast," she says, remembering the bag of rubbish she'd left on the front step, ready to take to the bin. Eudora hauls herself to her feet, hurrying with some effort to the door. Hobbling down the path, she reaches the pavement in time to see the lorry pulling off.

"Blast!" she repeats with more venom. She hasn't noticed Stanley talking to Rose, as his yelping dogs weave in and out of their legs. Stanley has seen her though. He hands the dogs' leads to Rose and approaches with a smile.

"Do you want me to take that?" he asks, holding out his hand. Eudora looks around in surprise, drawing the bag out of reach as if fearful he's trying to rob her. Stanley laughs and peers in the direction of the lorry. He plants his fingers in his mouth and issues a loud, confident whistle.

Eudora is appalled, while Rose stares at him in awe. "Please can you teach me how to do that?"

"'Course I can."

One of the binmen glances in his direction. "You missed one!" calls Stanley. The man gives a thumbs-up and jogs back to fetch the bag.

"Sorry, Stan," he says with a grin. "Thanks, darlin'," he adds to Eudora, wresting it from her grasp. She can't remember the last time anyone addressed her in such a fashion and is surprised to feel her cheeks grow hot.

"That was cool," Rose tells him.

"Thank you," says Eudora.

Stanley gives a gallant bow. His dogs are up to their usual tricks of barking and trying to trip up everyone in sight.

Resisting the urge to kick one of them, Eudora turns away.

"Do you both want to come to my house for tea?" asks Rose.

Eudora regards her for a moment. She doesn't want to but is starting to realize that it's difficult to refuse Rose.

"I would love to, but I think I should leave these menaces at home," says Stanley, gesturing toward the dogs. "I'm sure you agree, Miss Honeysett?"

"I do," admits Eudora.

"Why don't you come 'round at about four o'clock then?" suggests Rose. "And we could use our surnames like you just did. So you can be Mr. Marcham and I'll be Miss Trewidney. It'll be like something out of olden times." She hugs herself with delight.

"Very well, Miss Trewidney, Miss Honeysett. I shall look forward to the opportunity of taking tea with you both at four of the clock," says Stanley with a deep bow.

Rose giggles. "This is going to be so much fun."

Eudora is perturbed as she makes her way back inside her house. She doesn't want this. She doesn't need their company. She has managed perfectly well for many years without unnecessary acquaintances. She wants to be left alone to put her affairs in order and put an end to all this. Why can't people leave her be?

However, Eudora Honeysett prides herself on never being impolite. Besides, it is just tea. She will show willing this time and extricate herself at the earliest available opportunity.

At precisely 3:58 P.M., she leaves her house and makes her way up Rose's front path. "I knew you'd arrive on the dot," says a voice behind her. She turns to see Stanley walking through the gate, carrying a delicate bunch of sweet peas and a cake tin.

"Of course. It's bad manners to be late," says Eudora, ringing the doorbell.

"Quite right too."

Rose flings open the door. Eudora had been alarmed by her outfit from the day before, but this one is even more startling. She wears a purple T-shirt with the words "Girls Rule" written in rose-colored sequins, a pair of striped orange shorts, a fluorescent green feather boa, and a huge gold bow in her hair. "Good day, Miss Honeysett, Mr. Marcham!" she cries with a clumsy curtsy.

"Good day to you, Miss Trewidney!" replies Stanley, ushering Eudora in before him. "Ladies first."

"Hello," says Eudora, refusing to go along with their ridiculous charade.

Maggie appears in the hallway. "Hi there. Lovely to see you again, Eudora. And you must be Stanley." They shake hands. Maggie's chaotic hair is tied with a red-and-gold scarf and she is wearing a pair of paint-splattered denim dungarees over a white T-shirt. Eudora notices for the first time that she is pregnant. "Excuse my appearance," she adds, patting her hair. "I'm busy decorating the nursery."

"Ahh, so you're going to have a new baby brother or sister," says Stanley to Rose.

"Sister. She's called Daisy," reports Rose, sounding bored.

"We moved up from Cornwall because of my partner's job," explains Maggie. Eudora is momentarily confused by the word "partner" before remembering that it's modern parlance for "other half."

"Shall we take tea in the garden?" asks Rose.

"Sounds perfect," says Stanley. "These are for you, by the way." He hands over the flowers and cake tin. Eudora is embarrassed by her empty hands.

"Thank you," says Rose. "Mmm, don't these smell lovely, Mummy?"

She holds out the flowers for her mother, who inhales deeply. "Heavenly," says Maggie.

Eudora catches the fragrance. It transports her momentarily toward a memory, which leaves her breathless with sadness. "Is the garden this way?" she asks, pointing her stick toward the back door, hoping that this will move things along.

"It is," says Maggie. "Everything's on the table. Rose and I made a jug of peach iced tea and a sponge cake."

"I brought a sponge cake too!" says Stanley. "But then, as my Ada used to say, there's no such thing as too much cake."

*There is if you don't know when to stop*, thinks Eudora.

"I'll leave you in Rose's capable hands then," says Maggie.

"Miss Trewidney," corrects Rose.

"Sorry—*Miss* Trewidney. I'll be upstairs if you need anything." As she smiles, Eudora is struck by how beautiful she is. It's the natural beauty of someone who is content within their own skin. Eudora envies and admires her for this.

Rose leads them into the garden. Someone has made a half-hearted attempt to cut the ailing lawn and there's a sagging trampoline at the far end opposite the shed. The garden is surrounded by towering shrubs punctuated with the odd rose or lavender bush. They sit at the garden table underneath a green parasol. It's still hot but there's a pleasant breeze wafting through the leaves.

"Well, isn't this lovely?" says Stanley.

"Mmm," admits Eudora.

Rose pours brimming glasses of iced tea and cuts generous slabs of cake. "Here you go."

"Thank you," says Eudora.

"Thank you, Miss Trewidney," echoes Stanley.

"So was Ada your wife?" asks Rose, taking a large bite of cake.

Stanley nods sorrowfully. "My angel. We were married for nearly sixty years, but my darling girl couldn't hold on to celebrate that particular anniversary."

"That's sad," says Rose. Eudora says nothing. She's not a fan of the open discussion of feelings.

"It is but I feel lucky to have known her," says Stanley. "We had the best life and a long one too. We met at school when we were younger than you," he tells Rose.

"How old?" she asks, enthralled.

"Six," says Stanley, smiling fondly.

"Six!" cries Rose. "So cute. And was it love at first sight?"

"Oh yes," says Stanley. "Ada was the prettiest girl in the school, with huge blue eyes and blond ringlets. And she had this beautiful laugh, like a little bell ringing. I used to do everything I could to make her laugh. She said I was the class joker, but then everyone loves a joker, don't they?"

*Not necessarily*, thinks Eudora. Her suspicions about Stanley Marcham are turning out to be true. He really did like the sound of his own voice.

"I think it's romantic that you found your true love at age six," declares Rose. "I can't imagine that happening to me. Most of the boys I know are plonkers."

Stanley laughs. "A lot of boys are plonkers."

"What about you, Miss Honeysett?" asks Rose. "Have you ever been in love?" Eudora frowns. "Meddlers for nosy parkers?" suggests the little girl.

"Precisely."

"Sorry," says Rose. "Shall we talk about your cat then?"

"If you like."

"How long have you had him?"

"Twelve years." Eudora had bought him soon after her mother died in an attempt to dilute her grief. It didn't work.

"Why did you call him Montgomery?"

"Let me guess. After the Field Marshal?" suggests Stanley.

"Not really," says Eudora. He is right but Eudora's not going to let him know it.

"Did you ever think about getting a dog?"

"No."

"I reckon you're either a cat or a dog person," says Stanley.

*Of course you do,* thinks Eudora.

"My Ada loved dogs, whereas we always had cats growing up."

"So you're a cat person," says Rose. "Like Eudora."

Stanley nods. "But Ada had always wanted a dog, so I couldn't say no. I'd have lassoed the moon if she'd asked."

"*It's a Wonderful Life*," says Eudora.

"What's a wonderful life?" asks Rose.

Stanley smiles. "That line. About lassoing the moon. It's from a film called *It's a Wonderful Life*, starring the great Jimmy Stewart."

"And Donna Reed," adds Eudora.

"She was a beauty," says Stanley. "It's a great film. You'd like it, Rose."

Rose was gazing at them both, her elbows resting on the table. "I like listening to you two talk." Eudora and Stanley exchange glances. "So what kind of dogs are Chas and Dave?"

"Cavalier King Charles spaniels," says Stanley. "They call them that because their ears make them look a bit like King Charles I."

"The second," interrupts Eudora. Stanley stares at her. "They're named after King Charles II—the restoration king."

"I stand corrected," says Stanley with a bow.

"You certainly do," replies Eudora.

"How old are they?" asks Rose.

"Ten. We had other dogs before them, but I think these two were Ada's favorites." Stanley's eyes mist. "They're all I've got left of her now. Little blighters."

Rose stands up and puts her arms around Stanley, squeezing him to her small frame. Eudora watches, appalled and intrigued. "You must miss her," says Rose.

Stanley nods and, to her horror, Eudora realizes he's crying.

"It's okay, Stanley," says Rose. "It's good to cry sometimes. It always makes me feel better."

Eudora is panicked at this public outpouring of grief. She reaches into her handbag, retrieving a clean handkerchief. It's the only way she can think to make him stop. "Here," she says, handing it over.

"Thank you," says Stanley, smiling at her. "I'm sorry. I get a bit down sometimes. It comes over me all of a sudden. You must think I'm a silly old fool."

Eudora welds her lips together.

"Not at all!" cries Rose. "You miss your wife and you're sad. We all need to cry sometimes and we're your friends, aren't we?" Rose gazes at Eudora with dark brown eyes that draw you in and refuse to let go.

"Why don't we have another piece of cake?" suggests Eudora. It's the best she can do given the circumstances.

"That's an excellent idea," says Rose.

"Thank you," says Stanley, his voice husky with sadness. "You're both very kind." Eudora nods and Stanley nudges her. "We're like peas in a pod, aren't we? Two old duffers together!"

"Speak for yourself," says Eudora.

Stanley laughs. "Maybe you and I should trip the light fantastic one evening? Go for a meal? Or the flicks?" Eudora frowns. "Or a nightclub?" She looks horrified. "I'm joking!" He grins. "You're a funny one, Miss Honeysett."

She shoots him a sideward glance. "Takes one to know one, Mr. Marcham."

"Touché," he replies.

"It's lovely to make new friends, isn't it?" says Rose. "BFFs forever!"

"BFFs?" asks Eudora.

"Best friends forever!" cries Rose.

Eudora is weary. She isn't used to such frivolity. "I think I shall go home now. Thank you both for a"—she searches for the right words—"pleasant afternoon."

"Oh, thank you for coming. It was so much fun," says Rose, following her down the hall. As Eudora is about to leave, Rose wraps her arms around her middle. Eudora freezes at the rare experience of human warmth. It's an awkward sensation but unexpectedly comforting too. "I'll see you soon," Rose tells her.

Once home, Eudora deadlocks the door on the world and puts the chain across. She is exhausted and confused. She wasn't lying when she said it had been a pleasant afternoon. She finds Stanley irritating but Rose is a force of nature. However, Eudora doesn't have time for this. She has a death to plan and can't allow the distraction of human kindness to stand in her way.

## 1948
## SIDNEY AVENUE, SOUTH-EAST LONDON

Eudora bought the sweet-pea seeds on a whim. It had seemed like a good idea at the time. Something to cheer her mother and occupy Stella. Her father used to grow sweet peas. Eudora recalled vases on every surface when she was small, filled with delicate pastel clouds of perfume. She thought it would be a happy memory, a comfort, like looking at his photograph or listening to one of his favorite songs. But if Eudora had realized the trouble they would cause, she would have left the seed packet in the shop.

Moving back to their family home at the end of the war had made Eudora feel as if she were losing her father all over again. Everything reminded her of his absence—the tang of tobacco, his dressing gown hanging on the back of the bedroom door. She watched her mother move around the house, wearing widowhood like a cloak. The expression on Beatrice's shrunken face was that of a woman who couldn't quite comprehend that this was her life now. Eudora understood that she needed to take action before the grief swallowed them all whole. She had only been thirteen at the time, but it was as if her childhood had accelerated into adulthood without notice or permission.

Eudora knew her father's words to her in the air-raid shelter had never been more salient. It was her duty to look after her mother and sister, and now that he wasn't around, to protect them too.

She encouraged her mother to accept a job at the primary school, which Stella attended. Beatrice seemed to enjoy the work, and it meant Eudora could go to her own secondary modern school safe in the knowledge that her mother wasn't sitting at home, dwelling on her loss. Eudora always made sure she was there to collect Stella after school and did a lion's share of the chores. She realized that if she took some of the stress out of her mother's daily life, they were more likely to avoid an argument.

These conflicts always involved her younger sister.

Much to Eudora's regret, Stella had failed to grow out of her defiant phase. If anything, she was wilder, having developed an almost feral streak during carefree years spent in the countryside. She was forever in trouble at school, receiving the slipper for her efforts on countless occasions. Eudora tried to reason with her, but Stella would merely shrug and insist she had no idea why she did the things she did. Beatrice had no patience with her at all. The shame she harbored at having such a willful child and the ever-present burden of widowhood only served to fuel her anger toward the brazen girl. Eudora lived her life on tenterhooks, a reluctant go-between in whichever battle raged next.

And yet, there were moments when she saw a sweetness and eagerness to please in Stella. This was one of the main reasons she'd bought the seeds.

"I've got a surprise," she told her one afternoon. Their mother was working late at school so Eudora thought it would be a good time to start her secret mission.

"What surprise, Dora?" asked Stella, eyes glinting with expectation. It was a look that made Eudora's heart swell with love, particularly as the little girl bore an uncanny resemblance to their father.

"I've bought some sweet-pea seeds. I thought we could plant them together as a surprise for Mummy."

Stella folded her arms. "I don't want to."

Eudora realized she'd taken the wrong tack. "Oh please, Stella. I think you'll love the flowers once they've grown. They smell wonderful. You could use them to make some of your perfume." Much to her mother's annoyance, the little girl had a habit of pulling petals from roses and storing them in jam jars filled to the brim with water. It made Eudora smile when she presented her with yet another sticky jar of stagnant water, declaring it to be Chanel No. 5. She could imagine her father erupting into laughter at such a scene.

Stella chewed a fingernail before giving her decision. "O-kay, Dora. Show me how."

Eudora and Stella spent a happy hour carefully filling trays with compost and sowing the tiny seeds.

"We'll keep them on the windowsill in the back bedroom until they germinate, and then we can plant them in the garden. We need to keep an eye on them, mind, and make sure they don't dry out."

Stella gave an earnest nod. "I'll check them every day."

"Good girl. And let's keep it a secret between us for now, all right?"

"Shh," replied Stella, drawing a finger to her smirking lips.

It didn't take long for the seedlings to develop. "When can we plant them in the garden?" asked Stella on the day they were delighted to find sturdy green shoots pushing through the compost.

"Tomorrow after school," said Eudora, remembering that her mother was working late again.

"I can't wait to smell the flowers," said Stella. Eudora rejoiced in a thrill of victory. She was making progress with her sister. All would be well.

Eudora found the homemade obelisk of bound canes that her father had used when he grew sweet peas tucked in the back of the cobweb-laced shed. She carried it to a bare patch of soil and pushed the spikes into the earth. "Now we must dig little holes all around the outside and carefully transplant the sweet peas so that they can climb up the canes."

"Okay, Dora," said Stella, waving her trowel in the air.

Eudora was impressed with the care her sister showed as she dug, planted, and patted the soil around their precious seedlings. When they were finished, they stood back to admire their handiwork.

"Well done, Stella. It won't be long until we've got flowers—provided we keep them watered."

"And then I can make my perfume?"

"And then you can make your perfume."

Stella wrapped her arms around Eudora's middle. "I love you, Dora."

Eudora planted a kiss on the top of her head like her father used to do to her. "I love you too."

One Saturday morning a few weeks later, Stella came running into the kitchen. "Dora, Dora, there are flowers! Come see! Come see!"

Eudora followed her sister into the garden and sure enough, the sweet peas bore an array of beautiful, fragrant flowers.

"Let's pick some!" cried Stella.

Eudora fetched some scissors and snipped a dozen stems. "Here's some for you," she said. "And I'm going to put the rest in a vase for Mummy."

"Thank you," said Stella, accepting the blooms with the tenderness of a new mother cradling her baby.

Eudora was changing beds later that day when the shouting began.

"Where did you get them, you wicked girl?"

"Dora and I planted them. They're mine!"

"Liar! You're a liar. You must have stolen them from someone's garden."

"I DIDN'T! THEY'RE MINE!"

"HOW DARE YOU SHOUT AT ME?"

"YOU'RE SHOUTING AND I DON'T CARE. I'M NOT LYING! I WISH YOU WERE DEAD!"

Eudora rushed down to the kitchen in time to see her mother deliver a stinging slap, which sent Stella flying. "Mummy, stop! Please stop!"

Her mother turned, face contorted with ugly rage. "Did you hear how she spoke to me, Eudora? Her own mother. She wishes her own mother dead."

Stella's face was a mask of anger but there were no tears. Later in life, Eudora would muse on the fact that she never saw her sister cry. "It's true," said Stella quietly. "I do."

"DEVIL!" shrieked Beatrice, lurching toward her. Stella darted out of the way as her mother stumbled to the floor.

"I HATE YOU!" screamed the little girl, disappearing out through the kitchen door.

Eudora knelt next to her sobbing mother and tried to console her. "She doesn't mean it, Mummy. She was upset because you wouldn't listen to her. We did plant the sweet peas together. It was meant to be a surprise. For you."

Beatrice gazed up at her daughter with such sorrow. As the years progressed, this look became as familiar to Eudora as the reflection of her own face. "For me?"

Eudora nodded. "We thought you might like them. Would you like to come and see?"

Beatrice gave a brief nod, allowing her daughter to help her to her feet. They made their way into the garden together but stopped in their tracks at the sight of Stella. She had pulled the entire tangle of sweet peas, canes and all, from the ground and thrown them onto the grass. She was now ripping them apart like a wolf setting upon its prey. She glanced up but didn't stop. She kept her gaze fixed on Beatrice as she pulled apart every stem and petal with a cold determination that chilled Eudora to her core.

# Chapter 5

DESPITE THE OPPRESSIVELY sticky summer night, Eudora wakes the next day feeling unusually refreshed. She recalls a bizarre dream in which Stanley was weeping over a wilting posy of sweet peas, while the young Stella begged Eudora to save her from some unspecified threat.

"Please, Dora. You're the only one who can help me now."

Eudora longed to look away but was transfixed as Stella's face distorted and twisted into that of Rose, who continued to plead. "Help me, Eudora. I need you to help me. Please. I'll share my Haribo Cherries with you."

She hauls herself to a sitting position in a bid to shake the remnants of this foolish dream from her brain. The sun beams through a gap in the curtain like a demanding toddler, urging her to be up and on. Montgomery seems to reinforce this point by issuing an insistent meow as he pushes his way in through the bedroom door, which is ajar. He leaps up onto the bed and fixes Eudora with a look of astonishment, as if to say, *For heaven's sake, woman, what on earth are you still doing in bed? Don't you know you have a cat to feed?*

Reaching out a hand to scratch his bony head, Eudora is rewarded with a thin purr of satisfaction.

"This is quite a transformation. I can't ever remember you making that sound before."

It doesn't take long for Montgomery to tire of his new game, however, as the purrs give way to nips of impatience.

"That was short-lived," says Eudora, pulling her hand away. "Come along then." She makes slow progress, but for once the cat doesn't try to trip her up on the stairs. Instead, he nuzzles her ankles appreciatively as she prepares his food. Eudora sets about making her own breakfast and carries it into the living room, where she switches on the radio, settling into her usual routine of tea, toast, and berating any *Today* program contributors who have the misfortune to annoy her. The subject of Eudora's wrath this morning is a seventy-five-year-old American woman who is promoting a book about how great it is to be old.

"Age really is just a number," she tells the interviewer in a cheerful southern drawl, which makes Eudora mistrust her from the off. "If you live your life with positivity and love, surround yourself with beautiful things, eat well, and exercise often, you can literally live forever."

"Literally live forever?" scoffs Eudora, ignoring the fact that she agrees with her points on food and exercise. "What on earth is this imbecile talking about?"

The interviewer picks up her point. "But no one can live for*ever*, can they?"

The woman laughs. Eudora scowls at the sound. "Not necessarily in this life, but I believe that on passing from this world we are merely transitioning to another. And we therefore can and will live forever."

Eudora almost chokes on her toast. "Passing? Transitioning? What in heaven's name are you blathering on about? It's called death—D-E-A-T-H. For goodness' sake, stop talking in euphemisms, you foolish woman!"

"Some people might say that you are failing to face the

reality of life and death by using this kind of language," says the interviewer.

"And some people would be right," says Eudora, nodding at the radio with approval.

But the interviewee is undeterred. "I understand. We are all entitled to our own views and must respect those of others. I can only tell you how I live my life and that it is a full and happy one. I wanted to share my knowledge because I thought it might help others."

"You really needn't have bothered," Eudora tells her.

"I truly believe that you are meant to enjoy your life for as long as possible. This is merely my philosophy. If people want to mock or tear down my beliefs, that is up to them. They have my sympathy because, probably, deep down, they're not happy themselves."

Eudora is furious. "You have no idea whether I'm happy or not, you sanctimonious harlot! How dare you pollute my morning's listening with your half-baked theories?" She turns off the radio with a flourish. "I'll show you who's happy or not." She hauls herself to a standing position, ready to gather her belongings and head out for a morning swim.

For Eudora, the biggest frustration of getting older is the speed at which she now moves. Everything from making a cup of tea to going upstairs to the lavatory takes a level of effort she finds maddening. Eudora understands entirely why people get frustrated with the elderly. There is nothing agreeable about some doddery old fool getting in your way, but what dismays her most of all is the fact that she is now one of them.

She watched her own mother's decline with a mixture of sadness and indignant anger. How could the woman who had given her life be reduced to a shriveled husk of a human, staring out at the world through frightened eyes? How could old age be so cruel?

Eudora is determined that it will not happen to her. The more her body winds down like a neglected antique clock, the more determined she is that she will leave this world on her own terms. *My death. My way.* It's becoming something of a mantra now.

She knows it's unorthodox. People don't talk about death. Not really. People fear it. Ignore it. Deny it. They're happy to blow one another's heads off in those infernal video games or devour horrific films where people are murdered in the most gruesome of ways, while refusing to face the reality of what death is or to have a grown-up discussion about what it means. Eudora adopts the opposite approach. Perhaps it's her background growing up during the war or the fact that death was like a series of punctuation marks in her life. Whatever the reason, she neither fears it, ignores it, nor denies it. In fact, as old age creeps through her veins, she welcomes its approach like a treasured friend.

It takes Eudora a good half hour to get herself ready. She tries to lessen the frustration with the notion that the swim will be a reward for her patience. She is on the point of leaving the house when the telephone rings. Eudora hesitates. It will probably be one of those nuisance callers—a bored nineteen-year-old trying to sell her pet insurance or, worse still, one of those idiotic recorded messages telling her that she's been in a recent accident at work and can claim compensation. Yet another thing she won't miss about this noisy, moronic world.

She pauses to listen. Eudora has an ancient answering machine—a vestige of when she tried to modernize the existence she shared with her mother, possibly purchased around the same time as those infuriating duvet covers.

"Hallo. This is Petra calling from Klinik Lebenswahl. I wanted to speak with Ms. Honeysett about her recent application."

Eudora almost stumbles in a bid to get to the phone. "Blasted knees. Why can't you move properly!" she scolds.

Thankfully, Petra is still talking by the time Eudora reaches the telephone. She snatches it from its cradle. "Hello? This is Eudora Honeysett."

"Ah, hallo, Ms. Honeysett. You are there. This is Petra from Klinik Lebenswahl. I have received your application and wanted to have a conversation with you. Is this a good time?"

Eudora experiences a thrill as all thoughts of her morning swim are replaced with an altogether more pressing matter. She sits down in her chair. "Yes, yes, of course. What would you like to know?"

"So. Do you remember we spoke before and I said that there were certain protocols we had to follow?"

"Yes. That's why I filled out the form. To make my wishes clear."

"I understand. Actually, let's do this properly. My name is Petra Konrad. Would you mind if I called you Eudora?"

She does mind but doesn't want to appear unhelpful.

This woman is the person who stands between Eudora and the thing she wants most. "As you wish."

"Okay. So, Eudora, you are eighty-five years old."

"Correct."

"And you have no husband or children?"

"No. On both counts."

"You live alone?"

"Yes."

"Would you say that you are unhappy?"

Eudora knows where she is headed with this question and is ready. "I am not depressed or lonely or sad in any way. I am simply old and increasingly affected by this. I have no family or friends." Rose's cheery face pops unexpectedly into her mind. Eudora blinks it away. "As I've said to you before, I do not want to end up dependent and decrepit in some terrible nursing home. I want to take control of my life by choosing my own ending. It is my own will. I am in complete possession of the facts and all my faculties, and I am fully prepared to sign whichever declaration is required. I will even administer the necessary drugs myself if that is possible."

"Eudora. I understand, really, I do. I am on your side. This conversation won't determine what happens, but it is our duty to talk to you properly, to discuss all options so that you and we are sure this is the right path for you."

"I am sure."

"Can I ask if you have discussed this with anyone else?"

Eudora is horrified. "No, I haven't and I don't need to.

I know you're only doing your job and you have various boxes to tick, but there really is no need with me. I've made up my mind. This is what I want."

Petra clears her throat. "I understand, but in life there is always doubt," she says. "We wouldn't be human if we didn't question our decisions, particularly one as important as this. My own grandmother—I think we spoke of her before—she had many doubts before she decided that voluntary assisted death was the right path for her."

"Was she ill?"

"Yes. Her quality of life was such that it became too much for her, but she didn't take the decision easily."

"Are you suggesting that I have?"

"No, Eudora, but I am offering myself as someone to talk to, as I did for my grandmother. You can share anything with me. It will go no further."

Eudora would rather walk along the street in her underwear than indulge the world's penchant for baring its soul. She decides to adopt a middle path: cooperative yet firm. "That is very kind of you, and I am happy to answer your questions. But I have thought about it for a long time and I'm not going to change my mind now."

"Can you remember when you first thought about it?"

Eudora considers the question. There are so many possible answers. In many ways, it's as if she's been contemplating this for as long as she can remember. "I suppose I started to think about it in earnest when I saw my own mother's decline."

"Did you care for her?"

"I did."

"For a long time?"

"I lived with my mother in this house all my life and looked after her until she died in 2005. She was ninety-five." Usually, when Eudora told people this, they would exclaim how Beatrice had had a good innings, but for Eudora, there'd been nothing "good" about the final years of her mother's life.

"This was hard for you," says Petra with an insight that impresses Eudora.

"At times. But she was my mother. We had no one else."

"You did your best."

An unexpected scratch of emotion catches at the back of her throat. "I hope so."

"Eudora, I must be honest with you."

"Please do."

"If I pass your application on to Doctor Liebermann, I suspect she will reject it."

"But why?"

"Because she and her colleagues will think you are depressed."

"I am not depressed." Eudora's voice is sharp with anger.

"Perhaps not, but given your circumstances, the fact that you are alone . . ."

"I am not lonely. I eat well, exercise, complete a daily crossword, listen to the radio. I am just old and I don't want to get any older!" Eudora immediately regrets the shrill edge to her tone.

"I understand. Really, I do. But we have regulations.

Voluntary assisted death is usually only for those who are sick and whose quality of life is too poor for them to continue happily."

"But surely it's my choice! Surely I should be able to decide if I live or die! We treat animals better than we treat humans. Why can't I be put down if it's my choice?"

"Because the world doesn't work like that. I'm sorry. I'm just being honest."

"Then maybe the world needs to change. Maybe it needs to grow up and have a sensible conversation about death."

"Maybe you are right."

"So you can't help me? I am destined for a life of adult nappies and being manhandled by strangers, am I?"

"Eudora, I want to help you. I've wanted to help you since we first spoke. You remind me of my grandmother."

"Was she a difficult old boot as well then?"

Petra laughs. It's a consoling sound. Eudora finds herself smiling. "She was very determined, like you, and she knew her mind like you."

"And you helped her to die?"

"I did."

"So will you help me, Petra? Please?" Her imploring tone seems to have the desired effect as Petra pauses before answering.

"I will try but I can't promise the doctor will agree. And also, I want you to promise me something."

"Yes?"

"That you will call me if you want to discuss any of this,

however small—any thoughts, doubts, or questions. I am here for you."

Eudora hesitates. She is so unused to human kindness that it catches her off guard. "Thank you," she says quietly. "So you will forward my application?"

"I will. And you will call me if you need to?"

"I will." Their promises are as sacred as wedding vows to Eudora.

"Okay, Eudora. I will be in touch and I will be here. Goodbye."

"Goodbye, Petra."

Eudora hangs up the phone with a mixture of hope and exhaustion. All she can do now is wait and pray. She sits back in the chair and closes her eyes, all thoughts of that day's routine postponed for now.

She is woken by a loud knock at the door. Eudora keeps her eyes closed and decides to ignore it. It won't be important. It's never important. There's another knock, louder this time and decidedly impatient.

*They'll give up and go away in a minute*, she thinks with a sigh.

Unfortunately, Eudora has underestimated the person doing the knocking. The next sound she hears is that of the letterbox being scraped open. A sinking realization descends upon her.

"Eudora! It's me. Rose. From next door."

"Of course it is," mutters Eudora under her breath. "Who else could it possibly be, shouting through my letterbox?" She decides to stay still and quiet in the vain hope Rose might get bored. She is out of luck.

"Eudora! Are you in there? I want to ask you something. It's very important."

"I sincerely doubt that," says Eudora to no one in particular. There is a pause, during which she experiences a glimmer of hope that Rose has finally given up.

"Hellooo! Eudora! Are you okay? I know you're home because I haven't seen you leave the house today."

"Good heavens above, it's like living next door to the Gestapo," says Eudora, heaving herself to her feet. "I'm coming!" she calls irritably.

"Okay! I'll wait here," says Rose in an obliviously cheerful tone.

Eudora huffs her way to the door and yanks it open, ready with a piercing glare. However, her furious scowl is quickly replaced with openmouthed astonishment. Rose is wearing her normal clothes—if you can call a fuchsia-pink ra-ra skirt, silver sequined flip-flops, and a fluorescent yellow T-shirt normal—but in addition, she has chosen to accessorize the outfit with a blue swimming cap and matching goggles. The overall effect is remarkable. Eudora is momentarily stunned into silence.

Rose seizes her opportunity. "Hello, Eudora. Would you like to come swimming with me?"

"What?" is the only word Eudora can find.

"Swim-ing," repeats Rose slowly. "With. Me."

Eudora is confused and appalled. "I don't think so, Rose. Thank you."

"Oh," says Rose, chewing the inside of her cheek. "Is it the walk that's putting you off? Because I'm sure Mum will drop us off if I ask her."

Eudora considers this. She would like to go for a swim but would rather go alone. "I'm just not quite sure why you'd want to go swimming with me," she says.

"We-ell, I'm a bit lonely and I think you might be too. And we both like swimming. And Mum's tired because of the baby so she can't take me. So will you? I'll buy you a slushy."

"I'm not lonely," says Eudora, her hackles rising. "I'm eighty-five and I like my own company, thank you very much. Don't you have any friends your own age with whom you could go?"

Rose shrugs. "My best friend, Lottie, is in Cornwall. You're the only person I know apart from Stanley and Mum and Dad. And Monty, but cats can't swim obviously, so . . ."

Something in Rose's hopeful face pricks Eudora's conscience. "Oh very well," she says. It seems that when it comes to Rose, resistance really is futile.

"Yessss!" cries Rose, punching the air.

During the stuffy journey to the pool, Eudora starts to lose patience with Maggie, who keeps checking if she is happy with the arrangement.

"I know how persistent my daughter can be."

"I can hear you, you know," says Rose from the back of the car.

"I'm just saying that if you don't want to, I would understand."

"I have said I will so there's really no need to ask again," snaps Eudora.

"Sorry," mutters Maggie. "And thank you. It's very kind of you."

Eudora is grateful that Rose allows her the dignity of her own changing cubicle, although she is obviously standing directly in front of the door when the old woman emerges.

"I stayed right outside in case you had an emergency," she says.

"Thank you," says Eudora uncertainly as they make their way to the poolside.

There's a chaotic "Family Splash" session taking place in the teaching pool, so they opt for the shallow end of the main pool. Eudora gazes longingly at the swimming lanes, wishing she could be making her usual steady progress back and forth.

"Shall we jump in?" suggests Rose.

"Certainly not," says Eudora. "I shall use the steps."

"I might jump in."

"As you wish."

Rose grins at her. "I love the way you talk. It's like something from the olden days."

"Mmm," says Eudora, lowering herself into the pool. The refreshing coolness of the water is almost healing after the stifling heat of Maggie's car. Eudora allows herself to float on her back, relishing a momentary respite from the burden of old age.

"Coming, ready or not!" cries Rose, jumping in from the side.

"Careful!" scolds Eudora, blinking away her splashes.

"I made sure I missed you," says Rose helpfully.

"Well, that's a blessing." Rose copies Eudora by floating on her back too. "Can you swim?" asks Eudora.

"Sort of," says Rose, flipping onto her front and doggy paddling her way around her swimming companion.

"Would you like me to teach you how to do front crawl?" asks Eudora as the whisper of a memory flits into her brain.

"Yes, please. I can almost do it, but sometimes it feels as if I'm drowning."

"Well, we can't have that. Show me how you do it."

Rose takes a deep breath and disappears under the water in a tangle of arms and legs before shooting above the surface with a loud gasp and then bobbing back down to begin the alarming process all over again. Eudora finds it both comical and terrifying.

"Stop, Rose. Stop!"

The little girl rises from the deep and stares wide-eyed at Eudora from behind her huge goggles.

"I can see why you feel as if you're drowning. You look as if you're drowning. Now stand here and watch me for a moment."

Rose does as she's told. Eudora swims back and forth along the width of the pool at a calm and steady pace.

Rose erupts into a splashy round of applause as she returns. "That was amazing! You look like a fish. Can you teach me how to do that?"

Eudora is buoyed by her eagerness to learn. "I'll try. The key is to keep your body flat so you glide through the water. You need to get into a rhythm, and you need to remain calm."

"Flat. Glide. Rhythm. Calm. Got it," says Rose.

"Now, try to kick from the hip but not too often and spear your arms into the water, putting your thumbs in first with your palms facing out."

Rose nods. "Okay, Eudora. I'll try."

Rose's first few attempts are clumsy and haphazard, but Eudora soon finds that she is an excellent pupil and a quick learner. She still flails her arms like a person having a fit, but she is beginning to move through the water in an altogether more measured fashion.

"That's very good, Rose," says Eudora. "You're getting it. Well done."

Rose beams. "Thank you. I don't feel as if I'm drowning anymore."

"I'm very relieved to hear it." Eudora glances at the large clock on the wall and realizes an hour has passed without her noticing. "I suppose we should be getting out," she says with a hint of regret. "Your mother will be here soon to collect us."

"Can we have just five more minutes? Pleeease? I could practice what you've taught me here and you could do some lengths."

The idea appeals to Eudora. "Are you sure you'll be all right?"

Rose nods. "I'll be fine. You're only in the next lane."

"Very well. Remember to keep those elbows high."

"Elbows high," repeats Rose.

Eudora makes her way back and forth, keeping an eye

on Rose, who soon bores of practicing her front crawl and seems content to climb out of the pool and jump back in over and over again. As Eudora rests at one end of the pool, she watches Rose star-jump, hop, and walk into the pool with irrepressible excitement. Eudora tries to remember if she was ever as carefree as Rose, if she ever viewed life as a joy rather than a chore. Sometimes, it's as if she had been born an adult, always taking responsibility for anyone who needed her. Eudora had fun of course but couldn't recall a time when she had been able to please herself. There had always been someone else in the background needing care or reassurance. She envies Rose a little and wonders, not for the first time, what life would have been like if her father had survived the war. There would have certainly been a great deal more joy to go around.

Eudora sets off on another length of the pool, deciding to make this her last. It has been an enjoyable afternoon, but she is tired now. As she nears the deep end, she spots Rose bobbing up and down.

"Help me, Eudora! I'm drowning!"

"Rose!" cries Eudora. Panicked, she bobs under the lane divider and with some effort pulls the little girl to the surface.

They emerge coughing and spluttering as Eudora realizes that Rose is laughing. "I'm not really drowning. I was just being silly."

Eudora's anger is immediate and white-hot. "You NEVER, EVER do that again. Do you hear me?" she shouts.

Rose's face falls. "I'm sorry, Eudora. I was only joking."

"You do NOT joke about such things. That is the end of

our swimming for today, and for good." She climbs out of the pool with Rose trailing after her.

They change in their separate cubicles before making their way out to wait for Maggie. Eudora's silence is deafening. Even the relentlessly cheerful Rose can sense her brooding fury. She glances up at Eudora. "I am very sorry," she says quietly.

Eudora gives her an imperious look but remains silent. She is exhausted now, not by the swimming, but by her anger. She longs to shake it off, but it has prompted a memory that is taking root in her mind, like a gnarly weed.

"Can I buy you a slushy to say sorry?" asks Rose.

"No, thank you," says Eudora.

The heavy mood is interrupted by the arrival of Maggie, bustling in through the entrance. "Sorry I'm late. The traffic out there is appalling. How was the swimming? Did you have fun?" She spots their expressions and grimaces. "Oh dear. What's happened?"

Eudora would rather go home than embark on this cross-examination, but Rose is ready to confess. "It was all going really well, Mummy. Eudora showed me how to do front crawl and I did brilliantly. Eudora said so. And then I did a silly thing and now Eudora is upset with me. And I'm very sorry."

Maggie winces apologetically at the old woman before kneeling in front of her daughter. Eudora looks away as she reaches out a hand to tuck a stray piece of hair behind Rose's ear. "What happened?"

Rose steals a glance at Eudora before answering. "I pretended I was drowning and it frightened Eudora."

"Oh, Rose," says Maggie.

Fat tears leak from Rose's eyes. "I know it was the wrong thing to do and I'm very sorry. Please forgive me, Eudora."

Eudora is aware that two sets of eyes are on her now, imploring her to forgive, expecting that a simple apology will make up for how she is feeling. "It was a very irresponsible thing to do," she says.

Rose nods. "I know. I promise I won't ever do it again."

Eudora glances at Maggie. Her expression is an open book, begging her to forgive her daughter, a mirror to Rose's. Eudora sighs. "Oh, very well. Now, please can we go home? I'm exhausted."

"Yes! Of course. Thank you," says Maggie. She reaches out to squeeze Eudora's arm.

*All these public displays of emotion*, thinks Eudora as they walk to the car. *No wonder the world is in such a mess.*

As soon as they reach home, Rose leaps from the car and opens Eudora's door. "Do you need help getting out?" she asks, eager to please.

"No. I'm perfectly capable, thank you," says Eudora, hauling herself to her feet and heading toward her house.

"Would you like to come in for a cup of tea?" asks Maggie.

"No. No, thank you," says Eudora without a backward glance. "Goodbye." Once inside the house, she shuts the front door and leans against it. Her hands are shaking. She's not sure whether it's from fear or anger. She does know, however, that this is the last time she's going to allow her feelings to be hijacked by a small girl with terrible taste in clothes.

## 1950
## BROCKWELL LIDO, SOUTH-EAST LONDON

"Can't catch me for a toffee flea!"

"Slow down, Stella. You'll slip over!" warned Eudora as her sister skipped out of the changing cubicle into the busy sunlit pool area.

"Don't be so boring, Dora. You sound like Mum," said Stella over her shoulder, although she paused long enough for Eudora to fall into step with her.

Eudora placed a hand on her head. "I need to keep you safe. You're my precious girl."

Stella beamed up at her sister. "Shall we jump in?"

"I'm not sure we're allowed to," said Eudora, glancing over at the list of pool rules attached to the wall.

"It says no bombing or diving but nothing about jumping. What's heavy petting?" asked Stella, frowning at the sign.

"It's er—"

"Hi, Eudora, I haven't seen you for a while."

Eudora turned to see Sam Buchanan, the most popular boy from her school days, standing in front of her. She kept her smile locked on his face in a brave attempt to avoid looking at his rather prominent pectoral muscles. "Oh, hello, Sam. Off for a swim?"

*Of course he's off for a swim, you foolish girl! Why else would he be at the lido?*

Sam nodded. "I'm here with Bill and Eric. We've already been in, but I might go for another dip in a minute."

"Dora," said Stella, pulling at her sister's arm. "Can we get in now?"

"Sorry," said Eudora, rolling her eyes at Sam. "Duty calls."

"Catch you later," said Sam with a wink.

Eudora can hear the pulse of her heart as she and Stella approach the pool. Sam Buchanan spoke to her! And he was pleased to see her too! She felt a thrill of possibility; a hint of something different in her humdrum life. It wasn't easy existing in a domestic bubble with her mother and sister. It was as if the pair of them had cast her in the role of piggy-in-the-middle and she was destined to play it until she could escape their situation. Eudora loved them both dearly but wasn't sure how much longer she could endure their enmity. The thought of a precious moment's escape with a boy like Sam gave her hope.

"Come on, Dora. Let's jump."

Eudora glanced over to where Sam was sitting on the side with his friends. He gave her another cheerful smile. She almost blushed at the fact that he had clearly been looking her way. Eudora dared a wink in reply as she grabbed Stella's hand.

"Jump!" she cried.

"Yippee!" shouted Stella.

Their giggling leap into freedom was short-lived as they made a terrific splash into the pool and were rewarded by the sound of a sharp, chastising whistle from one of the lifeguards.

"No bombing," he barked with a finger-pointing frown. "Final warning."

"We didn't bomb. We jumped," protested Stella.

"It's all right, Stella. We shouldn't have done it," said Eudora. "Sorry," she added, looking up at the lifeguard, her cheeks hot with shame. He nodded in reply. Eudora cast a look over toward Sam but he was nowhere to be seen.

"Come on, Dora," said Stella. "Let's try to talk underwater."

Eudora smiled. This was a game they liked to play. "Okay. One, two, three." They took deep breaths and ducked under. Stella looked comical as she mouthed words in an attempt to communicate. They giggled as they rose to the surface.

"What did I say?" asked Stella.

"I have no idea," replied Eudora laughing.

"God save the King!" cried Stella.

"Very good," declared Eudora. "Now, shall I teach you some swimming?"

"Aww, Dora, swimming is bor-ing," said Stella.

"Not if you don't want to drown. And besides, what are we doing here if not to swim?"

"To splash!" cried Stella, batting the water with her palms.

"Come on. Let's try. I bet I can get you to swim like a little fishy."

Stella rolled her eyes. "O-kay then. But just five minutes."

They felt like the longest five minutes of Eudora's life. Stella was a defiant pupil, refusing to do what her sister asked, continuing to make the same mistakes, splashing Eudora at every opportunity. "Come along, Stella. You're not even trying!" cried Eudora with exasperation.

"I am too! You're bossy and mean like Mother. I hate you!"

"Now, Stella. You don't mean that, and you mustn't be rude."

"I don't care. Leave me alone," she said, wading off in the opposite direction.

Eudora sighed. "Tricky pupil?" said a voice. She turned and very nearly bumped into the muscular torso of Sam Buchanan.

Eudora gave a casual laugh. "A little. She's not very good at being taught."

"Poor you." Sam smiled, and Eudora wondered what would happen if she kissed those lips. The idea made her shiver with illicit joy. "Listen, I've got to go now but I wondered if you fancied coming to the cinema with me one night? That new Cary Grant picture is playing at the Ritzy."

Eudora felt as if she were in a trance, a delicious, hopeful trance. "I would love—"

"Eudora! Help me!"

Eudora turned to see her sister's head bobbing up and sinking below the surface of the pool at the deep end.

"Stella!" she screamed.

Life seemed to move at double speed after that. The lifeguard who had scolded them earlier sprang into heroic action by diving in and pulling the trembling girl to safety. Eudora raced to Stella's side, fell to her knees, and held her sister tightly, stroking her head.

"Oh, Stella, I'm so sorry," she said after thanking the lifeguard. Stella remained silent and scowling. "Are you okay, my darling?" Silence. "Stella. Please speak to me."

Stella glared up at Eudora, her face a picture of haughty, unforgiving rage. "It was all your fault. It would never have happened if you hadn't been flirting with that stupid boy."

Guilt flooded through Eudora. "You're right. Of course you're right. I'm so sorry, Stella. I should have been watching you. I'm very sorry."

"Good. You should be sorry. You were mean to me. It was all your fault. You made me do it."

Eudora stared into her sister's eyes and saw the defiance. *You made me do it.* There was something about the way Stella said this that nagged at Eudora, something about her victorious air when Eudora had come running that bothered her. Eudora frowned. It was a ridiculous notion. She was far too young to think of manipulating her sister in that way. Besides, Stella loved her. Eudora knew this. She wouldn't pretend to drown just to get her attention. Eudora was immediately ashamed for entertaining these thoughts. She was just a child. It was Eudora's job to protect her. She kissed the top of Stella's head and wrapped the towel around her small body. "Come on. Let's go and find you some dry clothes."

Eudora saw Sam at the lido again the following week. "Is your sister okay?" he asked.

"Yes, thank you. Luckily, she's fine."

"I'm glad." His face softened into a smile. "So, when can I take you to the cinema then?"

Eudora cast her eyes downward. "Oh, I don't think it's such a good idea. Thank you all the same." The words tasted like medicine in her mouth—antiseptic and sour but necessary in order to absolve herself from the burden of guilt.

# Chapter 6

EUDORA STARES AT the long, drab hospital corridor stretching before her and questions the wisdom of whichever NHS operative decided to place the Geriatric Medicine Clinic at the end of it. Having negotiated the bus alongside a distressingly colorful cast of characters and walked in the shimmering heat to the hospital entrance, Eudora feels as if she has scaled the octogenarian's equivalent of Everest. What is more, she knows this appointment will be a waste of time, another item to be ticked off some poor overworked doctor's to-do list. And yet, Eudora has made the epic journey because for her the NHS is one of the last bastions of civilization in this morally bankrupt country. If they summon her, she will move mountains or catch the 194 toward Bexley in order to answer their call. It is her duty.

She inhales deeply, setting off along the seemingly endless corridor with fresh determination. Its walls are hung with cheerfully colored mosaics spelling different words, which Eudora reads were produced by St. James Primary School. She notices that the word "HAPPY," decorated in an eye-popping combination of pink and yellow, was created by seven-year-old Rosie. She decides that Rose and Rosie would no doubt be great friends, bonding over a love of disastrously clashing colors.

"Why, Miss Honeysett, fancy meeting you here!"

She turns to sees Stanley Marcham moving toward

her, grinning broadly, arms outstretched. Fearing he is about to embrace her, Eudora takes a step back. "Good morning," she says, undecided as to whether or not she is pleased to see him. Eudora finds him innately irritating, but there's a certain amount of relief in seeing a friendly face in this soulless place.

"Going my way?" asks Stanley, gesturing toward the clinic. She stares at him blankly. "The old duffers' clinic," he adds.

Eudora clears her throat. "I prefer to call it the geriatric clinic."

"Of course you do," says Stanley, eyes twinkling. "Would you allow me to escort you?" He offers his arm.

"I can manage quite well, thank you." She realizes this sounds brusque, so she adds, "But I'd be glad of the company if you don't mind walking at my pace."

"It will be my pleasure," he says. "My Ada was on a go-slow during her last few years. She used to say, *Why are people always hurrying, Stan? You miss so much when you're dashing here, there, and everywhere. You've got to take a moment to feel the sun on your face.*"

"She sounds like a wise woman."

"She was."

Eudora can hear a choke in Stanley's voice and decides to save them both the embarrassment by changing the subject. "Do you have any children?" she asks.

"Two," he says with obvious pride. "Paul, who's nearly fifty, and Sharon, who's fifty-two. They're both married with their own kids. They're good to their old dad."

"Quite right too," says Eudora.

Stanley smiles. "I'm lucky. I've got two wonderful kids, four amazing grandkids. I just wish Ada were here to share it with me."

"Here we are," says Eudora with relief as they reach the entrance to the clinic.

"After you," says Stanley, pulling open the door.

"Thank you."

They report to reception and take a seat in a couple of laughably uncomfortable blue plastic chairs. *God's waiting room*, thinks Eudora as she takes in her surroundings. She notices an elderly couple sitting together, the woman gripping her husband's arm, staring into the middle distance while he frowns at the *Telegraph*.

Another woman paces the floor, eyes flitting left and right, looking hopefully as if searching for something that may spring into view at any moment. She is tiny like a bird, with sharp, pointed features and straggly black-gray hair. She reminds Eudora of a crow with bead-bright eyes, always on the lookout. Her faded yellow sundress hangs baggy and misshapen over her shrunken body. Eudora recognizes a woman who no longer dresses herself, who has to trust this task to someone else, someone who dresses her for comfort rather than style. She recalls the day she visited her mother in the hospital to find her wearing tracksuit bottoms and shivers at the memory. The woman's gaze rests on Eudora. A flicker of recognition passes across her face. She darts forward and grabs Eudora by the arms.

"Margery, you naughty girl! Where have you been?"

Eudora glances nonplussed at Stanley, who seems to know exactly what to do. "Hello," he says, holding out his hand. "I don't think we've been properly introduced."

The woman gives Stanley what can only be described as a coquettish smile. "Of course we have, Peter. It's me—Enid!"

"Ahh, Enid! How are you?"

"Well, I'm all right but my flight's been delayed, so I've no idea how long I'm going to be here."

"Oh dear. What a bother," says Stanley. "Where are you flying to today?"

"New York," says Enid.

"Lovely."

"I prefer San Francisco but I have to go where my editor sends me. Follow the story and all that."

"Of course."

"Come along, Mum," says a frazzled-looking woman who appears at Enid's shoulder.

"And this is my editor, Catherine," says Enid, gesturing to her daughter.

"Pleased to meet you," says Catherine with the weary but kindly air of someone who is used to playing along with these games.

"Have they called our flight, dear?"

"They have, Mum. Let's go."

"Bye, Enid," says Stanley.

"Yes, goodbye," echoes Eudora.

"Goodbye, you two," says Enid, eyes sparkling with excitement. "Let's grab drinks at the Groucho when I'm back in town."

"We look forward to it, don't we, Margery?" says Stanley.

"Very much," says Eudora.

Enid's daughter flashes them a grateful smile before leading her mother toward the exit.

"Poor soul," says Eudora.

"She seemed very happy to me," says Stanley. "But I feel for her daughter. Ada was like that at the end; it's best to go along with it but it's not easy."

"I'm sure," says Eudora. "I thought you were very kind." She's not one for flattery but believes in giving credit where it's due.

Stanley shrugs. "It's what anyone would do."

*It's not though*, thinks Eudora. *The world isn't kind and understanding. It's impatient and full of judgment.*

"I almost forgot; I've got your handkerchief here," says Stanley, fishing it from his pocket. "Washed and ironed, just as madam likes them. Thanks for lending it to me. I've been carrying it around on the off chance I might see you."

"Thank you," says Eudora, impressed by his thoughtfulness. His incessant cheer may be annoying at times, but she is grateful for his presence today. She doesn't like hospitals and he is a welcome distraction.

"So I suppose it's a bit like prison," says Stanley.

"I beg your pardon?" asks Eudora.

"We're not allowed to ask each other what we're in for," he says with a chuckle.

Eudora rolls her eyes. It's exactly this kind of idiocy that vexes her. "For your information, I am attending the falls clinic."

"Ah right, I see. They're checking up on you after your

drunk and disorderly episode last year," says Stanley, nudging her arm.

Eudora ignores this immature attempt at humor. "What about you?"

Stanley taps his forehead. "Memory clinic. My son thinks I'm getting a bit forgetful since Ada died. I'm sure it's nothing but doesn't hurt to get it checked out, does it? Biscuit?" He pulls a packet of fig rolls from his pocket and offers it to Eudora. She eyes them with suspicion. "Don't worry, I haven't poisoned them."

"Thank you," she says, taking one. "You've come prepared."

"I know what the waiting times can be like in this place," he says, biting down on his treat. "Mind you, it's better than sitting at home feeling sorry for yourself, isn't it?"

"I try not to do that," says Eudora, reaching into her handbag for a book of crosswords.

"Ah, you're a puzzler, are you?" asks Stanley, gesturing at the book.

"You're not the only one who comes prepared for a lengthy wait. I make sure I do at least one crossword every day. It keeps one's brain ticking over."

"That's what my Ada used to say. She was a big puzzler—crosswords, word searches, the whole kit and caboodle. Never really appealed to me."

"Well, you should try it if you're worried about your memory."

"Use it or lose it?" says Stanley.

"Something like that," says Eudora, taking out her pen.

"Stanley Marcham," calls a brightly smiling nurse.

"At your service, madam," cries Stanley, leaping to his feet.

"Good luck," says Eudora.

"I don't need luck," says Stanley.

"I was talking to the nurse."

Stanley laughs. "Very good, Miss Honeysett!"

Eudora shakes her head and turns back to her crossword. It's a tricky one today, but she relishes the challenge, enjoying the moment of immersive concentration, searching for the right word. The *Times* crosswords have always been her favorite. Eudora used to have the newspaper delivered every day but canceled it when she realized she was only buying it for the crossword. At least with these compendiums at hand, she no longer has to deal with stories or images of the half-wits who are currently running the world. She dreads to think what Churchill would make of these dangerous fools.

Her pen is poised over seventeen across—"meaningless language" (12)—as she considers how many e's are in the word "gobbledegook" when her hand begins to tremble. A flurry of panic intensifies the shaking so that Eudora is forced to fold her arms and tell herself to breathe.

"Miss Honeysett?" calls a small, hopeful voice. Eudora looks up at the woman, wondering how someone who is barely old enough to drive can be summoning her. She notices her stethoscope and sighs.

"That's me," she says, rising to her feet, relieved that the shaking has stopped for now.

"Do you need a hand?" offers the doctor, venturing forward.

"No, I can manage." She regrets her abrupt tone as the doctor shrinks back. "Thank you."

Eudora follows her into a small, stuffy room with unprepossessing views of the car park. She spots Enid and her daughter making their way, arm in arm, toward their car. Enid says something. Her daughter laughs and kisses her mother's cheek. Eudora finds herself envying their connection. She can't recall ever having such a bond with her own mother.

"Please take a seat," says the doctor. "My name is Doctor Abbie Jarvis. I'm a registrar specializing in geriatric medicine working under Mr. Simons. I believe this is a follow-up appointment after your fall last year?"

"You believe correctly," says Eudora. "Although I'm not entirely sure why it's necessary." She looks at the young woman properly now. She feels guilty for dismissing her so readily. Eudora detects a sweet nature behind the doctor's huge bottle-top glasses but also a disastrous lack of self-confidence.

Doctor Jarvis's smile lights up her face. "Hopefully it's just routine and we can send you on your way as quickly as possible."

"Very well," says Eudora. She decides to help this young woman and resolves to be as cooperative as possible.

"Do you remember the circumstances of your fall?"

"I tripped over a loose paving stone. I complained to the council. There are hundreds of them all over the borough."

"And you didn't break anything?"

"Thankfully, no. I was concussed and bruised but no lasting damage."

"That's good. And you're still able to get around okay?"

"I have a stick now and that helps." Eudora's hand begins to tremble again. She tries in vain to hide it.

"Do you often experience shaking like that?" asks Doctor Jarvis with the hint of a frown.

"On occasion. I'm sure it's nothing."

"Any stiffness in your joints or slowing of movement?"

"Of course," says Eudora. "I'm eighty-five years old."

The doctor reaches forward and takes her trembling hand. "Would you mind if I brought Mr. Simons in for a second opinion?"

*Yes*, thinks Eudora. *I absolutely would mind. I want to be left alone. I'm just old. Why won't you listen?* Then she remembers her resolution to cooperate.

"Very well," she says.

Doctor Jarvis squeezes her hand gently. Her touch is cool and reassuring. "I'll be back as quickly as possible."

Eudora sits very still. She stares at her hand accusingly, commanding it to stop shaking. The consultant bursts through the door moments later without bothering to knock. He has the ham-faced look of a man who believes himself to be a great deal more important than everyone else. Eudora dislikes him on sight. Doctor Jarvis trails in behind him, and Eudora is struck by how terrified she looks.

"I'm Mr. Simons," he says in the bored voice of someone who has been told he has to introduce himself but finds the whole thing beneath him. "Doctor Jarvis suspects you may be displaying symptoms of Parkinson's."

Doctor Jarvis breathes in sharply. "I hadn't actually mentioned that."

The consultant sighs but makes no apology. "Any stiffness in your muscles or slowing in your ability to walk?"

"A little," says Eudora, pursing her lips. "But I put that down to age."

"Do you indeed?" he says. He turns to Doctor Jarvis. "These really are the most basic questions. Am I supposed to do your job for you?"

"No, of course not. Sorry," she says, looking as if she may be on the verge of tears.

Eudora begins to shake again. The consultant glares, seizing her hand as if he means to give it a sound telling off. He sniffs and drops it, looking faintly disappointed. "Tremors," he says. "Very common in the elderly." He turns to Eudora and addresses her with the patronizing slow-speak of the ignorant. "Are-these-affecting-your-everyday-life?"

Eudora's shoulders stiffen. "They're a nuisance but generally no."

"They can be caused by stress or anger or too much caffeine," he tells Doctor Jarvis. "Write to the GP and ask them to monitor," he adds, turning toward the door.

"I would put it down to anger then at this precise moment," mutters Eudora.

"I beg your pardon?"

"Yes, I think you probably should," she says, narrowing her eyes. Mr. Simons looks nonplussed. "May I ask you something?"

He folds his arms. "Very well."

"Is your mother proud of you?"

"I beg your pardon?"

"Your mother. I was wondering if she would be proud of the way you conduct yourself. I mean, you've clearly achieved a great deal in your professional life and yet you appear unable to behave in a civilized fashion." Mr. Simons opens his mouth to protest. Eudora holds up a hand to silence him. "I am an eighty-five-year-old woman with no time for bullies. I suggest you rethink your career, because to my mind you shouldn't be dealing with other people. You are rude, undignified, and unkind. You owe this young woman and me an apology."

Mr. Simons glares at her for a moment before clamping his mouth shut and storming out of the room without another word.

The young doctor and old woman stare at each other as a flicker of recognition passes between them. It's the look of two women who are united in support of each other, regardless of age. For Eudora, it is as if she's found her voice again and discovered, to her surprise, that she has something to say.

"I hope I haven't caused trouble for you by speaking my mind," she says.

"Not at all, Miss Honeysett," says the doctor, shaking her head. "I'm very sorry for what happened. Mr. Simons is . . ."

"A despicable human being who needed to be told," says Eudora, rising to her feet. She fixes the doctor with a steady gaze. "You have nothing to apologize for. I can't abide bullies, and I urge you to stand up to this one. You are a kind young woman and an excellent doctor. You deserve better."

"Thank you," says Doctor Jarvis. "Sometimes I feel as if I should find another career."

"Don't you dare," says Eudora. "You need to be strong and fearless, because you are more than capable. And besides, who will I visit when I come here for my next appointment? You have an important role to play."

The doctor studies her face. "I think we both do."

Eudora is momentarily caught off guard before she regains her composure. "So are we finished here?"

"Yes. I'll write to your GP, and if these tremors get worse, please get in touch." She holds out her hand. Eudora accepts it. "It was a pleasure to meet you, Miss Honeysett."

"And you, Doctor Jarvis."

Eudora's conversation with Doctor Jarvis sifts through her mind as she returns to the waiting room. The older she gets, the more redundant she feels. It's as if her life is a long corridor lined with different doors leading to activities past and present. In her youth, she could enter through any number of these doors. Going out to work, socializing with friends, trips to the seaside. Everything was possible. Now, most of the doors are marked with strict "no entry" signs. She is limited to hospital appointments, daily crosswords, and preparing easy-to-chew food. It's not the end of the world but it's a shrunken world, which makes her feel a lot less useful.

As she reaches the waiting room, she is pleasantly unsurprised to find Stanley waiting for her.

"I thought you might appreciate a lift home," he says.

"Thank you. That's very kind."

"How did you get on?" he asks. "Everything all right?"

Eudora decides not to mention the shaking or the bullying doctor. She hasn't quite worked it out in her own head yet. "Everything is fine. How about you?"

Stanley shrugs. "They want to keep an eye on me, but they always do at our age, don't they?"

"They've got us in an iron grip," says Eudora.

Stanley laughs. "True, but it all comes from a good place."

"I suppose it does."

He opens the passenger door for her as they reach his car. She climbs inside, relieved at not having to catch the bus home.

"You know, I'm always happy to give you a lift if you have an appointment," he says, settling behind the wheel and switching on the ignition, bringing a welcome breath of cold air from the air-conditioning.

"Thank you, but I don't mind public transport," says Eudora.

"You're not a very good liar," says Stanley. "Seriously. It's no bother. It helps get me out of the house. I'll give you my telephone number when we get back to yours."

"Thank you," says Eudora. She knows she'll never use it but is grateful for the gesture.

Stanley switches on the radio. Eudora winces as "Hound Dog" blares through the speakers. Instead of turning it down, Stanley joins in, howling and jigging about in his seat like a man possessed. He glances over at her. "Not a fan of the King?"

"He was a little after my time," says Eudora.

"Fair enough. But you used to go dancing, didn't you?"

"Of course." Eudora's eyes glitter at the memory. "Every Saturday night."

"Magical times," says Stanley.

"A long time ago now," says Eudora.

"Well. You're only as young as you feel."

"In which case, I feel about two hundred years old."

"Now then, Miss Honeysett. We can't be having that. So, I've got a proposal for you."

"Oh yes," says Eudora, wishing she'd caught the bus after all.

"It's my Paul's fiftieth birthday this weekend and I was wondering if you might like to come to the party with me? It's at the old dance hall 'round the corner. I don't really want to go on my own and it might be fun."

Eudora glances at him. Of course she doesn't want to go but how can she refuse? And besides, what harm is there in indulging him for one evening?

*Might as well make myself useful while I'm waiting to die.*

"Very well," she says. "But I'll need to be home by ten."

Stanley pretends to doff a cap. "Your wish is my command, Cinderella."

## 1952

## SIDNEY AVENUE, SOUTH-EAST LONDON

---

It was a missing button that started the argument. A fat brown button as shiny as a freshly uncased conker.

There had been three of them on Stella's blazer when she left for her first day at the local secondary modern, a picture of nervous excitement in her new uniform.

"Smart as a new pin," said Eudora, eyes brimming as she held her sister at arm's length. "And ready for adventure." She glanced over her shoulder at her mother, who watched them both without emotion. "Doesn't she look smart, Mum?" prompted Eudora, ever the appeaser.

Beatrice took a step forward. "You have a speck of fluff on your collar," she said, brushing it away with a scratch of her fingernail. "But otherwise you'll pass muster."

Stella glanced at her sister, who gave her a nod of encouragement. "See you later then," she said, picking up her satchel and heading for the door.

"Have a good day, precious girl," called Eudora. Stella flashed a brave smile before disappearing along the street. "I hope she'll be all right."

"She'll be fine," said Beatrice dismissively. "Don't be late for work, will you?"

Since she left school, Eudora had worked as a secretary in a bank in London. She enjoyed the job, but more than this, she loved commuting into the city every day. It made her feel important and necessary. She was providing for her family, looking after them just as her father had asked her to. She missed him every day and often wished he was there to provide respite from her mother's and sister's stormier episodes. She could imagine her and her father rolling their eyes at each other, diffusing the situation with a shared smile.

Eudora had hoped that Beatrice would soften toward Stella as the child became older and less demanding. Unfortunately, the brooding seed of resentment, which had been firmly planted the day her father died, had taken root, growing into something more permanent. Ridiculous as it sounded, it was almost as if Beatrice held Stella responsible for her husband's death. Her life had been settled before he was killed—Albert, Beatrice, and Eudora had been a happy band of three. And then the war came and stole her father away just as Stella made her dramatic, noisy entrance into the world. Unfortunate as it was for Stella, she was synonymous with tragedy in Beatrice's mind, and the child's sometimes cruel and demanding nature solidified her position as someone to be endured rather than adored.

Eudora took it upon herself to compensate for her mother's negative attitude toward her youngest child. It was a burdensome and often thankless task.

Work was a welcome refuge. Eudora's colleagues were friendly enough, and a couple of the older secretaries had taken her under their wing. Mr. Wells, her boss, was a kindly older man, who reminded her a little of her father when he called her "dear."

Eudora's mother still worked at the primary school that she and Stella had attended and was now in charge of the school office. Last year, a male teacher called Mr. Harrison had asked her mother to the theater.

Beatrice had been deeply offended by the suggestion, which Eudora secretly decided was a shame. She understood that her mother missed their father, but she couldn't understand why this meant avoiding all male company for the rest of her life. She was certain her father would want her mother to be happy, but for some reason her mother seemed unable to free herself from the weight of grief.

As Eudora let herself in through the front door that evening, she was looking forward to seeing Stella and hearing about her first day.

"Hello! Mum? Stella?" There was a heavy silence followed by a gasping sob from the kitchen. "Mum?" Eudora knew something bad had happened as soon as she spotted her mother's anguished face and the unpeeled carrots and potatoes on the counter.

"That child is a devil!" cried Beatrice.

"What has she done now?" asked Eudora, trying to mask her impatience.

"She slapped me! Her own mother!" Beatrice leaned toward Eudora and, as soon as her daughter embraced her, began to sob like a child.

"What happened?" asked Eudora softly, stroking her mother's hair.

"Well. When she came home from school, I noticed her blazer was missing a button, and when I asked her what had happened, she shrugged as if she didn't care. It made me so cross, Eudora. I told her that she was to sit down and sew it back on immediately, but she refused.

Can you believe it? And when I shouted at her to do as she was told, she shouted back at me and told me to go to hell! My mother would have shut me in the coal shed if I'd spoken to her like that."

Eudora sighed inwardly.

"She was about to leave the kitchen, so I grabbed her arm and that was when she slapped me. Here." Beatrice jutted her cheek upward to show Eudora the angry pink mark.

"Oh dear," said Eudora, a suffocating weariness descending.

"What are we to do about her?" said Beatrice. "She's out of control, Eudora. This would never have happened if your father was still alive. I'm sure of that."

"I'll talk to her," said Eudora.

"Oh, would you? Thank you. You're such a kind girl. Where would I be without you? Stella listens to you. I think she hates me! What I've done to deserve that, I'll never know."

Eudora climbed the stairs and tapped lightly on Stella's door. "Go away!" came a muffled, angry voice.

"Stella, it's me. Please can I come in?" She heard movement from within the room before the door opened a fraction. Eudora took this as a cue and stepped inside. Stella was sitting on the bed still in her uniform, scowling at the world. Eudora sat down beside her.

"I suppose she told you what happened," said Stella after a pause.

"If by 'she' you mean Mum, then yes." Eudora stole a

glance at her sister. Where Beatrice's reaction had been tearful, Stella's was brimming with fury. "You know you shouldn't have slapped her, don't you?"

Stella shrugged.

"Stella," warned Eudora. "You can't go around hitting people."

"She grabbed my arm really hard!"

Eudora swallowed. She knew their mother could be heavy-handed. "You still shouldn't have slapped her."

"Why do you always take her side? Every time. She hates me and you always stick up for her. It's not fair, Dora."

Eudora knew she was right, but then it wasn't fair that she came home night after night having to referee her mother and sister. "She doesn't hate you."

"She does," said Stella, folding her arms. "But it doesn't matter because I hate her too. She's a bitch."

"Don't say that, Stella. It's rude and disrespectful. She's your mother."

"So what?" said Stella, jumping to her feet, tearing open the bedroom door. She leaned over the banister. "You're a bitch, do you hear me, Mother? A B-I-T-C-H. Bitch."

"Eudora!" cried her mother from the kitchen doorway. "How can you let her talk to me like that?"

Eudora's shoulders sagged with fatigue as she let herself fall back onto Stella's bed. She tried to blot out the creeping realization that whatever she did, however hard she tried, she would never be able to make her mother and sister happy. As she turned her head, she spied the framed photograph of their father in full uniform, smiling his encouragement, from Stella's bedside table. Eudora sighed, hauling herself to her feet, ready to face her mother and sister and try, yet again, to broker peace in their bitter, endless battle.

## Chapter 7

AS EUDORA PULLS open the doors to her ancient mahogany wardrobe, she is hit with the scent of mothballs and lavender. She sifts through her limited selection of clothes with a resigned sigh. It's been a long time since she's been invited anywhere, and Eudora isn't convinced she owns the appropriate outfit for a fiftieth birthday party. Alongside her funeral suit, the rod is loaded with garments in every shade of gray, brown, and blue, all leaning toward the darker end of this palette.

"When did I get so drab?" she asks Montgomery, who is curled neatly on top of the bed. Eudora reaches over to scratch the top of his head. The cat stretches out and yawns, revealing sharp teeth, a warning that her actions are not currently welcome. "Well, you're not much use," she tells him, turning back to her disastrous excuse for a wardrobe.

Eudora has always been smart—she prides herself on her appearance—but she has never been adventurous when it comes to clothes. She is wondering if she regrets this. She is also wondering why she cares so much. It's only a birthday party with Stanley and a group of strangers. And it's not as if she knows him that well anyway. Or cares what he thinks. No. She definitely doesn't give two hoots what Stanley Marcham thinks.

However, she would like to make an effort for herself. Eudora always used to take pride in her appearance when she went dancing as a young woman. She can still recall the effervescent joy of getting spruced up on a Saturday night, of wearing a beautiful dress with newly curled hair and makeup—not too much, mind—before skipping off to dance the night away. It seems like a different lifetime now.

Eudora reaches disconsolately into the wardrobe, wishing for a large pumpkin and a fairy godmother. She pulls out a navy blue skirt, which she used to wear for gardening, and a blouse the color of over-steeped tea. Holding both items up for inspection, she tries to convince herself they might do. Perhaps a brooch would lift the whole effect? Or her mother's pearls? And should she dare to wear a pair of smart court shoes, or stick to her boring but comfortable slip-ons with the cushioned soles?

Eudora is so lost in thought that she jumps as the silence is broken by someone pressing the doorbell for a little longer than is strictly necessary. "Let go of the bell, Rose," calls Eudora over the banister.

"How did you know it was me?" asks the little girl, as Eudora eventually reaches the front door.

"Who else would it be?"

"I am very reliable," admits Rose. "Mum always says that I am the best and most loyal friend you can have."

"That makes you sound like a dog."

Rose giggles. "I like that."

"And to what do I owe the pleasure? Because I'm not going swimming today if that's what you're thinking."

"Oh, I know. You went this morning. I saw you come back."

Eudora isn't sure whether to be touched or terrified by

Rose's commitment to keeping her under KGB-level surveillance.

"I just popped 'round with this." She holds out a red-and-white-polka-dot cake tin. "To say sorry. It's lemon drizzle. I made it with Mum. She told me to drop it off and come straight home."

Eudora accepts the tin. "Oh. Well, thank you, Rose." The little girl stares up at her hopefully. "You're not doing a very good job of going straight home, are you?"

"Well, no," admits Rose. "But I thought it would be polite of me to offer to share the cake with you so you don't feel too piggy."

"How selfless of you."

"Thank you," says Rose, nodding proudly.

Eudora realizes she's not going to leave and can't think of a way of banishing her without appearing rude. "Would you like to come in for a slice of cake, Rose?"

Rose's face erupts with delight. "Yes please! Thank you, Eudora. Shall I make us some squash, or cor-dial, as you like to call it?"

Recalling the tooth-dissolving concoction she prepared last time, Eudora shakes her head. "Not for me. I shall make some tea, but you can have cordial if you prefer."

"I do prefer," says Rose, following her to the kitchen.

Eudora fetches a glass and the cordial bottle, then sets about making her tea. Rose pours out a good half glass, topping it up with the merest splash of water.

"You'll rot your teeth," warns Eudora.

"That's what Mum says. But I'm a really good brusher, so I think it'll be okay." She looks around the room. "Your kitchen is very bare. You don't have any magnets on your fridge or pictures on the cupboards like we do."

"True."

"I'll make you some pictures," says Rose.

"There's really no need."

"I don't mind. I love drawing."

Eudora sips her tea and thinks about the pictures she saw on the walls of the hospital and knows there's no sense in arguing. Besides, they might brighten up the place a little. What with her ill-stocked wardrobe and empty walls, life has steadily become a little less colorful.

"Were you having a nap upstairs when I rang the doorbell? My granny often has a nap in the afternoons."

"No. In actual fact, I was trying to choose an outfit."

"Ooh, can I help? I know a lot about fashion."

Eudora glances at Rose's current ensemble—a pair of pink khaki shorts, a purple T-shirt emblazoned with the words "Be More Unicorn," and a gold headscarf. Maybe Eudora is starting to get used to these affronts to fashion, or perhaps it's just too hot to protest. "Very well," she says.

"You always say that."

"Say what?"

"Very well. When you don't want to do something but decide to go along with it to be polite."

"Very well," repeats Eudora.

"You're funny, Eudora," says Rose, draining her drink before galloping up the stairs.

By the time Eudora reaches the door to her bedroom, Rose is standing with her arms folded, having reviewed and rejected her entire wardrobe. "There are too many browns and grays. You need something colorful," she says, confirming Eudora's suspicions. "Also, I was wondering what that is up there?" she asks, pointing to a large cardboard box marked "Eudora's Treasures."

"It's nothing," says Eudora, leaning forward to push the door closed.

"Meddlers for nosy parkers. Am I right?" says Rose proudly.

Eudora purses her lips. "Let's return to your critique of my wardrobe."

Rose frowns. "Does that mean you want me to be your style guru?"

"I prefer the term 'fashion advisor.'"

"Very well," says Rose, adopting a serious expression as she parrots Eudora. "I accept the challenge. When shall we go shopping?"

Eudora is determined to nip this ridiculous suggestion in the bud. "Is that entirely necessary, Rose?"

"Of course. You need a makeover and I am the woman for the job." Rose is bouncing from foot to foot like a toddler in need of the toilet.

"I'm not sure it's worth it for one evening out."

Rose is agog. "An evening out! Is it a party?"

Eudora nods. "Stanley's son's fiftieth."

Rose looks as if she's about to burst. "Then you have to get a new outfit! It's very important to make an effort and not let yourself go as you get older."

Eudora's lips twitch with amusement. "Is that so?"

Rose nods gravely. "It is."

"Well then, I suppose I'd better try," says Eudora, staggered that she is agreeing to this charade.

"Yesss! Wait here, I'll go and ask Mum."

Rose bounds off down the stairs, leaving Eudora wondering what has just happened. She isn't used to having such a force of nature in her life. This little girl is like a grenade packed full of joie de vivre, and Eudora has no idea why she's been chosen as a friend. Eudora is everything Rose isn't: old, disillusioned, and able to keep her emotions in check. Yet it's not unpleasant having the child around. She is infuriatingly persistent but unrelentingly kind. Eudora supposes Rose has singled her out because she misses her own grandmother. She has no doubt her enthusiasm will fizzle out once she starts school and meets people her own age. In the meantime, it's probably no bad thing for Eudora to have a distraction from the business of dying. And it might be nice to have a new dress. She could wear it to her funeral. Now, there's a thought.

Eudora makes her way downstairs, her mind set on making another cup of tea, as the first one has gone cold. The phone rings, and she diverts to the living room to answer it. Her heart beats a little faster as she registers the voice.

"Good afternoon, Miss Honeysett. This is Doctor Greta Liebermann calling from Klinik Lebenswahl."

Eudora's pulse quickens. "It's good to hear from you."

"It's good to speak to you too. Petra has passed on your application to me, so I wanted to call in person. I will be the one who effectively guides you through the process, and of course I will ultimately make the decision as to whether we are able to proceed."

"I see."

"Do you have time for a conversation about your application?"

Eudora glances at the door, fearing that Rose will come flying through it at any moment. "Yes. Of course," she says, wanting to sound as cooperative as possible.

"Good. First, let me introduce myself properly. My name is Greta Liebermann. Please call me Greta, and would it be all right if I call you Eudora?"

"Very well," says Eudora.

"So, everything is up to date on your form in terms of medical conditions?"

"It is."

"And have you had any more thoughts about your decision?"

Eudora bristles. "You mean have I changed my mind?"

"People often do."

"Well, I haven't."

"Okay. And have you discussed your decision with anyone?"

"Good heavens, no. Why on earth would I do that?"

"You could say that it really is a matter of life and death and therefore important to talk it through."

"Is this why you've called?"

"I want to make sure you understand the full implications of what this decision means."

Eudora gives an exasperated sigh. "I have explained this to Petra. I am eighty-five years old and done with life. My body is deteriorating and I want to have a choice about how I die. I am not depressed or unhappy. I just want to have a say about what happens to me before it's too late."

"Eudora, believe me, I do understand. But you must also understand that I need to ask these questions. I must be certain that you are sure before I make any decision."

Eudora inhales deeply. "I do understand. I'm sorry. I know you can't make this decision lightly."

"I can hear the determination in your voice, and I promise I will consider your application in full. I think what you say about having a choice in death as in life is very important. I cannot guarantee I will agree to it, but I will consult with my colleagues, consider everything you have told us, and contact you again for further discussions before I decide."

"Thank you," says Eudora. The doctor's words give her unexpected hope. Finally someone is listening to her. Finally someone understands.

There's a scrabbling sound in the hall as Rose returns. "Don't worry, it's not a burglar. It's me, Rose," she shouts. "I left the door on the latch like we used to in Cornwall, and then I was a bit worried that I shouldn't have because there are all sorts of violent criminals in London; I saw it on the news." She appears in the doorway. "Oh, sorry, I didn't realize you were on the phone."

Eudora stiffens. She doesn't want to be having this conversation with Doctor Liebermann while Rose is in the room. "I'm sorry, Doctor. I have to go. I've got a visitor."

"Yes, I heard her. But this is not your granddaughter, as you don't have family?"

"No. It's Rose. She's my . . ." Eudora fumbles for the right word.

"Fashion advisor!" shouts Rose, giving Eudora a thumbs-up.

". . . neighbor's daughter," finishes Eudora.

"I see," says the doctor with a hint of amusement in her voice. "I will let you go, but can I just say one thing?"

"Very well." Eudora rolls her eyes as Rose gives her a knowing look.

"Allow yourself to choose life while you are making the decision about your death. It's important to live life to the full while you can."

Eudora sniffs. "I'll give it some thought."

"Good. We will speak again soon. Goodbye, Eudora."

"That sounded intense," says Rose, wide-eyed, as Eudora replaces the handset.

"It was private business. Now, shall we have some of that cake?" says Eudora, keen to move things along.

Rose taps the side of her nose and winks. "Private business. Got it. Yes please to the cake. And Mum says we can go shopping whenever you like—we can be your fairy godmothers!" Rose is staring up at her hopefully. "You can just say 'very well,' if you like."

The doctor's "choose life" mantra echoes in Eudora's mind. "Thank you, Rose. That would be lovely."

"Yay! And now we can watch *Pointless* together while we eat our cake, if you like? My granny loves it."

"What an utterly ridiculous name for a television show," says Eudora.

"I know, but you'll love Richard Osman. All the old ladies do."

"I'm a very harsh critic."

"I don't know what that means, but okay," says Rose. "Shall I cut the cake and pour myself another cor-dial while you make more tea?"

"That would be helpful, thank you," says Eudora, leading the way to the kitchen.

Rose glances up from the haphazardly gigantic slices of cake she has cut for them. "Do you like your name?"

"I didn't have much choice in the matter," says Eudora.

"You could shorten it to Dora if you don't like the long version." Eudora is struck dumb by an emotional thunderbolt from the past. "Can I call you Dora? Like Dora the Explorer?"

"I would prefer it if you didn't," says Eudora in a shaky but firm voice.

"Why? It's much friendlier."

Eudora is surprised by the anger, which ignites immediately. "I don't want you to call me that, Rose. Please desist with this. I don't want to be called Dora. My name is Eudora!" She knows her fury is irrational, but she can't help it. Her dear father's face floats into her mind.

*"Adorable Dora!" he cries. "My little peach!"*

"Sorry," says Rose in a quiet voice. "I'm sorry I made you sad." Eudora is amazed by her intuition. "Do you want to talk about it?"

"No," says Eudora. "But thank you."

Rose nods. "Case closed, m'lud."

*This child is astonishing*, thinks Eudora.

"Come on, let's distract ourselves by watching *Pointless*," says Rose, balancing two plates of cake and her drink and leading them into the living room.

Eudora finds herself rather taken with both Richard Osman and the lemon drizzle cake as they watch television companionably. She enjoys identifying the missing words in certain categories and snorts with derision when a contestant suggests that John Steinbeck's novel is called "The Grapes of France."

"It's *The Grapes of Wrath*, you silly woman," she cries.

"You know a lot of stuff," says Rose, impressed.

"I've been alive for a long time," admits Eudora.

Rose finishes the cake, wiping her mouth with the back of her hand. "Are you scared of dying?"

Despite becoming more accustomed to Rose's direct approach to conversation, the question catches Eudora off guard. However, it doesn't take her long to find the answer. "No," she says. "Are you?"

Rose considers this for a moment. "I was until I watched *Coco*."

"What's that?"

"A film about the Day of the Dead, which is this really cool celebration they have in Mexico." Eudora watches Rose's face light up as she explains. "Basically, when you die, you hang out with all the other people from your family who have died, and then once a year the people who are still alive put up your picture and light candles and you go back to visit them."

"That sounds rather nice."

"I think so too. Mum says we can do it this year to

remember Grandad. She thinks I'm a bit obsessed with death, but I think it's important not to be scared, don't you?"

Eudora stares at her. "Yes. Yes, I do."

"I'm glad you're not scared because it would be easy to be frightened the nearer you get to death."

"Thank you for reminding me."

"Sorry. I'm talking too much again, aren't I? Do you want me to go?"

Normally, Eudora would welcome the idea of having her house back to herself, but for some reason, she's in no hurry today. "You can stay for a bit longer, if you'd like."

"Thanks. Anyway, I hope you live long enough to come to my birthday party."

Eudora swallows her amusement. "How long have I got?"

"It's the twenty-second of October."

"You'll want all your new school friends there, not some fuddy-duddy like me."

Rose is indignant. "I will want you there. And Stanley. And Montgomery, if we can persuade him. Please can you try to stay alive until then?"

"I'll do my best."

Their conversation is interrupted by a loud knock at the door. "Rose? Are you still in there?"

Rose pulls a face. "That's Mum. I better go. Thanks for sharing the cake and for the chat. I really enjoyed it."

"Me too," says Eudora.

Rose skips down the hall to let her mother in. Eudora hears Maggie scolding her daughter before appearing at the living room door. "Eudora, I'm so sorry. I told Rose not to stay too long."

Eudora holds up her hands. "It's quite all right. I invited her to stay. Please don't be cross with her."

"Are you sure?"

"Completely sure." Eudora notices that she looks weary. "How are you?"

Maggie runs a hand over her burgeoning belly. "Fine, thank you. A bit tired, but that's babies for you."

"I'm sure."

Maggie smiles. "Right, come along you," she says to Rose. "Have you said thank you?"

"Yes, Mum," says Rose, rolling her eyes at Eudora. "When shall we go shopping then?"

"Oh yes," says Maggie. "I understand we're taking you for a makeover."

"Apparently so."

Maggie smiles. "How about this Saturday?"

"That would be fine, thank you. The party is in the evening, so it will force me to be decisive."

"Fantastic. Shall we say ten o'clock?"

"Thank you," says Eudora. "Oh, and, Rose?"

"Yes?" says Rose with shining eyes.

"What does 'Be More Unicorn' mean?" she asks, gesturing at her T-shirt.

"Well, Eudora. It's all about being more sparkly and magical," she says, flinging open her arms like a singer reaching the finale of a big number. "Does that make sense?"

*Resistance is futile, Eudora. You should know this by now.*

"It does, Rose. I understand perfectly. See you both on Saturday."

## 1955
## THE ORCHID BALLROOM, SOUTH-EAST LONDON

The dress was pale blue and had a chiffon bodice finished with an A-line skirt. Eudora found it in Allders during a Saturday afternoon shopping trip with her best friend, Sylvia, and she had spent a good while trying to decide whether she should fritter nearly a month's wages on it.

"It's like something Grace Kelly would wear," said Sylvia with a dreamy look in her eyes.

"I'll take it," Eudora told the shop assistant.

As Eddie arrived to collect her the following Saturday, she made sure she was standing at the top of the stairs so she could sashay down toward him in the manner of a Hollywood film star. It didn't help that the staircase was carpeted in beige Axminster rather than made from the smooth gray marble of L.A. mansions, but she did her best to remain elegant. Eddie's face was a picture of admiration, and Eudora decided immediately that it had been worth every penny.

"Like the cat that got the cream," as her mother might say.

Beatrice disapproved of Eddie. Eudora could tell. She was always civil, greeting him politely but without warmth, twitching her nose as if she'd detected a bad smell. Eudora chose to ignore it. Eddie was her escape. There was something about his mischievous south-east London charm and noisy self-confidence that gave her hope. In a home life almost devoid of fun and laughter,

Eddie offered a joyful alternative. Encouraged by Sylvia, Eudora resolved that if she wasn't having fun at the age of twenty-two, she may as well give up.

"Seriously, Dor. You can't stay stuck at home with your mum and Stella going hell for leather at each other forever. You'll end up in the Bethlem."

Eudora knew her friend was right. Beatrice and Stella's loathing for each other had hardened into something as cold and solid as granite. Their communication was either cursory or like a lit fuse that threatened to ignite into conflict at any moment. As soon as Eudora walked through the door at night, her shoulders would tighten as the toxic atmosphere cloaked her.

Eddie was the antithesis of this world. She had met him at a dance one Saturday night, where she was playing gooseberry to Sylvia and her date, Ken. Eudora was usually happy to sit at the side and watch; the atmosphere alone was enough to serve as respite. She had noticed Eddie a few times and on first sight had shared her mother's reservations. He was loud, brash, and a little too sure of himself. As a result, he was never short of doe-eyed females with whom to dance. On this particular night, Eudora was sitting in her usual position at the side of the room, nursing a glass of lemonade and tapping her foot in time to the music, when Eddie appeared before her.

"Of all the dance floors in all the towns in all the world, she walks into mine," he said, putting his foot up on the chair next to her and leaning forward with a smirk.

Eudora knew it was clichéd, but there was something

about the way he had strode over and chosen her that made her laugh and blush. Taking this as an invitation, Eddie stuck out his hand.

"Eddie Spencer."

"Eudora Honeysett," she replied, longing for a more straightforward name.

"A beautiful name for a beautiful lady." Eudora's cheeks grew warm. "Smoke?" He offered her the packet.

"No, thank you. I don't smoke," she said, hoping this didn't make her sound superior.

"I like a woman who knows her own mind," said Eddie, tucking the packet back inside his pocket and flashing her a grin.

Eudora pressed her lips together, struggling to know what to say next. Luckily, Eddie was a dab hand. "How about we say it with music?" he asked, offering his arm. Eudora accepted, and as they danced, her body grew light with the possibility of how life could be.

In the weeks and months that followed, Eudora, Eddie, Sylvia, and Kenny became a happy band of four. To Eudora, Saturday was as sacred as a Sunday and she allowed herself to dream that she was on the path toward something new and wonderful.

Stella was the thorn in her side. She nagged and pestered Eudora to let her tag along, and when her sister refused, she flouted the rules and left the house anyway. After one occasion when fifteen-year-old Stella was brought home by a policeman, having broken into the local park with two other girls and been caught smoking, Beatrice had turned to Eudora with mournful eyes.

"Please, Dora. Just take her with you on Saturday night. I can't bear the shame."

Conscience suitably pricked, Eudora had agreed. She told herself it would be fine. Stella's level of defiance had intensified as she hit the teenage years, but Eudora's relationship with her sister remained strong. Or so she had thought.

"You can come along on Saturday, but you have to behave. No drinking or smoking, okay?"

"O-kay, Do-ra," sang Stella in a mocking little-girl voice.

"If you're going to be like that, I won't let you come."

Stella fixed her sister with a determined look. "Of course you will. Because if you don't, I'll escape and bring shame upon this house. Again. And you'll have to deal with Beatrice droning on and on about how life would have been so much better if our precious father hadn't been killed, blah, blah, blah."

"Stella!"

Stella's expression dissolved into one of raucous mirth. "I'm joking, Dora. Calm down. Of course I'll behave." Eudora looked deep into her sister's eyes, longing to believe her. Stella pulled a comical face before planting a kiss on her sister's cheek and whispering in her ear. "You can trust me, Dora. I won't let you down. Beatrice might hate me, but I know you love me."

Stella had taken to calling their mother Beatrice in a

bid to annoy her. For Eudora, it was another example of her being cast as the mother, torn between warring siblings. She loathed this role but endured it as best she could, hoping for brighter days ahead.

Stella started off the evening as good as her word. She wore a simple, pretty pink dress and helped Eudora with her hair. "You look beautiful, Dora," she told her sister as they smiled at their reflections in the mirror.

Their mother waved them off. "Be back by eleven and be good, Stella," she warned. Stella rolled her eyes.

The alarm bells should have rung during the car journey. Eudora sat in the front with Eddie, while Stella was in the back with Kenny in the middle and Sylvia to his left. Stella kept laughing too loudly at everything Kenny said. It was a sharp, tinkling sound designed to focus attention on her alone. At one point, she reached over and squeezed his knee.

"You're so funny, Ken," she told him.

Eudora could see Sylvia was fuming, while Kenny lapped it up.

In the front, Eddie and Eudora exchanged glances. "Your sister's a bit over the top, isn't she?" he muttered.

Eudora was mortified. After all she'd said to Stella, her selfish sister was going to ruin everything if she didn't act fast.

Eudora turned in her seat to see Stella leaning in to whisper something in Kenny's ear. From his shocked laugh and Stella's raised eyebrows, Eudora could tell that whatever she'd said was highly inappropriate. She stole a glance at Sylvia, who looked ready to explode.

"Stella," said Eudora. "May I remind you that you are fifteen years old and have been invited along tonight as my guest. If you don't stop embarrassing me in front of my friends, I shall take you straight home. Do you understand?"

"Yeah, cool it, little girl," said Eddie.

Stella's face clouded with shame. It was one thing to be told off by her sister, but Eddie's casual dismissal crushed her. She shrank back into her seat and didn't speak for the rest of the journey.

Stella stood next to Eudora in brooding silence as they checked their coats.

"Stella . . ." she began.

"I know you don't want me here. I wish I'd stayed at home."

"That's not true."

"Of course it is. You and your little friends hate me."

"No, Stella. We don't hate you. You just got off on the wrong foot."

"I was being friendly. Anyway, I don't care. You go and dance with your precious Eddie and I'll sit on the side like a good girl," said Stella as they entered the dance hall.

"Come on, Eudora," said Eddie, appearing next to them and grabbing her hand. "It's your favorite." Eudora allowed him to lead her to the dance floor, and she watched as Stella took a seat at the side, arms folded, face set in a pout.

"Ignore her," said Eddie. "She'll be fine. I'll keep an eye out."

Eudora looked into his eyes and planted a kiss on his cheek. "Thank you," she said.

"Anything for my girl," he told her, grabbing her by the waist and whirling her around.

Eudora's body, heart, and mind soared with hopeful joy. *This is living. This is how life is meant to be.*

About halfway through the evening, Eudora lost sight of Stella. She glanced over to where her sister had been sitting. Panic shot through her as she noticed the empty chair.

"Stella's gone," she told Eddie.

He cast around the room. "Don't worry. She's probably powdering her nose or something. We'll find her."

Eddie's reassurance was short-lived as Eudora spotted Stella in a far corner, laughing with a group of older teenagers. She was holding a glass of what looked like cherryade. Eudora's heart sank when she spotted one of the boys surreptitiously pull out a hip flask and pour some into Stella's drink. "Eddie," she said, tapping him on the arm and gesturing in the direction of the group.

Eddie's eyes flashed with anger as he let go of Eudora's hand and charged toward them. She hurried after in fearful astonishment. Before Eudora could stop him, Eddie had the youth with the hip flask pinned up against the wall.

"What the fuck do you think you're playing at? She's fifteen!"

Eudora was horrified, not only by the violence of Eddie's reaction but by the way her sister watched the scene unfold with calm, smiling indifference. It was almost as if she'd planned it. The boy was flailing his hands and struggling to breathe as his friends watched on in stupefied fear. Eddie was older than these youths and had a reputation as someone to be respected and even feared. Eudora reached out a trembling hand and touched him on the shoulder. "Eddie. Let him go. Please."

Eddie shot a glance in her direction. Eudora saw a coldness in his eyes she'd never noticed before.

"Eddie. Mate. Let him go, eh? He's just a kid." Kenny had joined them now.

Eddie loosened his grip enough to bring the boy down to eye level. "Pull a stunt like that again and I'll break your fucking arm, do you hear?" he said, before letting go and walking away in disgust. Kenny hurried after him, leaving Eudora staring at her sister as the other youths dispersed.

Stella stumbled toward her, wearing a smirk of triumph. "Isn't your boyfriend a hero? You're so lucky, Eudora." She pretended to trip, Eudora was sure of that, and her smirk deepened as the cherry-red liquid was flung across the front of Eudora's dress.

"Ohh noo! Your beautiful dress," cried Stella, hand on heart, standing back as if to admire her handiwork. "I do hope it's not ruined."

Eudora had scrubbed and scrubbed at the dress for weeks afterward, but the stain never came out and Stella never apologized.

# Chapter 8

AS EUDORA RINGS Rose's doorbell on yet another unbearably hot morning, she begins to wonder why on earth she agreed to this ludicrous idea. Her doubts are further heightened as Rose throws open the door and she spots Maggie waddling toward them from the kitchen, looking ready to give birth at any moment.

"Hey, Eudora. Are you ready to be made over?" cries Rose, doing a twirl so that Eudora can fully appreciate the sparkling "Fashion Guru" T-shirt teamed with purple Hawaiian shorts, silver flip-flops, and a matching bandanna.

"I very much doubt it," she says with a rising sense of dread.

"You must be the famous Eudora," says a scruffy-looking man, plodding down the stairs and holding out his hand. Eudora accepts with some reluctance. "I'm Rose's dad, Rob."

"Pleased to meet you," says Eudora.

"Excuse my appearance. It's been a crazy week and I'm having a lazy morning."

"I see."

"Right," says Maggie, slinging her bag over her shoulder, car keys in hand. "Let's go, shall we?"

"Are you sure you don't want me to take Rose and Eudora instead?" asks Rob, leaning over to kiss her.

Rose fixes him with a stern look. "No, Daddy. It's girls only."

Rob shakes his head. "So sexist." He rubs Maggie's back. "Will you be okay?"

Maggie smiles. "We'll be fine. See you later."

He gives a thumbs-up. "I wish you luck. Good to finally meet you, Eudora."

"You too."

As the unlikely trio make their way from the car park to the shopping center, Eudora wonders yet again at the wisdom of their mission. Maggie looks as if she might go into labor at any second. Both she and Eudora have to keep stopping to mop their brows and catch their breath, while Rose runs backward and forward in the manner of an overexcited cocker spaniel puppy.

Eudora is horrified by almost every person she sees: hooded teenagers shouting and shoving; overweight parents with overweight children stuffing yet more food into their bodies at just after ten o'clock in the morning; people stopping to stare, zombie-like, at their phones in the middle of the walkway with infuriating regularity. For Eudora it is a vision of Hades—the crowds, the noise, the pushing—all these individuals moving through their lives with scant regard for others. And why is everyone in such a hurry? They're shopping, for heaven's sake; surely that should be a leisure activity. These people look as if they're participating in some kind of gladiatorial tournament. Shop to the death. Consume or be consumed. It confirms her worst suspicions about humans and why she can't wait to be rid of them.

"Right," says Maggie. "I propose we go to Marks and Spencer . . ."

"I prefer Debenhams," interrupts Rose. "Their doughnuts are much nicer."

"Well, Marks and Spencer has a loo on this floor and your sister is putting all her weight on my bladder today, so I vote we go there."

Eudora clears her throat to register her distaste at Maggie's oversharing.

"Eudora doesn't like toilet talk, Mummy, but that's fine."

"Thank you," says Maggie, hurrying them into the store with relief. "Why don't you start to browse, and I'll come and find you in a minute."

"Okay. Come on, Eudora. Let's go and find the old-lady clothes."

"Don't try to soften the blow, will you, Rose?" says Eudora.

Rose looks sheepish. "Sorry. It's just that they're the clothes my granny likes, so I thought you might like them too. They're actually really nice." She is momentarily distracted by a floaty sundress in a shade of fire-engine red with gold piping decorating the neck and hemline. "Ooh, this is fancy," she says, holding it up for inspection.

Eudora frowns. "I own handkerchiefs made from more material."

"Yes, but still, it's pretty," says Rose, replacing the hanger on the rack with an air of disappointment.

Eudora knows she's being ill-tempered and realizes it has to stop. Rose may have the wearying positivity of a jack-in-the-box, but she is kindness personified. And she wants to help. So Eudora must let her. Anything else would be bad manners.

"Rose, I must apologize to you." Rose stares at her in surprise. "I don't enjoy shopping. I'm hot and bothered and don't like crowds of people. But you are trying to help me, and I shall do my best to be receptive to your ideas."

"It's fine," says Rose with a shrug. "Honestly. I understand. You're old and life's a bit much sometimes."

"Yes," says Eudora in astonishment. "That's exactly it."

Rose nods. "So how about this plan? You sit here with Mum"—she gestures to some fat, round teal-colored sofas set between the shoe and clothing sections—"and if you give me some idea of the clothes you like, I'll try to find them for you."

Eudora considers the idea. The shop is pleasantly air-conditioned and the sofas do look inviting. "That's an excellent plan, Rose." The little girl beams. "So. I would like a simple but well-fitting dress to my knees, with a high neck and short sleeves. I do not like red but will consider other colors."

"Leave it to me, Eudora. I won't let you down."

Maggie reappears, flushed and out of breath. "What did I miss?" she asks, lowering herself with care onto the sofa.

"Your daughter is on a mission."

Maggie smiles. "Rose has got a brilliant eye for style. Sure, she's unconventional with her own clothes but somehow they work."

"Mmm," says Eudora. She finds Rose's outfits to be an assault on the senses, but she takes Maggie's point. They watch in amused silence as the little girl darts from rack to rack, picking up, rejecting, and selecting. Eudora is nervous about letting a ten-year-old loose on her behalf but rather excited too.

"Ow," says Maggie, shifting in her seat, putting a hand to her swollen belly.

"Are you all right?" asks Eudora with a frisson of panic. She isn't ready to play midwife today—or indeed any other day.

Maggie sighs. "I'm fine. This baby is going to be a star striker with kicks like that." She rolls her shoulders and stretches out her arms. "It's been a while since I was pregnant. I'd forgotten how tiring it can be."

"How long have you got to go?" asks Eudora, largely to be polite. She has little knowledge of babies or childbirth.

"About a month, although Rose was early. I hope the birth isn't as difficult as it was with her." Maggie notices the horror on Eudora's face at this turn in the conversation. She clears her throat. "So, whose party are you off to?"

"Stanley's son's fiftieth. Although quite why he's invited me is anyone's guess."

"I expect he's just being friendly."

"Perhaps."

"He's a lovely man," says Maggie. "Rose thinks the world of him."

"Mmm."

"And I think he misses his wife."

"Well, I hope I'm not next in line," says Eudora with indignation.

Maggie laughs nervously. "I expect he's just glad for the

company. I know my mum has found it hard since Dad died. She's got lots of wonderful friends but it's not the same as having your husband."

*Here we go,* thinks Eudora. *Another one who insists on opening up at the drop of a hat. It's as if I'm a magnet for these people.* There's a silence that threatens to inch its way toward awkwardness. Eudora realizes it would be rude not to speak. "How long since your father died?"

"Three years. There isn't a day goes by that I don't miss him."

Maggie's unguarded honesty triggers something in Eudora. The words are out of her mouth before she can check them. "It's over seventy years since my father died. I feel exactly the same."

Maggie and Eudora look at each other, their mirrored grief giving way to a moment's understanding. "It must be hard for you," says Maggie.

Eudora sits up straighter, focusing on the rack of highly impractical heeled shoes in front of her. "It was a long time ago. You learn to live with it." She feels Maggie's eyes on her. They both know it's a lie. Eudora is relieved as Rose returns, her arms loaded with outfits. She has a shop assistant in tow, carrying even more.

"This is Beryl," says Rose. "She's been helping me."

Beryl smiles. "You're so blessed to have a granddaughter like Rose. She's a ray of sunshine."

"Oh, she's not my granddaughter," says Eudora.

"I'm her fashion guru," says Rose, hanging the dresses on a nearby rack and showing Beryl her T-shirt.

Beryl laughs. "You're an absolute poppet. These ladies

are lucky to have you," she says, adding her selection of dresses to the rack. "I'll leave you in Rose's more than capable hands. Let me know if you need anything else. Or if I can borrow her."

"Thank you, Beryl," says Rose, giving a little bow.

"Adorable," mouths Beryl to Maggie.

"So I got mostly dresses but also a few pretty tops in case you wanted to, you know, pep up your wardrobe a bit."

"I'll try not to be offended by that, Rose."

"Sorry. It's just that you did have a lot of grays. And browns. And dark blues."

"Yes. I'm well aware of the drab nature of my fashion collection. Very well. Show me what you've got, please."

Rose turns to the rack and holds up the outfits one at a time for Eudora and Maggie to judge. Yet again, Eudora is astonished. She likes almost everything Rose has selected, apart from a sparkly maroon jumpsuit.

"Oh no, that's not for you, Eudora. I picked it up because I like it and wanted to show Mum."

In the end, Eudora chooses a soft A-line dress with a delicate blue iris design and a bottle-green top decorated with small yellow birds.

"The dress is beautiful, Eudora," says Maggie, stroking the material. "It'll be lovely and cool too."

"Thank you, Rose," says Eudora. "You've excelled yourself."

"I'm not sure what that means, but it sounds a bit like 'excellent' and you look happy, so that's good. Do you want to try them on?"

Eudora shakes her head. "I had a dress very similar to this once, so I know it will fit, and the top looks perfect."

Rose claps her hands with delight. "You're going to be the belle of the ball!"

"Shall we go and pay?" asks Maggie.

"Good idea. I'll take the dress and top for me and the jumpsuit for my fashion advisor."

Rose's face lights up.

"You don't need to do that, Eudora," says Maggie.

"I know. But I would like to," says Eudora with a firm nod. Eudora also buys a card and a bottle of champagne for Stanley's son. "I don't know about you, but I could do with a cup of tea," she tells them both as they leave the shop. "I hear the doughnuts in Debenhams are superb."

"Can we, Mummy?" asks Rose, hopping from foot to foot.

"I think you've earned it," says Maggie.

"My treat," says Eudora. She can't remember the last time she uttered these words. The crowd seems to irritate her less as they make their way to the café. When they finally sit down with their doughnuts and she watches Rose bite into one, the little girl's murmurs of approval and jam-covered smile make Eudora wonder at how lucky grandmothers must feel to share in such moments.

As Eudora walks into the Royston Ballroom later that evening, it's as if she's stepping into a memory. True, the people gathered lack the style of the dance-goers of Eudora's heyday—there's a little too much exposed flesh and open necks for her liking—but the room is exactly the same and it takes her breath away. White silk drapes fan out from the middle to the corners of the ceiling, each one adorned with soft twinkling fairy lights. A glitter ball spins from the center, making everything shimmer with magic. Eudora finds herself thinking how much Rose would like this. She would already be hurtling around the room like an out-of-control spinning top.

At one end of the space is a stage on which the band is warming up. From the look of their lead singer, who is wearing dark glasses, a porkpie hat, and a tight suit, Eudora fears they won't be in for an evening of swing tunes. The furniture has been set up around the room in the manner of a café, with six chairs to every round table so people can sit and watch anyone brave enough to dance. Eudora approves of the white linen tablecloths and matching seat covers, which give it an air of sophistication. She is less sure of the fiftieth-birthday helium balloons, which a couple of particularly thuggish-looking children are currently using as punch bags, or the huge garish "Cheers to Fifty Years, Paul!" sign hanging over the bar.

"Here we are," says Stanley, returning with their drinks. "An orange juice, just as the lady requested."

"Thank you," says Eudora.

"You look lovely, Eudora," he tells her. "That dress really suits you."

"Thank you," she repeats, realizing that she needs to offer Stanley some kind of compliment in return. "And you look very smart."

Stanley smiles. "Shall we take a seat?"

"I thought you'd never ask." Eudora is impressed as Stanley pulls out a chair and waits for her to sit down before taking his place. She misses people with manners. It seems as if courtesy is heading the way of kindness these days. "I used to come here to dances many moons ago," she tells him.

"I bet you could show these young'uns a thing or two," he says, gesturing toward a couple of awkward thirty-something dancers, who look more like pecking chickens than graceful swans.

"Yes, and not just in terms of dancing."

"Life's certainly different these days."

"You can say that again."

"And did you come here with a significant other? Was there a man who stole Miss Honeysett's heart?" asks Stanley.

Eudora is about to tell him to mind his own business when they're interrupted by a taller, younger version of Stanley with more hair. "Dad! Here you are! Helen said she'd seen you."

Stanley leaps up to embrace his son. "Paul, my boy! Happy birthday." Paul pats his father on the back. Eudora is intrigued to see their obvious closeness. "Paul, I want you to meet Eudora—a good friend of mine."

Eudora bristles at the overfamiliarity but remains gracious as she reaches up to shake Paul's hand. "Pleased to meet you. Happy birthday. I've left you a present over on the table with the others." She is taken aback as Paul leans down to kiss her on the cheek. He smells of beer and cigarettes.

"It's lovely to meet you, Eudora. I'm chuffed you could make it. Dad's told us all about you."

"Oh?" says Eudora, glancing at Stanley.

"Only about you falling over drunk and always giving me a hard time," says Stanley with a teasing nudge.

"I see," says Eudora. "Well, perhaps you deserve it."

"Touché, Dad. Eudora's got the measure of you!" Paul and Stanley grin at each other.

"Can I get you a drink, son?"

"No thanks, Dad. I've got about six lined up. But listen, you'd better watch out. Gloria's on the prowl. Best stay here and let Eudora protect you."

Stanley puts a hand on his heart. "Thanks, son. I'll make sure I keep a low profile."

"You do that. Right, see you in a bit. Good to meet you, Eudora."

"You too." Eudora watches Stanley glance around the room nervously. "And who is Gloria?"

He squirms in his seat. "Paul's mother-in-law. She's been a widow for a couple of years and seems to think we should go on a date."

"And I take it you're not keen?"

"Definitely not. She's a man-eater! And besides, I'm not interested in anyone else. Ada was my one true love."

"Well then, I shall do my best to protect you."

"Maybe we could pretend this is a date?"

Eudora frowns. Today is one of the more bizarre days of her life. This morning she allowed herself to be made over by a ten-year-old girl, and this evening she is apparently required as an ersatz sweetheart. She's not sure if this is what Doctor Liebermann had in mind when she advised her to choose life, but Eudora realizes she isn't averse to the plan. "All right, but only for this evening."

Stanley clinks his glass against hers. "Cheers, Eudora. You're a pal."

The band strikes up their first song. Eudora isn't familiar with any of the tunes they play, but the musicians are accomplished and she finds herself tapping her foot in time to the music. A gaggle of children of all ages jig and skip around the dance floor, much to Stanley's and Eudora's amusement. She finds him to be an attentive host as he leans in so Eudora can hear him over the music, pointing out various relatives. Eudora soon realizes that Stanley is something of a celebrity in this company. She loses count of the number of people who stop to shake his hand or kiss his cheek.

"Hey, Pops," says a beautiful young girl wearing a shimmering dusky-rose dress.

"This is my Livvy," he tells Eudora, with a warmth that she finds touching.

"You must be Eudora. Pops never stops talking about you," she says, winking at her grandfather.

"This one's a worse joker than her grandpa," says Stanley.

"That's a beautiful ring, by the way," says Livvy, gesturing at Eudora's right hand.

"It was my grandmother's," says Eudora, her mind transported to another party where she'd worn it proudly. "They're rose-cut diamonds—quite unusual."

"It's gorgeous," says Livvy, smiling.

"Come on, Liv," says another, equally lovely girl, jumping on her back. "Let's dance! Oh hey, Pops!"

"And that's Ellie," says Stanley, blowing them both kisses as Livvy is dragged away by her sister. "They're my angels."

Eudora watches Stanley's face. He is rapt, gazing at them with adoration. Eudora remembers her father bestowing a similar look on her, and she feels weary with longing. She is about to tell Stanley it's time for her to go home when a drunken woman stumbles toward them.

"Hieeee, Stanleeeeeee, you're here! Paul said he didn't know where you were. Have you been hiding from me?" Gloria. Eudora can see straightaway that she has no filter in terms of appropriate dress or behavior. Her short dyed-black hair is standing on end as if she has been clutching a van de Graaff generator, and her gold lamé dress is too tight, too short, and too revealing. She is sweating so profusely that the makeup on her face has run, giving her a rather unfortunate ghoulish appearance. It would be easy to mock or dismiss this woman, but Eudora feels only sympathy. There's a desperation about her, a fear of being alone.

Stanley's face is filled with horror as Gloria slides herself onto his lap, wraps her arms around his shoulders, and plants a fat kiss on his cheek. "Ooh, sorry. I left a mark," she says, rubbing at the scarlet stain. "It's good to see you, Stanley. Now, when are we going to go on that date?"

Stanley's body stiffens as he throws a pleading look in Eudora's direction. She clears her throat and taps his admirer on the arm. Gloria turns, her painted-on eyebrows raised.

"I don't think we've been introduced," says Eudora, holding out her hand. Gloria's return handshake is the wet fish Eudora feared it would be. "I am Eudora and I'm here tonight with Stanley. I'm sure you don't mean to be rude, but I would prefer it if you removed yourself from his lap at your earliest convenience."

Gloria gapes at Eudora but does as she is asked. Paul's wife, Helen, appears at her elbow. "Come on, Mum. I think it's time we got you home."

Gloria gives Stanley a forlorn look before blowing him a kiss and allowing her daughter to lead her away. "Farewell, sweet prince," she calls, waggling her fingers in a clumsy wave.

Stanley turns to Eudora. "You were magnificent, Eudora. *I would prefer it if you removed yourself from his lap at your earliest convenience.* I don't think Gloria knew what hit her!"

"I'm sure she has a good heart underneath all those ill-fitting clothes," says Eudora. "In truth, I feel sorry for her, but you're not the answer to her prayers, so there's no sense in stringing the poor woman along."

"Let's just say Gloria's not the only one with a good heart, shall we?" says Stanley. Eudora gives a dismissive shake of her head but is quietly gratified. "I think this calls for a drink. Can I tempt you with a glass of bubbly?"

Eudora is about to say "Very well" but decides to take a different tack. "Why not? We must toast your son's health."

"Lovely stuff," says Stanley.

Eudora watches him disappear to the bar, glad she made the effort to come tonight. There is something pleasant about basking in the warmth of Stanley's easy relationship with his friends and family. They seem to genuinely enjoy one another's company and relish being together. It's a far cry from her own experience of family. Despite her best efforts, hers was a fractured, bitter mess. There were moments of happiness of course, but they never seemed to linger; like a feather on the breeze, they fluttered in front of her for a second before they were gone, out of reach, never to return.

"Are you having a good time?"

Eudora is roused from her thoughts by Paul, taking a seat next to her and placing his beer glass on the table.

"It's been a very pleasant evening," she says truthfully.

"I'm glad. Dad was over the moon you could come. I think you've made an impression on him. You give as good as you get. He needs that."

"A sparring partner?"

Paul laughs. "Yeah, if you like. To be honest, Eudora, we're worried about him."

"Oh?"

Paul grimaces. "He's getting a bit forgetful since Mum died. Not just losing things but forgetting what day it is and the things we've just told him."

"I see. I met him at the memory clinic the other day. He seemed very philosophical about it."

"Yeah, but I think he's scared. You know what men are like."

"I certainly do."

"Sorry. I don't mean to go on to you about it. I'm just glad he's met someone who keeps his brain ticking over."

"What are you two talking about?" asks Stanley, placing a bottle of champagne and two glasses on the table.

"Meddlers for nosy parkers," says Eudora.

"See what she's like, Paul?" says Stanley.

"I do. I think she's brilliant."

"Don't tell her that. She'll get bigheaded. Now then. Fetch yourself a glass, son. Eudora and I would like to toast your health."

Paul returns moments later, and as the three of them raise their glasses, Eudora makes a decision. She may not be here for much longer, but while she is she will do her best to help Stanley Marcham. She owes it to Ada, to Gloria, and to all the other people who love him.

## 1957
## SIDNEY AVENUE, SOUTH-EAST LONDON

As Eudora looked around the room, taking in the "Congratulations" banner and table heaving with plates of sandwiches, homemade quiche, and sausage rolls, she couldn't recall ever being as happy as she was in this moment. Eddie's proposal was like a long-wished-for gift after years of being the conduit for her mother's and sister's unhappiness. She would never say this out loud, but it was as if her father was sending her a message:

*You've done your bit, Eudora. It's your turn to be happy and live a wonderful life now.*

She was sure that her father would have approved of Eddie. He worked hard in his father's car repair garage, and she knew he would look after her. He had a bit of a temper but never toward Eudora. He had also worked hard to win over Beatrice. He fixed her aging Morris Minor for free and undertook odd jobs whenever they arose.

"It is nice to have a man around the place to help with these things," Beatrice told him one day as he emerged from under the sink, having fixed a leaking U-bend.

"My pleasure, Mrs. H. Things must have been hard for you after the war, but I'm here if you need me," said Eddie, flashing his customary charming smile.

Eudora noticed her mother's neck bloom red with the trace of a blush as she handed Eddie a cup of tea with one of the good biscuits balanced on the saucer. "You are too kind."

In the absence of a father, Eddie had sought Beatrice's permission for her daughter's hand in marriage. Eudora's own joy had been raised to new heights when she saw the lift it gave her mother.

"You deserve to be happy," she said later that day after they had finished the washing-up. She squeezed Eudora's hands, gazing at her through misted eyes. "And I want you to have something." Beatrice disappeared upstairs, returning moments later with a small green felt box. "It was my mother's."

Eudora smiled as she opened it to reveal a gold ring set with three rose-cut diamonds. "Granny's engagement ring."

"It's yours now," said Beatrice with satisfaction.

"Thank you," said Eudora, leaning over to kiss her on the cheek.

Beatrice's eyes sparkled with excitement. "We must

have a party to celebrate. And I shall bake a cake—something special for you and dear Eddie."

"Yes. We must have the very best for dear Eddie and darling Eudora," said Stella, appearing in the doorway. She said this in a neutral tone, but Eudora saw her raised eyebrow and knew the truth behind it.

"Yes. We must," said Beatrice, oblivious to her cattiness. "Now, if you'll excuse me, there's a program on the television I should like to see."

Eudora watched her go before turning to her sister. "Stella, I know things haven't always been easy between you and Mother, but I was hoping that you'd be happy for me."

Stella sighed. "Dear Eudora, when will you realize that life doesn't always go the way you want?" As Eudora's face fell, Stella laughed. "I'm joking, silly! Of course I'm happy for you. Oh my goodness, why do you always take everything so seriously?"

Eudora laughed along. "Sorry. Of course I know you're happy for me. And don't fret. I won't be far away if you need me."

Stella shrugged. "Oh, don't worry about me. I won't be hanging around here for any longer than I need to."

Eudora bristled. "Don't do anything daft, will you?" she said, looking into Stella's eyes.

Stella put an arm around her shoulders. "There you go again, worry, worry, worry. Honestly, you've got to stop that or Eddie will get fed up with you. I'll be fine. You take care of your happiness and I'll take care of mine." She reached out and pinched her sister's cheek a little too firmly so that later, when she looked in the mirror, Eudora could see a small red welt.

Eudora was relieved when Stella appeared true to her word at the party. It was a relatively low-key affair with a few neighbors and Eddie's family in attendance. Eddie had a cousin who was a couple of years older than Stella, and Eudora had been concerned that her sister might embarrass them by flirting. However, Stella wore a demure but pretty floral dress, handed around drinks, and seemed full of innocent chatter and smiles. As the afternoon wore on, Eudora began to relax. Stella was behaving, Beatrice seemed to be bonding with Eddie's mother, and Eddie kept flashing winks and smirks in her direction.

As promised, Beatrice had baked a stunning fruit cake, its royal icing top piped with "Congratulations Eudora and Eddie" in swirling blue font.

"When are you going to cut this beautiful cake?" asked Eddie's mother a while later, smiling at Beatrice.

"No time like the present," said Eddie, clearing his throat.

"Oh, I forgot the cake knife," said Beatrice.

"I'll fetch it," offered Eudora, making her way to the kitchen. She noticed Stella standing at the sink. At first she thought she was washing up glasses, but then Eudora realized that she was knocking back the remains of other people's drinks.

"Stella?"

Her sister spun around, a woozy smile on her face. "My darling Dora!" she cried.

"Are you drunk?" asked Eudora, glancing with concern over her shoulder.

Stella's slurring reply did little to reassure her. "Oh, stop worrying about your precious guests and what they'll think. I'm fine."

"Eudora? Have you got that knife?" called Beatrice with an edge to her voice. "We're all waiting!"

Eudora looked back at her sister. Stella's expression was defiant, as if issuing a challenge. She elbowed Eudora as she sloped past. "Come on. Mummy's waiting."

Eudora found the cake knife and followed Stella back to the living room. "Here she is," said Eddie, clapping his hands together. The room hushed to silence as he took his fiancée's hand. Eudora saw her mother's tearful smile and Stella standing behind her, swaying, a maniacal smirk on her face.

Eudora sent up a silent prayer. *Please let her behave today. Please let me have this moment.*

"I'm not a big one for speeches," began Eddie. "So I'll just say thank you for coming and thank you to Mrs. Honeysett for opening up her house to us and welcoming me into the family. I feel very lucky and hope I will make Eudora as happy as she makes me." A couple of his noisier male relatives whooped and whistled. Eddie grinned.

"I would like to say something, if I may," said Stella, sidling past her mother to the front of the room.

"Stella," warned Eudora as Beatrice's face paled.

"No please, Dora," said Stella, holding up a hand. "You have no one to speak for you, so I would like to."

"Just let her," growled Eddie.

"Thank you, Eddie," said Stella with a leering smile before flinging her arms wide as she spoke. "My sister Dora is a wonderful human being. She is kind and warm and full of love."

Eudora glanced at Eddie, who gave her a reassuring nod.

"Our mother, on the other hand, is cold and unfeeling, an embittered old hag."

"Stella!" Eudora grabbed her sister by the shoulders as gasps went up, along with embarrassed chuckles from various quarters. Beatrice stood still, her mouth gaping in horror.

Stella threw back her head and laughed. "It's true, Dora. You can't deny it."

"You're drunk and you're embarrassing us," said Eudora.

"Oh, I'm embarrassing you, am I? Well, I'm so sorry if I'm spoiling your perfect life and your happily ever after with Eddie the man. Let's not hold up the party. Come on, cut the cake!"

Eudora remained motionless, so Stella grabbed the knife and started to stab at Beatrice's cake. "I said. CUT. THE. CAKE."

Eudora shot a horrified glance at Eddie, whose reaction was immediate. He grabbed Stella's wrist, and as she dropped the knife, he pulled her out of the room into the hallway with Eudora following on their heels.

"Ow! Get lost, Eddie!" said Stella, trying to twist out of his grasp.

"I should put you over my knee," he told her.

Stella threw back her head and laughed again before fixing him with a provocative look. "In your dreams, you filthy bugger. Now let go of me." Eddie released his grip. Stella flexed her wrist as she slid her gaze from him to her sister and back again. "Sorry for spoiling your party," she said, before turning on her heel and walking out the front door without a backward glance.

"Silly little tart," said Eddie. "I need a drink." He stalked off toward the kitchen, leaving Eudora alone in the hall. She stood still, unable to shake the suffocating feeling that the walls were closing in on her. *Get ahold of yourself, Eudora*. She twisted her engagement ring, running a finger over the sparkling diamonds, smoothed her hair, and made her way back to the living room to comfort her mother.

# Chapter 9

THE SOCIAL WORKER is precisely seven minutes late and Eudora is vexed. She has never been late in her life and considers anyone who is as suffering from a weakness of character.

Her annoyance is heightened by her weariness. She enjoyed the party over the weekend, but it has left her tired and peevish. She longs for a swim to reenergize her fatigued soul. However, the summer's heat refuses to abate and so she is forced to spend yet another day imprisoned at home. What with Britain's scorching summers, monsoon-like autumns, and arctic winters, it feels as if there are only a handful of days a year when it's safe for the elderly to venture outside. Eudora often finds herself *harrumphing* at the television as another beaming Met Office presenter promises yet more inclement weather.

"There's no need to be so cheerful about it—black ice is no laughing matter when you're eighty-five!"

Eudora approaches the window, peers out at the moody-looking sky, and prays for rain. At least that would cool everything down a little. A small red car, which looks to Eudora like something a toddler might play with, pulls up outside. A harassed woman climbs out, darting an anxious glance toward the house. Eudora recognizes her as the social worker who visited before. Ruth, her name was, and she was very kind. The woman hauls a huge black bag and folder from the back of the car and hurries up the garden path. Eudora waits for the knock before making her way to the front door. She values kindness, but that won't save Ruth today.

"You are nearly fifteen minutes late," she says by way of a greeting.

"Yes, and I'm very sorry. My little boy was sick today, so I had to wait for my mum to come over to look after him," says Ruth, out of breath, her eyes creased with worry.

Eudora purses her lips. As far as excuses go, this one is difficult to counter. "Very well. You'd better come in."

"Thank you. And sorry again."

"There's no need to keep apologizing."

"Right. Yes. Sorry." Eudora raises an eyebrow. Ruth holds up her hands. "Force of habit. Got it. No more apologies."

"Would you like a cup of tea?"

"Only if you're having one. I can make it if you like?"

This feels like a test. "No. I'm perfectly capable, thank you. Why don't you go into the living room. I'll join you shortly."

"Okay. Thank you."

As Eudora makes the tea, she wonders what Ruth would say if she told her about her application to the clinic in Switzerland. She would be horrified of course. Human beings are only programmed to judge information based on their own experiences. Ruth spends her time ensuring that life is preserved and enhanced wherever possible. It's a noble cause, but what happens when someone like Eudora doesn't want her life to be preserved? It's not long before the hand-wringing starts, swiftly followed by pained expressions.

*But why would you want to die? You have so much to live for!*

*No.* You *have so much to live for. I don't and I'm absolutely fine with that. If I can have the choice of how I live my own life, why can't I choose how to die my own death?*

Eudora despairs of a world that can't at least have a sensible conversation about this.

She finishes making the tea and carries it into the living room. "Thank you very much," says Ruth, accepting the bone-china mug.

"So," says Eudora, sitting in her chair. "What is this all about?"

Ruth puts her mug on a coaster, a gesture that ingratiates her with Eudora. She pulls out a form. The dreaded forms. Eudora is touched by the NHS's unrelenting attention but is a little tired of answering the same questions over and over again.

*Name? (Honeysett. With two t's.)*

*Date of birth? (Pause while person filling in form registers that you are rather old.)*

*Do you live alone? (Pause while form-filler adopts a sympathetic expression as you answer in the affirmative.)*

*How do you feel about living alone? (Eye roll.)*

*Would you benefit from extra help around the home? (Shudder.)*

Eudora feels like a record on repeat as she tries to give each person the information they need, in the hope that they will leave her be. Their concern stems from kindness of course, but it also stems from that fundamental principle of preserving life at all cost.

Eudora is painfully aware that some healthcare professionals have no idea what to do when confronted with an old person. She recalls Mrs. Carter from three doors down who had a fall and was sent to A&E. For three years, she went back and forth between home and the germ-laced emergency department. Eventually, she died in the back of an ambulance, her final snapshot of life a flashing blue light and a kindly, overworked paramedic telling her she was going to be all right. Eudora is determined that this will not be the ending to her story.

"So, really, I wanted to see how you're getting on. I know you went to the falls clinic and they were very pleased with your progress."

*Gold star, Eudora.* "I am quite well, thank you," she says.

"That's excellent. And you're using the stick I gave you?"

"Yes. It's a godsend. I use it when I go to the swimming pool and manage well enough without it around the house."

"Wonderful. It's great to hear you still go swimming. You're an example to us all, Eudora."

"Thank you."

"And you're managing at home? With washing and toilet needs?"

Eudora is appalled. "Yes. Yes, thank you."

"How about getting up from your chair, and in and out of bed?"

"Everything is fine. Really."

"Good. What about your mental health?"

Eudora frowns. "There's nothing wrong with me."

"Oh, I wasn't suggesting there is. I'm just aware that you live alone." *Here we go,* thinks Eudora. "And I have some activities I could suggest, which you might enjoy—various groups and the like."

*Good heavens above. A place where all the miserable old people can sit together and moan about their ailments.* Eudora is reminded of the Groucho Marx quote: "I don't care to belong to any club that will have me as a member."

"I'm not sure it's for me. Thank you," says Eudora firmly.

"Okay," says Ruth. "I'll leave you some leaflets to peruse at your leisure."

"Mmm," says Eudora vaguely.

Their conversation is interrupted by Ruth's phone ringing. She glances at the screen and pulls a face. "Sorry, Eudora. I need to take this." She carries the phone into the hall.

Eudora takes a sip of her tea, hearing every word of the conversation that follows.

"Mum? Is everything okay. How's Max? Yes. Yes, he had some Calpol at eight. Is his temperature not coming down? Okay, try Nurofen and check it again in half an hour. Keep me posted. Thanks, Mum, love you. Give Max a kiss from me."

Eudora hears the shakiness in Ruth's voice. She doesn't claim to have firsthand experience of motherhood but does understand about caring for another human being.

Ruth returns to the living room, her face pale and fretful. "Right," she says, taking her seat again. "Where were we?"

"You should go," says Eudora.

"Pardon?"

"You should go and be with your baby. It's far more important than all this." Ruth stares at her with shining eyes.

Eudora fears she's about to cry, so she speaks quickly. "I am an old woman and I am perfectly fine. I appreciate your efforts, but you do not need to worry about me. You do, however, need to worry about your little boy. So please leave now or I shall be forced to call your office and complain."

It takes Ruth a moment to realize that Eudora is joking. She clutches her heart and gives a relieved laugh. "Are you sure? I think you might be right. I need to be with him, don't I?"

Eudora realizes that only she can grant this young mother permission. "Of course. You young women are trying to do it all. You need to give yourselves a break sometimes." She heard someone use this phrase on *Woman's Hour*. It sounds faintly ridiculous on her lips, but she decides that it's the correct thing to say.

Ruth nods rapidly. "Thank you, Eudora. You're absolutely right. Max has to come first. I'll go. Is it all right if I call you again, to finish our chat?"

"As you wish, but make sure your baby's well first. Otherwise I shall hang up on you."

Ruth smiles. "Thank you. You're very kind. Take care of yourself, Eudora."

"You too."

Eudora hears the door shut and sinks back into her chair, tired but satisfied. *For beauty lives with kindness*, she thinks as she closes her eyes and lets sleep descend.

It's around lunchtime when Rose knocks on the door. Eudora has just finished a very acceptable ham sandwich and is making good progress with the crossword. Usually, she would be irritated by the interruption. However, as she opens the front door, Eudora is unexpectedly cheered to see Rose, not least because today's outfit is extraordinary, comprising buttercup yellow, ecclesiastical purple, and neon orange. There's something surprisingly reassuring about Rose's questionable sartorial experiments.

"Good afternoon, Rose. How are you?"

"Hello, Eudora. I'm fine but I'm worried about Stanley."

"Oh?"

Rose's face is serious. "He hasn't been past with the dogs today and that never happens. And I remember he said he gets a bit down about Ada sometimes. Mum sent me 'round to ask if you know where he lives."

"Actually, I do. Are you going to go and check on him?"

"I am, but Mum is really tired because of the bloody baby."

"Rose!"

"Sorry. That's what Mum said. If you give me the address, I'll go and knock on his door."

Visions of this eccentric little girl shinnying up Stanley's drainpipe flood Eudora's mind. She would rather not get involved but feels as if her hand is being forced somehow. Besides, she is also a little worried about Stanley Marcham. "I'll come with you."

"Are you sure? Mum said not to bother you when it's this hot."

"It's perfectly fine. I think it's going to rain soon anyway. We'll go together."

"Okay. I'll tell Mum."

The sky is the color of anger, with grumbling thunder threatening in the distance, as Eudora and Rose make the short walk to Stanley's house. Rose is now accessorizing her outfit with an umbrella decorated with gold llamas as spots of rain start to fall. Eudora holds her stick in one hand and a functional burgundy umbrella in the other. A shiver of panic runs through her as she notices that the curtains to Stanley's house are still drawn.

She shakes her head. It's utter madness coming here alone with Rose. What if he's lying on the floor unconscious? She's too old for all this.

"Come on, Eudora," says Rose, leading her by the arm to the front door. Eudora steels herself, reaching forward to press the doorbell. There's a cacophony of barking from somewhere in the house but no sign of Stanley. She tries again. More barking but no other signs of life. Eudora glances down at Rose, who takes this as a cue.

The little girl pushes open the letterbox and leans in. "Stanley! It's Rose and Eudora! Are you there? We're worried about you!"

The barking begins afresh along with another sound, human this time. "All right. I'm coming." It's a small, reluctant version of Stanley's voice. They stand back as he opens the door. Eudora is shocked by his appearance. He looks so different from the larger-than-life character she is used to. She can hardly believe that this shrunken man is the same one with whom she drank champagne on the weekend. He is also still in his pajamas and dressing gown, which, to Eudora's mind, is an abhorrence, particularly given that it's well after two in the afternoon.

"Oh. Are you having a pajama day, Stanley?" asks Rose.

Stanley stares down at his attire and then at Eudora. She sees shame in his eyes and something else: a plea for help. "Well, I . . ."

"Let's all go inside," says Eudora, glancing at the steadily falling rain. "Before we get washed away."

"Oh yes, of course," says Stanley, moving back to let them in.

As Rose steps over the threshold she wraps her arms around his waist. "I'm so glad you're all right."

Eudora notices Stanley's face crumple and, fearing the avalanche of emotion that may follow, she asks, "Do you have any cordial?"

"She means squash," whispers Rose behind her hand. "It's Eudora's posh word for it."

Stanley's expression lifts to one of confusion. "Erm, yes, I think so."

"Right. Rose, unhand Stanley and go into the kitchen and make us three of your best glasses of cordial, please. Stanley and I will be in the living room."

Rose stands poker straight like a regimental soldier. "Aye, aye, captain," she says. "Do you want me to check on Chas and Dave too?"

Stanley looks as if he's remembered something important. "Oh yes. They're in the back room. They're probably hungry. The food and bowls are on the side."

Rose puts a hand on her heart. "Leave it to me, Stanley. You go and have a nice chat with Eudora."

Stanley stares at Eudora. "I didn't feel like doing anything today. I couldn't see the point."

"Let's go and sit down," says Eudora.

Stanley Marcham's living room is a shrine to a happy life. It's bright and cheerful, with two upright but comfortable Ercol chairs set against one wall opposite the television. An Ercol sofa flanks the adjacent wall. The red velvet curtains and peacock-feather flocked wallpaper are not to Eudora's taste, but she finds herself admiring them all the same. What is most eye-catching are the photographs lining each surface and wall, bordered by frames of every color and design. There are pictures of babies, elderly people, toddlers, teenagers, and lots of photographs of Stanley and Ada, smiling out at her. Pictures of love and happiness.

She hears the dogs yelp with excitement as Rose opens the door to the back room and delivers their food. Her voice is kind and reassuring and their barking immediately calms to an occasional yap.

Eudora takes a seat on the sofa as Stanley sinks into what she realizes is his usual chair. She notices his glasses case on the side table next to a framed photograph of a beaming woman who has to be Ada and a "Best Pops in the World" mug decorated with more pictures of Stanley with his grandchildren. Then she spots the empty chair to his right holding the large cushion decorated with a huge photograph of Chas and Dave, who stare out at her with optimistically eager eyes. Ada's chair.

"So what's this all about then?" asks Eudora.

Stanley adopts the expression of a small boy being questioned by his mother. He shrugs. "I don't know."

"Did something happen?"

His eyes grow misty with the promise of tears. "I miss Ada."

Eudora folds her hands in her lap. "I know you do."

Stanley gazes into the distance, lost in a moment's reverie. "I had this dream. We were about to go dancing. She looked so beautiful, all dolled up. I could smell her perfume. And I was so happy to see her. I thought she was still with me and that her leaving me had all been a dream. And then I woke up . . ." Stanley glances at his late wife's chair and starts to cry. He wraps his arms around his body and shakes as the sobs engulf him.

Eudora freezes, darting a glance at the door and hoping Rose might burst through it, but she can hear the little girl still fussing over the dogs and realizes it's down to her. She rises to her feet and approaches Stanley. He is hunched over like a man adopting the crash position, a picture of heartbreaking grief. She reaches out a hesitant hand, glancing toward the photograph of Ada on the side table and willing her to give Eudora strength. As her palm makes contact with Stanley's shoulder, he stops crying but remains curled over with sadness.

"There, there," says Eudora before realizing how inadequate this sounds. She searches her mind for the right words. "You mustn't upset yourself. Ada wouldn't want you to be sad."

Stanley looks up at her in bewilderment. "She'd think I was a silly old fool sitting here feeling sorry for myself."

Eudora nods. "Very possibly. Now, come along. Dry your tears. Rose will be back with her astonishingly sweet cordial in a minute. It will make you wince, but it might make you feel better."

"Made with love, eh?"

"Something like that."

Stanley fishes out his handkerchief and wipes his eyes. "I'm sorry, Eudora."

"What on earth are you sorry about? You miss your wife. You feel sad. It's perfectly understandable. You certainly shouldn't be apologizing to me."

"I just know you don't like all this weeping and wailing."

"Everyone is different," she says.

"Thank you for coming to check up on me."

"You would do the same for me," says Eudora.

"I would."

"Here we are," says Rose, carrying a tray into the living room. "And I found some chocolate biscuits, if that's okay with you, Stanley?"

As Stanley smiles and nods, Eudora sees a little of his old self return. "Of course, Rose. Anything for my two knights in shining armor."

"Can you have lady knights?" asks Rose with genuine interest.

Stanley gestures at them both with open palms. "It would seem that way."

"Are you feeling better?" she asks, handing him a glass.

Stanley takes a sip of the drink and winces before regaining his composure. "Much better, thank you, Rose."

"Good," she says, munching on a biscuit. "Because I've got an invitation for you both."

Stanley glances at Eudora and smiles. She gives an uncertain laugh before darting her gaze back toward the photo of Ada. Eudora sees the sparkle in her eyes, a spirit of adventure, and a deep kindness, which makes her wish they'd known each other. She sends her a silent promise. *I'll make sure he's all right, Ada. I'll do my best for you while I can.*

Rose is pogoing up and down in her seat with excitement. Eudora turns to her. "Come along then, Rose. Don't keep us in suspense any longer. What have you got in store for us now?"

## 1958
## SIDNEY AVENUE, SOUTH-EAST LONDON

The dress was perfect—a deferential nod to the exquisite gown Grace Kelly wore for her wedding only two years earlier, with a demure high-necked lace collar, empire waist, and elegant full skirt. It was everything Eudora could wish for. Her mother had cried and clutched Sylvia's arm when she saw her daughter wearing it. Even Stella had nodded and smiled with obvious affection. Eudora had been relieved when her sister agreed to their mother's idea of a shopping trip to London with fellow bridesmaid, Sylvia. Beatrice was adamant that they should do things properly.

"The mother of the bride must buy her daughter's dress. It's tradition," she said, eyes brimming with tears.

Eudora didn't want to put her mother to unnecessary expense, but she was glad her wedding was bringing Beatrice a rare moment of joy. She squeezed her mother's hands. "Thank you, Mummy."

There had been a truce of sorts between Beatrice and her youngest daughter over the past six months and a change in Stella, which Eudora welcomed like a cooling breeze on a hot day.

Stella had been attending the local church-run youth club and had even volunteered to run activities for some of the younger kids. Eudora was further reassured by the presence of Eddie, who often went along to teach mechanics to any teenagers who were interested. Having her fiancé there to keep an eye on Stella made Eudora feel as if life might finally be settling into something more hopeful. Eudora's future was there for the taking and she intended to embrace it with open arms.

With little over one month to go before the wedding, Eudora was skittish with excitement. Apart from the one extravagance of her dress, she had done her best to keep costs to a minimum. Although rationing was a thing of the past, she still harbored a strong sense of thriftiness. Eudora had rejected the idea of a fancy wedding reception for afternoon tea in the hall next to the church where they were to be married. She and Eddie would leave the reception at around six and catch a train to Eastbourne. There they would enjoy a week-long honeymoon staying in a bed-and-breakfast run by a friend of Eddie's mother, who had given them a reduced rate on a room with a sea view. Eudora was more than satisfied with their plans and couldn't wait to begin their life together.

Two weeks before the wedding, Sylvia suggested they go for afternoon tea up in town.

"My treat. It can be our last hoorah before you walk up the aisle. Ask Stella and your mum along too if you like."

Eudora had been relieved when her mother and Stella had each declined the invitation. She loved them dearly, but it would be more relaxing with just Sylvia.

"I've got to get on in the garden while the weather's fine," said Beatrice. "You go and have fun with Sylvia."

Eudora intended do just that. It was a beautiful, warm day and she was wearing her favorite summer dress. She stood in the hall getting ready to leave as Stella came down the stairs.

"That dress always looks lovely on you, Dora," she said, pausing to admire her sister.

"Thank you, Stella," said Eudora, looking up from the mirror as she smoothed her hair.

"I'm sorry I can't make it this afternoon."

Eudora turned to face her sister, noticing that her blue eyes were narrowed with concern. She patted Stella's arm. "It's all right. I understand. It's far more important that you help out at the youth club."

"Mmm," said Stella, staring at the floor.

Eudora reached out and lifted her chin. "Really. It's okay. It's only afternoon tea with Sylvia."

"Darling Dora," said Stella, flinging her arms around her sister and squeezing her tight. "You deserve to be happy."

Eudora smiled, holding her sister at arm's length. "I am happy."

Stella stared into her eyes and nodded. "I think you will be. And you won't need to worry about me anymore."

"I will always worry about you. It's my job as your sister," Eudora told her. "But I am proud of you. I know things haven't been easy, but I feel as if you've turned a corner."

Stella opened her mouth to speak, hesitating as if struggling to find the right words. "I think I have too. I love you, Dora. Always remember that."

Eudora planted a kiss on her forehead. "Silly goose. Of course I will."

It had been a wonderful afternoon with Sylvia. They had laughed and reminisced about those magical evenings, dancing the night away. Then they shared their hopes and secret wishes for the future. Sylvia longed for a proposal from Kenny. Inspired by her own fairy tale, Eudora reassured her that she was certain it would happen any day. They talked about their dreams of happy marriages and homes full of children, of the domestic bliss they were convinced was a heartbeat away.

When Eudora looked back on that afternoon, she viewed it as one of the last times she was truly happy. It all came as such a shock. She felt naïve for not having had the faintest idea of what was about to happen. As the freight train plowed its way through her life, she realized she hadn't even heard the whistle or the *click-clack* of the track.

The house was quiet as she entered later that afternoon. Eudora relished the peace after so many years of coming home to the battling of her mother and sister.

"Dora dear. Is that you?"

"Yes, Mother," she said, hanging her coat on the stand and making her way to the kitchen, where Beatrice was pouring boiling water into the teapot.

"Would you like a cup, dear?"

"No, thank you. I feel as if I've drunk gallons of the stuff."

Her mother smiled. "Did you have a nice time?"

"It was lovely. Is Stella home yet?"

"I haven't heard her come in, but then I've been in the garden all afternoon. I've planted out the runner beans and lettuces," she said, her mind clearly more focused on her horticultural endeavors than her younger daughter.

"Mmm, strange. Maybe she's in her room. I'll go and check."

Eudora padded up the stairs and pushed open the door to Stella's bedroom. It was uncharacteristically ordered, and Stella was nowhere to be seen. Eudora's mouth went dry as she took in her surroundings, reaching out a hand to open Stella's wardrobe. Empty. She cast around, realizing that all of Stella's personal items were missing, along with the suitcase that usually sat on top of the wardrobe. "She's gone!" cried Eudora, rushing out onto the landing.

"Gone?" said Beatrice, appearing in the hallway. "What do you mean 'gone'?"

Eudora hurried downstairs. "I mean, she's taken everything and left."

"Good heavens above. Should we call the police?"

Eudora realized at that moment that she would be forever responsible for her mother. Beatrice didn't have the first clue what to do. "Yes. I think we should." The telephone began to ring as she reached the bottom step. Eudora snatched it up. "Stella?"

"It's Eddie," said a voice.

"Eddie. Oh, thank goodness. You have to come 'round at once. Stella's gone missing. We're worried about her."

There was a moment's hesitation before he answered. "She's with me."

"Oh. Good. Where did you find her?"

Eddie cleared his throat. "The thing is, Dora . . . There's no easy way to tell you this, but, well, Stella and me, we've become close over the last year or so and, well, I'm sorry but the wedding's off."

Eudora knew she had to keep speaking, even though words were failing her. "What? What do you mean?"

"Yeah, I mean, we've fallen in love and we're getting married."

"You and Stella?" It sounded like a joke. A terrible, tragic joke.

Eudora detected a hint of impatience in Eddie's voice. "That's what I'm trying to tell you. I'm sorry but, you know, these things happen."

"But she's just a child."

"Well, no, actually. She's eighteen, so she can make up her own mind. Sorry, Dor, but you and me, it was never going to work. You're too . . ."

*Too trusting?*

*Too foolish?*

*Too naïve?*

"Too . . . ?" said Eudora, wondering at her perverse need to hear the awful truth.

"Too straight and too nice. You deserve better than me. I'm a bit of a joker and so is Stella. Listen, I know this is a lot to take in but it's for the best. You'll see. We want you to be happy, Dor. I think you will be with us out of the picture. Find yourself a nice, reliable bloke like Kenny."

"I don't know what to say."

"Look, we've got a train to catch. No hard feelings, okay? Oh, Stella wants to say something."

There was a crackle on the line as Eddie handed over the receiver. Eudora realized she was holding her breath.

"Dora? I'm sorry, Dora. I wanted to tell you face-to-face but Eddie thought it was for the best this way. I meant what I said. I love you and I want you to be happy. I think you will be with us gone."

Eudora's heart was pierced with white-hot hatred at the sound of her sister's voice. It was a slap across the face and the wake-up call she needed. "Never call this number again. You are dead to us," she said, before replacing the handset and crumpling to the floor.

# Chapter 10

EUDORA HONEYSETT IS more than a little baffled to find herself waiting in the queue for a merry-go-round. Like most extraordinary events in her life of late, it's Rose's fault. And Stanley's. But mostly she blames Rose.

The potent combination of Rose's wide-eyed delight on spotting the garishly opulent carousel ride teamed with Stanley's melancholy expression as he told them both how much Ada used to love a merry-go-round made it impossible for Eudora to refuse.

*I could be sitting at home waiting to die*, she thinks. *And yet here I am in the searing August heat, pretending to enjoy myself because of an ill-advised promise I made to a dead woman and the overexcitement of a young girl. What has happened to me?*

"This is going to be so much fun!" cries Rose. "Which one are you going to choose? I like the look of William." She points to a startled-looking horse, whose alarmingly clashing rainbow-colored body and golden mane could have come directly from the Rose Trewidney school of design.

Eudora considers her options. A rather dashing white stallion with a regal red-and-gold-painted saddle catches her eye. She reads the name. It's like a hand reaching out to her from the past. "I think I'll choose Albert," she says.

"Oh. Like your dad," says Rose.

"How do you know that?" asks Eudora, unsure of whether to be pleased or annoyed.

"You told me," says Rose. "I have an excellent memory."

"You might need to lend me a dollop of that, Rose," says Stanley.

"Anytime, Stanley. Anytime."

As they reach the front of the queue, the young man on the gate gawks at Eudora and Stanley as if he's never encountered a person over the age of sixty-five before. "Oi, Dave!" he shouts.

A man with a weathered, impatient face glares over at them. "What?"

The youth cocks his head at Eudora and Stanley. "Where shall I put 'em?"

"You could always push us off the end of the pier," mutters Eudora.

The older man shrugs. "I dunno. They can go in the double-seater, if they want," he says, gesturing toward a lower-level carousel car for two with a silver dragon design.

Eudora's patience has reached its limit. She pushes forward, squaring up to the young man, who looks terrified despite being nearly a foot taller and well over half a century younger than her. "Listen here, young man. I am going to ride Albert, do you understand? Now kindly allow me to pass so we can have our turn."

The older man cackles with laughter. "You tell him, sweetheart. Let them through, Dean, you doughnut."

Dean's face reddens to a shade matching Albert's saddle, but he does as he's told. Emboldened by her victory, Eudora sweeps up to her horse and carefully climbs aboard, thankful that Albert's design enables her to perch side-saddle while holding on tightly to his reins and pole. Rose and Stanley climb up onto the horses on either side of her.

"I thought you wanted to ride William," says Eudora to Rose.

Rose shakes her head. "It's more fun like this."

"You certainly put that lad in his place, Miss Honeysett," says Stanley with an admiring glance.

"Some people need to be told," says Eudora.

The reassuringly cheerful organ music strikes up as they set off, slowly at first but gradually picking up speed.

"Whee!" cries Rose as they race past her mother and father. "Mum, Dad, look at us! We're flying!"

It takes Eudora a moment or two to get used to the rise and fall of the carousel, but soon a sense of freedom—not unlike the way she feels when she's swimming—rises up inside her. She glances over at Stanley, who is laughing at Rose's enthusiastic whoops and cheers. Eudora wonders how they must look: two octogenarians and a small girl on a fairground ride; it's faintly ridiculous. As she glances up, Eudora realizes that people are pointing and smiling at them. She finds herself raising her hand, offering a regal wave to the crowd. The smiles become waves and cheers accompanied by delighted comments.

"She looks like the Queen!"

"Good for her and the old boy!"

"Hope I'm like that at their age."

Eudora breathes in cooling sea-salt air, exhilarated by this gloriously clamorous world. She catches Rose's eye. The little girl's gleeful grin is as infectious as her spirit.

"You're right, Rose," she tells her. "This is fun."

Rose gives her a jubilant thumbs-up.

Eudora is almost disappointed when the carousel eventually slows to a halt. Stanley slides down from his horse, offering her his hand. "Your majesty?"

"The cheek of the man!" says Eudora, but she accepts his help all the same.

"Wasn't that brilliant?" says Rose, as they rejoin her parents on the other side of the barrier.

"I'm a little dizzy but it was most enjoyable," admits Eudora.

"Praise indeed," says Stanley with a grin.

They find Maggie and Rob sitting on a bench in the shade. At first Eudora had been doubtful of Rose's suggestion that she and Stanley join her family on a trip to the seaside. However, not only was Eudora bound by her promise to Ada, but when she heard that they would be visiting Broadstairs, her heart leapt. She had fond memories of this place and was keen to take one last trip.

Maggie had offered Eudora a seat in the front next to Rob, but the sight of this heavily pregnant, weary young mother made it impossible for her to accept. Thankfully, modern life had done her a favor by inventing air-conditioning, ample legroom, and noise-canceling headphones, which meant Rose could listen to her beloved pop songs without disturbing her fellow passengers. Eudora chose to overlook her occasional tuneless accompaniment and even managed a nap during the journey.

She was intrigued by the idea of spending a whole day with Rose and her parents. Eudora didn't claim to understand the vagaries of modern family relationships but could see that the world had moved on in this respect. There was an egalitarianism to Rob's relationship with Maggie that was alien to Eudora but which she secretly applauded. However, it was the ease of Rob's relationship with his daughter that she found both cheering and familiar. It was like a timeless version of the bond she had enjoyed with her own father. It made Eudora feel unexpectedly safe.

"So who's for ice cream?" asks Rob.

"Me, me, me!" cries Rose, bouncing up and down in front of her father with her hand in the air.

Rob looks past her to Eudora and Stanley, maintaining a poker-straight expression. "No one? Eudora? Stanley? Can I tempt you to an ice cream because at the moment I've got no takers?"

"Daddee, stop it!" cries Rose.

"You're such a tease, Robert," says Maggie.

"Ooh, Robert," he says. "She called me 'Robert.' I'm in trouble now. If only there was some way of making it up to you all."

"You could buy us ice cream," says Eudora, surprising herself by being drawn into their jesting.

"What a good idea," says Rob. "Thank you, Eudora. Come along then. Ice cream for everyone except Rose, who would probably just like a carrot or something."

Rose replies by jumping on his back. Rob hitches her higher and gallops off toward the ice-cream kiosk.

"You're very lucky," says Eudora to Maggie as they follow

after. She glances at Stanley. "You too. You have wonderful families."

"You're welcome to be part of ours anytime you like," says Maggie.

"Thank you" is all Eudora can think to say.

Maggie steals a glance at her. "Do you have any blood relatives anywhere, Eudora?"

Eudora would usually refuse to be cross-examined in this way, but there's something about Maggie that draws out the sad truth. "No. My father died in the war and my mother died thirteen years ago."

"No siblings?" asks Maggie, running a hand over her belly.

Eudora hesitates before answering. "I had a sister."

Maggie hears her emphasis on the past tense. "I'm so sorry."

They reach the kiosk in time to see Rose receive her ice cream. "What is that?" cries her mother. "It looks incredible."

Rose takes a lick, rewarding them with a victorious sauce-covered smile. "It's vanilla toffee chocolate ice cream with nuts, sauce, *and* sprinkles."

"What can I get you, Eudora?" asks Rob.

"Well, Rose hasn't let me down when it comes to fashion, so perhaps I should trust her taste in ice cream too," says Eudora.

"That's a vanilla toffee chocolate ice cream with nuts, sauce, *and* sprinkles, Daddy," says Rose, puffing out her chest with pride.

"Thank you," says Eudora.

Rob grins. "Coming right up."

They carry their ice creams to benches overlooking the sea. Rose is sandwiched between Maggie and Stanley on one bench, while Eudora finds herself sitting next to Rob on another. She stares out at the cloudless hyacinth-blue sky, toward the pale sand where children are building sandcastles and skipping in and out of the water with squealing delight. Eudora remembers this beach and that sacred day when she'd dared to dream. Another life. A different world. She blinks away the memory.

"Your daughter has exceptional taste in ice cream," she tells Rob. "So how are you settling in to London life? It must be quite a change from Cornwall."

"You can say that again." He inhales deeply. "It's good to take a day to come here. We miss the sea, and I can't say I enjoy commuting into London, particularly in this heat." He glances at Eudora. "Have you always lived on Sidney Avenue?"

She nods. "Apart from when I was evacuated during the war."

"You must have seen a lot of people come and go."

"That's something of an understatement. You're probably the tenth or eleventh family to live next door to me."

"But we're the best, right?" says Rob, his eyes glittering with amusement.

Eudora finds his easy humor hard to resist. "That's still under review."

He laughs. "Very good. Then we shall do our best to win your heart. Although—and I know I'm biased here—I can't believe Rose hasn't already wheedled her way into your affections."

"She's certainly wheedled her way into my life," says Eudora. "She's quite a character. And we get along rather well, I think."

"Just a bit. All I get when I come home from work is *Guess what Eudora told me today, Daddy,* and *Eudora said the funniest thing this morning.*"

Eudora is astonished. "Really?"

"Really."

"I expect that will change when she starts school and makes friends her own age."

Rob stares out to sea. "The thing is, Rose has always struggled to make friends. She was bullied at her last school."

"Oh," says Eudora. "I'm sorry to hear that."

"The school tried to sort it out but there's only so much you can do. It was one of the reasons we decided to come here and make a new start."

"I see."

"Anyway, I for one am glad that the two of you are friends. I can already see how it's boosted her confidence." They look over to the other bench. Rose is on her feet entertaining Maggie and Stanley with a funky chicken dance. Rob laughs. "Okay, so she's a little eccentric at times."

"I think you'll find the most interesting people are," says Eudora.

Rob smiles. "See? I knew you got her. Thank you."

"What on earth for?"

"Your kindness. Maggie and I value it a great deal."

Their conversation is interrupted as Rose drags her father off to look through the telescope that points out to sea. Eudora watches them, reflecting on Rob's comments. It hadn't occurred to her that she was playing a significant role in Rose's life. It unnerves her slightly but pleases her too. She hasn't been needed by another human being since her mother died, and now it would seem she is being drawn into the lives of two individuals. Eudora isn't sure how this has happened but finds the whole notion a great deal less irksome than she expected. She realizes this adds a certain level of complication to her future plans but consoles herself that she is merely passing the time, rather like doing a crossword puzzle while waiting to see the doctor.

They arrive home late that evening after deciding to stay for a fish-and-chips supper so they can avoid the early evening traffic. Rose spends the journey drawing, and as they part company later she presents Stanley and Eudora with a piece of original artwork each.

"This is Stanley fighting off that seagull when it tried to steal his chips."

"The blighter," says Stanley.

"And this is Eudora and me, eating cake and watching *Pointless* together while Monty sleeps on the sofa. See? I've even drawn Richard Osman on the telly."

"It's a very good likeness," says Eudora.

"It's for you to put up in your kitchen," explains Rose. "To make it a bit more colorful."

"Thank you."

Eudora searches in the back of the cupboard among miscellaneous "just in case" pieces of string and redundant keys.

"Aha!" she cries, retrieving an ancient packet of Blu Tack, which, according to the yellowing price label, had been purchased for 75p from a now-defunct high-street chain. Eudora sticks Rose's picture onto the cupboard next to her "Adorable Kittens" calendar. It had been the only one left in the post office when she purchased it earlier in the year. Although it wouldn't have been her first choice, she has to admit that August's blue-eyed, soft gray kitten, who gazes out at her from a flowerpot, is rather charming.

"Look, Monty," she says as the cat saunters into the kitchen. "Rose drew a picture of us." The cat looks up at her with a bored expression before turning his attention to the biscuits she has just poured out for him. Eudora stands back, satisfied with her handiwork. She lifts the pages of the calendar, noticing the word "Freedom," which she had written barely a month before. She is about to make some tea when the telephone starts to ring. Eudora hobbles into the living room to answer it.

"Hello?"

"Eudora? This is Petra."

Eudora's heartbeat quickens. "Hello, Petra. I was wondering when you might call."

"How are you, Eudora?"

"I am quite well, thank you. I'm keen to know how my application is progressing. Do you have any news for me?"

"I don't, I'm afraid. I know you spoke to Doctor Liebermann last week and I'm telephoning to see how things are. I tried to call yesterday but you were not at home."

"I went out for the day." The words spill from Eudora's mouth before she has time to stop them.

"Did you go somewhere nice?"

Eudora is genetically programmed never to lie. "I went to the seaside with some friends."

"Oh, how lovely."

"Yes. It was very pleasant but very tiring."

"Hopefully it was worth the tiredness?"

Eudora remembers Rose's declaration as they parted company last night that it had been the "Best. Day. Ever." She dismisses the thought with a shake of her head. "It was an enjoyable day, but it hasn't changed my mind about my application. I still want to go ahead."

"I understand," says Petra. "Well, I know Doctor Liebermann is considering your application very carefully, so it shouldn't be too long before you hear."

"I see," says Eudora.

*More waiting and hoping, Eudora. But then you've had a lifetime of both so what's a few more weeks?*

"I must say that I am glad you're making the most of life, Eudora."

"It's better than sitting around waiting to die, isn't it?"

"You're absolutely right. You're a remarkable woman, Eudora. Don't forget that."

*Remarkable, my foot,* thinks Eudora as she replaces the telephone in its cradle. *I am merely being realistic about life and death. Surely that's the most sensible thing in the world.*

She struggles to a standing position, irritated by her uncooperative joints, and shuffles to the kitchen, her mind on a restorative cup of tea. As she spots Rose's picture on the cupboard again, she reaches for a pen and turns the calendar pages. She stares at the word "Freedom" for a while before adding a question mark beside it and giving a satisfied nod. It was important to be realistic about these things.

## CHRISTMAS 1958
## THE ORCHID BALLROOM, SOUTH-EAST LONDON

Sylvia had suggested the pre-Christmas outing to a Saturday-night dance. Eudora had tried to protest, but you couldn't reason with Sylvia once she'd gotten a bee in her bonnet.

"You need to get out of the house on the weekends, meet someone new, forget about . . . you know . . . what happened."

Eudora had forbidden her friends from mentioning Eddie and Stella by name. She wanted to blot them out, forget they had ever existed. It didn't work but she had to try.

Patrick Nicholson was one of the senior managers at the bank where Eudora worked, acceding to his position largely due to the fact that his father was on the board of directors. He was handsome with a whiff of Gregory Peck about him and had immaculate dress sense. Eudora didn't find him remotely attractive even though she knew most of the secretaries would give their eyeteeth to court him. So when he asked if she would like to go dancing sometime, she faced the weight of expectation from both Sylvia and the secretarial pool. She decided to give in, suggesting he join them at the Orchid Ballroom.

"He is such a dish," exclaimed Sylvia as they waited to check their coats. "And so courteous. The way he helped you out of the car . . . Good heavens, Eudora, if Kenny hadn't just proposed, I would be insanely jealous."

"He's certainly very charming," said Eudora, looking around at the familiar surroundings of the ballroom and wondering why she had agreed to come. She kept expecting to see Eddie. The very thought made her queasy with sadness.

The evening began well enough. Despite his outwardly debonair appearance, Patrick wasn't the most elegant dancer, but as he led Eudora in a passable foxtrot, she began to enjoy herself a little. Everyone was in a festive mood. The ballroom was festooned with crepe-paper streamers, honeycomb bells, and baubles. Eudora started to wonder if Patrick could be the answer to her problems. Maybe she was foolish to reject him out of hand; maybe she did deserve to be happy. Perhaps it was time to stop wallowing in self-pity.

As she excused herself to the powder room, Patrick kissed her hand in a way that gave Eudora fresh hope. However, while she was in the cubicle, she overheard two women discussing him.

"Did you see that guy who looks like Gregory Peck?"

"Did I? He keeps giving me the eye."

"Doris! You're shameless," her friend said, laughing.

"Yes, but can you blame him? Did you see the girl he's with? Talk about an ice queen. He probably just wants someone to have fun with."

Eudora closed her eyes and waited until their laughter died down and they had left the powder room. She emerged moments later, washed her hands, and went to find Patrick.

"Ahh, here she is!" he cried as she met him by the bar. "I thought you'd gotten lost. Can I get you a drink?"

Eudora wasn't a drinker. She could see that Patrick was already quite drunk, but the powder-room women's comments were echoing in her ears. "I'll have a Babycham, thank you," she said with as much sophistication as she could muster.

"Your wish is my command," said Patrick with a satisfied smirk.

Eudora took in her surroundings. Sylvia and Kenny were floating elegantly around the dance floor like a Hollywood couple. She swallowed down her envy as Patrick returned with their drinks.

"Babycham for the lady," he said, handing it to her. "Cheers!" He knocked his pint glass against hers, slopping some of his beer onto the floor.

"Cheers," said Eudora, forcing a smile. She noticed a gaggle of women standing nearby who were eyeing them with jealousy. "Shall we find somewhere to sit?"

"As the lady wishes," said Patrick with a clumsy bow.

Eudora led them to a table in the corner, realizing to her horror that it was a little darker than she had anticipated. She sipped her drink, wincing at its claggy sweetness. Patrick pulled his chair closer, putting an arm around her shoulders. Eudora remained perfectly still, keeping her eyes fixed on the dance floor. She felt

Patrick move closer, his breath hot and stale on her cheek.

"You're a remarkable woman, Eudora," he whispered, leaning toward her so she was hit with an overpowering aroma of expensive aftershave and cheap beer.

She picked up her glass, forcing herself to drink, trying to ignore the fact that Patrick had placed a hand on her knee. She kept drinking, downing every last drop and then holding up her glass with a flourish. She planned to ask him to fetch her another so she could move to a different, less-secluded table, but Patrick had other ideas. As soon as she placed the glass on the table, he lurched forward and pressed his lips to hers, pushing his tongue into her mouth. Eudora was caught off guard. Her immediate reaction was to shove him as hard as she could. Patrick fell backward onto the floor, much to the amusement of nearby partygoers.

"'Ere mate, I don't think she likes you!" shouted one man.

"Yeah, better luck next time," called another.

Humiliated, Patrick stumbled to his feet, glaring at Eudora. "Why did you do that? What's the matter with you?" he shouted.

"I'm sorry, Patrick. This was all a mistake. I should never have asked you here," said Eudora, as a tidal wave of panic rose up inside her.

"Oh, I see, you're one of those girls, are you?" he said, his charm now replaced with spite.

Eudora blanched as people turned to stare. "Please don't make a scene."

Patrick shrugged. "Why? Don't you want people to know what a tease you are? Leading men on, then giving them the cold shoulder."

"I'm sorry."

"You should be." Patrick's icy stare chilled Eudora as he added his final insult. "Prick tease."

Eudora was horrified. She pushed her way through the sniggering crowds, fetched her coat, and fled into the night.

She hoped Patrick might forget the events of this ill-advised evening, but she knew it was in vain when she returned to work on Monday to be greeted with whispers and nudges from her fellow secretaries. Eudora did her best to ignore it, telling herself that today's news was tomorrow's fish-and-chips paper.

However, as she was on her way to the bathroom, she overheard Patrick talking to the manager of the female staff.

"I don't like to speak out of turn, but what is wrong with Eudora?" he asked.

The woman sighed. "I'm not one to gossip, Mr. Nicholson, but I heard that her fiancé ran off with her sister," she said in less than sympathetic tones.

"Oh dear. How unfortunate. Well, it doesn't excuse her shameful behavior, but I suppose at least we have an explanation for it."

"Would you like me to speak to her, sir?"

"No. Thank you, Rosemary. However, might I suggest that you make a note of it on her personnel records?

She's clearly unstable. We need to keep that in mind for the sake of our customers."

"Of course."

"Thank you. I feel sorry for her, to be honest. Poor Eudora Honeysett will no doubt die an old maid."

Eudora heard the sound of Rosemary gathering her papers, ready to leave his office, and she rushed to the lavatory. Blinking back tears as she bolted the door behind her, she realized two things: first, she would have to leave her beloved job, and second, Patrick Nicholson's prognosis of her future life was almost certainly correct.

# Chapter 11

"LINE DANCING."

"What? It could be fun."

"I sincerely doubt it. Why on earth would anyone want to dance in a line?"

Stanley peers at another leaflet. "*Nordic walking*?"

Eudora frowns. "Can't people just walk?"

He sighs. "*Sit and Get Fit*?"

"Impossible."

"Fine," he says, fanning out the remaining leaflets. "Pick one." Eudora eyes the offerings with suspicion. Stanley shrugs. "You promised to go to a group with me, and so far you've rejected all my suggestions. Now you have to pick one."

Eudora knows he's right. Ruth, the social worker, had left the leaflets during her visit, and Eudora had decided that they presented a perfect opportunity to get Stanley out of the house. She was starting to regret this ill-thought-through promise now though. "Very well," she says, closing her eyes as she plucks one from Stanley's hand. Her expression lifts as she reads the text. "Actually, this might be rather good."

"High praise," mutters Stanley.

Eudora ignores this jibe and reads out loud, "'Those Were the Days—activities for the older generation, including puzzles, music, tea, and talks.'"

"Sounds good, particularly the music bit."

Eudora throws him a warning look. "You are strictly forbidden to embark on any flamboyant participation."

Stanley pretends to tug his forelock. "Yes, m'lady."

"Foolish man."

"It's why you like me."

"Mmm."

Eudora isn't sure how she would define her relationship with Stanley. She can imagine Rose proclaiming them to be "BFFs" and insisting that they high-five. There's a pleasingly familial aspect to their interactions, almost as if Stanley is a younger brother, content to be bossed and teased by his older sister.

They have taken to telephoning each other during the early evening. It was Eudora's suggestion after Stanley confessed that he missed having someone with whom to recount the details of his day. At first she feared it would become a bind, but now she looks forward to their "nineteen-hundred-hour debrief" as Stanley insists on calling it. Although most of Stanley's chatter is light-hearted nonsense, she relishes their easy banter and the way Stanley always has a daft anecdote. Often he reports that day's score in his music quiz, detailing the trickier questions while Eudora shares a selection of troublesome crossword clues from her daily puzzle. Invariably, their talk will turn to Rose and something amusing she has done. They rarely talk for longer than ten minutes, but it's enough.

"Night, John-Boy," Stanley always says in a dreadful Deep South accent.

"Good night, Stanley."

Eudora faces the prospect of the group the next morning with a hint of dread but decides to view it as the Queen might: with an overriding sense of duty. She is hopeful that if she goes along once, Stanley will be his usual gregarious self, make a host of new friends, and Eudora will be off the hook.

Good deed done.

Promise to Ada fulfilled.

Eudora has enlisted Rose to come along, partly as an overexcited distraction who will bounce them through the morning with her relentless enthusiasm but also to give Maggie a break. She's noticed how weary she's been looking lately. She told Maggie that she would take Rose on the strict condition that she get some rest.

Maggie's hollowed-out expression when she and Stanley call for Rose at ten o'clock on the dot vindicates her decision.

"Thank you," says Maggie, casting an accusing look at her bump. "I hardly got any sleep last night as Rose's sister decided to have an all-night party."

"Oh dear," says Eudora. "Well, make sure you get some rest now. We should be back around lunchtime."

"This is going to be so much fun!" says Rose, skipping down the stairs wearing a brilliant orange sundress, yellow-framed sunglasses, and sparkly silver sandals.

"I like your outfit, Rose," says Stanley. "You look like a burst of sunshine."

"Very summery," agrees Eudora.

"You're wearing that top we bought when we went shopping!" cries Rose.

"I wondered if you'd notice," says Eudora. She had nearly put it back in the wardrobe but had experienced a rare "seize the day" moment.

"It looks lovely."

"I can see I'm going to have to up my game," says Stanley, offering them an arm each. "Shall we?"

"Have a good time!" calls Maggie as they climb into Stanley's car.

It's a short but pleasant enough drive to the group. Eudora doesn't even mind Stanley's choice of radio station, its incessant chatter interspersed with music. The DJ has an inoffensive and occasionally witty style. She listens as he chats amiably to a member of the public who has called in to participate in Stanley's favorite quiz. The DJ plays a song by Ella Fitzgerald. Eudora nods her approval.

"My dad loves *PopMaster*," says Rose.

"Good chap," says Stanley.

"I've no idea what you're talking about," says Eudora.

"It's that quiz I'm always telling you about," explains Stanley.

"You'll love it, Eudora," says Rose. "But you have to be very quiet so you can hear the questions."

"I can't quite believe you're telling *me* to be quiet, Rose."

"Shhh—it's starting!" says Rose as the song ends and the DJ addresses the caller.

*So, Phil, you have a choice of "Hits of the Sixties" or "Sexy Songs."*

"Good grief," exclaims Eudora.

*"Hits of the Sixties," please, Ken.*

*"Hits of the Sixties" it is. Okay. Here we go.*

As the quiz begins, Eudora is surprised to notice Stanley's face grow serious with concentration. What's more, he seems to know the answer to every question.

*And now for the "Hits of the Sixties" question: Lonnie Donegan achieved a 1960s number one with which song about a refuse collector?*

"'My Old Man's a Dustman'!" chorus Phil and Stanley at the same time.

*Correct. In which musical did Elaine Paige and Barbara Dickson's 1985 chart-topping hit "I Know Him So Well" feature?*

"*Chess*!" both men cry.

"Ada was a big Elaine Paige fan," confides Stanley with a fond smile.

Eudora glances at Stanley's animated expression and wishes she could join in. Alas, she has eschewed popular culture over the past forty years. She doesn't miss it. You can't miss what you've never had, after all. It would just be pleasant to be able to share in his enjoyment.

*And now for our final question: What was the title of the Top 10 hit by Laurel and Hardy that was featured in the 1937 movie* Way Out West *and found its way onto the UK chart in 1976?*

"*The Trail of the Lonesome Pine*," cries Eudora in tandem with Stanley and Phil.

Stanley laughs. "Well done, Miss Honeysett; six points to you!"

"You're a dream team!" cries Rose from the back.

Eudora's initial impression of the group is favorable. She admires the early-twentieth-century manor house where this and a host of other community-based activities are held. She gazes at the fine plastered ceilings and marble fireplaces, inhaling the reassuring aroma of history. A cheerful-looking woman with purple-tipped hair welcomes and directs them to a side room.

It is as Eudora enters this dark wood-paneled space and notices the thirty or so other decrepit individuals who look just like her that her heart sinks. It's such a nuisance that elderly people have to look so old. This shrunken, prune-like appearance, as if someone is slowly deflating them, is most unprepossessing. Eudora has no great desire to sit with these people, to effectively stare into the mirror at a constant reminder of what she has become. And yet here she is.

"Welcome! Welcome!" cries a small, efficient-looking woman carrying a jug of juice. "My name is Sue. And you are?"

*Wishing I were anywhere but here*, thinks Eudora.

Rose takes the initiative, and Eudora gives thanks for the impetuosity of ten-year-olds. "I'm Rose. I'm not over sixty-five, but Eudora thought it would be okay if I came along. This is Eudora, by the way, and that's Stanley. We're not related—just friends."

Sue beams. "Well, you are of course all very welcome. Please take a seat wherever you can find space and then you can make your name badges. Don't be shy. Do please introduce yourselves to others. There are all sorts of puzzles, games, and activities for you to enjoy. Oh, and help yourself to refreshments. We don't charge—it's voluntary contributions only. The talk will be starting in about half an hour."

"Thank you, Sue," says Stanley, flashing his usual charming smile. Eudora shakes her head when she notices the effect it has on this woman.

"I'll come and check on you in a bit," she says.

"Name badges?" mutters Eudora in disgust. "I know people regress as they get older, but really."

"It's okay, Eudora," says Rose. "I'll make you one. I love being creative. Ooh, glitter pens!"

They find space at a table where another couple is already seated. Rose gets to work immediately, selecting foam letters, glue, and all the glitter pens she can find.

"Good morning," says Stanley.

"Hello, hello, hello," says a man who looks about the same age as him. "The name's James but everyone calls me Jim."

"Hello, Jim," says Stanley. "This is Eudora and Rose."

The woman sitting next to Jim smiles. "Eudora. What an unusual name. I'm Jim's wife, Audrey. Aren't you a busy little bee?" she says to Rose.

"I do like to make stuff, Audrey. Can I ask how long you've been married, or is that nosy?"

Audrey smiles. "Not at all. It's been nearly fifty-six years. How about you?" she asks, looking at Eudora, who recoils in horror.

"We're not married," says Stanley. "She couldn't afford

me." Eudora rolls her eyes. "No. We're friends. And Rose is our minder." Rose strikes a weight lifter's pose, kissing each of her biceps in turn.

Audrey laughs. "You're very lucky to have one another. We hardly ever see our grandchildren," she adds.

"That is sad," says Rose. "I could probably come and visit you, if you don't live too far away." Audrey looks as if her heart has melted. "Right. Here's your name badge, Eudora. I tried not to be too over-the-top because I know you don't really like that."

Eudora looks at the fluorescent orange badge, purple foam letters, and green glitter decorations. "Good heavens, Rose. If this is subtle, I'd hate to see your extravagant version."

"Whereas I would like you to go all out with mine, please, Rose," says Stanley. "Every color of the rainbow and as bright as you can make it."

"Yessir!"

Stanley turns to Eudora. "Would her majesty like a cup of tea?"

"Are you going to insist on calling me that?"

"Probably."

"In that case, I would love a cup of tea, please. And an acceptable biscuit, if they have one."

Stanley clicks his heels to attention. "Very good. I'll ask the chef if he can rustle up some cucumber sandwiches while I'm at it." Eudora purses her lips. "Juice for you, Rose?"

"Yes please, Stanley."

"Can I get anyone else anything?"

"No, thank you," says Audrey.

"Right-ho. Back in a sec."

"What a lovely man," remarks Audrey, watching Stanley go.

"Mmm," says Eudora.

"It's important to have friends as you get older, isn't it? For extra support."

"I suppose so," says Eudora. She follows Audrey's gaze, which lingers on Rose for a moment. The little girl is intent on her badge-making project, spreading glitter as if her life depends on it.

"Toilet, Audrey, please," says Jim, looking scared.

Audrey's gaze snaps back to reality. "Of course, my love. Come along," she says, helping her husband to his feet. "Most of our friends keep their distance these days," she tells Eudora before leading Jim toward the door. "They don't know how to deal with Jim."

"I'm sorry," says Eudora because she doesn't know what else to say.

Audrey's face is weary with resignation. "It's how life is."

*Yes, but it shouldn't be. It shouldn't be like this at all*, thinks Eudora. *We're living longer but not better. We're doing it all wrong.*

Eudora casts around the room at the rest of the assembled company. There are people doing jigsaws and others playing dominoes, while some just chat or drink tea. It's not an unpleasant atmosphere and the people seem friendly enough. She feels sure Stanley will enjoy coming here.

"Here we are," says Stanley, returning with a tray containing their drinks and a plate of biscuits.

"Ooh, Oreo cookies. I love those," says Rose, helping herself to one.

"Thank you," says Eudora, taking a sip of her tea. "Not bad at all."

"Right. Good afternoon, everyone!" cries Sue. "It's wonderful to see so many new faces and lots of old friends too; you are all very welcome here. I hope you've found some people to chat to and find this group supportive and friendly. As many of you know, it's one of my personal missions to make sure older people continue to feel empowered."

*Empowered?* thinks Eudora. *Most days I'm just happy if I can find my glasses. I haven't got the strength for empowerment.*

"There is nothing I detest more," continues Sue, "than the stripping away of people's independence so they lose confidence and, ultimately, control over their own lives. And as those of you who are regulars will know, I never shy away from discussing difficult subjects. I was pleased how useful many of you found the recent talk about lasting power of attorney and how to fund care as and when you need it. So today's topic is something we all need to face . . ." She pauses for effect. "Death."

"Ooh," says Rose as the rest of the room seems to hold its breath. Eudora sits up straighter in her chair.

"Now, I don't want you to worry. This is not going to be depressing because I have a rather wonderful speaker who is going to tell us about what it is to have a good death. I have heard this lady speak before, so I know we are in safe hands. Please give a big Those-Were-the-Days welcome to Hannah Reeve, who is a death doula. Hannah."

Eudora is astonished by the aura of calm that ripples through the assembled company as Hannah rises to her feet. She casts her eyes over the audience, radiating positivity, her dark curly hair framing her face like a crown. The effect is immediate as the room falls completely silent and still. Even Rose stops fidgeting.

"Thank you, Sue. It's wonderful to be here. I must reiterate what she has said. You don't need to worry. This will not be a depressing talk. In fact, my sole aim is to uplift and educate you as to what a death doula does. All you need is an open mind and heart." Her voice is soothing and gentle and there's a quiet authority to every word she utters. Eudora finds herself leaning forward, noticing that Rose does the same. "My dearest wish is that people are able to have a good death. I would like us to consider for a moment what that might be. Would anyone like to make a suggestion?"

"Dying at home," says Stanley. "Like my Ada did." There are sympathetic murmurs around the room. Eudora notices Rose pat him on the shoulder.

"I am sorry for your loss," says Hannah, gazing at him kindly. "I very much appreciate you sharing your experience."

"Surrounded by love," says Audrey, patting Jim's hand.

Hannah smiles and nods. "Absolutely. I'm going to write these on my trusty board, if that's okay?" She fishes a marker pen from her pocket and begins to write on a whiteboard. People are emboldened by the other suggestions, and soon

Hannah has a long list, including "no pain," "without fear," and, on Rose's suggestion and to everyone's amusement, "having just eaten a big pizza and drunk a can of cherry Coke." Hannah turns back to face the room. "These are all wonderful contributions—thank you. I notice that no one considers a good death to be one that takes place in the back of an ambulance following emergency intervention." The room buzzes with disapproval. "Of course not. No one wants that. And yet, it's what happens to a large number of people in the UK today."

"That's terrible," says Rose.

"I agree with you, Rose."

"She knows my name," whispers Rose to Eudora.

"But I have good news," continues Hannah, "because if we all do one small thing during our lives we can avoid this ending. Does anyone know what that is?" There are nervous glances around the room. "It's all right," says Hannah. "It's not a test but it is very simple. All you need to do is talk. You need to share your wishes about what kind of death you'd like. Write it down in a living will or on a piece of paper for your loved ones, but above all, tell them what you want." Eudora inclines her head forward. "Because death is as important as birth. We celebrate one but fear the other. We don't need to do that anymore. In my job, I have the privilege of walking alongside people and their families as they experience this most significant of moments, and I can tell you that it is a time filled with love, laughter, tears, hope, and joy. There are moments of fear, but I am there to reassure; there may be pain, but I work alongside palliative teams to ensure that it is minimal. Above all, I seek to facilitate a good death and an enduring positive memory for the people who live on without their loved ones. I want to ensure that people leave this world feeling comforted and unafraid. Because death is inevitable, but it needn't be feared."

If Eudora were a different woman, she would have leapt to her feet and given Hannah a standing ovation. Instead, her heart beats faster as if applauding the most sensible thing she's heard for a long time.

Hannah continues. "If we learn to discuss it in a calm and rational way, we can dispel our fears and face death with an open and positive heart." She smiles at them all. "I hope this has given you a good insight into what I do. I am around for the rest of the afternoon, so please come and ask me any specific questions and I will do my best to answer them. I have some living will forms for anyone who would like one and leaflets about my work. Thank you for listening."

There is a polite smattering of applause, which doesn't surprise Eudora. People are loath to hear the truth, particularly when it's so final.

"I want to go and talk to Hannah," says Rose. "Will you come with me?"

"Erm, I'm not sure. Maybe Stanley could . . ."

"Stanley's talking to that lady," says Rose. Eudora turns to where she is pointing. Stanley is deep in conversation with a woman of about the same age as him. She is wearing a fire-engine-red jacket, which contrasts strikingly with her snowy-white hair.

Eudora curses the fact that he is doing exactly what she

wanted him to. "Very well." She follows Rose over to where Sue and Hannah are chatting. Hannah looks around and smiles with a warmth that's hard to resist. "Can I ask you a question, please?" asks Rose.

"Of course," says Hannah.

"Why don't people want to talk about death?"

Hannah glances at Eudora before answering. "I suppose it's mostly because they're afraid."

"Of dying?"

"Precisely."

"I was frightened of swimming in the sea, so Dad and I talked it all through and I stopped being frightened. I think talking about the stuff that scares you is very important."

Hannah nods. "I couldn't agree with you more. I suppose people are scared of death because it feels so final."

"But it's not because the people who've died come back on the Day of the Dead. At least that's what I think."

"You're wise, Rose. Keep holding on to those beliefs and keep talking too."

"Don't worry, Hannah. I like to talk. Don't I, Eudora?"

"Indeed," says Eudora. "In fact, sometimes I worry that you're going to run out of breath or words."

Rose laughs. "You're so funny. Luckily, I never do. So, Hannah, do you have any advice for my friend Eudora, because, you know, death is a bit nearer for her."

Hannah suppresses a laugh. "Is there anything you would like to know, Eudora?"

"Apart from how to stop Rose from constantly reminding me of my own mortality?" says Eudora.

"I get the feeling she has your best interests at heart," says Hannah. "Would you consider completing a living will? That way you can let people know what your wishes might be if the situation changes."

"You should definitely do that," says Rose.

"I suppose it can't hurt," says Eudora, accepting the form from Hannah.

"It's pretty straightforward. You just need to get it witnessed by your GP."

"Very well. And thank you for your talk today. It was very interesting and you're right. People should talk more about death."

"Thank you, Eudora. Here, take one of my cards in case you ever need me."

Eudora looks into her dark brown eyes as she takes the card and sees nothing but kindness. She could imagine that Hannah would be a great source of reassurance in your final moments.

"I think I'd make an excellent death doula," says Rose as they leave the group.

"It would certainly be a chatty end for your clients," says Eudora.

"I don't like silence."

"I've noticed that."

"I'm happy to be your death doula when the time comes, Eudora."

"I'll bear that in mind."

"Hello, ladies. Did you enjoy that?" asks Stanley, meeting them in the entrance hall.

"It was very . . . interesting," says Eudora.

"I enjoyed the badge-making, the biscuits, and the death chat," says Rose. "How about you?"

"I liked getting out and meeting new people. I met a lovely lady called Sheila, who lost her husband at around the same time as I lost Ada."

"Sounds like a positive experience all 'round," says Eudora.

"Thanks for coming!" calls Sue as they head for the door. "Do come along on September the twelfth—Chris the Crooner will be entertaining us with songs across the decades; he's very popular."

"Can't wait," says Stanley.

"I think I might have a doctor's appointment that day," fibs Eudora. Stanley looks disappointed. "But you should go," she tells him. "I'm sure Sheila will look after you."

Back at home later that afternoon, Eudora takes out the living will form that Hannah gave her. Her eyes dart back and forth as she reads, searching for something it simply doesn't offer. It's all about refusing treatment when it's too late, when she can't make decisions for herself. What about those people who are tired and ache from old age and too much life? Where's the option for them to be allowed to go gently and with dignity? Eudora throws the form to one side and closes her eyes. *A good death.* It sounded simple and yet felt as plausible as a trip to the moon.

Eudora wakes with a start to the sound of the telephone, knocking her half-empty teacup all over the discarded form as she struggles to answer it.

"Blast!" she says, trying to mop up the spillage with her handkerchief as she picks up the receiver. "Hello?"

"Eudora?"

Eudora drops her makeshift wiping-up cloth as she registers the accent. "This is she."

"Hallo again, Eudora. This is Greta Liebermann from Klinik Lebenswahl. Is this a good time?"

Eudora sinks into the nearest chair. "Yes, it's fine," she says, watching the spilt tea soak into her once pristine handkerchief embroidered with an E. It had been a present from her mother.

"Good. So I have been considering your application in conjunction with my colleagues as I told you I would, and I would like to have a further discussion with you about it."

Eudora's mouth is dry. She curses spilling her last drop of tea. "I see."

Greta continues. "I have reviewed your form, in which you have given me all your medical information. Is this still correct?"

"It is," says Eudora with as much authority as she can muster.

"Good. And I have spoken with Petra, who has explained your situation to me."

A germ of hope takes root in Eudora's mind. She knew Petra wouldn't let her down. "Then you understand."

"I do," says the doctor. "But as I mentioned before, we must have proper, rigorous discussions before any decision is made."

"I'm not sure what else I can tell you aside from what you already know."

"Well, let me ask you some more questions. Aside from the conditions you have listed, are you suffering from any other illnesses?"

"No, but I would have thought that old age and its associated indignities and ailments would be sufficient. People certainly don't hesitate to alleviate an animal's suffering in this regard."

"True, but humans have a choice and a voice. We must be sure that an individual is of sound mind before we proceed."

"I can assure you that I am."

"And you live alone and have no family?"

Eudora knows what she is getting at and is ready. "Yes, but I am not depressed. I am merely done with life."

"How do you know you are not depressed?"

Eudora sighs. "I live as active a life as I can. I try to swim or at least leave the house every day. I eat well and sleep reasonably. But I am old and I want to exercise my right to choose how I die."

"Eudora, believe me, I understand what you are asking and the reasons. You are not the first person to request this, but you have to understand that we need to be sure you are making the right decision."

"I will sign any document you require."

"I am glad you have said that because I would like you to complete a living will."

Eudora glances at the ruined, tea-stained form sitting on the side table. "Very well. Do you have a copy you can send me, please?"

"Naturally. I will send it today."

"Thank you. Anything else?"

"Yes. I will need up-to-date medical forms from your doctor, but I advise that you don't tell them what they are for."

"I understand."

"Only when I have all this information will I be able to properly make a decision."

"So you're not rejecting my application?"

"No, but I'm not promising I will approve it. I can hear your determination and understand your conviction, but I would not be a responsible member of the medical profession if I did not request these documents. I also need to ask you to continue to think seriously about what you are proposing. If you have any doubts or reasons to change your mind, then you should. Life is precious and as long as we have a reason to continue, we should follow that path."

Montgomery wanders into the living room and jumps onto Eudora's lap, nuzzling his head against her chin like a positive affirmation of the doctor's words. "I will," says Eudora. "And I'll fill out the form and collate the documents too."

"Good. Thank you. Promise me you will phone Petra or myself when you need to talk."

"I will," lies Eudora. "Thank you, doctor—Greta."

"You are welcome. Goodbye, Eudora."

Eudora's hands are trembling as she places the phone back in its cradle. It's as if a coin has been flipped. It's constantly spinning, and Eudora has no idea which way it will land. Heads, you're granted the thing you've wanted for so long. Tails, you stay and live out your days as you are. Montgomery is still nudging her hand in a surprising display of affection.

"Would you miss me then, Monty? Or would you simply go and bother Rose?" The cat replies by butting her chin with his cold, wet nose. "I appreciate your sentiment," she tells him, scratching the top of his head. He leans in to her touch, moving his neck from side to side. "But what if I stay here? It's still just you and me in this house. You're not exactly going to phone an ambulance if I need one, are you?" The cat sits up and stares at her unblinking. "Not that I'd want you to." Eudora glances at the smiling photograph of her with her parents. She'd do anything to go back to that time of pure, uncomplicated happiness. "Everything's a moment. Nothing lasts forever," she murmurs. Montgomery is tired of Eudora's introspection and nips at her hand to tell her so. "Ow! Get off, you fractious feline!" she cries, shooing him away. Eudora can't predict how the coin will land but is determined to do all she can to ensure she has some influence over the matter. She picks up the telephone to make an appointment with the doctor.

## 1959
## SIDNEY AVENUE, SOUTH-EAST LONDON

"Happy birthday, Dora dear."

"Thank you, Mum," said Eudora, leaning down to kiss her mother's cheek. "Shall I make some tea?"

"No. You have a seat. I'll make it. I thought we could

have a nice breakfast together. Boiled eggs and soldiers, followed by toast and marmalade. I bought some Rose's Lemon and Lime especially. Your favorite."

"Thank you," repeated Eudora, taking a seat at the kitchen table and wondering why she felt so weary. Weary to her twenty-six-year-old bones. She glanced at the small pile of cards on the table. "Are these for me?"

Beatrice nodded. "Why don't you open them while I make breakfast? I'll give you mine afterward."

"Thank you."

"Here, use your father's letter opener." Beatrice handed over the miniature silver sword. Eudora stared at it for a moment and longed for a time machine to take her back to that afternoon in Piccadilly, to the exact second when it was her and Albert in the tea shop before the air-raid siren wailed. Before life went sour.

"Come on, Dolly Daydream!" cried Beatrice. "Aren't you going to open your cards?"

"Sorry," said Eudora, slicing through the first envelope and pulling out a card. "Love from Auntie Doris and Hazel."

Beatrice sniffed. "Birthdays and Christmas. They're the only times they get in touch. It's shameful."

Eudora didn't reply. *They* were her father's siblings, who had never got on with Beatrice and had scarcely been in touch since Albert died. Eudora can't remember why they fell out. She was fairly certain her mother had forgotten too. Eudora often fantasized about contacting these mythical relatives. It would be nice to have another family member aside from her mother, maybe a couple of cousins near to her own age. They could go on day trips to Clacton or holidays to Eastbourne like Sylvia did with hers.

Eudora opened the next card. Speak of the devil.

*Sorry I can't come out with you on your birthday, Dor–we're having lunch with Ken's parents to talk about the wedding–not long now! Let's go to the flicks just the two of us soon, my treat.*

Eudora placed the card to one side, her chest tightening. She missed Sylvia and knew it was only going to get worse. Marriage, babies, a house to run. They would be Sylvia's priorities from now on. And what did Eudora have? A job working in the bank, where her cards were marked, and life at home with Beatrice.

Eudora felt an immediate pang of guilt. She loved her mother and wanted to protect her. It was still her duty after all these years, and besides, who else did Beatrice have? Her own parents were long gone, and she was an only child. It was all down to Eudora. She would have to make the best of it. Besides, life wasn't all bad. Her mother was grateful for every kindness Eudora showed. She would cup her daughter's cheeks and stare into her eyes.

"You're the best daughter in the world, Dora. I don't know where I'd be without you."

Beatrice was humming as she moved around the

kitchen preparing breakfast. Eudora took a moment to relish her mother's happy mood. It wasn't always like this. "The eggs will be ready in two minutes."

"Lovely," said Eudora.

The eggs weren't lovely. They were almost hard-boiled. And the tea was stewed. But the marmalade saved the day.

"I'm so sorry, Dora," said Beatrice, tears forming in her eyes. "I've ruined your birthday breakfast."

"No, you haven't," exclaimed Eudora, reaching out a comforting hand. "The toast is delicious!" She laughed.

Her mother gave a weak smile. "Darling Dora. You always see the best in everything. Here, open your present."

Eudora accepted the soft, fat parcel as big as a newborn baby, wrapped in brown paper and tied with string. She opened it, uncovering a sage-colored hand-knitted cardigan with large brown buttons. "I made it for you," said Beatrice. "I hope it fits okay."

Eudora tried and failed to dismiss the overriding thought as she slipped her arms into the sleeves. *I am twenty-six years old, living at home with my mother, who is still knitting cardigans for me.* "It's lovely. Thank you, Mum," she said in a tight voice.

"And now, what are your plans for today?"

"I was thinking of taking a stroll in the park. It's such a lovely day. We could go together."

Beatrice blinked rapidly as the shutters of her mind descended. Apart from her job at the school, she rarely left the house. The back garden was her only exception to this rule. Beatrice drew a hand to her throat. "I thought there was rain forecasted later," she said.

"No. I don't think so," said Eudora, unable to suppress her indignation. It was her birthday for heaven's sake. Couldn't her mother make an effort today of all days? Eudora's mind swam with a vision of her slamming her fists on the table, unleashing a Pandora's box of long-suppressed fury as she demanded to be treated like a daughter for once. Eudora tossed the idea back and forth in her mind before swallowing her annoyance. Yet again. She would never behave like this because it reminded her of Stella. Eudora prided herself on being the antithesis of everything Stella was. No. She would always be better than her traitorous sister. It was her only consolation.

"So will you come to the park with me, please?" asked Eudora. "I'll treat you to an ice cream." She flashed her mother an encouraging smile. *Keep smiling. Keep moving. Keep calm and carry on.*

"Oh, very well. How can I say no to my daughter on her birthday? And I'll buy the ice creams today."

The park was the jewel in the crown of this corner of south-east London. Its circular walk took you on a pleasant, but not too taxing stroll around a large lake populated by a noisy ensemble of ducks and swans. The green space that surrounded the lake was punctuated with oak and chestnut trees looking as pretty as brides on their wedding days. The herbaceous borders were a riot of midsummer color—blue, yellow, orange, and pink all mingled to stunning effect.

Eudora and Beatrice walked arm in arm in the July sunshine. They bought ice creams and sat on a bench overlooking the lake. Eudora closed her eyes, relishing the warmth of the sun on her face, tempered by a gentle summer breeze.

"This is lovely," she murmured.

"It's a little chilly in the wind," said Beatrice.

Eudora's shoulders stiffened an inch as she did her best to breathe away the irritation. Her mother couldn't help finding fault with everything. Life had dealt her a raw deal. She wasn't the only woman to be widowed in her thirties in 1944 but that didn't make it any easier. And of course the situation with Stella hadn't helped. They'd both borne the brunt of her wild behavior, and then there was the "episode" as they referred to it now. The details were never discussed, and Eddie and Stella were certainly never mentioned by name. Eudora had wondered if her sister might get in touch at least to let them know she was safe. She didn't and in truth, it was a relief. No news was good news surely. It meant that Eudora was able to get on with her life as best she could.

Of course she thought about her sister. You didn't merely switch off sibling love like a light. However, Eudora found that whenever Stella came to mind, her thoughts quickly turned white-hot with anger, and the love that had flowed easily through her veins before became dark and viscous with hatred. There would be no forgiveness this time.

Beatrice had behaved in an almost maternal fashion in the weeks and months following Stella's departure. She baked cakes for her daughter, placed a consoling hand on her shoulder, and made endless cups of tea.

"Tea and sympathy," she would say every time she placed the cup and saucer carefully in front of her daughter before busying herself with some other task. She never actually delivered the sympathy, never tried to impart sage words or offer advice. It didn't surprise Eudora. To be honest, she would have been rather horrified if her mother had attempted to share any wisdom. The only words Eudora ever heard her utter were about Eddie on the day it happened.

"I always knew he was a bad apple," she said before shaking her head and returning to her sentry position in the kitchen. Eudora watched her go with a sense of loneliness so sharp and overwhelming that she had to tell herself to keep breathing.

Eudora finished her ice cream, wiping her fingers on a handkerchief. She noticed a familiar figure walking in their direction and her heart leapt. Sam Buchanan. The boy she'd rejected out of loyalty to her sister. The boy, now a man, who could have been the one . . . or if not the one, an encounter that gave her the courage to keep searching. He was a distance away but there was no mistaking his confident gait and muscular frame. Sam Buchanan. Strolling toward her in the sunshine, arm in arm with a pretty young wife, carrying a small boy on his shoulders as a little girl with yellow ribbons in her hair skipped in front of them. A perfect family of four.

Eudora hurried to her feet. "I think you're right, Mum, the wind's got up. Let's go home, shall we?"

They were preparing dinner later that evening when the telephone rang. Pork chops, tinned potatoes ("Let's have a night off the peeling, shall we, Dora?"), and mixed veg, followed by birthday cake.

"I'll go," said Eudora, trailing down the hall. "Edenham 7359?"

There was a pause on the line before a voice answered. "Dora."

Eudora said nothing. She had been waiting for this call for a long time, had practiced in her head all the things she might say, but words failed her. All she could hear was her heart pumping in her head and her sister's breathing.

"Dora. Are you there?"

"Yes."

"Listen. I know you probably hate me, but I had to call today to wish you a happy birthday. I think about you all the time. I miss you. Do you think about me?"

Stella sounded much younger than her nineteen years. Eudora might have felt sympathy if it weren't for the plaintive, needy tone, which brought to mind all the reasons Eudora despised her.

"NEVER call here again," she said before replacing the handset and walking slowly back to the kitchen.

"Who was that?" asked her mother.

"Interference on the line," said Eudora. "It was no one."

Beatrice put an arm around her daughter's shoulders

and kissed her cheek. “Are you having a good birthday?” she asked.

Eudora stared into her eyes and saw her mother’s desperation. “It’s been lovely, thanks, Mum,” she lied, tipping the tinned potatoes into a pan and carrying them to the stove.

# Chapter 12

EUDORA IS OUT shopping the next day when she sees the sunflowers. There's something about their huge yellow blooms that reminds her of Rose. She thinks Maggie will appreciate this too. Eudora also spots a bag of "Unicorn Foamies" in the sweets aisle and places them in her basket, along with the flowers and a handful of other items.

Eudora walks back from the shops in the sunshine, enjoying the sensation of warmth on her face, relieved that summer's relentless heat has tempered into something more palatable. She quickens her step, eager to reach Rose's house and deliver her gifts. Eudora has barely set foot on the garden path when the door flings open.

"Eudora!" cries Rose, standing on the doorstep wearing an unusually conservative white blouse on her top half and bright pink knickers on her bottom half. "Are you coming in?"

"If you're not busy," says Eudora, casting a questioning glance at Rose's ensemble.

"Mum is making me try on my school uniform, which is obviously incredibly boring, so no, we're not busy at all. I'm glad you're back. I saw you leave about an hour ago and was starting to get worried."

Eudora steps over the threshold. "Just for my own information, Rose, do you spend most of your time checking my movements?"

Rose seesaws her head from side to side as she considers

this. "Not just you. I look out for Stanley too. And Daddy obviously. Although he's not usually home until approximately 7:13 P.M."

"Approximately?"

Rose nods. "His train gets in at seven-oh-five and it takes him eight minutes to walk up the road."

"And woe betide him if he's a minute late," says Maggie, appearing in the hallway. "How are you, Eudora?"

"A little concerned that my every move is being monitored by the secret police," she says. "But apart from that, I am quite well. How are you today?"

"Tired and uncomfortable but hopefully it won't be for much longer. Would you like a cup of tea or coffee?"

"Tea. Please."

"Come through," says Maggie, leading them to the kitchen.

"These are for you," says Eudora, offering her the flowers. "As a belated thank-you for the trip to the seaside."

"Oh, you didn't need to do that," says Maggie, accepting them. Eudora always wonders why people say this. Of course no one needs to do anything. She is caught off guard by Maggie leaning over to kiss her cheek. "Thank you, Eudora."

The scent of strawberries that she catches from Maggie is comforting. "And these are for you, Rose." She offers the sweets, bracing herself for the inevitable hug.

Rose doesn't disappoint. "Unicorn foamies! Thank you, Eudora. You're the best," she says, wrapping her arms around her middle.

Eudora catches sight of Maggie pausing to catch her breath as she fills the kettle. "Rose, why don't you help me make the tea so that your mother can sit down?"

"Good plan," says Rose. "That way I can make it for you every time I come over to your house too."

Eudora isn't sure if this is a threat or a promise. "Very well. Fill the kettle, please, and fetch the teapot," she says, taking a seat at the kitchen table.

Maggie heaves herself into the chair opposite and pulls a face. "Sorry, Eudora. We don't own a teapot."

Eudora winces. "No wonder civilization is on its knees. Very well. What do you have?"

"Erm, mugs and tea bags?"

Eudora narrows her eyes. "What kind of tea?"

"Yorkshire?"

"Thank heavens for small mercies."

Rose laughs. "Don't you just love the way Eudora talks, Mummy?"

Maggie smiles. "I do."

"Now then, Rose. Place a tea bag in each mug and pour on the boiling water the second it boils. This is very important."

"Aye aye, captain," says Rose. She follows Eudora's instructions with care. "Now what?"

"We allow it to steep for about three minutes, which means we leave the tea bag in the water to help the flavor develop."

"Steep. I like that word." Rose begins to fidget. "Is it time yet? Has it steeped?"

Eudora fixes her with a stern look. "You're not very patient, are you, Rose?"

Maggie clears her throat in agreement.

"I just don't like waiting," says Rose, jigging from foot to foot.

"How about you go and put on the bottom half of your uniform to show me and then I'll tell you a secret."

Rose's eyes widen. "I love secrets!"

"I thought you might," says Eudora, watching her skip back to the living room.

"How did you know to do that?" asks Maggie, impressed.

"I haven't always been this old. I can just about remember what it was like to be young."

Maggie laughs. "It sounds as if you had an interesting trip to the group. Rose is now committed to becoming a death doula."

"It was interesting, but I hope you didn't mind her being there. I hadn't realized that talk was taking place. You might not have wanted her to sit through a presentation on death."

Maggie smiles. "We've never shied away from talking to Rose about death or any other tricky topics. She had to face it when Dad died, and I've also had several miscarriages."

Eudora's shoulders stiffen. "I'm so sorry to hear that," she says, forcing herself to meet Maggie's eye.

"Thank you, Eudora," she says, her expression twisted with sorrow. "I find the best way to deal with these things is to talk." Eudora clears her throat. "But I know that's not for everyone," she adds kindly.

Eudora holds her gaze for a moment longer. "You look exhausted, if you don't mind me saying."

Maggie sighs. "Life is tiring, Rose is full-on, and being pregnant doesn't help. I haven't been sleeping that well either."

"It must be uncomfortable," says Eudora.

"Yes, but it's not only that. I'm also worried about my mum. We moved here because of Rob's work and as a fresh start for Rose, but she's struggling without us. I miss her too."

"Could she move nearer?"

Maggie shakes her head. "There's no way she'll leave Cornwall. She's got good friends around her but life's been hard since Dad died."

"How long were they married?"

"Over fifty years. Everybody deals with grief in different ways. It's an entirely personal thing, but I think it molds you into something better if you let it. It's certainly made me think about what kind of person I want to be."

Eudora leans forward, her interest piqued. "And what kind of person do you want to be?"

Maggie fixes her with a clear blue gaze as wide-open as the ocean. "When Dad died, everyone was so kind. People who I hadn't heard from or barely knew got in touch to tell me how sad they were or how much he was loved. There's great comfort in kindness. I value it above almost everything else these days. Do you know what I mean?"

"I do," admits Eudora.

Maggie continues. "I always used to think it was silly

when people said life was short, but I completely get that now. We're here for such a limited time. The least we can do is try to be kind to the people around us. Humans seem to forget that so easily."

Eudora is swept along by her words, as if a great truth has unexpectedly landed at her feet. "If only more people shared this sentiment."

"Oh, but I think they do," says Maggie. "We only hear or notice the negative stuff. There is definitely more good than bad in the world."

Eudora stares at her, longing to believe this but knowing from her own experience that it simply isn't true. "It's a noble belief."

"I'm ba-ack and ready to hear the se-cret!" cries Rose, skipping into the kitchen. She is now wearing her complete school uniform but in true Rose fashion has adapted the outfit. Her blue-and-white-striped tie is a bandanna, her collar is undone, and her blouse is tied in the middle, revealing a good half-inch of belly.

"Right. Let's sort the tea and then we can turn our attentions to your sartorial issues," says Eudora.

"Does that mean you'll tell me the secret?"

"Only if your tea passes muster."

Rose takes the rest of the task very seriously and it's not long before they are drinking tea and eating the unicorn sweets. Eudora then teaches Rose to tie an acceptable Full Windsor before persuading her to wear her uniform as it was intended. She gives an approving nod. "You look very smart. The reason I wanted you to dress properly is because you're going to the primary school I attended when I was your age."

"Really?" says Maggie, impressed.

"Oh. Is that the big secret then?" says Rose, folding her arms.

"I thought you'd be pleased to be going to the same school as Eudora," says her mother.

"I am." Rose's face clouds. "It's just that I'm not sure if I want to go."

Eudora studies her expression. She detests the modern penchant for sharing every last worry, but she notices the frowns creasing Rose's usually carefree face and doesn't like it. "What's the matter, Rose?"

Rose shoots her a sideways glance. "What if the girls at this school are as mean as the ones from my last school?" she says quietly.

"I'm sure they won't be . . ." begins Maggie in soothing tones.

"Then you come to me and I will help you deal with them," interjects Eudora with a vehemence that surprises even her. Maggie smiles.

"Really?" says Rose. "How?"

Eudora purses her lips. "I have my methods. I may well trip them up with my walking stick."

Rose's face brightens. "You'd do that for me?"

Eudora looks into her eyes. "I am very old and have no truck with bullies. I am therefore excellent at dealing with them and fully prepared to teach you everything I know."

"A bit like when Mum says she's 'got my back'?" asks

Rose, her expression lifting with hope. Maggie reaches out, pulling her daughter into a tight hug.

"If you like," says Eudora, touched by their easy affection. The world may indulge itself with grotesque oversharing these days, but it also knows when to fold the disheartened into its arms.

"Well, I've got your back too. And Stanley's."

"Thank you, Rose."

"Did you know it's Stanley's birthday tomorrow?"

"I didn't."

"And are you free tomorrow night?" asks Rose, flashing a conspiratorial grin at Maggie.

"What are you two up to?" asks Eudora.

"Nothing," chorus Rose and Maggie with glee.

Eudora folds her arms. "Out with it."

Maggie smiles. "Stanley told me that he always went with Ada to that pizza place on the high street on his birthday, and I know he's not seeing his family until the weekend, so Rose and I thought . . ."

"That you and I should go with Stanley to help him celebrate his birthday!" cries Rose triumphantly.

"Pizza?" says Eudora in horror, recalling with a shudder the countless takeaway leaflets bearing images of greasy, oozing cheese on top of something professing to be bread.

"This isn't any old pizza, Eudora. It's all freshly made, and their olives are to die for. I think you'll like it," says Maggie.

"Pleeease?" says Rose. "For Stanley?"

Eudora stares at them both for a moment before

throwing up her hands in defeat. "Oh, very well. Let's just hope they make an acceptable salad."

The Numero Uno pizzeria, nestled between a nail bar and a betting shop on the high street, turns out to be something of a revelation to Eudora. She has lost count of the number of times she has passed its unassuming red-canopied frontage, and yet, once inside, it is as if Eudora has been transported to the Mediterranean. The walls are decorated with murals depicting views of the Italian landscape—the Amalfi Coast, the villages of Puglia, St. Mark's Square in Venice—and the low-beam ceilings are hung with lanterns and garlands of foliage that look to Eudora as if they might be fashioned from olive and bay leaves.

"Ooh, I love it in here; it's so cozy and welcoming," says Rose, echoing Eudora's thoughts.

"Welcome, welcome, welcome, Mister Stanley," cries a short, round man with a smart mustache, hurrying forward to shake hands with him. "I reserve my very best table for you and your guests."

"Thank you, Francesco," says Stanley. "It's good to see you."

"You too, my friend. We still miss your beautiful Ada, but we know she is eating grissini in heaven, no?" Stanley nods sadly and Francesco pats him on the back. "And who are these beautiful ladies?"

Rose beams at him. "I'm Rose. And this is Eudora. We've come to help celebrate Stanley's birthday with him."

Francesco claps a hand to his forehead. "But of course, it's Mister Stanley's birthday. Thank you for reminding me, Miss Rose. Gino!"

A cheerful-looking man with dark curly hair looks up from where he's mixing a cocktail at the bar. "Yes, boss?"

"A bottle of prosecco and some of our special olives on the house for my friends here, please."

"Coming right up, boss."

Francesco bows to their table. "I wish you a wonderful evening, and if you need anything at all, please ask."

"I like that man," says Rose, watching him go. "You're like a celebrity in here, Stanley."

"Ada and I always came here for high days and holidays. She was the real celebrity. I can remember her singing 'That's Amore' with Francesco up there," he says, gesturing to the mezzanine. "I just watched her and thought, *How did I get so lucky?*" He brushes away a tear.

"Here, have a menu," says Eudora.

"Thank you, Eudora. So, what do you think of the place?" asks Stanley, his eyes glittering with hope.

"It has a very pleasant atmosphere," says Eudora, perusing the menu. "I think I might choose the salade Niçoise."

"You should try their pizza—the Quattro Stagioni is really something," says Stanley.

Eudora frowns. "I'm not really one for pizza."

"This isn't any ordinary pizza though. It's all fresh ingredients." Eudora watches as a waitress brings out a large pizza on a wooden board and places it on the table next to them. It's certainly not what Eudora imagined. The smell of garlic and herbs is intoxicating.

"I love all pizza, even ham and pineapple. Although Dad says it's the food of the devil."

"Your father is a wise man, Rose," says Eudora.

"Aww, he likes you too, Eudora."

The waiter appears with their drinks and olives. He opens the prosecco with a loud, satisfying pop and pours a glass each for Eudora and Stanley. "Would you like a drink?" he asks Rose.

"Could I have lemonade, please?"

"Coming right up."

Rose pops an olive into her mouth. "Man, these are good. Try one, Eudora."

"Very well." She chooses a fat green olive and is amazed. It's like nothing she's ever eaten before—salty, creamy, and absolutely delicious. "That's very pleasant," she says, placing the stone on the saucer under the olive bowl. Once Rose has her lemonade, Stanley picks up his glass for a toast.

"I would like to thank you for making my birthday so special—I am honored to be here with you both tonight. Cheers."

"Cheers!" they chorus, raising their glasses in reply. Eudora takes a sip. The fresh, crisp fizz is unexpectedly welcome.

"I've made you something, Stanley," says Rose, handing him an A4 envelope.

"What do we have here then?" asks Stanley, pulling out the card. He breaks into a huge grin when he sees the picture. "Is that you, me, and Eudora?"

Rose nods with glee.

"It's wonderful, Rose. Look, Eudora—it's us on the merry-go-round."

Eudora takes the card and can't help but chuckle. It's a warts-and-all appraisal of the three of them. Both her and Stanley's faces are as wrinkled as old paper bags, while Rose's eyes are comically huge. They look wildly happy.

"I copied it from a photo Daddy took," says Rose, her voice laced with pride. "It took ages."

"I bet," says Eudora. "You're a very lucky man," she tells Stanley.

"Don't worry, Eudora," says Rose. "I'll do the same for you on your birthday, and it will be a different picture because we will have had lots more adventures by then."

A shiver of regret courses through Eudora's mind as she considers the possibility that she may not be around to experience any of this. She brushes away the thought and reaches into her bag. "I've got something for you too, Stanley."

"Oh. Thank you, Eudora," he says.

Eudora hands him a parcel wrapped in plain brown paper. "Sorry I didn't have fancier wrapping."

Stanley holds the parcel, turning it in his hands. "This is very kind, Eudora. I'm touched."

"O-pen it! O-pen it!" chants Rose.

Stanley smiles. He tears at the paper like a little boy who's just discovered his bulging stocking on Christmas morning and pulls out a book. He chuckles when he sees the title. "Crosswords! That's very thoughtful. Thank you." Stanley leaps up and plants a kiss on Eudora's cheek.

Rose looks as if she's about to explode with delight,

while Eudora is momentarily stunned into silence before her words tumble forth. "Well, I thought it might be useful. You're always saying you need to keep your noggin ticking over."

"Noggin!" says Rose. "I love that word."

"I've written a message inside, so give them a try and see how you get on. I'm happy to help if you get stuck."

Stanley opens the front cover and reads. "To Stanley, keep your pencil sharp and your brain sharper. All the best on your birthday, Eudora." He rests a hand on his heart.

"That's lovely, Eudora," says Rose, hugging herself.

"It's only a little something," says Eudora.

"It means the world to me," says Stanley. "Really. I feel very lucky to have met you both and to be able to share my birthday celebrations with you. To make new friends at my age, well, it's quite a thing. I have to tell you that when Ada died I never thought I'd be happy again. Don't get me wrong, my family are wonderful, but they've got their own lives and friends. But you two have given me new hope. And I can't thank you enough." Stanley's eyes are brimming with tears.

Eudora used to find his outpourings distasteful, but his words strike a chord tonight. She wants him to stop crying, but not for her. She doesn't like to see him upset. She wants this funny little man to be happy. It's the very least he deserves. "No tears tonight, Stanley," she says. "Ada wouldn't want that. She'd want you to enjoy your birthday." She raises her glass. "Here's to Ada. And to you, Stanley. Happy birthday!"

Stanley sniffs back his tears and clinks glasses with them.

"Thank you, Eudora—for keeping me on the straight and narrow."

"It appears to be my job now," she says with a knowing smile.

"Excellent speech, Eudora," says Rose.

"Are you ready to order?" asks the waiter.

"I'll have the Quattro Stagioni, thank you," says Stanley.

"Same for me," says Eudora, closing her menu and glancing at Stanley. "But if I don't like it, I shall blame you."

"I reckon I'm safe."

"Sal-sicc-ia pizza for me, please," says Rose, reading carefully from the menu. She gazes up at the waiter with hopeful eyes. "Did I say that right?"

"*Perfetto*!" says the waiter, beaming at her.

Later that evening, Eudora scrapes the last morsel of tiramisu from her bowl and wipes her mouth with a napkin. She can't remember a time when she enjoyed a meal more. She glances over at Rose, whose face is covered in chocolate, having just licked her bowl.

A waitress appears. "How was everything?"

"Wonderful. Thank you," says Stanley.

She smiles and starts to clear their plates. "Thank you," says Rose as she picks up her bowl.

"Your granddaughter has beautiful manners," she says to Eudora and Stanley. "She's a credit to you."

"Thank you," says Eudora, avoiding Stanley's gaze.

"So we're adopting Rose now, are we?" asks Stanley as the waitress disappears.

"For one night only," she says, grasped by an unexpected split-second wish that life had dealt her a different hand—a life of small sticky faces and hand-drawn birthday cards.

"I'm happy to pretend to be your granddaughter anytime," says Rose, patting Eudora on the shoulder.

"Thank you, Rose. I appreciate that," says Eudora, shifting in her chair. "Now, I think we should get the bill. And I don't want any arguments. I'm paying."

"Thank you, Eudora," says Rose.

"I know never to argue with a determined woman, so thank you from me too," says Stanley.

"My pleasure," says Eudora.

"Although I must say that if I'd known you were paying, I would have had the steak," says Stanley, winking at Rose. She giggles.

"Foolish man," says Eudora.

"Oh, and before I forget," says Stanley, "Paul's invited you both to the family barbecue on Saturday."

Rose adopts a serious expression. "Will there be sausages?"

Stanley nods. "And burgers."

"Then I'm in."

"Eudora?"

Eudora has never been to a barbecue in her life and, up until this evening, would have happily gone to her grave without ever attending one. But she hadn't eaten pizza until this evening either and that has turned out rather well. "Thank you. That will be very—"

"Pleasant!" chorus Stanley and Rose. Eudora stares at them in amazement.

"You always say that when you like something more than you want to let on," says Rose, high-fiving Stanley.

"Do I indeed?" says Eudora, her lips pursing into a smile. "For your information I was *going* to say that it will be very enjoyable."

"Fibber!" says Stanley. "I'm glad you can come though. The family all enjoyed meeting you at Paul's do."

"Oh. Well, that's lovely," says Eudora, folding her napkin carefully and placing it on the table, realizing to her surprise that she is rather looking forward to it. "Now then, I promised your mother we'd have you home by ten o'clock, so chop-chop!"

As she falls asleep later that night, a sense of calm descends over Eudora. It might be the food or the prosecco, but she finds herself playing the same thought over in her head as she drifts off to sleep.

*Life is precious and as long as we have a reason to continue, we should follow that path.*

## 1961
## SIDNEY AVENUE, SOUTH-EAST LONDON

---

The bootees were the most darling thing Eudora had ever seen. She cupped them in her palm, running a gentle finger over the soft white wool and satin ribbons. They were perfect. She laid them on the table next to the matching matinee jacket and bonnet. It was the third set her mother had knitted this month.

"You've got to have one in each size," said Beatrice with a satisfied smile. "Babies grow so fast."

Eudora patted her mother's shoulder, pleased she had found happiness in her knit-one-purl-one industry. The *click-clack* of her knitting needles while she listened to the *Light Programme* every evening was a reassuring sound for Eudora. It signified that Beatrice was as content as she could be.

Eudora dreaded returning from work to a silent house, whose only noise was the heavy ticking of her father's Enfield clock. Inevitably, she would find her mother sitting in a gloomy kitchen, staring without seeing. A cup of stone-cold tea by her side was a positive sign that she had at least brewed a pot following her return from the school. It meant that Eudora would be able to rouse her into an evening routine. But no tea, silence, and darkness were the holy trinity of desperation for Eudora; a signal that there was a long night ahead.

So she was delighted that the news of a baby had inspired Beatrice into a frenzy of activity. Eudora didn't even mind that the baby wasn't hers. She had given up hope that she would marry and have children now and was delighted for Sylvia. Motherhood mattered to her friend. It was the thing she longed for most.

"Oh, Dor, I can't wait for the baby to come," she cried, patting her rounded middle and linking her arm through Eudora's as she led her into the nursery. Eudora took in the sparkling new crib and the neat piles of folded nappies and was relieved that it was Sylvia instead of her about to embark on this journey.

"I'm so happy for you," she said.

Sylvia gripped her friend by the shoulders and stared into her eyes. "It's not too late for you, you know. I'm sure your prince charming is just over the next hill."

"I'm happy as I am. Really."

Sylvia cocked her head to one side, her face folding into a look of deep sympathy. "You're very brave, Dora. I don't know how you do it."

*What choice do I have?* thought Eudora as she walked home later that afternoon. *And besides, I am happy. Or at least, I'm not unhappy.*

This was true. She still enjoyed her job and, thankfully, Patrick Nicholson had been sacked after an indiscretion with one of the partners' wives. *Dipping his nib in the company ink* was how one of the younger, coarser secretaries had put it. It meant that her role at work was safer, and as a more senior secretary, she was afforded greater respect and a modicum more money. What's more, her life at home with Beatrice had improved with her mother's new phase of contentment. She scarcely ever gave a thought to Stella. Out of sight, out of mind. It was better that way.

So really, Eudora couldn't complain. She had enough money to go to the cinema when she wanted and lived a comfortable existence. At one stage she might have liked a husband and a family, but you couldn't mourn what you'd never had. This was enough for her. There were plenty worse off, not least all the poor souls who had perished during the war so that she might enjoy her freedom. No. She had no right to grumble at all.

She opened the front door to the deafening quiet, broken only by the clock's ticking.

"Mum? Are you here?" she called, hoping that perhaps Beatrice had stepped out for a moment. There was a tiny yelp of affirmation from the kitchen. Eudora's heart quickened as she rushed forward. "What's wrong, Mum? What's happened?"

Beatrice was sitting in her usual position, a tea towel clutched in one hand, her handkerchief in the other. She looked small and scared, like a child who needed its mother. Eudora reached out a hand, touching her on the shoulder. "Mum? Tell me what's wrong," she said softly.

"Stella," said Beatrice, uttering the name with a mixture of anguish and despair. "She telephoned."

"Oh," said Eudora. "What did she want?"

"She wouldn't tell me," cried Beatrice. "Her own mother and she wouldn't speak to me. She said she wanted to talk to you and that she would phone again."

Eudora sighed. "Did she sound okay?"

Beatrice shook her head. "I don't know. I don't know!"

Her sobs intensified. Eudora pulled her close. "Shhh, Mum. It's okay. You don't need to upset yourself."

"But I've failed," said Beatrice through hiccupping sobs. "Failed as a mother."

"No, you haven't," said Eudora. "Stella made her own choices. It's not your fault."

Beatrice nodded, wanting to believe her daughter. "Why does she hate me so much, Dora?"

"She doesn't hate you. She's just lost her way. Now come along, let's have a nice cup of tea. That will make us feel a bit better, won't it? And I can tell you all about Sylvia. She loved the jacket set, by the way."

"Did she?" asked Beatrice, brightening.

Eudora nodded. "She really did. She said she's going to write to thank you."

"Well, I know it must be hard for her having lost her own mother. I wasn't sure if she'd have anyone else to knit things for the baby."

"That's kind of you." Eudora was a little envious that her best friend was on the receiving end of Beatrice's maternal empathy. She couldn't recall ever being rewarded in such a way herself. She set about filling the kettle and placing it on the stove as the telephone began to ring.

"Oh," wailed Beatrice, clutching her handkerchief to her throat.

"It's all right," said Eudora. "I'll deal with whoever it is." She strode down the hall, her mind racing. She picked up the receiver with a trembling hand and tried to inject her voice with more courage than she felt. "Edenham 7359."

"Dora. It's Stella. Please don't hang up."

Eudora hesitated. Even after all this time, after the betrayal that had set hard in her brain like concrete, she found it hard to refuse. "I told you never to call here again."

"I know but I'm in trouble and I want to come home."

Eudora's laugh was bitter. "Really."

"Please, Dora. Just hear me out."

"Well, come along then. What is it now? Has Eddie abandoned you?"

"No, but I am pregnant."

"Congratulations."

"Dora, please. This isn't easy for me."

It was as if a dam had burst. Eudora's words flowed fast and savage. "Oh, and you think this is easy for me, do you? To be abandoned, to be betrayed, to be left behind. By the one person you should always be able to trust. You think this has been a stroll in the park for me, do you?"

Stella's voice was small and hollow. She sounded different to Eudora, older but diminished too. "No. And I know you won't believe me, but the thing I regret most is hurting you, Dora. You were always so kind to me."

"Well, that's a turn up, because the thing I regret most, Stella, is ever being kind to you."

There's a pause. "I'm scared, Dora." Eudora said nothing, so Stella continued. "It's Eddie. He's drinking too much and he's, well, he's not very nice to be around. I'm frightened for the baby. I need somewhere to go. You're the only person I can ask, Dora. Please. I'm begging you. If not for me then for the child."

Eudora thought about her conversation with her mother, about her life now, relatively calm and peaceful, about the hurt she'd worked so hard to banish. It had taken a long time but she'd managed it.

"Dora? Please help me. Please?"

Eudora glimpsed the photograph of her father in full uniform staring out at her from its position on the telephone table, his face unusually grave apart from the customary softness around his eyes.

*So, will you look after Mummy and the baby for me? Please?*

His words rippled back to her from the past, tangling their way into her brain.

*I said I would, but I didn't realize you meant forever. I thought you'd come back. I didn't know I'd have to do it alone.*

"Dora?" pleaded Stella.

Eudora closed her eyes. "Where are you?"

"I'm—" There was a *click-whirr* as the line went dead.

"Stella? Stella?" Eudora pressed the receiver button repeatedly in a vain attempt to bring her sister back. She held it against her forehead for a moment, trying to breathe away the relief and regret that snaked around her brain. The clock struck six o'clock. "Time for tea," she murmured, avoiding the gentle gaze of her father as she replaced the receiver in its cradle and made her way back to the kitchen.

# Chapter 13

"WHO'S FOR ANOTHER sausage then?" asks Paul, holding up a plate.

"Me please!" cries Rose, darting her hand into the air like a school pupil trying to get the teacher's attention.

"You'll pop if you eat any more," warns Eudora.

"It's a risk I'm willing to take," says Rose, sweeping two sausages onto her plate. "Thank you, Paul."

"You're welcome. Eudora?"

"No, thank you," she says. "I am replete."

Rose laughs. "Don't you just love the way Eudora talks? 'Replete.' So funny. What does that mean?"

"Sated," says Eudora with a wry smile.

Paul and Rose exchange nonplussed glances. "Full," says Stanley. "It was the answer to a clue in one of those crosswords the other day. I had to look it up."

"Bravo, Stanley," says Eudora, applauding him.

He gives a modest curtsy and Rose laughs. "This is so much fun. Much better than being at home with boring Mummy."

"Now then, Rose. You mustn't be so hard on your mother. She's very tired," says Eudora.

"Yes. Because of the stupid baby."

"Don't worry, Rose. I didn't like my sister when she was born either," says Stanley's granddaughter Livvy, taking a place in the chair next to Eudora. "But it's actually quite handy when you get older and you need to borrow clothes."

"I hope she shares my excellent taste in fashion then."

Livvy takes in Rose's leopard print leggings paired with a neon-orange T-shirt and smiles. "Well, as big sister you'll have to teach her."

"Oh, don't worry, I've already started a list of everything she needs to know. And I've made a big 'Keep Out' sign for my bedroom door too."

"Very wise," says Livvy.

"Didn't you have a sister?" says Rose to Eudora. "Or am I being nosy again?"

Eudora stares at the ice cubes bobbing up and down in her drink. "You are being nosy, Rose, but it's all right. I did have a sister. Once."

"Oh," says Rose. "I'm sorry. I don't want to make you sad."

"No. I don't mind," says Eudora. There's something about the way that Stanley's family wraps everything in love that puts her at ease. "She was called Stella. She was seven years younger than me."

"Stella," says Rose, trying it out. "I like that."

"It means 'star,'" says Stanley.

"It does," says Eudora.

"Wow, you had seven years between you? I thought two was bad enough," says Livvy.

"There's ten years between Daisy and me," says Rose, puffing out her chest. "So, did you get on or was she annoying?"

Eudora's eyes soften at the memory. "I adored her when she was small. She was full of spirit and fun. A bit like you, Rose."

"Aww, thanks, Eudora. And what happened? Did you stay besties when she grew up?"

Eudora's body stiffens. She'd forgotten about Rose's forensic quest for facts. A sentimental stroll down a lane of happy memories was one thing, but veering toward a dead end of bitter truths was wholly undesirable. Eudora clears her throat. "Not really. She moved away and we never really saw each other again."

"Oh. That's so sad. You must have missed her."

"It was a long time ago." She can see that Rose is poised, like a sniffer dog on the hunt for clues. She turns to Stanley's daughter-in-law. "So, Helen, your clever daughter has been telling me that she wants to work in television and her sister hopes to train as a vet?"

"I don't know where they get it from," says Paul, joining their conversation. "It must be their mum's influence," he adds, winking at his wife.

Helen smiles. "They're good girls," she tells Eudora. "Always have been. I keep them close. We've had a few trials this week, haven't we, Liv?"

Livvy nods slowly. "I broke up with my boyfriend. We've been together since we were fourteen."

"Oh. That's so sad," says Rose.

"Terrible," echoes Eudora, relieved that she is now distracted by another tale of heartbreak.

"I should have gone 'round and had a word," says Paul. "No one cheats on my girls."

"And I should have come with you," says Stanley.

Livvy and Helen roll their eyes at each other. "But thankfully, they didn't," says Helen. "Instead we ate two tubs of Ben and Jerry's and watched a whole season of *Friends*."

"Well, I have no idea who Ben, Jerry, or these friends are, but it sounds as if you've got the best mother in the world," says Eudora. She thinks of Beatrice. She couldn't imagine anyone more different from Helen. "Trust me, you are extremely lucky."

"I am," says Livvy, putting an arm around her mum. "She told me I can do a lot better and I believe her."

"And so you should," says Eudora. "Any man who makes you feel less than you are isn't worth a jot of your time."

"I know. It's just that we'd been together for ages and we were good mates, you know? I'm sad that our friendship had to end as well."

"The truth is that sometimes even those you're closest to can let you down. There's nothing you can do about it. You're a confident, intelligent young woman. I have no doubt that you will find a man who is worthy of you. And if you don't, I suspect you'll be magnificent regardless."

"Thank you, Eudora," says Livvy. "That's a lovely thing to say."

"Am I a confident, intelligent young woman?" asks Rose hopefully.

Eudora and Livvy exchange amused glances. "You're one in a million, Rose," says Eudora.

"Right. Who's ready to sing?" They all look up to see Helen, carrying in a large rectangular cake. It's decorated with the words "Happy Birthday Pops!" and a fondant icing model of Stanley wearing sunglasses, lying in a deck chair, with a handkerchief on his head. The twenty or so candle flames dip and waver in the breeze, but somehow Helen manages to keep them alight as they sing. Eudora looks around at these people, turning their smiling faces toward Stanley, like flowers in the sun. She envies their easy companionship, their pure, uncomplicated love for one another.

"Make a wish!" cries Rose as they finish singing, and Stanley blows out the candles. It takes him several attempts to extinguish all of them.

"Lucky we didn't stick the right number of candles on there, Pops! We did try but we couldn't get the fire insurance," says Paul.

"Dad!" cries Ellie, rolling her eyes. "You tell that joke every year."

"That's because it's such a good one," says Paul, ruffling her hair.

Ellie holds up her hands. "Never. Touch. The Hair. Dad."

Paul laughs.

"What? Do you mean you actually meant your hair to look like that?" says Livvy, arching a brow.

Ellie purses her lips. "What? Do you actually mean your face to look like that?"

"Girls," says Helen, putting an arm around each of them. "Let's not fight about nothing today, shall we?"

"JK, Mum, chill."

"Yeah, Mum. We're joking. Chill."

Helen turns to Eudora and Rose. "Remember what I said about them being good girls? I take it all back."

Ellie and Livvy link arms with their mother and plant fat kisses on her cheeks. "Oh, Mummy, you don't mean it."

Rose giggles. "I want Daisy and me to be just like them when we grow up."

Eudora's smile is tempered by a shiver of melancholy at the thought that she won't be around to see this. "I hope you get your wish, Rose," she says. "Now, shall we get you home? I expect your mother will be wondering where you are."

Eudora waves Stanley off and lets herself in through the front door. It's cool but gloomy in the hall compared with the dazzling brightness outside. She experiences a momentary sensation of dizziness, which she puts down to that afternoon's exertions. It's been enjoyable but exhausting.

"Tea and a sit-down is all I need," she tells Montgomery, who greets her from the kitchen doorway with an impatient meow. "And yes, I'll give you some food too. Don't worry."

The persistence with which he weaves himself around her ankles until she complies with his wishes is another stark reminder of why she is relieved she never had children. Demanding and needy. Two of the least attractive traits known to man. Of course, her mother was needy at times, but there was gratitude lurking not far behind. Even at the end of her life, Beatrice was always thanking Eudora for the smallest of kindnesses. It squeezes her heart to think of this now.

As she waits for the kettle to boil, Eudora notices a magpie in the garden filling the air with rasping chatter.

*One for sorrow.*

Another magpie hops onto the grass beside the other. "Two for joy," she murmurs with relief.

Cat fed, tea made, Eudora settles in her chair, breathless and tired. *I'm eighty-five*, she tells herself. *I'm not used to such busy social activities with all these people to talk to and the irrepressible Rose in tow. It's hardly surprising I'm exhausted.*

Eudora notices the answering machine flashing red with a message and presses "play."

"Hallo, Eudora. This is Petra. I know you spoke to Doctor Liebermann and I wanted to know how you are. Please call me if you want to chat. Anytime."

Eudora sits back in her chair and takes a sip of tea.

*How are you, Eudora? How are you feeling? Really.*

Much as she rallies against these open discussions of feelings, she knows it's important to answer them, that Petra and the doctor won't help her unless she does. And yet, the truth is that she fears the answer. Which is why, for the time being, she resolves to remain silent. Silence is powerful. Silence neither agrees nor disagrees. It buys time and actually, that is what she wants at the moment. A little more time. A little more life.

It was a chance meeting that brought this notion more sharply into focus for Eudora. She was leaving the leisure center after a swim, wondering how on earth she would manage the walk home. Fatigue was a daily feature of her eighty-five-year-old life but for some reason, she was feeling particularly worn out today.

"Hello. It's Eudora, isn't it?" said a voice as soothing as treacle. Eudora turned, nonplussed, inhaling the warm spice of the woman's perfume. "I'm Hannah. You came to one of my talks. With that little girl—Rose, was it?"

"You have an excellent memory," said Eudora.

Hannah's smile puts Eudora immediately at ease. "How are you?"

"Still above ground."

Hannah laughed. "I remember that gallows humor. You were the only one brave enough to speak to me afterward. Most people seem to think I'm the grim reaper in disguise."

"It's a very good disguise," said Eudora. "Actually, it was Rose who wanted to speak to you."

Hannah nodded. "A lot of kids want to talk about death. They're trying to figure out how it fits into the grand scheme of things, but lots of adults won't talk about it. Too depressing." She drew air quotes as she said this.

"Mmm," said Eudora, keen to be on her way. "Well, it's nice to see you again."

Hannah glanced at Eudora's stick. "Can I give you a lift somewhere? I only popped in to drop off some leaflets."

"Oh, there's really no need."

"It's no bother."

"Very well," said Eudora with some relief. "Thank you."

"So I presume you heard about Jim?" said Hannah, once they were in the car and on their way.

"Jim?"

"Audrey's husband from the group?"

"Oh, I've only been along once, but I did meet them both. Is everything all right?"

Hannah cleared her throat. "Jim died over the weekend. I had the privilege of being with him and Audrey at the end."

"Oh. Poor Audrey."

"Yes," said Hannah. "She'd had a difficult few years, so I know she was glad his death was gentle and surrounded by love."

"It's the best you can hope for," murmured Eudora.

"I believe so, yes."

They drove in silence until Hannah turned onto Sidney Avenue and Eudora pointed out her house. She pulled into the space outside and switched off the ignition. Eudora unbuckled her belt. "Can I ask you something?"

"Of course."

"Do you think people should be able to choose how they die?"

Hannah fixed her with a gaze of pure kindness. "Within reason, yes. I think the first thing we need to do is talk about death. We need to reclaim the D word and have grown-up discussions to dispel the myth and do away with the fear."

"But what if you're not afraid?"

Hannah held her gaze. "Then you should embrace life for as long as possible—cherish and value it. I don't know you very well, but I've seen you with Rose and can tell you have a special friendship. You're one of the lucky ones. Wouldn't you say?"

"Yes," admitted Eudora. "I suppose I am."

⁂

Eudora cradles the cup in her hand, inhaling the sweet aroma of tea, and takes a deep breath. She was listening to a program on the radio earlier about mindfulness. Normally, she would dismiss these ideas as hokum. However, the expert spoke with a quiet, measured authority, which reminded Eudora of the way Hannah conveyed her truths. She found it utterly compelling. She looks around the room, at the photographs of her parents on the telephone table, the fireplace, her books, the curtains, and the tall, elegant standard lamp that bathes everything in a warm apricot glow. She feels the gentle, comforting heat of the cup snug in her hand. She watches Montgomery saunter into the room, leap up onto the sofa, and turn 360 degrees twice before settling into a tidy parcel of steadily breathing fur. Eudora scans her body for pain and apart from her weariness and the usual aches, which are eased by her seated position, all is well. In this moment, at this time, all is well and that is enough for now.

Her inner peace is brought to a swift end by an urgent, persistent knocking on the front door, followed by a prolonged pressing of the doorbell. There's only one person it could be.

"For heaven's sake, Rose. What is it now?" she cries, having struggled down the hall to open the front door. "A trip to the moon? A nighttime raid on London Zoo?" Eudora stops in her tracks when she sees the little girl's ashen face. "What is it, Rose?"

"It's Mum. She needs you. The baby's coming."

## 1961
## SIDNEY AVENUE, SOUTH-EAST LONDON

Eudora could remember almost every minute detail of that day. It had started in a very ordinary fashion, but whenever she looked back, she found she could recall even the most mundane aspects. She remembered what she'd had for breakfast (a boiled egg followed by Golden Shred on toast) and that she had bumped into Mrs. Cooper on the way to the bus stop, who told her that her youngest grandson, Anthony, had caught chicken pox, poor mite. It was as if the shock of what followed brought everything into sharp focus and replayed it forever. A film reel rolling over and over in her mind.

It was a Friday. Eudora had taken the day off to spend it with Sylvia and her new baby. She was looking forward to it. Ever since baby Philip arrived, she had felt a renewed sense of purpose. Eudora would probably never have children of her own, but she fully intended to cosset and spoil her best friend's new son.

Eudora decided that the word "cherubic" could have been invented with Philip in mind. His wide-eyed gaze and pleasingly chubby thighs could melt the stoniest of hearts. Eudora was besotted with him on sight, and it was clear the feeling was mutual. The first time they met, he grabbed her finger and stared into her eyes as if reading her soul.

"I think he likes you, Dor," said Sylvia. "And it's a good thing too, seeing as we'd like you to be his godmother."

Eudora stared at her and Ken in amazement and then back at Philip. "Are you sure?" she asked.

Ken and Sylvia exchanged indulgent smiles. "Of course," said Sylvia. "Who else would we ask?"

Beatrice had been almost as delighted as Eudora and set about knitting a jacket for Philip's christening. "I'll edge it with lace. To make it extra special." Eudora patted her shoulder. After the drama of Stella's phone call, their world had returned to its usual quiet routine. Thankfully, Beatrice seemed to have forgotten about it altogether. Eudora was relieved. It was better that way.

She set off to Sylvia's after breakfast, armed with a parcel of assorted scarves, hats, and mittens for the baby. Sylvia and Ken had recently moved out to the suburbs. Their house was a very pleasant 1930s semidetached with three bedrooms and a large garden.

"Room for Philip to kick a football with his dad," said Sylvia, now the model of domesticity. She had recently acquired a twin-tub washer and was almost as clucky about it as she was about Philip. "It's so handy with the nappies, Dor," said Sylvia. "It's changed my life."

Eudora walked up the front path. It was early September and the leaves were turning, but Sylvia's roses were in full bloom. She leaned over to inhale their scent and was rewarded with a perfume so sweet and fresh. It made her body lift with hope at this rare moment of uncomplicated joy.

"You're here!" cried Sylvia, opening the front door. Philip sat alert and smiling in his mother's arms. He reached out his pudgy little hands as soon as he saw Eudora.

"Hello, my little man," Eudora said, taking him from Sylvia and planting a kiss on his forehead. She had been fearful of what would happen once Sylvia got married and became a mother but realized now that there'd been nothing to worry about. If anything, she and Sylvia were closer than ever, almost like sisters.

As an only child with no mother and a father she rarely saw, Sylvia had come to think of Eudora—and by extension, Beatrice—as her surrogate family. "Come through," she said, leading Eudora down the hall. "It's a lovely day. Let's have coffee in the sunroom."

Eudora smiled. Sylvia liked to bestow grand names on the rooms in her house. She would talk about the "drawing room" and "master bedroom" with great enthusiasm. Eudora didn't mind. Taking pride in one's house was an admirable quality.

"So how have you been?" she asked as Sylvia brought in a tray holding a matching coffee set, including a sugar bowl and tongs, and started to serve. Philip sat facing Eudora on her lap. They had just enjoyed several rounds of pat-a-cake, which to her delight had provoked multiple gurgles of pure happiness from her godson.

"Yes. We're all fine, really. Ken's busy at work, but it's the price you have to pay for the good life, isn't it?"

"I suppose it is. But you're happy, aren't you, Sylvia?" she asked, detecting a note of caution in her friend's voice.

Sylvia pursed her lips. "I'm fine. Absolutely fine. How about you? How's life at the bank?"

Eudora could tell that Sylvia was hiding something from her. "Yes, everything is good, thank you. I've just been given a small promotion."

"Oh, but that's wonderful," cried Sylvia, placing Eudora's coffee cup on a coaster. "You'll be running the show soon."

"I don't know about that, but it is nice to get some recognition."

"And how is your mother?"

"She's fine. Sends her love and a whole host of knitted items for this young man too," said Eudora, reaching out a hand to stroke his downy hair. She glanced up at Sylvia and noticed that she was crying. "Oh, Sylvia, whatever's the matter?"

"Oh, Dor, I don't know how to tell you."

Panic rose in Eudora's chest. "Tell me what, Sylvia? What's the matter? Is there something wrong with Philip?"

Sylvia shook her head rapidly. "No, he's fine. Sorry, I shouldn't have scared you like that. The thing is, Dor, Ken has been offered a new position in the company."

"But that's marvelous," said Eudora. "He really will be running the company soon."

Sylvia gave a weak smile. "They want him to open up a new office."

"Oh. Where?" asked Eudora, willing her to say Scotland.

"Canada."

"Canada?"

Sylvia nodded. "I'm so sorry. I didn't know how to tell you."

"And he's definitely going to take it?"

"I think so. It would be a very good career move. And Canada is so beautiful."

"It's so far away, Sylvia," said Eudora, a sob catching in her throat.

"I know." Sylvia nodded as they both started to cry.

Philip stared at them with huge, questioning eyes. Eudora pulled him to her and kissed his head. "It's all right, little man. I'll come and visit you. I promise," she said, unsure as to whether this would even be possible.

"And we can write," said Sylvia, trying to sound hopeful.

"We won't lose touch," said Eudora. "We'll always be there for each other. Whatever happens."

Eudora returned home heavy with sorrow. They had tried to make the best of it, to tell each other that nothing would change, but it was all lies. The lies you tell to make yourself feel better. As she neared the house, Eudora noticed a policeman walking toward her: a constable, barely older than her. He was staring up at the rows of terraced houses, trying to read the numbers.

"May I help you?" she asked as they met by her own front gate.

"No, thank you, Miss," he said, touching the peak of his helmet. "This is the one I'm looking for."

"But this is my house," she said in alarm.

The police constable blushed, his eyes wide in an expression that reminded her of Philip. "Oh, well. Could I speak to your father, please?"

"He's dead," she told him.

"I'm sorry. Your mother?"

"She's . . ." Eudora's voice trailed away. "You'd better come inside."

"Thank you."

Eudora opened the front door to the sound of music playing and knitting needles clacking. A good sign. "Mum? There's someone to see you." She led the policeman into the lounge, where Beatrice was knitting by the fire, a cup of tea at her side. She looked up and smiled, the picture of contentment. Eudora would often wonder afterward if this was the last time she ever saw her like that.

The policeman took off his helmet and cleared his throat. "Mrs. Honeysett? I'm afraid I've got some bad news."

Beatrice looked from Eudora to the policeman and back again, as if trying to work out what on earth could be the matter given that her eldest daughter was present and correct. "What is it?" she demanded with a hint of irritation.

"It's your daughter, Stella. I'm afraid there's been an accident."

"Dora?" cried Beatrice in alarm, reaching out for her daughter.

"It's all right, Mum, I'm here," said Eudora, turning to the policeman. "What kind of accident? Is she okay? What about the baby?"

"What baby?" cried Beatrice.

Eudora squeezed her mother's hands. "What's happened?" she asked the constable.

The policeman's face was ghostly. Eudora wondered if this was the first time he'd ever had to deliver news like this. "I'm sorry to say that she had a fall down some stairs and unfortunately she sustained fatal injuries."

"She's dead," said Eudora.

The policeman nodded. "I'm sorry."

"She's dead," repeated Eudora. "And her baby?"

The policeman shook his head again. "I'm sorry."

"What happened? Why did she fall? How did it happen?"

The policeman shifted uncomfortably. "She was pushed."

"By her husband," said Eudora. "It was him, wasn't it?"

He gave the briefest of nods. "He's in custody. I'm very sorry. Please accept my condolences."

Eudora could remember everything that happened that day up until this point, but what followed remained a blur. She probably made some tea, tried to comfort her mother, eventually prepared a meal, but she couldn't remember any of this. All she knew was that she had never felt so lonely, so wretched, or so guilty in her entire life. You made your choices and you had to live with them. And Eudora knew, from that moment onward, that the choice she'd made would haunt her until the day she died.

## Chapter 14

"EUDORA? EUDORA, DID you hear me? We need your help. The baby's coming."

Eudora is jolted back to the present, but the tang of the past lingers like sour milk. "I can't."

Rose blinks. Once. Twice. Eudora can see that the threat of tears is imminent. "But there's nobody else. You're the only one I can ask."

A shutter-click memory of a desperate plea from the past rattles her.

*You're the only one.*

Eudora does her best to banish it. "Wouldn't it be best to phone the emergency services?"

Rose shakes her head. "Mum doesn't do hospitals. We've called Beth, the midwife, but she's not going to get here for another half hour and Mum says the baby's coming now." Eudora hesitates. Rose touches her on the arm. "Please, Eudora."

Eudora stares past Rose. "I'm too old for this."

"And I'm too young."

They stare at each other in a moment of mutual, ageless understanding.

*We're the same, you and me. The helpless ones. And we must stick together.*

"Fetch me my stick, please."

Rose moves quickly and without any of her usual chirpiness. "Here you go," she says. "Now, please don't think I'm being rude, but we need to get back to Mum. She's making a terrible noise and I don't think she should be on her own."

"Of course. Yes. Come along." Eudora follows behind Rose, doing her best to hurry. She is pleased to note that she no longer feels tired. Adrenaline is a powerful thing. "Where's your father?" she asks as they enter Rose's house to be greeted by what sounds like an animal keening. Eudora's heart quickens.

"On his way back from somewhere or other. I can't remember the name. I'm giving him half-hourly updates."

Rose leads her down the hall into the lounge. Maggie has her back to them. She is standing with arms and legs wide, like a human star, bracing herself against the wall, puffing in and out. She takes a deep breath before emitting a low, steady roar. Eudora finds herself unable to do anything but stare.

"Mummy? Are you okay?" asks Rose, fear edging her voice.

Eudora realizes that she needs to take charge but remains paralyzed with fear.

"S'okay, s'okay, Rose," says Maggie, glancing over her shoulder. "The baby's coming and I need to push when I get the contraction." She breathes. Maggie winces as another contraction arrives. She screws up her face as she pushes and bellows again.

"Eudora?" says Rose in a small voice, eyes pleading and desperate. "Please help her."

Tentatively, Eudora reaches out and touches Maggie lightly on the shoulder. She responds by turning to face her and grasping her hand. Her touch is cool but strong. It emboldens Eudora.

"I'm here," she says. "And so is Rose. Everything is going to be fine. You're doing very well." She hopes this is true. *Please let this baby be all right. Please let her be all right.*

Maggie nods rapidly.

"Rose, I think we could do with some towels. As many as you can find, please. And do you remember how I taught you to boil the kettle? Could you do that too?"

"Aye, aye, captain," says Rose, back to her old self. She dashes out the door. "I remember this bit from episodes of *Call the Midwife*. I'm glad you're here, Eudora. I was getting a bit scared."

Eudora looks into Maggie's eyes and squeezes her hand. "She'll be fine. And you will too."

Rose returns moments later with half a dozen towels, just as Maggie stops puffing again and begins to push and roar anew. "Is Mummy okay?" asks Rose, her face pale.

"She's fine," says Eudora, sending up a fresh prayer. "But we have to support her. I need you to put down some of the towels so she can stand on them. And then you hold her other hand so she knows you're here."

Maggie moves onto the towels, which Rose has placed on the floor. She takes Rose's hand and kisses it. "Don't be scared. I know what I'm doing. I remember it from when you arrived in the world. I love you and I'm glad you're here."

"I love you too, Mummy," says Rose, tears forming in her eyes as her mother pushes again.

Eudora watches with horrified fascination as the top of the baby's head appears. "Is that . . . ?" begins Rose, gaping at Eudora.

Eudora nods, all fear elbowed out of the way by new life. "Your sister is coming, Rose. All right, Maggie? You're doing very well. Keep going."

Maggie is puffing and nodding. "This time," she breathes. "I think it will be this time."

"Okay, Rose," says Eudora. "You keep holding your mother's hand and I will be ready with the towel to take the baby."

"Like in rugby when the ball pops out of the scrum?" asks Rose, eyes wide and eager.

Eudora gives her an encouraging smile. "If you like." She notices Maggie screw her eyes tightly shut. "Come on, Maggie. You can do this," she says, holding out a fresh, clean towel.

"Yes, Mummy, you can do it!" cries Rose.

Maggie lets out the roar of women the world over, announcing new life, new hope—a gift to the universe. Eudora accepts the gift, a tiny, bloody form, sticky and perfect. As Maggie lowers herself to the floor, Eudora wraps this new being in the towel, gently wiping her nose and mouth. The baby replies with a piercing cry as if announcing herself to the assembled company.

"I hope she's not going to do that all the time," says Rose.

They laugh as Eudora hands over the precious parcel to her mother. "Congratulations."

"Thank you. Really, Eudora. I don't know what we would have done without you."

"It was all down to you, Maggie. You were magnificent," she tells her with a shiver of admiration.

There's an urgent knock at the door. Rose runs off to answer it, returning moments later with a cheery, bustling lady. "Now then. I hear someone has delivered their baby all by themselves," she says. "Congratulations."

"I couldn't have done it without Eudora and Rose," says Maggie.

"Well done. Both of you," says the woman. "I'm Beth. Sorry I missed all the fun. Now, Rose, would you like to cut your sister's cord?"

"Okay," says Rose. "We boiled some hot water. Do you need it?"

"You're amazing," says Beth. "Take me to the kitchen and I will sort everything."

Rose leads her away. Eudora is left watching Maggie nurse her new daughter.

"She's perfect," says Eudora, admiring the baby's delicate features.

"Thank you," says Maggie.

"I've decided I want to be a midwife when I grow up," says Rose, returning with Beth. "I already have experience, and Beth says that bringing new life into the world is the best job there is."

"It's true," says Beth, as she sets about clamping the cord so Rose can cut it. "Here you go, Rose," she adds, handing her the scissors.

"I declare this cord cut!" cries Rose. Everyone laughs.

"Excellent work," says Beth. "And now I need to check

your mum over and help her deliver the placenta. Would you like to watch?"

"Ew, no, sounds disgusting," says Rose.

Beth laughs. "Perhaps this job isn't for you after all. Could you and Eudora look after your baby sister for me while I do that, please?"

"Of course," says Rose. "Although it might be better if Eudora holds her."

"All right," says Beth. "Why don't you sit on the sofa in there," she suggests, pointing toward the room next door.

Eudora does as she says, and Rose settles next to her. Beth places the baby, who has drifted off to sleep, in Eudora's arms.

"Hello, Daisy," says Rose. "I'm your big sister, Rose. And this is my best friend, Eudora." Her words wrap themselves around Eudora's heart as she looks down at the world's newest inhabitant. "She doesn't do much, does she?" says Rose.

Eudora laughs. "True, but it won't be long before she's running rings 'round you."

Rose shrugs "I'll have to come to your house if she gets annoying." Rose leaps to her feet. The baby's eyes snap open. "I forgot to call Daddy!" she cries. "Back in a sec."

Eudora and the baby eye each other. "That's your sister," she tells her. "She never stops moving. I know you're going to have a lot of fun with her. You're a very lucky girl. Please be kind to her always. Don't treat her like Stella treated me."

The baby gives a small squeak as if she understands

and continues to gaze up at her. Eudora knows that babies can't focus at this age, but there's something about the way Daisy's eyes travel over her face, as if she's drinking her in, studying her soul. That gaze is like a blessing to Eudora, reminding her of a time when she could have helped another mother and child but didn't. This time she did help. It's only when she notices a tear land on Daisy's cheek that she realizes she's crying.

Eudora takes her leave when Rob returns, despite Rose begging her to stay and celebrate.

"We're going to wet the baby's head or something," she says.

"Thank you, but I'm going to go home. I'm rather tired after all this drama," she tells her. "I'll see you soon."

"Tomorrow?"

"Rose," warns her father.

"Eudora doesn't mind. She likes it," says Rose.

Eudora doesn't contradict her. "I daresay." She smiles at the brand-new family of four. "Congratulations. She's beautiful."

"Thank you," says Rose, who is nestled very close to her mother and sister on the sofa now.

Rob walks Eudora to the front door. "Are you sure you'll be all right from here?" he jokes.

Eudora smiles. "Take care of them."

"I will." He leans forward and kisses her on the cheek. "Thank you for being there. You saved the day."

Eudora holds his gaze for a moment. "It was a privilege."

She experiences that same light-headed feeling as she retreats back to her house. *It's all the excitement*, she tells herself, *all that adrenaline coursing 'round my body.* Eudora is exhausted but knows she won't be able to fall asleep for a while. She makes some tea and settles once again in her armchair. She looks around the room, as if searching for someone with whom to share the wonderful news. Montgomery sleeps, oblivious, on the sofa.

"Well, you're not much use," she says. She glances at the phone and a thought enters her mind. Would it be too late to call? She's not sure if the number is a home or work one but decides to try all the same.

She hears a long, steady ring, followed by another and another. She is about to give up when a voice answers.

"Konrad?"

"Is that Petra?"

"Yes. Is that Eudora?"

"How did you know?"

"I recognize your voice. Plus, I don't get many calls from English people at home."

"Is this a good time?"

"Oh yes, of course. I told you to call anytime and I'm very glad you did. I am pleasantly surprised, as you like to say."

Eudora is drawn in by the warmth in her voice. It makes her want to tell Petra everything. "I wanted to share some good news."

"Oh yes?"

"Yes. My neighbor, Rose? Her mother had a baby. And I helped deliver her."

"Oh, Eudora. That's wonderful. I know it's not your baby, but I congratulate you. And to help deliver the child. That must have been incredible."

"It was like a miracle, Petra."

"The miracle of life, right?"

The pause says everything. "Yes. Yes, it was exactly that."

"I am glad you called to tell me this, Eudora. You sound so happy."

Another pause, this time as the idea sinks in. "I am." She would like to tell Petra her truth, to share the story of her sister and the baby who died because of her, of how Daisy's birth feels like an absolution. She will always carry the guilt, but its burden has lightened somehow.

"Thank you, Eudora."

"For what?"

"For calling. I am honored that you wanted to share this news with me."

"Thank you, Petra."

"Take care of yourself, Eudora."

"You too."

Eudora decides it really is time for bed now. The cat follows her upstairs, and as soon as she is in bed, he leaps up and settles by her feet. Eudora is surprised. He is a habitual night prowler and a prodigious mouser. However, she finds his gentle breathing to be a welcome presence as she drifts off into an unusually easy and deep sleep.

## 1961
## EDENHAM CREMATORIUM, SOUTH-EAST LONDON

The chapel building looked resplendent in the mid-morning autumn sunshine, its tower cloaked in a thick layer of blood-red ivy. Eudora shivered at the sight of it, pulling her collar up around her throat, quickening her pace as the sky darkened and sharp darts of rain began to fall. The priest greeted her in the doorway with a cursory nod. He was a serious, distracted-looking individual, who had been more than a little offhand when they met to discuss the arrangements. Eudora supposed he didn't relish having to deal with a woman, but then she didn't relish having to arrange her twenty-one-year-old sister's funeral. Life was unfair sometimes.

She took her place at the front of the chapel, eyes fixed forward. She didn't want to acknowledge the other mourners or the fact that there were so few of them. She was the only family member present. Her mother had refused to come and wouldn't allow Eudora to let the relatives on her father's side know about Stella's death.

"They will pity us," she said with a hint of venom. "And I will not be pitied."

Eudora could hear the whispers and sniffles behind her now. She recognized a couple of the voices as friends of Stella's.

"I can't believe it."

"She was so young."

"How could this happen?"

"She wrote to me last year. Said she wanted to come home."

"Why didn't she then?"

The speaker lowered the volume of her voice so that her reply was inaudible to Eudora, but she knew what she was saying.

*It's her fault. Her sister wouldn't speak to her. She's so bitter and spiteful. She couldn't see past her selfish feelings to help her own flesh and blood.*

Eudora's version of the truth churned over and over in her head as it did constantly these days.

"Please stand," said the priest.

Eudora kept her eyes fixed forward as her sister was brought in. She heard the sobs intensify and watched as the pallbearers placed the coffin on the supports with care, laid the small spray of yellow roses on top, and bowed before taking their leave.

It was a short service, but it seemed like an eternity to Eudora. There were no hymns or music, no celebration of a life well-lived. Eudora didn't listen to the priest's words, to his prayers or blessings or hollow eulogy. There was no comfort or consolation to be garnered today. This was the time to accept her responsibility, to face the guilt and pain. She stared at the coffin, thinking about the two people inside. Two lives lost: one half-lived, the other never begun. She could have saved them both.

The rain was hammering on the windows now, the wind rattling at the doors. Eudora looked around fearfully as if her sister were the cause of the tempest. She wouldn't put it past her. Stella had thrived on drama in her life. Why should her death be any different?

The priest had to raise his voice to give the final commendation and blessing before the curtains were drawn around the coffin and the mourners departed. Eudora remained, motionless, gazing at the pink velvet curtain. She didn't want to speak to anyone. She would wait until everyone had gone before taking her leave.

"Eudora?"

She started at the voice close behind her. She turned and hurried to her feet in surprise. "Sam." Instinctively, she held out her hand.

He shook it gently, staring into her eyes with smiling kindness. "I'm so sorry for your loss, Eudora."

"Thank you. I'm touched that you came."

"How is your mother?"

There were a dozen ways she could answer this, leading to another dozen excuses and lies. "She's not well, which meant that she was unable to come today." It was only a half lie.

"I'm sorry to hear that. Please pass on my condolences."

"I will. Thank you." They looked around at the empty chapel, sensing that it was time to leave.

"Would you like a lift home?" asked Sam.

"That's very kind of you, but I thought I might take a stroll around the gardens. Clear my head a little."

"Of course." This was Sam's cue to leave but he stayed where he was. "Would it be all right if I accompanied you? We don't need to talk, unless you want to. I could do with clearing my head too."

"Oh. Well, of course."

Eudora took one final glance at the closed curtain before walking out into the open with Sam. The rain had stopped but a chill wind remained as the sun struggled to break through the haze. Eudora tucked her scarf up around her neck for warmth as they made their way through the graveyard.

"Funny place for a stroll, eh?" said Sam.

"Mmm," agreed Eudora. "At least it's peaceful." It was a beautiful setting, the graves and gardens well-tended. The golden leaves on the surrounding trees made everything look majestic.

"And how are you, Eudora?" asked Sam. His voice sounded serious.

"I'm all right, thank you." It was the best she could manage.

"Sorry," he said. "Daft question."

"It's all right. It's kind of you to ask. How are you? I heard you got married and had children. Congratulations." She hadn't actually heard this. She'd only seen them in the park.

Sam sighed. "Thank you. I do have two children. But unfortunately, my wife and I are getting divorced."

"Oh."

"That's what my mother said when I told her. And then she ranted about the shame I would bring on the family. And she hasn't spoken to me since."

"Oh dear. I'm sorry."

Sam shrugged. "Don't be. You've got bigger fish to fry."

Eudora looked up at him. He had aged well. His face had a lived-in appearance, but he was still handsome, with flecks of gray peppering his neatly Brylcreemed hair. "It's nice to see you."

Sam smiled. Eudora was ashamed to feel her heart lift. She was supposed to be in mourning. Sack cloth and ashes and no joy. And yet, it felt good to spend a moment like this. "It's nice to see you too, Eudora. I've often wondered how you were getting on. Would it be presumptuous of me to ask if we could keep in touch?"

The rain was starting to fall again. Eudora put up her umbrella and gazed at him. "Not at all. I'd like that."

When Sam had gone, Eudora walked back toward the chapel cloisters, where floral tributes were displayed after services. She thought about going to take one last look at the flowers, to keep one to press, but decided against it. Instead, she kept on walking in the wind and rain. She folded away her umbrella and gritted her teeth, wanting to feel each stinging drop.

The pale roses trembled in the storm, their butter-yellow petals flecked with water droplets. A card flapped in the breeze, its words melting away in the rain. Two words. One plea.

"Forgive me."

The storm raged on.

# Chapter 15

THE WALK TO the doctor's office feels especially strenuous today. It usually takes Eudora a while, but she has always derived satisfaction from her ability to scale her own version of K2. Today feels different though.

"You're an example to us all, Miss Honeysett," says the postman, who is walking by as she sets off. "Got to keep going, right?"

"Right," she replies. She has noticed that he's started to exchange a nod or wave with her again. She isn't sure what has brought on this change of heart. It might be down to Rose, who has been telling anyone who'll listen about her part in Daisy's birth. Either way, Eudora welcomes this softening of attitude.

There is a distinct pinch of autumn in the air today. Eudora is grateful that the hot summer is at an end. Usually she detests autumn, with its air of melancholy decay, but this year is different. As nature turns in on itself, green becomes brown and plants shrink to dust, Eudora has discovered solace in the new life taking root next door to her.

For a small, newly arrived being, Daisy seems particularly eager to announce her presence as frequently as possible. Eudora hears her all through the night and day; she hears squeals and wails and Rose's desperate pleas for her sister to "shut the flip up!" She hears Maggie's soothing tones and Rob's gentle singing when they're trying to persuade Daisy to sleep. She hears crashing and banging and screams as Rose loses her temper with the situation, and then patient reasoning from one or the other parent followed by quiet as she is comforted. Eudora hears life going on with all its drama and love and smiles to herself. In times gone by, the noise and bustle of other people's lives served as a stark reminder that she was cut off from the world, but Rose's presence has curbed this notion. Since the advent of Daisy, Rose demands Eudora's attendance in their house on an almost daily basis. Eudora finds herself pleased to accept.

"I need you, Eudora. Mum needs you. Please can you come?"

Invariably, Eudora will turn up to face a level of chaos to which she is wholly unused but unexpectedly able to deal with.

"I thought I was tired before all this, but now . . ." said Maggie one day, her voice trailing off as if she is too exhausted to find the words.

Eudora likes to think of herself as an army general, drafted in to manage a military crisis. Rose enjoys this game too. "Right, Captain Rose, can you bring me up to speed on today's situation, please?"

"Yes, ma'am," says Rose with a salute. "The enemy woke at two A.M."

"Please don't call your sister 'the enemy,'" mumbles Maggie.

"Sorry, Mummy. The baby woke at two A.M. and basically . . ."

". . . hasn't been to sleep since," says Maggie, as if resigned to a lifetime of wakefulness.

Eudora looks at her hollow, red-rimmed eyes and then at the baby in her arms. Daisy's eyes mirror her mother's as they dart left and right, her facial muscles twitching as if she has no idea which expression to adopt.

"Food? Nappies?"

"Done. All done," says Maggie.

"Very good. Right, give the enemy—sorry, I mean, the baby to me. And you go to bed," says Eudora.

Maggie looks as if she might cry. "But . . ."

"That's a direct order," says Eudora.

Maggie stares at them both before handing over Daisy. "Thank you," she breathes.

Eudora turns to Rose. "Right, we need soothing music, Rose, and the sound of the washing machine."

"On it," says Rose. Fifteen minutes later, Daisy has been lulled to sleep by the calming tones of "Brahms's Lullaby" interspersed with the *chug-churn* of a spin cycle. Eudora places her in the Moses basket in the living room and sets about playing a fiercely competitive game of dominoes with Rose.

"I'm glad you're here, Eudora. Things are pret-ty intense in this house at the moment."

"I'm pleased I'm able to help."

"I start school next week," says Rose, her eyes fixed on the tile she's just placed.

Eudora knows enough of Rose to understand that this is a cue. "And how do you feel about that?"

"Terrible. I'm trying to persuade Mum to homeschool me instead."

Eudora glances over at Daisy's snuffling form. "I think she might have her hands full at the moment, Rose."

Rose's eyes widen. "Maybe you could do it."

"I don't think that's a very good idea."

"Why not? You know everything and Stanley could help too. We could go on educational trips to museums and stuff. It would be great for all of us."

Eudora places a hand over Rose's. "You need to be with people of your own age."

Rose stares at the dominoes as tears form in her eyes. "But I don't like people of my own age. They're mean."

"Not all of them. Just as not all older people are kind."

"You are. And Stanley is. You're my best friends," says Rose. A tear plops onto the line of dominoes.

Eudora reaches out her other hand and cups Rose's between her own. "All will be well," she says.

"Promise?" Rose stares up at her, eyes brimming.

"Have I ever let you down?"

"No."

"Well, there you are then. Now, come along. Let's finish this game. It's two-one to me. You really need to buck up your ideas."

Eudora reaches the doctor's office now. It's taken her twenty minutes longer than usual, largely because she needed to pause to catch her breath more than once. Part of her wishes she'd asked Stanley for a lift, but it's only a very small part. It's against her nature to ask for help, even from him.

If the individual who designed this doctor's office had intended to make it as uninviting as possible, they've done an excellent job. The reception area is reached via a narrow alley and two heavy doors. Eudora is thankful that a man who is leaving pauses to hold them both open for her. The interior is slightly worse than the exterior. It looks to Eudora like a less fun version of a World War II bunker. The dark, oppressive surroundings are enhanced by a bank of blinds covering the windows at the far end. Eudora has been coming to this office for as long as she can remember but can't recall ever seeing the blinds raised. A radio shouts out music from one corner of the waiting area; the background din does little to lighten the atmosphere. The walls are emblazoned with terrifying posters warning of life-threatening diseases alongside more mundane notices advertising coffee mornings and knitting groups.

Eudora approaches the desk and looks at the poster warning her that aggressive behavior will not be tolerated. It is therefore ironic that the words "passive aggressive" could have been invented for the woman behind the counter, such is her disinterest and contempt.

It takes the woman a good two minutes to acknowledge Eudora's presence, and when she does, she stares at her with cold indifference. "Yeh?"

Eudora opens her mouth to speak but is interrupted by the woman raising a hand to silence her as her telephone begins to ring and she makes the baffling decision to answer it. "Juss a minute."

Eudora purses her lips and stares past the woman's dirty-blond bouffant and overly made-up face. A cheerful blue-and-white-polka-dot cardboard box sits on the shelf behind her head, announcing its contents to be "Death Certificates." Eudora considers catching the next available flight to Switzerland as the woman puts down the phone with a perfectly manicured hand.

"Yeh?" she says again without apology.

Eudora takes a deep breath. "Eudora Honeysett. I have an appointment with the doctor."

"Which doctor?"

At first Eudora is confused, thinking she has said "witch doctor," but then the penny drops. "I have no idea. I seem to see a different doctor every time I come here."

The woman sighs heavily and rolls her eyes. "Date of birth?"

Eudora would like to take this woman down a peg or two, to admonish her for her rudeness, but it occurs to her that she is probably unhappy. Eudora bites her lip. "The twentieth of July, 1933."

The woman's face softens. "My mum's birthday," she murmurs. Eudora can see from her face that her mother is no longer alive, and gives her a brisk smile. "Wass yer name, darlin'?"

"Eudora Honeysett."

"Ah yeah, I got yah. Take a seat. Doctor Khalid is running half an hour late."

"Thank you." Eudora was hoping there would be a delay. She wants to reread the living will form she has completed before she goes in. She glances at the radio and then back at her new friend. "Would it be possible to switch off the radio, please, if no one is listening to it?"

The receptionist's brow furrows as if Eudora has requested that she redecorate the waiting room rather than merely silence it. "We usually have it on, but I don't mind, do you, Sam?" she says to her colleague.

"Nah," says Sam, shaking her head. "Be nice to have a bit of p and q for a change."

"Thank you," repeats Eudora.

"No bovver, darlin'," says the receptionist, reaching over her desk to switch off the clattering din.

Eudora breathes out as she takes a seat in the far corner of the waiting room. The place is packed with people but is relatively quiet apart from the odd wheezy breath or squeaking child. Eudora retrieves the form and casts her eye over her shaky handwriting. A sharp tightness in her chest catches her unawares. She takes a deep breath and places a hand over her heart to calm herself. It subsides. Eudora dismisses it as a side effect of her exertions.

"Eudora Honeysett?" calls the doctor, a stressed-looking woman, who barely waits for Eudora to follow before hurrying back to her consulting room.

Eudora taps on the door before entering.

"Come in!"

She does as she's told, entering the stuffy room and making her way over to the vacant chair. The doctor is already back at her desk, tapping away at her computer. She doesn't look up as Eudora sits down. "How are you, Ms. Honeysett?"

"I am quite well, thank you." She's decided not to mention her recent dizzy spells or the tightness in her chest. Ignorance is bliss.

"That's good. So, what can I do for you?"

Eudora sits up straighter in her chair. "I wanted to ask you to witness this form for me, please," says Eudora, handing it over. "And may I have a copy of my medical records?" She delivers the form with a smile, trusting that this will coax the doctor to do her bidding.

The doctor reads the form and glances up at Eudora. "Have you discussed this with anyone close to you?"

"I live alone. It's just me now but I have given it a great deal of thought."

The doctor glances at the clock. Eudora hopes the doctor's lateness will play to her advantage. "And you're sure about all aspects of this form?"

Eudora answers without hesitation. "I am. I'm eighty-five. I've had a long time to consider my life."

Her certainty and no-nonsense approach clearly does the job, as the doctor smiles. "I think you're wise to get it all written down. If you sign in the box, I will witness it."

"Thank you," says Eudora, doing as she's asked before handing it back to the doctor. She winces as her chest tenses again.

"Are you all right, Ms. Honeysett?" asks the doctor, looking concerned.

"Indigestion," says Eudora with a reassuring nod.

The doctor hesitates, her pen poised over the form. "Would you mind if I examined you?"

*Yes*, thinks Eudora. *I would mind a great deal.* "Of course not."

The doctor unfurls her stethoscope and listens to Eudora's chest. For an overworked woman, she takes her time.

Eventually, she returns to her chair. "I think you may have a chest infection. I'm going to prescribe some antibiotics, and I'd also like you to go for an echo test on your heart."

The irony of the fact that Eudora's heart sinks at this news is not lost on her. "Very well. Are you still able to sign my form, please?"

"Of course," says the doctor. She signs her name and clicks her mouse rapidly. The printer whirrs into action. "Here you are." She hands the form back to Eudora, along with her records and prescription, still warm from the printer. "You'll get a letter soon about the echo test. If your breathing doesn't improve over the next couple of weeks, please come back to me."

"Thank you," says Eudora, making her way to the door. She tucks the papers into her bag, deciding that she will send them to Doctor Liebermann after all. Life may be precious but it's uncertain too. It's wise to be prepared for all eventualities.

## 1964
## JOSS BAY, BROADSTAIRS

Eudora lay back on the red tartan picnic rug and gazed up at the sky.

"Cerulean," she murmured.

"What's that, darling?" asked Sam.

"The color of the sky. It's cerulean. I remember that word from school. Hadn't thought of it since, until now."

Sam propped himself on one elbow and leaned over to kiss her. "My clever Dora darling. I love you."

She smiled. "I love you too."

Theirs had been a straightforward courtship, at least as far as their feelings for each other were concerned. Eudora had known from the second she saw Sam at Stella's funeral that they were meant to be. She had loved him since school but hadn't been able to permit herself these feelings until that moment. The second he approached her and asked if he could walk with her, she knew.

Of course, the others who made up their respective worlds were a different matter. Sam and his ex-wife, Judith, had given mutual consent for the divorce; it had been a "marry in haste" affair and they were both pleased to be released from a loveless future. However, as soon as Eudora appeared on the scene, Judith was less cooperative, particularly in relation to the children. Eudora understood this to a certain extent; a mother must protect her offspring. However, when she began to use the children as bargaining chips in an endless game of one-upmanship, Eudora lost all sympathy. She comforted Sam as he wept when he wasn't allowed to see them for the umpteenth time, while boiling with rage at the calculating cruelty of humans.

Sam also had to contend with the constant disapproval of his parents, a campaign that was spearheaded by his mother. Consequently, Eudora and Sam were never invited to his parents' house together. All family celebrations had to be undertaken separately. It was wearying but, ironically, Sam and Eudora's relationship emerged unscathed and strengthened. They were a perfect unit of two, united against the world, strong and desperately in love.

The breeze had picked up a little now. Eudora shivered. Sam wrapped a shawl around her shoulders, pulling her in for a kiss. "Fancy a stroll?"

"That makes me think of the day we found each other again," she said, taking his hand, allowing him to help her to her feet. "We took a stroll around the crematorium gardens. Do you remember?"

"Happiest day of my life," said Sam, kissing her hand and staring into her eyes. "Apart from when James and Sarah were born of course."

"Of course."

Eudora didn't mind playing second fiddle to Sam's children. This was exactly as it should be. She'd met them on a couple of occasions and found them adorable. She liked the idea of playing stepmother to them, particularly as she'd given up hope of having children of her own. Eudora relished the presence of a child in her life. Despite Sylvia's assurances, Eudora hadn't seen her or Philip since their move to Canada three years earlier. Sylvia sent letters and photos of course. Eudora treasured them but it wasn't the same as having Philip close by, watching him grow.

She walked hand in hand with Sam, smiling at the children splashing in the sea. Eudora wondered what life would have been like if she hadn't refused Sam's invitation to the cinema all those years ago. Would they have married? Had children of their own? It was a pointless thought but still, she couldn't help wishing that they'd had a better shot at this, something more straightforward.

"There's something I need to discuss with you," said Sam, turning to face her.

"Sounds serious," said Eudora, gazing up at him, shielding her eyes from the sun.

"It's Judith."

Eudora sighed. "What's she been up to now?"

"She's moving."

"Moving. Where to?"

"Norwich. She wants to move back to where her parents live."

"Oh, you poor thing," said Eudora, reaching out a hand to stroke his cheek. "You'll never see the children."

"I know," said Sam. "So I'm going to move there too."

"What?"

Sam grabbed her hands. "I want you to come with me." He went on before she had a chance to answer, his eyes imploring. "Just think about it, Dora. It could be perfect. I've made some inquiries. We could rent somewhere for a while and then perhaps buy a place when we're ready. I've got money from the sale of the house and it's much cheaper in Norwich."

"But what about my life in London? What about my mother?"

Sam's gaze was steady. Eudora longed to give in to him. "I'm sure she'll be happy for you. For us. She's been very understanding about us. Far more than my parents."

This was true. To Eudora's astonishment, her mother had made little comment about Sam's situation. She didn't exactly welcome him with open arms but had patted Eudora's hand and told her, "I just want you to be happy, dear." Beatrice had never been demonstrative, so Eudora took this as a positive sign. She knew her mother carried the weight of guilt for Stella—as she did too—but they never spoke of it. Life had consequently fallen into a new rhythm, where Eudora allowed herself to nurture the idea of happiness again. It had felt very good indeed, but now she wasn't so sure.

"I can't just abandon her."

"Perhaps she could come with us?"

"You mean live with us?"

"Not necessarily. If she sold her house, she could afford to buy something herself."

"And what about other people? What will they think?"

Sam stared deep into her eyes. "The world is changing, Dora. It doesn't care what people think. You and I are the most important ones in this decision. I vote for a life of happiness with you."

Eudora looked out to sea as the idea sifted through her mind like a pebble in the tide. Whether it was the sun on her face or Sam's encouragement, Eudora felt alive with hope at the idea. After so many disappointments, this had to be her time.

She turned to Sam. "I'll talk to Mum."

Sam scooped Eudora into the air and spun her around and around as she threw back her head and laughed. Like that afternoon with her father in the tea shop in Piccadilly, this would be a memory she would always treasure.

It was starting to get dark by the time Sam dropped her home. He switched off the engine and turned to her. "Do you want me to come in and talk to your mother with you?"

Eudora shook her head. "No, it's all right. Let me speak to her first."

Sam reached over to stroke her cheek. "You know I love you, don't you?"

She leaned over to kiss him. "Of course," she said before climbing out of the car. "I'll call you tomorrow."

As she opened the front door, Eudora knew immediately that something was wrong. The house was silent. Her skin prickled as she put down her bag and made her way to the kitchen. "Mum?" she called, although it came out as a fearful whisper.

The kitchen was empty and spotless, all the dishes cleared away, everything tidy and sparkling. Eudora saw the envelope with just her name written across it on the kitchen table and her heart began to thump. She ripped it open, scanning the words in a frenzy. Then she dropped it and ran. Hurling herself up the stairs, she flung open her mother's bedroom door. An empty bottle of sleeping tablets had been placed carefully on the bedside table next to her mother's water glass etched with a pretty flower design. Eudora shook her mother by the shoulders.

"Mum! Mum! Can you hear me?" she shouted.

"Ugh," said her mother.

"Mum! What have you done?" she cried, anger and fear rising like bile. "Why have you done this?"

Her mother was mumbling something now.

"What are you saying? I need to call an ambulance. What is it?"

Beatrice slumped toward her daughter's ear. "Want you to be happy, Dora," she murmured before falling back onto the bed.

# Chapter 16

"EUDORA?" SAYS STANLEY, waving a hand in front of her face.

"Mmm?"

"I said, would you like a cup of tea?"

"Oh. Yes, please. Thank you."

Stanley frowns. "Are you all right?"

"Yes. Yes, I'm fine. I'll have a custard cream too if they've got one, please."

"Coming right up."

Eudora watches him go and wonders at her declaration that she is "fine." Such an innocuous word and yet so loaded with opposite meaning. She isn't fine of course. Hasn't been since her consultation with the doctor last week. She is feeling little effect from the antibiotics and the notion of a heart scan is unsettling. If Rose hadn't been otherwise engaged at a meeting with her new teacher, Eudora might have asked her to deputize today, but Stanley had turned up like an eager little boy. She hadn't the heart to send him away.

Stanley is taking his time with the tea. Eudora looks up to see him chatting with a woman she recalls from the last meeting. This must be the famous Sheila. Stanley makes a comment and the woman laughs, resting her hand on his arm as if afraid that his sparkling wit will throw her off balance. Eudora shifts in her seat, turning her attention elsewhere. She notices Audrey coming in through the door. They've made eye contact before Eudora has a chance to turn away. Audrey obviously sees this as an invitation.

"Hello, Eudora," she says, taking a seat. "I wasn't sure whether to come today so it's lovely to see a friendly face."

Eudora has never considered that her face might be friendly, but she is pleased to be able to offer some comfort to Audrey. She's been around death enough to understand the seismic shifts of grief. "I was sorry to hear about Jim."

"Thank you," says Audrey. "I was very glad to have Hannah there. Do you remember her? The death doula." Audrey smiles. "What a title, eh?"

"Quite. Yes, I know who you mean. She's a remarkable woman. I bumped into her the other day, actually. She said she'd been with you and Jim at the end. That must have been consoling."

Audrey nods. "It was. She's a very special lady. I didn't know what a good death was until I met her. And I'm glad Jim had that. He deserved it. He was a wonderful man. The last couple of years have been very hard, so it's a comfort that he left this world surrounded by love."

Eudora surprises herself by reaching out to squeeze Audrey's hand. Their eyes lock in a moment of shared understanding. "And how are you?" she asks.

Audrey takes a deep breath. "Would you think me a monster if I said I was relieved?"

"No," says Eudora without hesitation. "I could see how difficult your life was. I think relief is entirely natural and understandable."

Audrey blinks back tears. "Thank you, Eudora. You

have no idea what that means to me. My son doesn't understand at all, probably because he hardly saw his dad. He's so angry at the moment."

"That will be the guilt. And it's his guilt. Not yours. He'll have to deal with that in his own time."

Audrey nods gratefully. "Where's Stanley today?"

"Did somebody mention my name?" says Stanley, appearing before them with Sheila at his side. "Meet my glamorous assistant," he adds as she places two teas in front of Eudora and Audrey and curtsies to play along. Stanley laughs. "Have you met Sheila?" he says to Eudora.

"No, I haven't had the pleasure," she replies with a thin-lipped smile.

"Pleased to meet you, Eudora," says Sheila, shaking her hand warmly. "And Audrey, my love. How are you?" she asks, reaching out her arms and folding her into a tight embrace. Eudora's shoulders stiffen.

"I'm not too bad, thank you, Sheila," says Audrey. "Eudora is being very kind."

"She's got a good heart deep down, that one," says Stanley, winking at Eudora, who rolls her eyes.

"I used to find it hard coming here after Vic died," says Sheila, cupping Audrey's hands in hers. "But everyone was so supportive. It always made me feel much better."

"Hear, hear," says Stanley. "It's been hard since I lost Ada, but having people around who understand helps."

"We should form a support group," jokes Sheila, squeezing Audrey's hand. She turns to Eudora. "Are you a widow, Eudora?"

Eudora bristles. "No. I've never been married."

"Oh," says Sheila, looking unsure. "Well. I'd better get back to help with the teas. It was nice to meet you. Take care, Audrey."

"Thank you, Sheila," says Audrey, patting her on the arm.

"What a smashing lady," says Stanley after she's gone.

"Oh, Sheila is wonderful," says Audrey. "I was having a wobble in the chilled aisle in Sainsbury's the other day. She saw me and gave me the biggest hug."

"Ahhh. That is lovely, isn't it, Eudora?" says Stanley.

"Lovely," echoes Eudora.

"Do you know that we share the same birthday?" says Stanley.

"No," says Audrey with a level of astonishment that Eudora finds baffling.

"And we were born in the same year so we're practically twins!"

"Well, there's a thing," says Eudora, wondering how long they are going to spend discussing the merits of Sheila. Stanley stares at her for a moment before they are distracted by Sue calling them to attention.

"Good afternoon, everyone! It's fantastic to see you all. I'm so pleased that some of our newbies have returned." She smiles at Eudora and Stanley. "I am delighted to welcome one of our absolute favorites back this afternoon, so without further ado, please put your hands together for Chris the Crooner!"

Eudora almost jumps out of her seat at the volume of the whoops and cheers that greet Chris. He grins and waves like a Hollywood star. "Good afternoon, everyone!" he cries. "My name is Chris the Crooner and I'm going to take you on a musical journey through the forties, fifties, and beyond. Feel free to sing, dance, or throw money!"

*Saints preserve us*, thinks Eudora.

Chris the Crooner flicks a switch and the opening bars of "Memories Are Made of This" begin to play. Eudora is amazed at the excitement he creates almost immediately. Three-quarters of the people present are already on their feet, while others tap and sway in time to the music.

One of the organizers spots Audrey and approaches, offering his hand. "Never miss a chance to dance," she says, accepting with shining eyes, reminding Eudora of her old friend Sylvia, who always used the exact same phrase. Eudora senses Stanley, who is swaying from side to side in his chair, itching to join in.

"He's not bad, is he?" says Stanley.

Eudora sniffs. "He's no Dean Martin. But he has a passable voice, I suppose."

"I don't suppose you'd care to dance, Miss Honeysett?" he asks.

Eudora arches a brow. "No. Thank you."

"Oh," says Stanley with obvious disappointment. "Well, do you mind if I ask Sheila?"

"Why would I mind?" says Eudora. "It makes no difference to me." She deliberately keeps her gaze fixed forward.

"Well, in that case, I will," he says, rising to his feet. "I'll come and check on you in a bit."

"There's no need. I'm not an invalid," calls Eudora after him, but he's already approached Sheila, bowing extravagantly like a courtier. Shelia responds in kind with an over-the-top curtsy before allowing Stanley to lead her around the dance floor in an impressive waltz.

"Birds of a feather," mutters Eudora, sipping her tea, trying to ignore the fact that she is just about the only person not dancing. Even an old lady in a wheelchair is being pirouetted around the dance floor by an exuberant volunteer.

The singer is working his way through the hits of Perry Como, Bobby Darin, and Frank Sinatra. Stanley's right. He is a good singer, but Eudora finds herself unable to take pleasure in it. There are too many memories woven into music, too much of the past that she'd rather forget. It's fine for others to pretend that reminiscences are a comfort, but for Eudora, it's a sudden reminder of all the activities she can no longer enjoy and the episodes of her life she has long since packed away.

Chris the Crooner has now become Chris the Pelvis-Wiggler as he dons an Elvis wig and launches into a medley of the King's greatest hits. Eudora watches in horror as Stanley embarks on a personal tribute to his favorite singer. He may be less physically able than Chris, but what he lacks in ability he more than makes up for in passion and energy.

The singer pulls Stanley next to him, hands him a spare Elvis wig and sunglasses, and the two of them embark on an enthusiastic duet, much to the delight of the assembled company. Stanley's singing is some of the most tuneless Eudora has ever heard, but the whole room—except her—is joining in now, cheering and singing along. Sheila thrusts two fingers into her mouth and issues a loud, uncouth whistle.

Eudora has had enough. She grabs her stick and hoists herself to a standing position. She throws a look toward Stanley and his adoring fans, who all have their backs to her. It's as if she's standing alone on the other side of a wall. The song is reaching its denouement now as Stanley turns to Sheila to deliver the final line:

"That's the won-der, the won-der of yoooooou!"

Eudora can bear it no longer. She turns away from the circle of swaying, whooping onlookers and hurries toward the door.

"Are you okay?" asks Sue, meeting her in the entrance hall.

"I need to get home," says Eudora with an unexpected gasp of emotion.

Sue rests a hand on her arm. "Come and sit down, Eudora. You seem upset."

Eudora is horrified. Stanley's and Sheila's demonstrative outbursts must be contagious. She takes a deep breath. "I am not upset. I just need to get home to feed my cat." Sue studies her face for the truth. "Please," says Eudora with a trace of desperation.

"Are you sure you won't wait for Stanley? I could fetch him."

"No," says Eudora with a little more force than she intends. "Thank you. I don't want to bother him. If you could just direct me to the nearest bus stop, I would be most grateful."

Sue chews her lip for a second before answering. "All right. But at least let me put you in a cab. There's usually a few waiting outside."

"Thank you," says Eudora. "That's very kind."

Eudora is relieved to return to the silent haven of home. The noise and clamor of the morning have exhausted her. She decides not to ruminate on what caused her to flee with such urgency but is sure that she made the right decision.

With a certain amount of effort, she manages to make some lunch and feed Montgomery. "Why am I so tired?" she asks the cat as she mashes his food with a fork. "It's as if I'm wading through treacle."

Montgomery jumps so that his front paws are resting on the work surface beside her and nuzzles her hand with his wet nose. "I know you're merely impatient for your food, but I appreciate the interest," she tells him, placing his bowl on the floor. He glances at her for a second before tucking in.

Eudora jumps as the doorbell pierces the silence. It's followed by a loud knocking and Stanley's worried voice calling to her. "Eudora? Are you in there?"

Eudora considers pretending that she's not, but the fear in Stanley's voice pricks her conscience. "Yes, of course I'm here. Where else would I be?" she says, shuffling down the corridor. As she opens the door, she spots Sheila sitting in Stanley's car, peering toward them with concern.

"Why did you run off like that?" asks Stanley. "You had me worried."

Eudora folds her arms. "I'm sorry but I needed to get home."

Stanley scrutinizes her face. "Why?"

"That's really none of your business."

He frowns. "What's the matter?"

"Nothing. Nothing is the matter. I'd merely had enough of the group and wanted to leave. You were otherwise occupied," she says with a fleeting glance toward Sheila. "So I decided to leave you to it."

"Without telling me?"

Eudora sees the hurt in his eyes. "I'm sorry. I should have told you but, as I said, you were busy. I told Sue I was leaving and assumed she would mention it."

"I see," says Stanley, looking at the floor. "Well, I was going to suggest that the three of us go for lunch, but if you're busy . . ."

"I am. Thank you for the invitation. You go. Sorry for worrying you unnecessarily." She nods at Sheila, who smiles in return.

Stanley fixes Eudora with a look. "You're a funny one, Eudora Honeysett."

"Takes one to know one, Stanley Marcham."

"I'll phone you later."

"As you wish. Goodbye," says Eudora, closing the door on his bewildered face. She can't offer him a further explanation because she has none. All Eudora knows is that she wants to shut the door on the world and be left alone for a while. She's too tired for all this nonsense.

The following week, Rose starts school and summons Eudora to meet her at the school gates with Stanley after the first day.

"In case I need you to trip up someone with your stick or something."

"Is that likely?"

"It depends how friendly the other children are."

"Very well."

Eudora arrives at the school with plenty of time to spare. She looks around at the parents gathering in the playground—a noisy, cheerful community of different nationalities and ages. She is impressed to notice that she's not the only octogenarian and watches as a tiny child, brightly daubed painting in hand, zigzags his way across the playground into the waiting arms of her contemporary. To his credit, the elderly man manages to scoop up the giggling boy and spin him around before planting the child on the ground and kissing the top of his hot little head.

"Eudora!" cries Rose, waving from the other side of the playground as if her life depends on it. Eudora is pleased to see that she is arm in arm with another girl.

She gives them a polite wave as Stanley appears by her side. "Made it," he says, hand on his chest as he tries to catch his breath.

Eudora looks pointedly at her watch. "I think you'll find that you are two minutes late."

"Sorry. Sheila and I went to the garden center this morning and we lost track of time."

"I see," says Eudora, avoiding his gaze.

"Eudora! Stanley! You came!" cries Rose, rushing over, dragging her new friend with her.

The girl stares from Eudora to Stanley and back to Rose. "*These* are your best friends?" she says.

"Yes!" cries Rose, oblivious to the girl's disdain. "Eudora, Stanley—this is Jada."

"Pleased to meet you, Jada," says Stanley with a gallant bow. Jada pulls a who-is-this-weirdo face.

"Hello, Jada," says Eudora, fixing her with a look.

"'Lo," says Jada, sounding bored.

"See you tomorrow, Rose," says a boy of the same age with messy hair and a lopsided smile as he runs past.

"Bye, Tommy," says Rose.

"He's such a loser," mutters Jada. "Okay, Rosie-Posie, I gotta go. See you tomorrow, yeah?"

"Okay, Jada," says Rose, pulling her new friend into an awkward hug. "See you then."

She slopes off, reminding Eudora of a big cat on the prowl for fresh prey. "Isn't she lovely?" says Rose. "She's already told me that I can be her best friend. I don't know why I was so worried about school. Everyone is really nice."

"As long as you're happy, Rose," says Stanley, widening his eyes at Eudora. "Now, who's for a milkshake and a doughnut?"

"Me please!" cries Rose, darting her hand into the air.

They walk to the café on the main road, an unusual band of three. Stanley ushers them through the door and fetches the drinks while Eudora and Rose seat themselves at a table by the window. The cream-colored plastic chairs, whiff of stale chip fat, and tinny background music aren't to Eudora's usual taste, but the tea Stanley brings is an acceptable color and Rose declares the doughnut to be "epic."

"So," says Stanley. "Tell us everything."

"Well," says Rose, wiping sugar from her mouth with the back of her hand. "My teacher is called Mrs. Lovely."

"Really?"

"No. That was a joke. That's the name of a character in a book I like. My teacher is called Mrs. Simpson and she is strict but kind."

"She sounds like a good woman," says Eudora.

Rose nods. "She's a bit like you, Eudora. The kids in my class seem really nice but Jada is my favorite."

Eudora catches Stanley's eye. "Is she kind, Rose?"

Rose shrugs. "Yeah. She likes to tease but it's just bants."

"Bants?"

"Banter," says Stanley with authority.

"As long as she's not laughing at other people's expense," says Eudora.

Rose shakes her head. "She's been lovely to me, letting me be part of her group."

Eudora fixes her with a look. "Just make sure you're doing what you want to do, not what someone else wants you to do."

Rose gives an earnest nod. "'Kay, got it. Thanks, Eudora."

"Hello, Rose," says a voice. They look up to see the boy from the playground waving from another table.

"Oh, hi, Tommy," says Rose. Tommy smiles before turning back to the phone he's holding.

"He seems friendly," says Stanley.

Rose leans in to whisper. "Yeah, but Jada says he's a prick, whatever that is."

Stanley suppresses a chuckle. Eudora glares at him. "I

don't think you should be using that language, Rose. And neither should Jada."

"Oh. Okay. Sorry," says Rose.

"And, what's more, you need to make up your own mind about people. He seems like a pleasant boy," says Eudora.

Rose nods. "Okay. I'll try." She jumps up. "I just need to go to the toilet. Back in a sec."

"Goodness," says Eudora after she's gone. "What do you make of that?"

"I'm not sure about Jada," admits Stanley.

"Mmm. Do you think we should tell Maggie?"

Stanley shakes his head. "She's got enough on her plate. Let's keep an eye out."

"Agreed."

"Eudora?"

"Yes?"

"I wanted to ask you if you were all right after the other day. You seemed a bit . . ."

"What?" demands Eudora.

"Jealous?"

Eudora snorts with laughter. "Jealous? Of whom?"

Stanley fiddles with his teaspoon. "Well, Sheila, I suppose."

Eudora shifts in her seat. "Why on earth would I be jealous of Sheila? You're not my husband."

"No, I know, but . . ."

"But what?"

"Well. You were acting strangely at the group, then you rushed off and you've been a bit off ever since."

Eudora sits up straighter in her chair. "For your information, I didn't enjoy the group and wanted to leave. I don't think I am being 'off,' as you call it. I'm here today, aren't I?"

"I suppose. It's just that . . ."

Eudora folds her arms. "What?"

Stanley stares at the cup in front of him. "I was wondering about asking Sheila out for dinner and wanted to know what you thought."

Eudora hesitates before answering. "It's really none of my business what you do, Stanley."

"Oh. Okay. I just thought you might have an opinion. As my friend."

Eudora brushes an invisible crumb off the table. "No. Not really. If you want to spend time with Sheila, it's entirely up to you."

Stanley nods uncertainly. "So you wouldn't think badly of me? I mean, I don't have any romantic intentions. She's just a nice lady who likes the same things as me."

Eudora holds her hands up to silence him. "Please. You don't need to explain yourself."

Stanley looks hurt. "But I value your opinion, Eudora."

She clears her throat. "As I said, it is none of my business what you do. You must make up your own mind. I am not about to tell you how to live your life."

Stanley scowls as Rose reappears, oblivious to the tension between them. "I've thought about what you said and decided that I'm going to be friends with everyone."

"Good idea, Rose," says Stanley, giving Eudora a pointed

look. "Best not to put all your eggs in one basket. Friends can be fickle sometimes. Shall we go?"

### 1977
### SIDNEY AVENUE, SOUTH-EAST LONDON

Sylvia's letter had said that they would arrive at noon, but Eudora was ready for her visitors by 10:30 A.M. She wanted everything to be perfect. She had no idea what Philip might like to eat so she had prepared a variety of dishes for lunch, some of which reminded her of the early years of her friendship with Sylvia. She stood back to admire the spread. Eudora was using her mother's special table linen, china, and cutlery—the best of everything for her best friend.

She had even decorated the mantelpiece with some of the flags and banners left over from the Jubilee street party last month. Beatrice had been reluctant, but Eudora insisted that they decorate the front of the house and go along to the party for a while. Their family had given the neighborhood enough cause to tittle-tattle over the years. Eudora wasn't about to add fuel to the fire by staying away.

She rearranged one of the flags, nodding with satisfaction. Excitement and nerves mingled in the pit of her stomach. Sylvia's monthly letters were always laced with affection, but sixteen years was a long time. Still, Eudora nurtured the belief that theirs was a strong friendship that could endure the test of time and distance.

"Someone's been busy," said Beatrice, standing in the doorway. Eudora smiled and put an arm around her mother's shoulders. Beatrice had never been what you might call a sturdy woman, but she seemed frail as a bird to Eudora now. She felt her mother's shoulder bone digging into her arm and pulled the shawl snugly around her.

"How are you feeling today, Mum?"

Beatrice shivered. "Chilly. Should we put the heating on?"

"It's the middle of summer. I don't think we need it. Why don't you sit out in the garden for a bit and I'll bring you a nice cup of tea."

Beatrice looked unsure. "All right. What time is Sylvia getting here?"

"Noon. We've got plenty of time. I just wanted everything to be ready."

Beatrice leaned in to her daughter. "You're a good girl, Dora, doing all this. I should have got out my knitting pins and made something special for Sylvia's baby."

Eudora was used to her mother's memory lapses. They were an unfortunate side effect of the shock treatment she had received following that terrible day. It was as if time had stood still for Beatrice. Looking around at the same four walls every day, Eudora understood this feeling sometimes.

"It's all right, Mum. I've got a present for Philip. Now, come on, let's make that tea and find some biscuits."

⁂

The doorbell rang shortly after twelve. Eudora checked her appearance once more in the hall mirror before hurrying forward to answer it. She knew the woman standing with arms outstretched was Sylvia, but it felt as if her friend had arrived from another era. She wore a bright orange sundress with a flared princess skirt and huge sunglasses, like something Sophia Loren might choose. Eudora smoothed her own navy blue pinafore before pulling her friend into a tight embrace.

"It's good to see you," she said, an unexpected swell of emotion rising inside her.

"It's good to see you too, Dor," said Sylvia. As she moved forward, Eudora caught sight of Philip, now nearly a foot taller than his mother and striking in his resemblance to her. He stared at his godmother shyly from behind a curtain of dark hair. Eudora was swept back to the time when she first looked into those soft hazelnut eyes. He had smiled easily back then but she was a stranger to him now.

"Philip," she said, holding out a hand. He glanced at his mother, who nodded encouragement, before accepting. Eudora longed to hug him but opted for a gentle handshake instead. "I suppose it would be foolish to comment on how much you've grown, seeing as the last time I saw you, you were a baby in arms!" Sylvia put out a hand and squeezed her friend's shoulder. Eudora smiled. "Oh, but where are my manners? Keeping you waiting in the hall. Come in, come in. Mum will be so pleased to see you. Lunch is ready and waiting."

"Thank you, Dora," said Sylvia.

"You sound so different," said Eudora as she led them to the dining room. "You've definitely picked up an accent."

"Have I?" asked Sylvia in surprise. Eudora could tell she was pleased by this comment. "You should hear Phil talk." She turned to her son. "Actually, Phil, have you even said hello to your godmother?"

Philip looked at his feet. "Hello," he said. "It's good to meet you."

Eudora stared at Sylvia. "My goodness! I'd forgotten that Philip grew up there. You're a proper Canadian boy." She turned to her mother, who was already seated at the table, napkin tucked under her chin in readiness. "Mum, you remember Sylvia, and this is Philip—all grown up now."

Beatrice squinted at them both as if trying to clear the fog from her mind. "Ah, Sylvia, of course. How are you, dear?"

Sylvia leaned down to kiss her. "It's good to see you again, Mrs. Honeysett. Say hello, Phil."

"Hello," said Philip with an awkward wave.

"Isn't this lovely?" said Eudora. "Shall we take a seat and have some food? What can I get you to drink? I expect you might like a nice cup of tea, Sylvia. What would you like, Philip?"

"Do you have any soda?" asked Philip.

Eudora looked flummoxed.

"It's okay, Dora. Water is fine for both of us," said Sylvia. "I hardly drink tea these days. We Canadians are fueled by coffee."

*We Canadians.*

Eudora swallowed down her disappointment. "Oh. Of course. That's absolutely fine. Take a seat. I'll fetch you both a glass."

She returned to find the three of them sitting in uncomfortable silence, Sylvia wearing a fixed bright smile, while Beatrice eyed these strangers in her midst with suspicion and Philip looked as if he'd be more than happy for the ground to swallow him whole.

"Here we are. Please do help yourselves. I made Quiche Lorraine and Coronation Chicken for old times' sake, and Black Forest Gateau for dessert."

"Goodness. You needn't have gone to all this effort," said Sylvia, with a faintly critical edge to her voice.

"I wanted to. I thought as you weren't here for the Jubilee celebrations, we could have our own feast in honor of the Queen."

"That's very thoughtful," said Sylvia, helping herself to a minuscule portion of chicken.

"And, I've got you a little present, Philip," said Eudora, handing over a parcel. "I hope it fits."

"Thanks," said Philip, opening it up and pulling out a commemorative Jubilee T-shirt.

"Oh, that's very kind, Dora," said Sylvia, patting her friend's arm in a bid to cover her son's bewilderment.

Eudora gave a breezy smile. "And now you must tell us all about life in Canada. We're dying to hear, aren't we, Mum?"

"Is there any salad cream?" asked Beatrice through a mouthful of quiche.

After lunch, Sylvia persuaded Philip to take Beatrice for a walk around the garden. Eudora was grateful to have a little time with her old friend. It was clear from their forced lunchtime conversation that they had lost touch. Eudora hoped they could reconnect a little without Philip and her mother in the room.

"Philip's such a handsome boy," said Eudora. "You must be very proud."

"I am, but I keep looking 'round every time you call him Philip. Everyone calls him Phil."

"Oh. Sorry."

"It's fine, Dora. You weren't to know. Anyway, how is your mother? She seems a little confused."

Eudora pursed her lips and tried not to sound defensive. "She's fine. Life's not been easy for her." She'd never told anyone about what her mother did. She had hoped she might confide in Sylvia today, but something was telling her to keep her counsel.

Sylvia inclined her head toward Eudora as she nodded with sympathy. "And what about you now, Eudora? How is life?"

"It's . . ." Eudora hesitated. "It's fine. It was my twenty-fifth anniversary of working at the bank this year. They gave me a carriage clock."

"Fancy," said Sylvia in a teasing tone that Eudora didn't care for. "And what about living here?"

"It's fine. Mum and I get along just fine."

"Really?" Sylvia raised her eyebrows.

Eudora felt her hands ball into fists. "Mum needs me."

"But what about you, Dor? What about what you need? You were so happy when you met Sam again. Why didn't you move away with him? What on earth stopped you?"

Eudora wasn't sure if it was the judgmental note in Sylvia's tone or her endless boasting about their perfect life in Canada—her four-bedroom town house, their summer cabin by the lake, Ken becoming the youngest CEO in the history of the company—but something made Eudora snap.

"I had no choice. Mum needed me, and Sam had to move away so he could see his children. The two situations were incompatible."

"But you gave up your happiness, Dora. Again."

"You don't know what you're talking about."

"Dora. This is me. I know you."

Sylvia jumped as Eudora banged her fist on the table. "No. You don't know me. Not anymore. You know about society life in Toronto and coffee and soda! I haven't seen you for sixteen years, so you don't have the first idea how I feel. Now, I would appreciate it if you would mind your own business, Sylvia. I have made my choices and I stand by them."

Sylvia held up her hands. "Okay, okay, I'm sorry. I was just trying to help."

"I don't need your help. I don't need anyone's help."

Sylvia and Philip only stayed an hour longer. Eudora was relieved when she announced they would be leaving. It's one thing to know in your heart that you have remained frozen in time while the world moves on but quite another thing to be told it by the person you trust most.

Sylvia hugged Eudora before holding her at arm's length and staring into her eyes. "Take care, Dora, okay?"

Eudora saw the pity in her eyes and knew this would be the last time they ever saw each other. "You too."

As soon as they'd left, she picked up the plate holding the last of the Black Forest Gateau and threw the cake into the bin. Some things simply weren't to be.

# Chapter 17

THE PHONE CALL arrives out of the blue. Eudora hasn't been giving her application much thought lately. A month ago, it had preoccupied her every waking minute: the right to choose the ending to her story. In recent times, however, the clamor of death has been drowned out by the noisy distraction of life.

Eudora is listening to the radio, draining the last drop of tea after a late breakfast, her mind set on that day's crossword. Normally, she would be heading out the door for a swim, but she's been unable to muster the energy over the past week. She is doing her best to ignore a creeping apprehension that she may not be able to keep to her rigorous daily routine for much longer. It's been a tiring summer. She's sure the fatigue will pass.

Eudora starts as the insistent chirping of the telephone interrupts her peace. She wonders if it might be Stanley. Their evening calls have become more sporadic of late. Last night, Eudora didn't get to the phone in time. Stanley's message lacked its usual warmth:

"Eudora? Are you there? Just checking in as usual. Call me if you want to speak. Bye."

She had tried to call but the phone line had been engaged so it wasn't as if he was desperate to speak to her. He'd probably phoned Sheila instead.

Eudora picks up the receiver on the third ring and answers with a casual air.

"Hello?"

"Eudora?"

Eudora sits up straighter in her chair as she recognizes the voice. "Oh. Hello."

"Hello, Eudora. This is Greta Liebermann. Have I telephoned at a bad time?"

"I have a moment in my packed schedule," says Eudora.

The doctor hesitates.

"That was a joke, by the way," she adds.

"Ah yes, English humor, a useful tool when facing difficult subjects."

"Quite."

"Well, I'm sure you know why I am calling."

Eudora's hands begin to tremble. "You've made a decision about my application."

"Exactly. Thank you for sending your forms and all the information. I have now considered everything in full and have consulted with my colleagues."

*It's a refusal*, thinks Eudora, clasping her hands around the receiver to lessen the tremors.

"I want you to know that I have thought very hard about this."

*Please. Just tell me.*

"Having spoken to you and Petra and considered everything you told me, and having read your medical reports and living will"—the doctor pauses as if announcing the winner of a talent show—"I have come to the decision that we are able to help you, if it is what you really want."

"Oh." Eudora knows this is a rather understated reaction after what seems like a lifetime of waiting and hoping, but it's all she can manage as she tries to catch hold of her feelings. Her heart is beating so fast she feels as if it might burst from her chest. She squeezes her hands tight to stop the trembling. The doctor is still talking. Eudora knows she must listen, but all she can think is:

*Finally. Someone has heard me.*

"You must understand that we will keep asking you and checking right until the end. You can change your mind at any time, and of course you don't have to go ahead at all. It is your choice. Always."

*The end. Your choice.*

Eudora knows that this "deny death because we're really going to live forever" world would find the very notion depressing, but she doesn't. It's the answer to a question she has been asking for the longest time.

She exhales. "Thank you."

"So, Eudora, I can appreciate that this is a lot to take in. To be honest, this is the start of a big decision for you. Do you have any questions for me now?"

"What happens if I decide to go ahead?"

"We would make all the necessary arrangements for you to come over—flights, accommodations, and so on."

"And how long . . . ?"

"If you decide to proceed, you can come in a matter of weeks."

*Weeks.* It's a dizzying thought.

"But I want you to think hard about whether this is what you want. Nothing is decided. Talk to Petra or phone me. We are here for you. Please remember that."

"Thank you. Thank you very much."

"Take care, Eudora. Goodbye."

"Goodbye." Eudora sits, receiver in hand, unsure of what to do next. Her hands have stopped shaking but her heart is a drumbeat to her thoughts.

*This is it. This is it. The thing you want. An unexpected gift. Low-hanging fruit. Take it. You should take it. This is it.*

The very idea gives her a surge of unexpected energy. She hauls herself to her feet.

"I must go for a walk to clear my head," she tells Montgomery, reaching down to stroke him. The cat nuzzles her hand for a few seconds before stretching out his body, yawning and falling back asleep.

As Eudora makes her way down the front path and onto the street, she spots Maggie pushing the pram through her own front gate. "Eudora! I haven't seen you for a while. How are you?"

*Trying to contemplate my mortality in peace*, thinks Eudora. "I'm quite well, thank you. How are you all?"

"We're pretty good, thanks. Rose seems to be enjoying school, which is obviously a big relief, and this little madam," she says, pointing toward a beaming Daisy, "actually slept through the night last night."

"That's good to hear. You look a lot less tired, if I may say."

"Thank you. Anyway, I'd better get her inside. Let's have tea soon, shall we?"

"That would be lovely," says Eudora, relieved that Maggie has gifted her an excuse to be on her way. "See you later."

Eudora keeps her head down as she walks. She doesn't

want any more distractions today. She falls into a slow but steady rhythm as the realization of her conversation with Doctor Liebermann sinks in. The coin has landed.

*Heads, you win, Eudora. This is what you want, isn't it?*

*Isn't it?*

She doesn't remember walking into the shop until she inhales the smell of fresh bread and realizes that she's staring at a packet of French Fancies.

"It's too tempting sometimes, isn't it?" says a voice beside her.

Eudora turns to see Audrey. Her face is smiling but tired. Eudora recognizes the empty look of a hollowed-out soul, worn down by grief. "Hello, Audrey. How are you?"

"Lonely," blurts out Audrey, surprising them both. "Sorry. You're not supposed to say that, are you? You're supposed to pretend you're fine."

"Yes, you probably are, but I'm not always sure that's the best way," says Eudora.

Audrey nods. "I come here every day because the ladies behind the registers are so friendly. Apart from the group, I hardly ever see anyone. And sometimes I'm fine. I can potter around at home, listen to the radio, or do some gardening, but . . ." Her voice trails off as her face falls. "It's the mornings and the evenings I can't bear with no one to talk to. My son says I should get a pet." She snorts with derision.

"Maybe you should," says Eudora. "I've got a cat. He's a little bad-tempered but I'm quite fond of him."

"More reliable than a human, eh?" says Audrey.

"More constant perhaps," says Eudora.

"I know it's the grief talking and I won't always feel like this, but you just wonder what the point is sometimes, don't you?"

Eudora fixes her gaze on Audrey. "Yes," she says. "Unfortunately, you do."

A few days later, Eudora is finishing the crossword and hoping Rose might pop in after school. She hasn't seen her or Stanley since their trip to the café. Despite relishing the quiet, Eudora misses the nonsense. Her only constant is Montgomery, who has scarcely left her side of late. He is still highly demanding when it comes to food, but rather than prowling the neighborhood, he prefers to seek her out, stretching long on the sofa, dozing, or watching her through one narrowed green eye. He's even stopped biting her.

"Maybe you're mellowing in your old age, eh?" she says, scratching under his chin. He juts out his jaw in approval. After twelve years, Eudora finally understands all the fuss about the constant companionship of pets. She must tell Audrey about this when they next meet.

The room darkens as if someone has dimmed the lights and a low growl of thunder echoes in the sky. Montgomery looks up in alarm.

"It's all right," Eudora reassures him. "Nothing to worry about." Montgomery fixes her with a look as if he understands before his eyes grow heavy and he falls back to sleep. Eudora can hear the excited chatter of schoolchildren on their way home. She makes her way to the window and peers out through the net curtains.

"Heaven help me," she mutters. "I'm becoming one of those old people who stare out at the world hoping it might notice them."

Still, the steady stream of children of all shapes and sizes running and skipping along the street proves to be an enjoyable spectacle. The bruise-colored sky and whipped-up breeze is making many of them excitable at the prospect of a storm. Small fingers point to the sky in surprise as another flash of lightning brings a distant rumble of thunder and squeals of delicious fear. Eudora smiles at their wonder.

It's not long before she spies Rose, ambling along the street, but to Eudora's dismay she is arm in arm with Jada. Eudora isn't surprised to notice that Jada is doing all the talking while Rose hangs on her every word. As they approach Eudora's front gate, she hears Rose interject.

"That's where Eudora lives," she says, nudging her friend.

Jada looks toward Eudora's hiding place behind the net curtain and pulls a face. The girl can't see her, but it feels to Eudora as if the contemptuous expression is aimed directly at her. Eudora takes a step back. "That old lady?" says Jada in disgust.

"She was young once like us," says Rose in a small, brave voice, which makes Eudora long to hug her.

"Whatever," says Jada. "Let's go to yours. I want to see the baby."

"Okay," says Rose, glancing back toward Eudora's house before turning to follow her friend.

Eudora watches an empty polystyrene container toss in the wind as the storm takes hold, ripping the leaves from the trees. She draws the curtains and puts on the lamps in a bid to make everything cozier.

"Come on," she says to Montgomery. "Let's have some tea and watch that program Rose likes."

Eudora has decided that Richard Osman is a fine man: intelligent, articulate, and extremely witty. She enjoys spending half an hour in his company but has to admit that it's not as much fun as when Rose is there, shouting out the answers. Despite the fat raindrops pelting the windowpane, Eudora can still hear the sound of life next door: Daisy crying and Rose shrieking with laughter at something her new friend has said. Normally, Eudora would have found this reassuring, but tonight it serves only as a reminder of her solitude.

At six o'clock, the newsreader with the kind face delivers the headlines. As soon as Eudora is satisfied that nothing has changed, that there is still no one in charge able to make a sensible or competent decision, she switches it off and makes her way to the kitchen to prepare dinner. She's not particularly hungry but knows she must eat and opts for a tin of soup. Cream of tomato seems to offer the correct level of comfort tonight. Eudora is emptying the can into a pan when there is a brilliant white flash followed by a vicious crack of thunder, which shakes the whole house, sending Montgomery darting past her ankles and out through the cat flap.

"Don't go out, silly cat!" she cries before realizing there is no point. He'll no doubt find a bush to shelter under until he feels safe enough to return inside. She turns back to her soup-stirring. The next sound Eudora hears is a screeching of tires. She switches off the stove and hurries to the front door as quickly as she can, even though in her heart she knows and fears what she will see. A large, expensive car has been left at an alarming angle in front of Rose's driveway, its lights shooting a beam into the darkness, illuminating the darts of rain. The driver's door has been left flung open. Eudora can hear a woman's shaken voice, talking to someone on Rose's doorstep.

"It came out of nowhere. I had no time to stop!"

"Come inside. I'll go and see," says a voice, which Eudora recognizes as Rob's.

"Daddy? Is it Monty? Is he . . . ?"

"Wait here, Rose," says Rob. Eudora watches as he walks toward the road. She sees his body shrink despondently as he discovers the cat. Very carefully he takes off his coat and scoops Montgomery into his arms. As he turns, he registers Eudora standing at the door. His expression says everything. "Shall I bring him in?" he asks. Eudora gives the smallest nod.

"Daddy?" cries Rose. "I want to come with you!" She darts out into the street and follows him up the path into Eudora's house.

Rob carries Montgomery into the living room. "Where shall I . . . ?"

"On the sofa, please. He likes it there," says Eudora, a choke catching in her throat.

"I could call a vet or we could take him in our car . . . ?" suggests Rob. Eudora gives a small shake of her head.

She feels Rose take hold of her hand as they stand back and gaze at Montgomery. His breathing is rapid with increasingly longer pauses in between.

"He's dying, isn't he?" says Rose through her tears.

"Yes. He is," whispers Eudora. "But he's not in pain. I remember this happening to a cat on my uncle's farm during the war."

"I'm very sorry," says Rob.

"Thank you," says Eudora.

"It was Jada's mum. He ran out in front of her car," says Rose in an accusing tone.

"It's not her fault," says Eudora. "It's no one's fault."

Rose wraps her arms around Eudora's middle and sobs. "Why is life so sad sometimes?"

Eudora doesn't try to suppress her tears this time. "Perhaps it's the universe's way of making you appreciate the happier times."

"That makes sense," says Rose. She turns to Eudora after a while. "Maybe we should take turns telling Montgomery what he means to us, so that he knows."

"I think that's a very good idea, Rose," says Eudora, exchanging a glance with Rob. "You go first."

Rose kneels in front of Montgomery and strokes his head. "You were the best cat ever. Thank you. I love you and I will never forget you."

She turns to Eudora, who approaches and takes a seat next to him. "Montgomery. Monty." Her voice falters. Rose reaches out and touches her on the arm. Eudora takes a deep breath and continues. "I'm going to miss you. Who is going to bite me now and try to trip me up on the stairs?" She sighs. "I don't know what I'm going to do without you. Life won't be the same." She rests a hand on his head. He lets out a small shudder and is still. "Goodbye, old friend," says Eudora. "I'm glad you didn't suffer." And with that, Eudora Honeysett knows exactly how her story will end.

## 2005
## SIDNEY AVENUE, SOUTH-EAST LONDON

It was the fifth time her mother had called an ambulance that week. Eudora had recently received a letter from the London Ambulance Frequent Caller department telling her that they were aware of the situation and would review her mother in six months. Eudora didn't know whether to laugh or cry, because the letter didn't make a jot of difference. Beatrice still called and the paramedics always came. Eudora would often beg them not to take her mother to A&E. They were very kind and understanding but had little choice because of Beatrice's age and frailty. She would complain of a stomachache, usually caused by inactivity, or a headache because she refused to drink water, and they would "pop her in for a checkup." She would be whisked away for eight or nine hours and then returned to Eudora confused and exhausted before the whole cycle began again the next day.

"Why do you do it, Mum? You're like the little boy who calls wolf."

Beatrice fixed her with rheumy, scared eyes. "I like the ambulances and I feel safe in a place with doctors."

Eudora tried not to feel insulted that she didn't feel safe at home with her. She also wondered at her mother's desire to spend the best part of twenty-four hours in a place where you were likely to leave with more germs than when you arrived. So far this year her mother had suffered with hospital-contracted pneumonia, MRSA, and bedsores. Eudora was exhausted. She knew the bus timetables and visiting hours by heart and most of the nurses by name.

"Back again?" asked a particularly friendly nurse called Helen.

"It would seem that way," said Eudora wearily.

"They should give you a loyalty card."

Eudora gave a weak laugh.

Of course she was grateful to the NHS for all their efforts. The paramedics, doctors, and nurses were patient, good-humored, and always kind to her bewildered mother. It just didn't seem like much of a life for either of them, traipsing back and forth from house to hospital in a bid to preserve the existence of a ninety-five-year-old woman. Eudora felt sure that Beatrice Honeysett was the most examined, tested, and treated woman ever. While she was pleased that they cared so much, she had to question the quality of life it delivered for them both.

Beatrice Honeysett had lost her husband and happiness in 1944. As a result, she had been unfortunate to live a long, unhappy life. Eudora had done her best to make her mother happy but now, as she started to embark on her own twilight years, she wondered what the point had been.

That's not to say there hadn't been joyful times. Eudora loved her mother. They had enjoyed holidays and outings together, but theirs had been a life held back by their shared history, by the war, by the loss of Albert, and the tragic death of Stella. The past had anchored Beatrice to an existence mired with regret and sadness. Despite her best efforts, Eudora had become entangled in its murky depths too. She often found herself wondering not when but if there would ever be an end to it.

The end came unexpectedly for Beatrice, as it happened. The fifth emergency call turned out to be well-founded: a heart attack followed by a prolonged period in the hospital. Dutifully, Eudora visited every day, still thinking her mother would last forever. The hospital staff seemed to think so too. There were teams of occupational therapists eager to get Beatrice shuffling up and down with a walker; a rehabilitation coordinator, who talked of a spell in a community hospital; and wearily smiling doctors, who made positive noises about Beatrice's "markers." Eudora wished she hadn't listened to any of them. She could see what was happening before her eyes: that her mother wasn't eating, could barely speak, slept almost all day. She didn't want to "get going" or eat flabby fish pie and overcooked broccoli. She wanted to leave this world with a little dignity and respect, not with a breathing tube up her nose and a team of overworked nurses having to turn her onto her side every day because of bedsores.

Eudora wished she'd been stronger. She wished she'd taken her mother home and nursed her, dressed her in a clean nightie, tucked her up in a freshly made bed, brushed her hair, and told her that she loved her until she slipped away. But it didn't happen like that.

Instead, she returned home exhausted after another day at her mother's bedside, another day trying to get her to drink water through a straw like a child and accept a spoonful of mashed potato like a baby. She left feeling furiously angry but had no idea with whom. She hadn't told her mother that she loved her or smoothed her hair before she left. She arrived home, too tired to eat, and had fallen into bed. She was woken six hours later by the phone ringing. The friendly nurse's voice was quiet and laced with sorrow.

"I'm sorry to tell you that Beatrice passed away half an hour ago."

Eudora thanked her for calling and replaced the phone in its cradle. Then she wrapped her arms around her body and sobbed.

## Chapter 18

EUDORA MAKES THE call to the clinic the very next day. She doesn't need to linger over this decision any longer. She is resolved. Eudora's never been surer of anything. It's time. She is relieved as Petra answers.

"I'd like to go ahead," says Eudora without a hint of doubt.

Petra pauses before answering. "Can I ask what has changed, Eudora?"

Eudora isn't sure how truthfully to answer this. Nothing has changed. That's the point. Nothing ever changes. And now she wants to call an end to it all. She selects her words with care. "Nothing has changed. I have merely considered everything in full, and, given my medical conditions and inevitably deteriorating health, I know the time is right."

"Have you discussed this with anyone?"

"There's really no need. I've made up my mind."

"What about Rose?"

Eudora flinches. "I hope you're not suggesting that I talk to a ten-year-old about my impending death."

"No, of course not, but I get the feeling that you have a strong relationship with her. How will she feel about this?"

Eudora sighs. "I don't know. I will write her a letter to explain. She's very bright. She'll understand one day."

"It is your choice, Eudora, and Doctor Liebermann is satisfied with what you have told us."

"Precisely. My death. My choice."

"Okay. Then let me give you the details of the documents we will require and the logistics of your journey. Will you be traveling alone?"

"Yes."

"In which case, would you permit me to meet you at the airport and accompany you on your final journey?"

It's as if she has reached out through the telephone and offered her hand. "Thank you, Petra. That would be very kind."

They bury Montgomery underneath the apple tree because it was his favorite place to sit while contemplating the chattering blue tits above his head. Rose insists that they have a "proper funeral with singing and prayers and stuff." Eudora decides to indulge her one last time, although she is starting to regret it now as the early October chill nips at her bones.

She stares into the faces of her fellow mourners. Rose has taken the funeral arrangements very seriously. She appointed Rob as chief and only pallbearer. He is now dutifully holding the old banana box containing Montgomery, which Rose decorated with "all the glitter I could find." The effect is startlingly beautiful as the box seems almost alive with color, sparkling in the pale autumn sunshine.

Rose had instructed everyone that black clothing is not

allowed, even though Montgomery had worn the color all his life. Instead, they must wear something that reminds them of him.

Maggie is wearing a scarf decorated with tiny smiling cats, which Daisy is currently trying to stuff into her mouth. Rose distributes cat-ear headbands to those who can be cajoled into wearing them. Eudora has chosen a brooch whose color reminds her of Montgomery's steely yellow-green eyes and politely refuses Rose's offer of a headband. Stanley has invited Sheila along to this strange ceremony. Eudora watches as she falls upon the headband and encourages Stanley to wear one too. Rose laughs as they both plonk them on their heads. Eudora finds this ridiculous. She hasn't spoken to Stanley since their disagreement in the café. Actually, disagreement is too strong a word. It was a silly misunderstanding. Eudora knows she behaved badly but doesn't have the first idea what to do about it. Eighty-five is not the age at which to develop a demonstrative side to one's personality, and yet she misses their evening chats. She misses the carefree silliness.

Rose's outfit is predictably overstated in its cat theme. She wears a T-shirt emblazoned with a photograph of a tabby cat's face and the word "Purrrrrfect!" and black leggings decorated with miniature gold cats. As self-appointed minister for the proceedings, Rose takes her place in front of the deep hole that Rob dug the day before.

"Dearly beloved, we are gathered here today to celebrate the life of our good friend Montgomery."

"Eee!" exclaims Daisy from the comfort of her mother's arms.

"Thank you, Daisy," says Rose. "That is my sister's way of telling you that she is sad for the loss of Montgomery. I now invite you all to do the same and then we will sing a song and say a prayer before the . . . What's it called, Mum?"

"The committal?"

"That's it. The committal."

Eudora sighs. She pulls her coat and scarf tighter around her shoulders. The cold is making her bones and soul ache today.

"Are you all right, Eudora?" whispers Stanley as Rose embarks on a lengthy eulogy to her friend.

"Fine, thank you," says Eudora, keeping her eyes fixed forward.

"I could fetch you a chair, if you like," offers Sheila.

"No. There's really no need. I'm quite all right." She notices Sheila shrink a little and regrets her tone. Stanley pats Sheila's arm.

"Eudora, would you like to say a few words?" asks Rose.

Eudora really wouldn't, but everyone is staring at her now. She sighs. "Thank you for being a constant companion. May you rest in peace."

Rose stares at her. "Is that it?"

"It is."

"Okay. Let's sing our song then. I couldn't find one about cats, so we're going to sing 'All Things Bright and Beautiful' because Mummy says everyone knows that."

The sound they produce is enough to bring all the cats

of the neighborhood into the garden. Eudora winces as they try and fail to hit the high notes.

"That was lovely," says Rose. Maggie catches Rob's eye and giggles. "What? Mummy, don't laugh. This is the serious bit."

Eudora has had enough. She's cold and miserable and in desperate need of a cup of tea. "Can we please just get on with it," she says.

Rose looks crestfallen. "Sorry. I just wanted to make it special."

"It is special, Rose," says Maggie. "Sorry. I shouldn't have laughed. Go on, do your next bit."

Rose looks unsure but nods to her father, who carefully places the box in the hole. Rose picks up a trowel and scoops some earth out of a compost bag.

"Earth to earth, ashes to ashes," she says, flicking the soil on top of the box. "Dust to dusty. We know Major Tom is rusty."

Rob starts to laugh and it's not long before Maggie, Stanley, and Sheila join in.

"Oh, for heaven's sake," says Eudora, turning on her heel and retreating to the house. Once inside she switches on the kettle and tries to warm her shivering joints on the radiator. Her hands are shaking uncontrollably and she feels faint.

"Eudora. I'm sorry. We should have reigned Rose in," says Maggie, appearing in the doorway.

"It's all right," says Eudora. "I'll be fine once I've had a cup of tea."

⁂

The tea helps a little. Eudora lets the chatter wash over her as Maggie and Rose hand out sandwiches and cakes. She doesn't feel like participating today. She is so tired.

"Was it all right?" asks Rose, coming to sit by Eudora, worry creasing her face.

"It was lovely," says Eudora. "You did Montgomery proud."

"That's good. I wanted it to be special. I'm sorry if I went a bit over the top. I do that sometimes."

"Do you, Rose? I'd never noticed," says Eudora. Rose laughs.

As the afternoon wears on and endless cups of tea are made and drunk, Eudora finds herself wishing that they'd all go home. She doesn't want to be part of this anymore. She looks at Rose playing peek-a-boo with her sister and the way Rob and Maggie smile at each other. She sees Stanley sharing a joke with Sheila and knows he'll be all right. *It's enough*, she thinks. *It's time to go.*

Eudora has already decided to tell them that she's going on holiday. She will write letters before she leaves explaining the truth. She will leave them with the solicitor when she goes for her meeting tomorrow, instructing her to distribute them after she's gone. It's better that way. Eudora doesn't want anyone to be an accessory or to try and talk her out of it. *My death, my way* is her mantra now.

"A holiday? I love holidays! Can we come?" asks Rose, clapping her hands together.

"Unfortunately not. It's during term time."

"Awwww."

"I know."

"Where are you going?" asks Stanley. It's one of the few times he's spoken to her today.

"Switzerland."

"Switzerland?" he says in surprise.

"Oh, it's lovely there," says Sheila. "Vic and I went on a few walking holidays around the mountains. Where are you going?"

"Basel," says Eudora. "I thought it would be good for my health." *Oh, the irony.*

"Well. There's a thing," says Stanley. "Funny, you've never mentioned it before."

Eudora can see a cloud of suspicion in his expression and knows she must nip it in the bud. "It was an impulse decision. I saw an advertisement in the newspaper and thought, why not?"

Stanley fixes his eyes on her as if trying to glean the truth. She holds his gaze. "I should come with you. I could do with a holiday."

"You should!" cries Sheila. "It's a wonderful place."

"That would be most agreeable," says Eudora. "But unfortunately, it's all booked and I'm going next week."

"Next week?" says Stanley.

"That's right. Maybe next time," she says, turning away.

"I'll see you before you go, won't I?" asks Rose.

Eudora hasn't considered this. The thought sends shivers through her body. "I'm only going for a short while. There's no need for tearful goodbyes."

"Okay. Might you be able to get me one of those massive

Toblerones, please? Dad brought me one back when he went on a business trip there. They're mega."

"I'll try," says Eudora, longing for the conversation to end and for the assembled company to leave.

As she is finally ushering everyone to the door, Stanley turns to her. "Tell you what, I'll take you to the airport. Where are you flying from?"

"Gatwick, but there's really no need."

"I insist," says Stanley, his face grave with intent.

"You have to let him. He won't take no for an answer," says Sheila. She leans in and kisses Eudora on the cheek. "Have a great trip. We'll miss you."

Eudora is momentarily glad that she's leaving Stanley with this generous-hearted woman. "Thank you. And thank you, Stanley. It's a very kind offer." Stanley nods before following everyone else out the door.

Eudora doesn't wave them goodbye, not today. She closes the door with relief. The silence of the house draws her in. Soon there will be nothing but silence. A shiver of panic quickens her heart. She catches sight of her father's photograph gazing out at her with smiling kindness. She places a hand over her heart and then touches the picture.

"All shall be well," she says. "Won't it, Dad?"

## Chapter 19

EUDORA CONSIDERS LYING to Stanley about when she is leaving for Switzerland. It would be easy enough to slip away like a fugitive one day. Less emotionally charged somehow. She has decided to keep her emotions in check from this moment on. What's required now is practical focus.

Petra has been particularly helpful. Once she understood that Eudora's decision was final, she made the flight and accommodation arrangements on her behalf and will be there to meet her at the airport. Eudora takes comfort in this. Even though they've never met, she senses that she can rely on Petra.

Eudora is satisfied that the loose threads of her life have been put in order. Last week she visited her solicitor. It was a cursory hour-long exchange with a woman Eudora had never met, who looked young enough to be her great-granddaughter. For once, Eudora was grateful for the casual indifference of the world. The woman was courteous enough but kept glancing at her phone, whose green light flashed constantly like a pulse.

This was another trait of the modern world that Eudora detested. No one ever gave you their full attention. There was always an urgent news flash about a royal princess buying shoes or a constant spewing of the same story about Trump or Putin or that infernal Brexit nonsense, the same story told with the words regurgitated into a slightly different order. Eudora had even caught Radio 4 in the act recently. It made her want to pack her bags and leave immediately.

On this occasion, however, the solicitor's disinterest suited Eudora well. She wanted to ensure that the letters to be opened once she died were filed along with her will and that this woman gave her the final documentation she required for her trip without question. The woman performed both tasks without comment. Eudora left the offices after the meeting confident that she was making the right decision.

On the day before Eudora is due to leave, she wakes early. A dazzling streak of sunlight is forcing its way through the curtains. She is about to struggle out of bed to feed Montgomery when she remembers. He's gone and soon she will be too.

"No time to waste," she tells the empty house. "We must keep moving."

She starts to pack after breakfast. It doesn't take long. Eudora tries not to dwell on the fact that she only requires a certain number of outfits now. She puts her official documents in the orange foolscap folder she bought specially and lays it on the bed alongside her small wheeled suitcase. It had been a gift from the bank when she retired. "For all your future adventures, with best wishes," said the card. If only they knew.

Eudora stands back and appraises what's left of her life. It doesn't look like much, but then what are humans when it comes down to it? We arrive with nothing, accumulate far too much, and leave with nothing. The thought makes her breathless with dizziness and also resolved to telephone Stanley. The last thing she needs on her trip to the airport is a yawning hollow of silence in the back of a taxi, forcing her to contemplate the enormity of what she is about to do.

He answers after three rings. "Stanley? It's Eudora. I wanted to ask if the offer of a lift to the airport still stands."

"Of course. I'm a man of my word. What time's your flight?" His tone is cursory. Eudora regrets the loss of their jocular, easy chatter in some ways, but it will make things easier in the long run.

"Thank you. I'm traveling tomorrow. My flight leaves from Gatwick at 1:50 P.M."

"Okay. I'll pick you up at ten o'clock to give you enough time."

"Thank you. That's very kind."

"Right-ho."

Eudora stares at the handset for a moment after he's gone. *It's better this way. Better for everyone.*

The journey to the airport is mercifully short. Luckily, Stanley has the radio on and they're playing the music quiz he likes. Eudora doesn't join in this time. She is struck dumb with nerves. She wants to get to the airport and get on with it now. As they approach Gatwick, she notices Stanley following the signs to the car park.

"You can just drop me off at the terminal. I don't want to put you to any trouble."

"It's no trouble at all, Eudora," he says. "I can help you with your bags and make sure you check in okay."

Eudora can see how determined he is. She doesn't want an argument today and besides, she would appreciate someone to help her find her way. "That's very kind."

Stanley is true to his word. He escorts her all the way inside, waiting while she checks in for her flight.

"Thank you, Stanley. I'll be fine now," says Eudora. She's not sure how to say goodbye. She sincerely hopes he's not going to try and hug her.

Stanley glances at his watch. "You've got hours to wait. How about a coffee before you go through?"

*Or a stiff whisky*, thinks Eudora. She is surprised to realize how welcome she finds his suggestion. She thought she would be happy to banish Stanley and face this alone, but in the cold light of day, and with the hours stretching before her, a little human company is precisely what she needs. No sense in dwelling on the inevitable. "Yes, very well. Thank you."

Eudora finds a table while Stanley fetches the drinks. It's the first time she's ever been to an airport and is finding the hum and chatter of its constant activity rather dizzying.

"Here we are," says Stanley, setting the drink in front of her. "A white coffee just as the lady likes it."

"Thank you," says Eudora, momentarily thrown by the thought that it is the last time they will do this together.

She bats away memories of that magical night at the pizza restaurant with Stanley and Rose.

*Focus, Eudora. The wheels are turning. This is no time for emotion.*

"Are you looking forward to your holiday then?"

Stanley's question pulls Eudora back to the present. For a second, she wonders what on earth he's talking about and then remembers her half-truth. Eudora doesn't enjoy lying. It's not in her nature. Part of her longs to tell him the truth, to share it all. It would be a relief in some ways, but she knows it's impossible. He would never understand. She hopes he might comprehend it a little after he's read her letter. She regrets the fact that there's no alternative to her course of action but consoles herself that he has Sheila and Rose. They will survive without her. "It will be good to get away," she says, stirring her coffee with a teaspoon.

"Shame you didn't give me a bit more notice. I might have come with you."

Stanley's hurt tone pricks Eudora's conscience. "It's best this way," she mutters.

He frowns. "What's going on, Eudora?"

She studies her cup, avoiding his gaze. "What do you mean?"

"I mean that you've changed."

"No, I haven't," she says indignantly, starting to regret her decision to agree to coffee.

Stanley fixes her with a look. "Yes, you have. Ever since Rose started school, actually."

"I don't know what you're talking about." She longs for him to leave, longs to be on her way and for this all to be over. She doesn't want Stanley to lift the lid on the feelings she has carefully packed away.

"Oh, don't you? Then let me spell it out for you. You've become distant and unfriendly. I thought you were someone I could rely on. A friend. But when I wanted to talk to you about Sheila, you cut me off like you didn't care. And I found that hurtful, Eudora. I thought we were friends."

Eudora doesn't know what to say. She stares straight ahead.

"See?" continues Stanley. "You can't even look me in the eye, can you? You think so little of me. Why is that, Eudora? Why can't you let people reach out to you? Why do you push us all away?"

Eudora is breathing fast now. This is exactly what she wanted to avoid, but it feels as if she's at the top of a hill about to hurtle down the slope. She can't hold back much longer. Maybe it's time to speak the truth. Stanley is staring at her now, waiting. She knows she owes him an explanation, that she's let him down. Eudora keeps her eyes fixed forward as she speaks. "Everyone I've ever cared about has left me. And you will too."

"What do you mean?" asks Stanley, frowning as he tries to understand. "I'm not going anywhere."

Eudora takes a deep breath. *No going back now.* "No. But I am."

A shadow of fear clouds Stanley's face. "What are you talking about? You're going to Switzerland."

She turns to face him. She needs to look him in the eye

as she says it. "To die, Stanley." She is surprised by the sense of calm that descends on her when saying this out loud.

Stanley slumps back in his seat. It takes him a while to speak. "No," he says, shaking his head in disbelief. "You can't do that."

Eudora folds her arms. "I've decided. I wasn't going to tell you, but you may as well know."

He's still shaking his head. "I don't understand. Why would you do that?"

She fixes her gaze on him. "Because I'm old and tired and done with life. My body is failing me. It's time. I want to choose the way I die, and this is the only way to do that."

"But what about the people left behind. What about Rose?"

Eudora shifts in her chair. "Rose has her family and school friends. She will be fine. She will forget about me. And so will you," she says quietly.

Stanley shakes his head rapidly. "You're lying to yourself and you're wrong. We're your friends. We care about you. We want you to be happy."

Eudora sighs. "You can't make people happy. I tried to make my mother and my sister happy but I couldn't. People make their choices, and this is mine."

A bloom of red rises to Stanley's cheeks. "And that's it. You've made your choice and to hell with Rose and me?"

Eudora glares at him. His refusal to see her side of things galvanizes her determination. "Of course not, but I need to be in control of my death. Surely you can understand that."

Stanley shakes his head. "I don't understand at all. I

watched my Ada die right in front of my eyes. It was the most peaceful thing I've ever seen. She slipped away."

"That's what I intend to do. I want a good death like Hannah described when she gave the talk at our group. But it's not possible in this country. Everyone is so busy trying to save your life rather than just letting you go."

"But you're going too soon. You've still got life to live."

Eudora purses her lips. "I've made my decision. I'm sorry you can't respect that."

Stanley throws up his hands. "And that's it, is it? You're just going to go all on your own, chasing after your so-called good death."

"I can assure you, Stanley, that my chasing days are far behind me."

His eyes flash with anger. Eudora has never seen him like this. "Well, let me tell you something, Eudora, and I never thought I'd say this. I think you're a coward."

Eudora is affronted. "I am not a coward. It is *my* life and *my* death, and I will end it as I see fit."

"And you think this will be a good ending, do you, alone in some stuffy room instead of surrounded by people who love you? You'd rather some strangers did it for you? Why can't you let it happen naturally?"

Eudora is angry now. *Why won't this infuriating man understand?* She jabs a finger as she speaks. "Because I don't want to end up like my mother, dying alone in the hospital, my life prolonged unnecessarily. I want to go on my own terms." She bangs her fists on the table as she says this, slopping coffee into the saucer.

Stanley lets out an exasperated sigh. "You're not your mother, Eudora. Why can't you realize that? And you have so many reasons to live, people who care about you and need you, who love you, who'd be there for you to the end if only you'd let them!" Eudora shakes her head. She doesn't want to hear this. It's too late. Stanley's phone begins to ring. He forces his gaze from Eudora to the screen. "It's Rose. She's trying to FaceTime me."

"You'd better answer it then," says Eudora, grateful for the interruption.

"Hello, Rose. No school today?" says Stanley, glancing at Eudora as he answers.

"No, I've got a cold. I thought I'd phone to see if you'd arrived at the airport? I love airports."

"Yes, we're here," says Stanley. "I'm just having coffee with Eudora." He holds up the phone so that Eudora can see Rose's face.

Eudora's throat goes dry. She forces herself to speak. "Hello, Rose. Sorry to hear you're not well."

"I'm okay," says Rose. "Are you excited about your holiday? I wish I could come with you."

Eudora avoids Stanley's gaze. "I think you'll have more fun with your new school friends."

"Mmmm. When will you be back?"

Eudora sees sadness in her eyes. "What's wrong, Rose?"

Rose sniffs. "Nothing. Shall I show you a coin trick? Stanley taught me."

"What's wrong, Rose?" repeats Eudora. "Is it Jada?"

The little girl shrugs. "It's nothing."

"Tell me, Rose. I can't help you if you don't tell me."

Tears spring quickly to Rose's eyes. "She's being mean. She started off all friendly, but now she won't talk to me and she won't let anyone else be friends with me either. It's exactly the same as at my last school." She sobs as the words tumble from her. Eudora catches sight of Stanley's worried expression. "Sorry," says Rose, wiping her tears with balled-up fists.

"It's all right, Rose," begins Eudora.

"So when are you coming back?" she asks, her face hopeful with forced bravery. "It's my birthday soon. I need you to help me plan my party."

*I need you.* Eudora swallows. She can feel Stanley's eyes boring into her. "Listen carefully, Rose. This is very important. You are the most remarkable little girl I have ever met. You are clever and funny and wise. Jada doesn't deserve a friend like you. You must ignore her and find another friend—someone who is worthy of you."

"You're my friend, Eudora. You're the most remarkable old lady I've ever met, and I bumped into Mary Berry with Mum once. She's lovely but nowhere near as lovely as you."

Eudora doesn't realize she's crying until she notices the teardrop on her hand. She hears a voice in the background at Rose's house. "That's Mum calling me for lunch. Sorry, Eudora. I've got to go but I'll see you soon, okay? I miss you. Bye."

Eudora dabs at her eyes with a freshly pressed handkerchief as the little girl's face disappears from the screen. "Goodbye, Rose," she says. "I'll miss you too."

## AUGUST 1940
## SIDNEY AVENUE, SOUTH-EAST LONDON

"More tea, dear?" asked Beatrice, gesturing toward the Sadler teapot nestled in its hand-crocheted cozy. The cozy was the product of a recent period of intense domestic activity on Beatrice's part, which had also resulted in a room-by-room spring cleaning, three new dresses for Eudora, and several pairs of socks for Albert.

"Your mother is nesting," said Albert to Eudora one night when he was tucking her in to bed. "It's something mummies do when they're getting ready for their baby's arrival." Eudora wished her mother would stop. The whole thing was making Beatrice extremely irritable. Eudora didn't see why it was necessary to hang new curtains in the living room. It wasn't as if the baby would notice. Her mother seemed to be wearing herself out. The thought of being left alone with her after her father's departure was making Eudora sick with nerves.

"I've got time for one more cup," he said. "Thank you, darling."

Beatrice's face lit up. As the years rolled by, Eudora would often return to the truth that no one ever made her mother smile as her father had. She reached for the milk jug. "Oh dear, we've run out of milk. Eudora, would you be a dear?"

"Of course," said Eudora, carrying the jug to the kitchen. She could hear her parents talking in low voices. Eudora lingered by the door so she could eavesdrop on what wasn't meant for her ears.

"I don't know how I'm going to manage, Albert."

"You will, my darling. Dora is a good girl. She'll help you."

"But she's just a child. I wish you didn't have to go."

"I know. So do I."

"What will happen, Albert? What will happen to you?" Beatrice's voice had a hysterical edge, her words melting to tears. Eudora heard her father's chair scrape against the floor as he moved forward to comfort his wife.

"It's all right, my darling. Everything will be all right. Shhh now, don't cry. You have to be strong and promise me you'll go back to Suffolk at the first hint of danger."

"I promise," she said in a muffled voice.

Eudora waited until she heard her mother's sobs subside before returning with the milk. Her father stood up as she entered the room and smiled at her. He placed a hand on Beatrice's shoulder and held out his other to Eudora. She put down the milk jug and reached for it as Beatrice looked up, resting a hand on top of Albert's.

"My wonderful girls," he said. A shaft of sunlight was streaming through from the garden and everything was bathed in light. Eudora would recall this moment whenever she was in need of comfort. She had felt so loved, standing in the radiant warmth of her father's presence.

Eudora accompanied her father to the end of the road. Beatrice accepted his advice to stay at home and rest. They both knew it would be too much for her. Eudora had hopscotched up and down the pavement while she waited for them to say goodbye.

"Careful you don't step on the cracks, or the bears might get you," said Albert with false cheer as he joined her on the street and they fell into step.

Eudora gave a weak smile but inside her stomach was churning. She reached for his hand. He squeezed it in reply as they walked in silence. She wanted this moment to last forever and she most certainly didn't want to let go of his hand. Albert kept a steady pace. Eudora's heart sank as they neared the end of the road.

"Can I walk with you to the train station?"

Albert gazed down at her. "I'm sorry, Dora. Your mother would worry and so would I. Let's say our goodbyes here, eh?"

Eudora panicked. They hadn't even reached the end of the road. There were at least a dozen paces to go. Albert saw her distress and knelt down in front of her, hands resting on her shoulders.

"All shall be well, and all shall be well, and all manner of thing shall be well," he said. "You don't need to worry, Dora. Whatever happens, I'll always be here." He placed a reassuring hand over her heart, kissed her on the cheek, and took his leave. Eudora blinked back tears, wiping her eyes with the handkerchief her mother had pressed for her yesterday. She had to be as brave and strong as her father now. She turned swiftly and marched back along the street, taking care above all else to avoid the cracks in the pavement.

# Chapter 20

THE KITTEN IS Eudora's idea. She checked with Maggie and Rob first of course before asking for Stanley's help in finding a suitable candidate. He agreed without hesitation. Their relationship had changed since that day at the airport. After Eudora had finished the call with Rose, she told him everything: about her father, mother, Stella, and even Sylvia. She wept as she recounted Stella's sorry story and the lifetime of regret she had packed away as a result. At first, Eudora was mortified at her own open display of feelings, but when she saw Stanley's face, so understanding and compassionate, she realized there was no need.

"You do understand that none of this was your fault, don't you?" he said, eyes wrinkled with kindness. "You did your best for your mother and sister, but you're not responsible for their lives and how they chose to live them."

Eudora stared at him openmouthed before a great gaping sob rocked her body. Stanley shuffled his chair nearer and, without hesitation, Eudora buried her face in his shoulder. He held her close and let her cry. He didn't need to speak. His steady embrace was enough.

Eudora now knew that she couldn't go to Switzerland. She hadn't been able to help Stella, but she was going to make sure she helped Rose. She wouldn't leave while there was unfinished business to attend to.

As luck would have it, Stanley's neighbor Barbara has a cat who had recently delivered a litter of kittens. The

Saturday before Rose's birthday, Eudora and Stanley call 'round to collect her. Maggie opens the door, grinning conspiratorially.

"Rose!" she calls over her shoulder. "You have visitors!"

Rose bounces down the stairs as if on springs. "Eudora! Stanley! I'm so happy to see you. How was your trip, Eudora?"

Eudora glances at Stanley. "Actually, I only made it as far as the airport. I had a change of heart."

"Oh. I'm sorry you missed out on your holiday."

"It's all right. And don't worry, I still managed to buy this for you at the airport," she says, handing over a large bar of Toblerone.

Rose's eyes bulge. "Wow! That's even bigger than the one Dad bought. Thank you. Shall we share it now?"

Eudora smiles. "Actually, we'd like to take you out for an early birthday surprise if you're not busy?"

Rose looks fit to burst. "I love surprises. Is that okay, Mum?"

"Absolutely," says Maggie, winking at Stanley.

"Cool. Let's go!" she says, grabbing a fuchsia-pink bobble hat from the coat stand and plonking it on her head.

"Er, Rose," says Eudora.

"Yes?" she replies, eyes bright with excitement.

"Stanley and I are well acquainted with your sartorial experiments, but I'm wondering if it might be wise for you to perhaps change out of your pajamas?"

Rose stares down at her rainbow-patterned nightwear and giggles. "Oh yeah. Give me two secs."

Rose walks between Stanley and Eudora, nattering all

the way. They cover every topic from David Attenborough ("I wish he'd marry my granny") to the best flavors of Haribo ("tropical is nice but cherry's better"). Eudora is struck by the realization that this chitchat would have been a great source of irritation to her three months ago but now she hangs on every precious word.

It takes them a while to reach Barbara's house. Eudora blames the cold weather as she needs to pause to catch her breath on more than one occasion. These are the only moments when Rose breaks off her chattering.

"You okay, Eudora?" she asks, gently touching her elbow. Eudora nods as she regains her breath.

"Take your time, Eudora," says Stanley. "No hurry."

"Are we going to your house for tea?" asks Rose as they reach his front gate.

"Not today. It's just a little farther."

"So this must be the birthday girl," says Barbara on opening the door. Eudora can hear a faint mewing as they enter the hall. Rose's eyes widen. "Come through."

They follow Barbara into the conservatory where six tiny kittens are play-fighting while their mother, a beautiful brown tabby, looks on. Rose gapes at Eudora and Stanley.

"Happy birthday, Rose," says Eudora. "Now all you have to do is pick one."

As Rose flings her arms around Eudora's waist and whispers a heartfelt "thank you" before dissolving into a tidal wave of happy tears, Eudora understands the joy of grandmothers the world over. She wipes away her own stray tear and shares a smile with Stanley as Rose kneels down. The kittens nudge one another out of the way in a bid to climb onto her lap. One particularly small kitten, a tiny caramel-tabby chaos of fur with a smut of black on his nose, can't get close. He sits behind the rest, staring up at Rose with luminous blue eyes. Rose reaches forward and picks him up. They stare at each other for a moment.

"Hello, Osman," she says. "Would you like to be my cat?" The kitten mews in the affirmative. Rose beams.

"Osman?" asks Stanley, bemused.

"After Richard Osman," says Eudora with authority.

"Well, he's a lucky cat to be going to live with a family like yours," says Barbara, smiling at them all.

"Yes," says Eudora. "He certainly is."

The following Saturday is Rose's birthday party. Stanley calls to escort Eudora to the door.

"Are you keeping an eye on me?" she asks as he offers an arm. "Because you don't need to worry. I'm not about to do a midnight flit." Eudora's not about to do anything particularly strenuous. She's been feeling even more tired than usual lately. She puts it down to the change of season. Autumn can make one feel distinctly peaky.

Stanley grins. "No. I'm just being my usual chivalrous self. Sheila says I'm like a knight in shining armor."

"How is Sheila?" asks Eudora.

"She's great," says Stanley. "I enjoy her company."

"Very good," says Eudora, ringing Rose's doorbell.

The birthday party couldn't have been more Rose-themed if Maggie had arranged for a live unicorn to appear. Everything sparkles with color and joy. There are unicorn balloons in each corner, a rainbow-shaped piñata, and a unicorn cake decorated with a golden horn and pastel pink roses. Shimmering silver, pink, and purple foil banners hang across the length of the room and an iridescent "Happy Birthday Rose" sign glimmers in the glow of the fairy lights, which Maggie has placed at regular intervals around the room.

"It's like a grotto in here," says Stanley as he enters, carrying a box-shaped parcel wrapped in pink glittery paper.

"I know. Isn't it the best?" cries Rose, pirouetting around and around with sheer delight.

"We thought Rose deserved a special celebration this year," says Maggie.

"Plus, there's the other factor that once my beloved starts on something like this, she can't stop," says Rob.

"It's why you love me," says Maggie, nudging him in the ribs.

"I can't deny it," admits Rob.

"I think it's wonderful," says Eudora. "And may I say that you have excelled yourself with your outfit today, Rose."

"I'm glad you like it, Eudora. I couldn't decide which color to wear so I thought I would just put them all together at once," she says.

"Dazzling," says Eudora.

"I'm glad you're both here," says Rose. "It wouldn't be the same without you."

Stanley and Eudora exchange glances. "This is a little extra something from Eudora and me," says Stanley, holding out the parcel.

"But you already got me Osman," says Rose, scooping up the kitten, who until that moment had been speeding around the room like a five-year-old after one Haribo too many.

"We didn't like to come empty-handed today," says Eudora. "Stanley saw it and we thought you'd like it."

"Thank you," says Rose, handing Eudora the kitten and accepting the gift. Osman nudges Eudora's cheek. She inhales warm fur and precious life. Rose rips off the paper and opens the packaging inside to reveal a smooth honey-colored wooden box carved with letters and a pink rose design. "Rose's Treasures," she reads as she lifts the lid.

"How beautiful," says Maggie.

"It's a keepsake box," explains Eudora. "For all your treasures and memories. I've got one of them at home. We thought you'd like it."

Rose beams. "Thank you. I know exactly what to put in here first." She leaps up and plucks a photograph from the fridge. "Daddy took it when we went to Broadstairs." Eudora peers at the picture of Rose, Stanley, and her on the carousel.

"You look like the Queen," says Stanley to Eudora. "All serene and dignified."

"Naturally," says Eudora. "Whereas you look like a loon."

"What do I look like?" asks Rose, laughing.

"You look exactly as you do now. Happy and full of fun," says Eudora.

Rose leans close, threading her arms around Eudora's. "We *all* look happy." Eudora nods with satisfaction.

The doorbell rings as the first guests arrive. Rose bounces

down the hall to let them in and soon the room is filled with the excited chatter of ten- and eleven-year-olds. Eudora is surprised to see Jada among them, but Rose greets her with a friendly hug, so she assumes that all is well. Rob puts on some music, which is too tinny and clamorous for Eudora's taste but which the assembled company seems to enjoy. There are about ten children present and half of them are boys. Eudora recognizes one of them as the friendly boy from the café and notices too how easily he makes Rose laugh. After a time, Rob calls them to attention.

"Okay, guys, we're going to play some games in a minute, but first I would like to present the magnificent, marvelous, magical Marvin!"

Eudora watches agog as Stanley appears from the back of the room wearing a bow tie, tuxedo, and top hat. "Hello, girls and boys!" he cries, pulling a plastic bouquet of flowers from his sleeve and handing it to Rose. She accepts the flowers with a giggle.

Eudora notices Jada, who is sitting on the floor right in front of Rose, whispering to the girl next to her. She overhears Jada's barbed comment. "Games and a magic show? So lame." The other girl rolls her eyes in agreement.

Stanley is now embarking on one of the most unconvincing magic shows Eudora has ever seen, but for some reason the children seem to be lapping it up.

"Pick a card, any card," he says to Rose's friend Tommy.

Tommy does as he is told.

"Okay, now you look at it but don't show me. Now place the card back in the pile."

Tommy follows his instructions. Stanley shuffles the pack before cutting it with a flourish. "Is this your card?"

"No," says Tommy with regret.

"Oh my God," whispers Jada to her sidekick. "This is embarrassing."

Undeterred, Stanley cuts the pack again. "How about this one?"

"Er, no," says Tommy.

"Okay," says Stanley. "But what about this one?" He pulls a card from his inside pocket.

Tommy's mouth drops open. "How did you do that?"

Stanley taps the side of his nose. "Magic, my friend. Pure magic."

The audience erupts into whoops and cheers of delight. Even Jada claps along.

Maggie appears with Daisy in her arms and takes a seat next to Eudora on the sofa. "How's he getting on?"

"Actually, he's doing rather well," says Eudora, smiling at Daisy, who reaches out her chubby arms. "Shall I take her for a while?"

"If that's okay? She's had a long nap and I've just changed her so you should be safe," says Maggie, placing Daisy on Eudora's lap. They eyeball each other for a moment before Eudora pulls a face and is rewarded with a throaty chuckle followed by a gummy kiss.

"It would seem that both my daughters are really quite fond of you, Eudora," says Maggie.

Eudora strokes Daisy's kitten-soft hair. "I can assure you that the feeling is mutual."

"I'm sorry you didn't get to go on your holiday," says Maggie. "I hope you're not too disappointed."

"It wasn't the right time," says Eudora.

"Maybe next year, eh?"

Eudora watches as Stanley performs a trick with Rose as his assistant. He keeps handing her the wand, but every time Rose takes hold of it, it flops in half. Rose, along with most of the audience, is doubled over in hysterics. "I don't think so. I'm too old for all that. I think I'll stay put from now on."

Maggie pats her hand. "I don't think I told you, but Mum has met a nice man."

"Oh. How do you feel about that?"

Maggie shrugs. "Well, obviously he'll never replace Dad, but I'm pleased for Mum. She seems much happier."

"That's good. It's important to grasp these moments of happiness whenever you can."

"Aaa!" says Daisy.

"You see," says Eudora, "Daisy agrees. Clever girl."

After the magic show finishes to rapturous applause from everyone except Jada, Rob takes Stanley's place at the front of the room. "Thank you, Magical Marvin, that was brilliant! Right, now we're going to have a few games before food. So, if you could all sit in a circle, please."

Jada stands up and folds her arms. "I don't want to play games," she says to Rob. "It's babyish."

A few of the other children look unsure. Eudora notices a flicker of panic dart across Rose's face. "Don't be boring, Jada," says Tommy. "It's Rose's party and we're having fun. If you don't want to play, you can just sit out."

Jada's eyes boggle with fury. She glances at her sidekick. "What about you, Amy?"

Amy shrugs. "I like playing games. They're doing that chocolate one where you have to throw a six and eat it with a knife and fork. I want to play."

"Why don't you come and sit by me," says Eudora.

Jada isn't used to being challenged but can see she has little choice. "'Kay. Can I hold the baby?" she asks, plonking herself beside Eudora and holding out her arms.

Daisy stares at Jada as she's passed onto her lap before grabbing a handful of her hair and giving it a sharp tug.

"Ow!" cries Jada. If Eudora didn't know better, she would swear Daisy was doing it out of loyalty to her sister.

"Oh dear," says Eudora, gently prying Daisy's hand away. "Now, Daisy, that's not very friendly, is it?"

"It's okay," says Jada. "She didn't mean to do it."

"No," says Eudora. "She's only a baby. She can't possibly take responsibility for her actions. But you can, Jada."

Jada gives Eudora a sideways glance. "What do you mean?"

"I mean that we all have choices. You do too. My advice is to choose kindness above everything else."

Jada frowns. "'Kay."

Eudora fixes her with a steady gaze. "I am very old, so I can say exactly what I think. I'm probably going to die soon too, and I promise you that if you are unkind to Rose or anyone else, for that matter, I will come back and haunt you. And not in a nice way. Be kind, Jada. Always be kind."

Jada seems to shrink at her words but gives a barely discernible nod.

"Eeee!" squeaks Daisy.

"That's right, Daisy," says Eudora. "Jada is a clever girl and has understood exactly what she needs to do from now on. Now, why don't you go and join in, dear? You don't want to miss all the fun."

Jada passes Daisy back to Eudora and goes to join the other children, who are now out in the garden, attacking the piñata. Eudora watches as Rose takes a step back and offers Jada the stick. She accepts with a smile, hitting the piñata with all her might. A handful of sweets fall to the floor. Jada picks up one and offers it to Rose. "Very good," murmurs Eudora.

"Remind me why we agreed to have this party in the first place," says Rob, peeling a fruit pastille from the bottom of his shoe later that afternoon.

Maggie gestures toward the garden where Stanley, Rose, and Tommy are blowing up balloons, screeching with laughter as they let go and watch them fart majestically around the garden. "That's why," she tells him.

"Oh yeah," he says with a grin.

The doorbell rings. "That'll be Tommy's mum," says Maggic, heading toward the hall. "She said she'd be a bit late. She's coming straight from work."

"Shall I take her from you?" says Rob to Eudora, who is still on the sofa with a sleeping Daisy nestled in her arms.

"I'm fine for now," she says. "You finish clearing up." In actual fact, Eudora is perfectly content. Daisy's steady breathing is calming and peaceful. She relishes her time here with this family and knows that they feel the same.

"I'm so sorry I'm late," says Tommy's mum, following Maggie into the kitchen. "I got held up at work."

"It's no problem at all. They're happy as anything."

Tommy's mum beams at Eudora. "Ahh bless, look at the babby with her nan."

Maggie flashes an amused look at Eudora, who purses her lips into a smile.

"Tommy! Time to go."

"Aww, Mum. Do we have to?" he groans, sloping in from the garden followed by Stanley and Rose.

"Yes, Tommy. Did you ask Rose about next weekend?"

Tommy traces a pattern with his foot on the floor. "No."

"Well, go on then. Don't be shy," says his mum.

Tommy turns to Rose. "Rose, would you like to come to the cinema to see the new Avengers movie and then go to Nando's afterward?" he asks in a quick-fire robotic voice.

"I told Tommy he could ask one friend and he chose Rose," says his mum, smiling.

Rose glances at Maggie, who gives an emphatic nod. "I would love that. Thank you!" she says.

Tommy's mum ruffles his hair. "See? I told you she'd say yes. Okay, we'd better go. Say thank you, Tommy."

"Thank you," he says, his neck flushing pink.

"You're welcome," says Rob, following them out to the door.

Rose scoops up Osman from under her feet and flops down next to Eudora on the sofa. "Best. Birthday. Ever."

"I'm very pleased to hear it," says Eudora. "And everything is all right with Jada?"

"Mhmm," says Rose. "I thought about what you said and I'm not just going to stick with her. I'm going to be friends with everyone. It's better that way."

"You're wise beyond your years, Rose. Tommy seems very nice."

"He is. Boys are plonkers but they're funny too."

Eudora glances up at Stanley. "They can be," she says. "Now, it's time I went home."

"Come along then, your majesty," says Stanley, as Eudora hands Daisy to Rob. "I'll help you up and see you home."

"It's only next door," says Eudora, shuffling to the front of her seat and taking hold of her stick.

"Yes, but a gentleman must always escort a lady," says Stanley, helping her to a standing position. "Are you okay?"

A wave of dizziness sweeps over Eudora. She grasps his arm for support. "I'm fine. I just got up a little too quickly."

After they say their goodbyes, Eudora allows Stanley to lend an arm as she makes the short walk home. She tells herself that the breathlessness is down to tiredness. It's been a long, exciting day. She needs tea and rest. Eudora is grateful as Stanley helps her up the front step.

"Well. Wasn't that a wonderful party? I'm so pleased for Rose."

"Me too," says Eudora, trying to catch her breath.

"I'm glad you decided to stay, Eudora," says Stanley, helping her inside the house.

Eudora is about to tell him that she is glad too when the world begins to distort and the floor comes up to meet her. The last thing she hears is Stanley's voice calling to her, but it's fading into the distance and she is simply too tired to answer.

## 2018
## ELSEWHERE

The dream is a kiss of relief, inevitable, consoling, exactly as she imagined it would be. Her father is there of course, arms outstretched, ready to welcome her. He's wearing his big coat with the buttons that look like chocolate. He lifts his hat and smiles. She catches the tang of his tobacco, the warmth of his embrace. Safe. You are safe now. Beatrice stands by his side, tea towel twisted between her hands. She is smiling, eyes creased with worry. Always the worry. The cares. But she looks happy, as if she's finally where she is meant to be. Another figure steps out of the shadows. She is young, slight, carrying a baby. Stella. Oh, Stella. Her gaze is cool, one eyebrow raised, chin jutted upward with defiance. Ever headstrong and haughty. Frozen in time that way. She never had a chance to change. A lifetime of regret for what might have been. Sisters. Aunties. Friends. Who knows what might have been? Stella turns toward her and holds out the baby. Take her. My gift to you. I absolve you.

Eudora moves forward to accept. Reaches out her arms.

She pauses as she hears the sound. It's faint at first. She leans in to listen. The sound becomes louder and louder until it's all Eudora can hear. The unmistakable sound of Rose singing at the top of her lungs, belting out a heartfelt and utterly tone-deaf rendition of her favorite song. Eudora opens her eyes.

# Chapter 21

EUDORA CAN'T REMEMBER the journey in the ambulance, but Rose is keen to tell her that she almost died. When she wakes up in the hospital, Eudora is adamant that she needs to leave as soon as possible.

"It was a mild heart attack, Ms. Honeysett," says the doctor, a bright young woman with eyes full of hope. "But you do have some underlying problems."

"My valve," says Eudora. "I've always known it was compromised."

"Yes. We could operate."

"No," says Eudora. The doctor's face crumples. "Please don't be upset. I'm eighty-five. It's the right time."

Eudora hadn't realized how much bureaucracy is involved in being permitted to die at home. She is harangued on an almost daily basis by all manner of nonmedical staff regarding her care arrangements. In the end, it is Sheila who saves the day. Eudora is delighted to learn that this woman is almost as bloody-minded as she. She liaises with the hospital, contacts Hannah the death doula, and organizes a rotation of people to care for Eudora when she arrives home.

"I organized it for Vic when he was dying," Sheila tells Eudora, her chin set with determination. "Best decision I ever made."

"Thank you, Sheila," says Eudora. Sheila pats her hand.

⁂

Eudora stays in bed most of the time now. She had wanted to be downstairs in her chair with the radio beside her for company, but Ruth, the social worker, persuaded her that "one-level living" was the best way. She is now Eudora's "allocated caseworker" and has been visiting as often as she can. Eudora knows she doesn't need to drop in as often as she does but is grateful. Ruth arranged for her favorite furniture, radio, and television to be moved upstairs along with her photos. She was on the verge of organizing carers four times a day as well when Maggie intervened.

"We'll look after Eudora," she said.

Ruth looked unsure. "That's a lot to take on. She needs someone with her nearly all the time."

"I can hear you, you know," said Eudora.

"Sorry, Eudora. I just need to make sure that you're safe and properly cared for."

"We'll sort it, dear," said Sheila. "I'll draw up a rota with Maggie, Stanley, and Hannah. It will be fine."

Ruth looked at Eudora, who shrugged and said, "I wouldn't stand in the way of these determined women, if I were you. Now, shouldn't you be getting home to that little boy of yours?"

Ruth smiled. "Very well. But call me if you need anything. I'll pop in as often as I can."

"Thank you, Ruth," said Eudora.

⁂

They fall into an easy routine. Either Stanley or Sheila is there in the mornings. Eudora prefers Sheila's tea but enjoys doing crosswords with Stanley.

"Eight across. Five letters. The clue is 'fool.'"

"Idiot," says Eudora.

"How rude," says Stanley. "Actually, that's not right. The first letter is 'm.'"

"Moron," says Eudora.

Stanley clutches his chest. "Ms. Honeysett! How can you be so cruel?"

Eudora laughs. There's something about Stanley's gentle humor that reminds her of her father. She couldn't give in to it when they first met, couldn't allow herself. Now it brings her nothing but comfort. "I never thanked you properly," she says.

"For what?"

She fixes her gaze on the laughter lines at the corners of his eyes. "For saving me."

Stanley puts down his pen and turns to face her. "That's what friends are for. After all, you saved me when I was in the doldrums."

Eudora reaches out to him. Stanley looks surprised but responds in kind. "Thank you, Stanley," she says. "Truly."

Stanley leans forward and kisses her hand. "It's a pleasure and a privilege, Eudora."

They hear the front door open. "It's only us!" calls Maggie up the stairs.

"Eee!" confirms Daisy.

"Right," says Stanley, giving Eudora's hand a gentle

squeeze before letting go. "I'd better take those pesky hounds for a walk."

Eudora nods. "Later potater, as Rose is fond of saying."

Stanley smiles. "Later potater," he says, issuing a swift salute from the doorway before he leaves.

Moments later, Maggie appears with Daisy in her arms.

"Eee, eee, eee," says Daisy, reaching out toward Eudora.

"Will you be okay with Daisy while I make your lunch?" asks Maggie.

"Of course," says Eudora. "It's the least I can do. Come here, madam," she says, sitting Daisy on the bed beside her.

"What would you like for lunch today? Soup maybe?"

Eudora wrinkles her nose. Her appetite has been draining away from her like water disappearing down a plughole. "Just some toast and tea, please, Maggie."

"Coming right up."

Eudora turns back to Daisy. Aside from Rose, Daisy is the best at entertaining her. Eudora could watch her all day. She marvels at the way Daisy approaches the world in a state of constant astonishment—everything is a wonder to her. Right now she is staring at Eudora with the studied concentration of a mind reader.

"You needn't look at me as if I'm going to expire at any moment," Eudora tells her.

"Aaaaaa!" says Daisy, grabbing hold of her hands.

"Precisely," says Eudora.

Eudora's favorite time of day is around four o'clock when Rose appears. She flings open the door and shouts, "Eudora! Are you still alive?"

"Yes, thank you, Rose!" she replies.

Hannah was visiting one day when Rose made this particular entrance and she laughed for nearly ten minutes. "That is one of the most hilarious and refreshing things I have ever heard."

"That's Rose for you."

Eudora often rediscovers her appetite when Rose is around. She always manages a slice of Sheila's homemade cake while they spend time discussing Rose's day or Eudora's mortality.

"I want to show you something," says Eudora as Rose enters the room one day, carefully carrying a mug of tea, which she places on the bedside table. "Can you reach my treasures box in the wardrobe, please?"

"Of course. You know how much I love treasures," says Rose, throwing open the doors and embarking on a thorough search. Eventually, she finds the cardboard box labeled "Eudora's Treasures." She blows off the dust and carries it to the bed. Eudora lifts the lid and stares inside. It's all there. Photographs, tickets to dances, a postcard from Joss Bay. A whole life. Rose looks as if she's about to explode with excitement.

"Dive in, Rose," says Eudora. "Ask away."

She tells her everything: about her father, her mother, Stella, Sam, Sylvia, and the baby who never was. Rose's face reflects the joy and sadness as she listens. She holds up a photograph of Sam and Eudora taken at Broadstairs. "He's very handsome and you look beautiful, Eudora."

"Thank you, Rose."

"I hope Daisy's never as mean to me as Stella was to you."

"It was a different time, Rose. I think you'll be fine."

"I love the sound of the dances you went to with Sylvia."

"We had fun," admits Eudora.

Rose looks at the scattered memories and fixes Eudora with her steady, honest gaze. "I know you had sad stuff with your dad and your sister, but you've had a good life."

Eudora stares at Rose and smiles. "Yes," she says. "On balance, I suppose I have."

One day, Rose brings Tommy to visit. He's a little shy at first, eyeing Eudora fearfully. "It's all right, Tommy, you don't need to be scared. Eudora is going to die but probably not today," says Rose. "That's right, isn't it, Eudora?"

Eudora nods. "You're quite safe, Tommy, and very welcome."

Tommy seems to relax a little. "So we thought we'd watch *The Greatest Showman* with you," says Rose. "Tommy's never seen it and it's pretty much the best film ever. I know all the words to all the songs."

"Sounds as if we're in for a treat, Tommy."

Eudora is too weary to follow the plot of the film. Instead, she delights in gazing at the faces of the two children as they watch. At one stage, a woman with a beard performs a rousing song about being an unapologetic version of yourself. Rose leaps up and joins in, her face absorbed in the moment. It's a Hollywood-glazed, but nonetheless powerful, sentiment of having confidence and self-belief. Eudora watches the little girl in awe and notices Tommy do the same. Rose seems transformed these days: assured and brave. Eudora is overwhelmed with pride. She knows that this child will always change other people's worlds for the better. She feels melancholy that she won't be here to see it but takes sheer delight in this truth.

As autumn blusters toward winter, Eudora watches the light on the ceiling change from the color of ripe wheat to a pale yellow. The year is fading and so is she. Every day she eats a little less and sleeps a little more. Hannah is a constant companion, observing, filling the space with kindness.

Stanley has volunteered for night shifts. Rob offered but Stanley refused. "You've got a family and work. I have time."

He sleeps in what used to be Eudora's old room under the rainbow-colored blanket that Beatrice crocheted in a different lifetime. "Best night's sleep I've had in ages," he tells her every morning as he brings in a cup of tea. He always taps lightly on the door before entering. Ever the gentleman.

As she reaches the end, Eudora is hardly ever on her own. Having spent aching chasms of time alone, she is grateful for the constant stream of district nurses, friends, and loved ones. Stanley's granddaughters call 'round to read to her and Helen, their mum, brings casseroles, flowers, and good humor. Rob always pops in on his return from work. They usually talk about how wonderful Rose is. Eudora feels shored up and safe.

She starts to struggle with her breathing and is given oxygen. It helps but she is tired. She feels as if she's being pulled backward. Away from all this. She doesn't resist.

Rose appears later that day. Hannah and Stanley are downstairs waiting to intercept her. Eudora hears their muffled voices, calm, resigned. Rose hops up the stairs and taps on her door.

"Come in, Rose," says Eudora.

Rose approaches her bed and sits down. She is carrying Osman in her arms. "I brought him to see you."

"That's kind. Hello, Osman," says Eudora, her voice rasping with tiredness. She reaches out a frail hand, relishing the feel of his silky fur. Rose places him on the bed. He turns three times before curling into a perfect ball.

Rose looks at the breathing tubes and places a smooth hand over Eudora's wrinkled one. "You're dying, aren't you?"

Eudora would laugh if she had the energy. "I think so."

"What does it feel like?"

"At the moment I feel quite relaxed."

"That sounds nice."

"I wouldn't go that far."

"I suppose it's worse for me."

"Is that right?"

"Yes, because you'll be able to go and see your mum and

dad and sister, wherever they are. And then you can come back for Day of the Dead and still see me. But I won't be able to see you."

"Don't worry. You'll know I'm here."

"How? Are you going to haunt me?"

"I'll try."

"Cool." There's a pause. "Can I hug you now?"

"If you must."

Rose climbs up beside Eudora on the bed. "Let's just be quiet together, shall we?"

"Do you think you can manage that, Rose?"

"I'll try for you, Eudora."

"Good girl."

Eudora watches the pale lemon sunlight cast a dappled shadow from the last straggly leaves gently blowing outside in the breeze. She feels Rose's warmth, her small perfect form, her steady breathing, two breaths to her one.

Stanley peers around the door. "I just wondered if you needed anything?"

Eudora shakes her head. "No. Thank you. Come and sit if you'd like to."

Stanley nods and brings the dressing-table chair over beside the bed. He smiles at them both before taking a seat. A faithful sentry. Osman has settled into a gently wheezing sleep.

Eudora closes her eyes, relishing the quiet. A long-forgotten, cherished sentence floats into her mind.

*All shall be well, and all shall be well, and all manner of thing shall be well.*

She knows this is true now. She feels nothing but peace,

along with the presence of an old man who shares his feelings a little too readily and a small girl with terrible dress sense.

She loves them. They love her.

*All is well.*

## Acknowledgments

A HUGE THANK-YOU to my agent, Laura Macdougall, who has been with Eudora and me from the start. She is a brilliant editor, incredible agent, and valued friend. Thanks also to the wider team at United Agents for your help in bringing this book to life.

Thank you to Emily Krump and the team at William Morrow in the US, who love Eudora and Rose almost as much as I do.

Thank you to Charlotte Ledger and the team at One More Chapter in the UK for your infectious enthusiasm and passion.

Love and gratitude to Team Laura (my UA fam), the London Writers, HQ authors past and present, and RNA friends for your wisdom and generous support.

Thanks to my Beckenham and Biggin Hill creative writing students—writing and running courses for you has taught me so much.

Thank you to the incredible bloggers and online community who read, review, and share the love for my books—your support means everything to me.

Thank you to Lisa Stevens and Kay Fox for sage advice about midwifery and veterinary issues respectively. Thank you to the lifecircle organization in Switzerland for information and guidance about voluntary assisted death.

All love and gratitude to Helen Abbott, Sarah Livingston, and Melissa Khan—my book soul mates, who always know when I need a message of encouragement or a good book recommendation.

Finally, and most important, thank you to Rich, Lil, and Alf for love, support, and endless episodes of *Brooklyn Nine-Nine*.

Book Recommendation

*With the End in Mind: Dying, Death, and Wisdom in an Age of Denial* by Kathryn Mannix was a huge source of inspiration to me while I was writing Eudora's story. I recommend it wholeheartedly for its insight, compassion, and truth. It's a stunning and important book, which I hope encourages people to talk more and fear less.

## About the Author

After a career in bookselling and publishing, Annie Lyons published five books in the UK, including the bestselling *Not Quite Perfect.* When not working on her novels, she teaches creative writing. She lives in south-east London with her husband and two children.